ADVANCE PRAISE FOR
ALLOW ME TO INTRODUCE MYSELF

'I loved everything about this book, from the original portrayal of social media and influencer culture, to the excellent humour, to the way it never paints anyone as entirely bad or entirely good, but allows the intricate threads that weave us together as people to create characters who are fully realised, flawed and relatable. Once again, Onyi Nwabineli tells a story that is wise, captivating and unforgettable.'
Ore Agbaje-Williams, author of *The Three of Us*

'A tack-sharp, beautifully told tale of agency and reclaiming your power. Nwabineli creates deeply drawn characters, uses perfect metaphors, and possesses an immersive storytelling style that never releases its grasp on you as you journey into the darkest recesses of her characters. Nwabineli is the queen of flawlessly blending serious topics with witty contemporary prose. Her way with words is an incredible gift.'
**Lola Akinmade Åkerström,
author of *In Every Mirror She's Black***

'An unputdownable read! Skilfully and delicately written, *Allow Me to Introduce Myself* helps us behave more ethically in this age of social media obsessions. Onyi Nwabineli is an immensely talented writer whose pen is sharp and unflinching.'
Nguyễn Phan Quế Mai, author of *Dust Child*

'Rich with emotion, heartbreaking, and timely. A fresh and compelling perspective on living online.'
Peace Adzo Medie, author of *Nightbloom*

Also by Onyi Nwabineli

Someday, Maybe

To learn more about Onyi Nwabineli,
visit her website, onyi-nwabineli.com.

ALLOW ME TO INTRODUCE MYSELF

ONYI NWABINELI

MAGPIE
BOOKS

A Note from the Author

Allow Me to Introduce Myself deals with a number of themes, including alcoholism and mental health. The book also mentions suicide.

A Magpie Book

First published in the United Kingdom, Republic of Ireland and Australia
by Magpie, an imprint of Oneworld Publications, 2024

Copyright © Onyi Nwabineli, 2024

The moral right of Onyi Nwabineli to be identified as the Author of this work has been asserted by her in accordance with the Copyright, Designs, and Patents Act 1988

All rights reserved
Copyright under Berne Convention
A CIP record for this title is available from the British Library

ISBN 978-0-86154-687-9 (hardback)
ISBN 978-0-86154-868-2 (trade paperback)
eISBN 978-0-86154-688-6

Printed and bound in Great Britain by Clays Ltd, Elcograf S.p.A

This book is a work of fiction. Names, characters, businesses, organisations, places and events are either the product of the author's imagination or are used fictitiously. Any resemblance to actual persons, living or dead, events or locales is entirely coincidental.

Oneworld Publications
10 Bloomsbury Street
London WC1B 3SR
England

Stay up to date with the latest books,
special offers, and exclusive content from
Oneworld with our newsletter

Sign up on our website
oneworld-publications.com

For all the kids who wish to be a little less visible.
And for my niece, nephew and godchildren—the stars of my heart.

PROLOGUE

This is the tool Aṅụrị's stepmother used to launch her empire:

- Blogger

These are the tools she then used to expand it:

- WordPress
- YouTube
- Twitter
- Instagram
- Snapchat

This is the number of followers and subscribers her stepmother amassed over the course of five years:

- Year one: 26 thousand
- Year two: 334 thousand
- Year three: 1 million
- Year four: 2.4 million
- Year five: 4 million

These are the products her stepmother released using Aṅụrị's likeness before she was three years old:

- Desktop wallpapers (ages six months to two years)
- Socks (age eighteen months)
- Natural baby wipes

These are the products her stepmother launched using the money made from the products she released using her likeness:

- High-end scented candle range
- Subscription service for "Curated Samples of Elite Living"
- *Raising Aṅụrị*, a #1 *New York Times* and *Sunday Times* bestselling book
- *Monetizing Motherhood*, a #1 *New York Times* and *Sunday Times* bestselling book
- Ophelia May range of natural haircare products

This is the number of attempts made to abduct Aṅụrị before she turned twelve:

- One

And this was how old Aṅụrị was when she decided enough was enough:

- Fourteen

ONE

Her last meal, she had decided, would be gelato. The craving eclipsed all other senses. She would savor it and then she would die. It was a Sunday afternoon, four years prior. Aṅụrị, twenty-one at the time, had chosen her method and left it in her living room. She spent part of the morning on the bathroom floor, the tile stamping its memory into the left side of her body. However, the inconvenient doggedness of life steered Aṅụrị down another path.

Ammah was not supposed to be working that day. The gelateria staff, however, were, and yet they were nowhere to be seen, and as Aṅụrị pressed her brow against the shuttered West London shop front, she repeated this heartbreak in a whispered, distraught loop: *You're supposed to be open. You are supposed to be open.* She could not die without a final taste of pistachio melting on her tongue, so she would call them, and they would arrive and rectify the mistake. She misdialed the number on the wooden shop sign and Ammah answered, deftly cutting through Aṅụrị's garbled desperation and identifying a more urgent distress. Ammah tossed death out onto the street. Aṅụrị knew that she, without hyperbole, quite literally owed Ammah her life.

Before that day, luck was for others; a remarried father, an astute stepmother. The moment she stepped into Ammah's office, Aṅụrị believed it might be for her as well.

Of the five therapy practitioners Aṅụrị had tried before that Sunday afternoon, two murdered her name with their mouths despite gentle then pained correction. One sought tears in a way that bordered on sociopathic. The other two were fans of Ophelia—an affliction even years of training failed to smother or at the very least shroud. Before Ammah, therapy, Aṅụrị decided, was yet another facet of normalcy that would remain out of her reach. How painful to possess the privilege to access the method of fixing, yet to remain unfixed.

Today, a Thursday, and most of Ammah's office was in shadow. A fact that made little sense to Aṅụrị as this was the room where said therapist bathed her in the kind of light she often found inconvenient—the type that reached with soft but insistent fingers into the recesses she would rather keep hidden. She sits in this office, in a sienna-colored armchair, and spills her guts onto the limewashed oak flooring, and when they are done, she wades through the viscera, pausing at the door to say "Same time next week?" as if it was not always the same time. As if they would not repeat this dance with a slight variation in choreography.

Ammah's micro-locs were twisted into a snake that coiled down the back of her head and made an attempt on her spine. Aṅụrị noticed new growth. The new growth would have been there the last time Ammah turned the spotlight on her, but last time, Aṅụrị was pushing her words out around shallow breaths. After too many exchanges with her father's voicemail culminating in a sleepless night, her mind was black. Ammah's questions chased her around the room. Aṅụrị saw her without seeing her. Today was different. Aṅụrị was calm enough to see that it would take her just shy of four hours to retwist Ammah's entire head.

She could almost feel the gel on her fingers and they twitched involuntarily until she squeezed them between her knees.

"Do you think a part of you wishes to be immortalized?" Ammah asked, and this was what it meant to be in that room. The softness of your underbelly was never safe. You simply felt less fraught about it being cut open.

"I think," Aṅụrị told her, "I would be more open to immortality if it was my choice."

In Ọdịnanị, the traditional religion of the Igbo people, Chukwu is the High God or the supreme being, responsible for first determining and then allotting the other deities their roles and tasks. Aunty Nneoma said Chukwu hand selected Aṅụrị to be a conduit for the awe and inspiration of others. That she was God-ordained to open eyes and peel away the veil that allows people to see only filtered versions of themselves—a mirror wrapped in five feet and ten inches of dark skin and darker eyes, topped with copper-streaked hair. Aunty Nneoma said this because she loved Aṅụrị. The truth was more brutal.

There is no perfect way to describe what it means to exist in a body that is not your own, that never really was. To walk on legs, speak with a mouth, a tongue to which others have laid claim. Before Ammah or any of the others, Aṅụrị learned to move through the world gingerly, to tread as if she were made of glass. Understanding that a misstep could mean breaking into unsalvageable pieces. She was accustomed to, but ever disturbed by, eyes sliding in her direction or an elbow digging into the ribs of an oblivious companion. The accompanying whispers.

You play like it doesn't bother you and you almost believe it. Until. Until the first guy you sleep with—an oversized collection of languid limbs whose face you tattoo on the inside of your eyelids because you are craving a connection that has nothing to do with bits and bytes—waits until after he has reached his all-too-hasty climax, then lazily traces the appendectomy scar on your stomach and informs you it looks different in person. His mother, it turns out, is a fan of yours, and he knew parts of your body before *you* knew he even existed. You cease to be a human then, under his hands, and revert again to a collection of parts; a commodity to be consumed by others. This happens and there is a weekend of blurred half memories lost in the bottom of innumerable bottles; smudged against the rim of martini glasses. The invisible line in the sand—the one separating your online life from your "real" one—bursts into flames. Simi and Loki had picked her up from the floor of a bar bathroom. Aṅụrị sought therapy for the first time four days later.

It was the seeming permanence of the entire thing that hurt the most. No doubt there would come a time when Aṅụrị would fade into the nothingness of human memory, but that knowledge did little to combat the anxiety of knowing she would be accosted again, but never knowing *when*.

Today, Aṅụrị recounted for Ammah how three months earlier, Sade warbled in her earbuds as she considered a shirt in cornflower blue, lifting the matte satin to her skin and wondering if her energy might extend to a trip to the fitting room when suddenly her wrist was wrenched away and the shirt floated to the ground. She knew the girl, the wrencher, meant no real harm. That she was propelled by an excitement that turned unintentionally aggressive, and it mattered not that she waylaid a stranger in a store in the middle of the day. What Aṅụrị also understood was that this girl did not consider her a stranger. You watch enough YouTube videos, spend enough time scrolling the archives of someone else's life, and you too may feel you know them, that you have some say in how their steps are ordered. This girl showed Aṅụrị her phone, the photos she had saved of Aṅụrị that she and her friends used as memes—private moments reduced to internet punchlines. "It's you, isn't it? God, isn't this amazing?" the girl said. Her friends were going to *die*.

It was then Aṅụrị decided that she had yet to break free of

Ophelia. There might be no new content with her name or face; a battle fought and won over a number of agonizing years, but no. Aṅụrị wanted that which existed to be erased. She wished to be wiped from the annals of Ophelia's personal yet public history. She left the cornflower shirt on the floor of the store and went to rage then weep at the desk of her lawyer, Gloria, a fellow Igbo woman and the one responsible for steering her through the choppy waters of previous litigation. Aṅụrị told her she needed it all gone: the videos, the blog posts, the merchandise. All of it would have to crumble before she could truly be whole.

"There is no real precedent here. It won't be easy. Ì màtàlù ife m kwùlù? You have to understand," Gloria said and when Aṅụrị nodded, she struck a match and began her best to try to burn it down.

Three months. And now it was time for Ophelia to be served. This was not the first fight through which Ammah had guided Aṅụrị. She asked her questions because Aṅụrị was backing away from the flame; refusing to attack this with her usual fervor. Ammah asked if Aṅụrị was dragging her feet.

"More like conserving my energy." Aṅụrị's calculated approach was mistaken for reluctance. "I'm picking Noelle up today, so I'll tell Ophelia about it when I drop her off."

Her eyes drifted to the brass-rimmed clock on the wall and she cut the session short.

In a world carved from hardness, Noelle was a soft landing. Aṅụrị waited for her outside the school gates where the supermums and the nannies no longer eyed her with the same curious contempt they had been cultivating since she bullied her father into adding her name to the safeguarding pickup list. There were some lukewarm attempts at camaraderie but over her twenty-five years, Aṅụrị's fake-bitch radar was honed to a knifepoint—a survival technique. Still, she knew that Elisa, the au pair for the Fords, smuggled her boyfriend into her basement quarters three times a week, and that Briony Gillespie was pregnant with Kid Four despite telling her husband she'd had her tubes tied. She knew that the sixteen-year-old stepson of Charmaine Parker-Green was sending such shock waves of chaos through the family that delicate Char had no other option but to embark on an affair with her husband's business partner. It was fascinating what could be absorbed after mastering the art of being visibly invisible.

That Thursday, the day before Good Friday, London was sitting under a blanket of premature warmth meant for later months. Decks had been hosed down, outdoor furniture hastily assembled, barbecue grills procured and fired up for impromptu gatherings awash with the bewildered gratitude of the English experiencing unexpected heat. Aṅụrị plucked at her shirt and trained her eyes on the exit. Somewhere inside the school, a bell rang. This was not the same place Ophelia and her father had sent her. This place, a sandstone architectural triumph set in a leafy London enclave, was different in that the children here had allotted time for something called "innovate free play," and model scouts had an ongoing agreement with the faculty and the parents to arrive quarterly and "observe." The similarities to Aṅụrị's school included the fees, which soared to the tens of thousands for the pleasure of being told that Araminta was—at this time—decidedly plain ("But there's always next year!").

Because it had always been this way, Aṅụrị felt Noelle before she saw her. On the day she was born, Aṅụrị stared down into the face of the child, her hair already springing into dark and damp coils, and felt part of her soul detach and fuse itself with her sister's. Since then, Noelle had only to breathe and Aṅụrị's heartstrings were pulled taut. The coils were longer now and had lightened in color, but Aṅụrị still wished to carve the image into her memory; make it indelible: her sister, spotting her by the gate, the realization moving from trickle to dam break; the miniature uniform hanging on slender brown limbs, the brightness not yet dulled in her eyes. Wishes were for children and hope for the deluded, so Aṅụrị, as she bent to receive the hurtling weight of Noelle into outstretched arms, comforted herself again with her secret: that this life would be salvageable. She would make it so.

They had to punch in a code to open the gates behind which sat the house Aṅụrị's life had paid for. The code changed every twenty-four hours and was texted automatically to the family members, to the staff and to Ophelia's business advisor. There was a separate state-of-the-art security system inside the house and had Ophelia managed to talk Nkem into it, Noelle herself would have been kitted out with her very own subcutaneous tracking device at birth.

"It's not my daughter you will stamp with the mark of the beast," Nkem said, in a rare display of dissent. And Ophelia, in an equally rare state of acquiescence, had not pushed the matter.

Inside, Aṅụrị knelt and slipped Noelle's shoes from her feet. She knew her sister was more than capable of doing it herself, but she enjoyed the giggling elicited from the tickling of toes, and she enjoyed the feeling of being useful. That was not something so easily shed. She listened to the ramblings of someone who had spent an afternoon learning about the colors of the rainbow and smiled at how children were tiny counterweights; your status, wealth, accomplishments rendered worthless under the gaze of those whose priorities extended only to *Paw Patrol* and the latest advancements in the world of coloring books. Noelle knew but did not care that a video of Aṅụrị had once garnered more than 1.2 million views in less than nine hours.

To Noelle, Aṅụrị was soft voice, shorn hair and the smell of jasmine. She was laughter and light and the baking of cupcakes, a spontaneous activity done only once because it was for fun and not for the internet.

"Are you going home now?" Noelle asked, her brow already beginning to crease.

"Nope. I'm yours all afternoon. What do you wanna do?" Afternoon sun spilled through the glass panes of the front door and turned Noelle's eyes golden.

Aṅụrị watched the wonder of possibility spread across Noelle's face. She knew better than anyone that presence without demand was one of the greatest gifts you could offer a person whose existence was shared amongst many. She tucked her sister's hands into her own, waited for her response.

When she turned thirty-seven, Ophelia developed a debilitating case of plantar fasciitis. She would leave the house clad head to toe in designer running gear only to slam back in minutes later, limping and cursing. Ten years and a team of physical therapists later, Ophelia could run once more but now owned a collection of custom calfskin slippers to help keep her arches intact. She wore them almost everywhere, even pulling them from her Bottega and swapping out her heels after she reached whichever destination required the initial crimson flash of a Louboutin sole. Because of the slippers, she moved through the house soundlessly, and so neither Aṅụrị nor Noelle heard her approach until her perfume tapped them on the shoulders. She wore a silk wrap shirt and wide-legged trousers, having abandoned the smocks and homely button-downs that endeared her to millions of mothers who looked upon her and thought *wow, she's just like me.*

"I thought I heard the alarm chirp." Ophelia bent to kiss Noelle's head. "Hi, poppet, how was school? Thanks for picking her up, Aṅụrị."

You would never think to look at the three of them there in that grand entrance hall that the silk-clad woman once swaddled the young woman with the short hair. It might seem incomprehensible that, as the young woman rose to her feet, her chest tightened at the memory of being welcomed home with a kiss from the same lips. Any warmth they possessed was now heaped onto the head of the child.

"Aṅụrị's going to play with me," Noelle informed her mother. "All afternoon."

"Oh. I'm sorry, poppet, but did you forget? Myla is here to show you some new clothes. She's waiting upstairs and she's got tons of pretty things for you to try."

"Myla?" Aṅụrị could not help herself. It was Noelle, and new names in conjunction with her sister put her on edge, made the hair on her arms rise.

"Stylist." Ophelia waited a beat, her eyes locking with her stepdaughter's, but Noelle's groan severed the stare.

"Mummy, I don't want to. I want to play with Aṅụrị!"

"Noelle—"

"She said she would play with me! I want to play with her!" Tears. The stamp of a tiny foot. "I don't want to try on clothes. I already have clothes."

"Noelle, darling, calm down." Ophelia crouched, took her child's face between manicured hands. "I need you to be super good for me today, okay? You try on some pretty dresses with Myla and Mummy will paint your nails tonight. You get to choose the color and everything."

Aṅụrị remembered the stylists. They came much later, after years spent at the mercy of Ophelia and her blood covenant with Zara Kids and OshKosh B'gosh. She remembered the solace in the cool darkness of the garden shed, in the dust that collected in the shadows under the bed. She remembered Ophelia's voice reaching her though she clamped her hands over her ears and closed her eyes; the dread crawling through her hair and finally, Ophelia's hands guiding her back to the clothes, the shoes, the camera. It took Aṅụrị a long time to reach the point of tantrums. Noelle learned quicker, but her distress still gnawed at Aṅụrị's fingertips and made her hands ball into fists. Finding her voice later in life meant Aṅụrị spoke a lot with her hands.

Noelle twisted out of her mother's embrace. "I want to play with Aṅụrị! I don't want to do my nails!"

"Alright, sweetheart." Ophelia's voice was soft. She reached out again and brushed the tears from Noelle's face. "No nails. How about we go and look at puppies at Tasha's? Hmm? Try on three outfits for Mummy and Myla, and I'll phone Tasha tonight. You do want Mummy to be happy, don't you?"

Aṅụrị wondered then, how long it took to learn how to manipulate a child. Was it something parents needed to harness for survival? She imagined it was, at least to some extent. There were school runs to make and offices at which to arrive, bosses and bills and myriad external factors that might necessitate the gentle nudging of a kid into a place or a space they would rather not be, like plying clay into a mold before it sets. She watched the negotiation between mother and daughter and, when Noelle's tears dried and a new game for her Nintendo Switch promised, she hugged Aṅụrị's legs and ran for the stairs, a svelte wearer of angular hair meeting her halfway. Myla.

"You shouldn't make promises like that to her without checking with me first." Ophelia was back to her full height and Aṅụrị thanked the god she sometimes struggled to still believe in for stretching her past her stepmother's tallest, then continuing to pull for another few inches.

"I have to check with you before telling my sister I can play with her?" Sometimes it helped, Aṅụrị found, to repeat Ophelia's words back to her if only to underline their absurdity.

"We might have avoided that little display if you had."

"Oh you managed it quite well." Aṅụrị's sarcasm, over time, had grown legs and other appendages until it became a separate thing; a law unto itself that neither Aṅụrị nor Ophelia could elude.

"Are you staying for dinner?"

"I'm just going to hang around until my dad gets home."

Ophelia nodded once. "He may be late."

"Then I guess I'll be here late."

Ophelia nearly let herself smile. The kid had a quick wit which, were it directed at anyone else, would have pulled laughter from her. But there was no warmth in Aṅụrị's delivery. And there was always something new Ophelia noticed whenever Aṅụrị came around: a piercing, a variation to the established looks of contempt with which she was familiar. She closed her eyes to extinguish the ache only an estranged mother can know, and turned away.

The house was large enough that Ophelia and Aṅụrị could retreat to different corners and see nothing of each other until Nkem's footsteps and voice alerted them to his arrival. He greeted his wife first and arranged his face from an expression of shock into one of delight when his firstborn entered the kitchen where he stood with his bottle of Supermalt, a beverage Ophelia failed to understand but kept stocked at all times.

"Dad." Aṅụrị nodded at her father; asked him how he was. "Ke kwanụ?"

Nkem acknowledged his daughter and returned the pleasantry. "Aṅụrị. Mma, gị kwanụ?" Even now, more than two decades after she first learned to speak, Nkem always felt wrong-footed by the Igbo Aṅụrị slid into conversation. He knew he was not responsible and this like so many other things formed another stone in the path of mistakes he continued to walk. He wondered again when he and his daughter stopped embracing with the innate ease that comes from loving and raising a human being. His feet, however, remained on the square of tile where he stood.

"I'm cool. I'm alright."

Nkem nodded and did so again. He set his drink down on a coaster. The kitchen island separating the two of them might as well have been Vesuvius. "Ophelia didn't say if you were staying to eat."

"Nah, no dinner for me. I was just waiting around to say hi to you and bye to Nell when she's done." Aṅụrị used the nickname Noelle coined for herself as a toddler; her infant tongue continually hampered by the second syllable. She raised an eyebrow and her eyes darted briefly to the time displayed above the keypad of the microwave. At some point, either on the journey from Noelle's school to the house, or when Ophelia opened her mouth, Aṅụrị's resolve to talk about the impending injunction shriveled and died. It couldn't wait, but it would have to.

Nkem shook his head. Too much about his daughter broke his heart. The slenderness of Aṅụrị's arms as they protruded from her sleeveless minidress, the slightness of her ankles disappearing into boots he felt should be too heavy for her to walk in; the words to tell her he was worried could not push past his lips. Food though, he could offer. "I'm sure she won't be much longer. Won't you stay? Biko, rie ihe."

"I'm not hungry. It's been hours. She wanted to play, Nell I mean. She was really excited about it but then got hauled off to try on clothes with someone called Myla. You know her?"

"There are background checks run on everyone who works with Noelle. We made sure of it. The girl—Myla—she's meant to be the best. It's not the first time she's been here."

She was still getting used to this, the sting of delayed information. Were she still living in this house, were her moments and movements part of the webbing that stitches a family together Myla wouldn't be a stranger to Aṅụrị. A few years of scar tissue, but her separateness still managed to pierce her. "You lot bribe her often? Or is that just an Ophelia thing?"

Nkem drained the bottle and tossed it into the glass recycling harder than he intended. This was the problem. Aṅụrị would arrive radiating judgement and he was to stand there and accept it. Was he not still a man in his house? Did she not still have a duty to respect him if not as her father then as an elder? "You..." He shook his head again. "How is work?"

"Tiring. Business is booming."

"Is that so? Which one, the candles or the hair?"

"Both, you know. Do you want me to bring you guys a couple new samples? I'm experimenting with some new scents." Aṅụrị watched her father's jaw tighten, stifled a smile at the petty joy this brought her.

"You went to Oxford. And Columbia. For you now to be peddling candles and making hair. Ekwetaghị m na ọ."

"And *thriving*. Believe it, o! You must be so proud, isn't it?"

The inevitable silence that followed pushed Nkem from the room. He glanced over his shoulder but Aṅụrị was reapplying lip gloss, using the behemoth of a coffee machine to check her reflection. And Nkem marveled like he always did when he saw his child, that she was now this adult whose puppy fat melted into cheekbones and whose eyes speared him in the same way her mother's had, and that he had disappointed her in many more ways.

Aṅụrị flew up the stairs and picked her way through the discarded clothes on the floor of the dressing room. Myla was zipping up the first of her enormous silver cases and Noelle was sitting in the corner, dwarfed by the armchair, her new game already downloaded to the Switch.

"I'm off, Nells Bells." She dropped a kiss into her sister's hair and when Noelle reached up to wrap her arms around Aṅụrị's neck, she wondered how fast she could run and how far she would get with the five-year-old in her arms.

LOWLYWORM17 IS NOW ONLINE

IJELE_RISING IS NOW ONLINE

LOWLYWORM17: Goddess, it's been so long. Where have you been?

IJELE_RISING: You're speaking before you're spoken to?

LOWLYWORM17: I'm sorry, Goddess. I'm sorry

IJELE_RISING: You're already wasting my time

LOWLYWORM17: Goddess, please don't go

IJELE_RISING: Blocking in 3...2...

LOWLYWORM17 IS SENDING A TRIBUTE: ACCEPT? YES/NO

IJELE_RISING: £200? Gutter trash, are you trying to insult me? 1...

LOWLYWORM17 IS SENDING A TRIBUTE: ACCEPT? YES/NO

LOWLYWORM17: I doubled it.

IJELE_RISING: Triple it.

LOWLYWORM17: You're so perfect

IJELE_RISING: Did I ask for a compliment or did I give a direct instruction?

LOWLYWORM17 IS SENDING A TRIBUTE: ACCEPT? YES/NO

LOWLYWORM17: I quadrupled it, Goddess

IJELE_RISING: You can't seem to follow simple instructions. It's truly pathetic. You are truly pathetic

LOWLYWORM17: I am. I'm a pathetic loser

IJELE_RISING: I don't remember giving you permission to describe yourself. What an interrupting useless smear on the surface of the earth. I've had enough of you. Get out of my sight

LOWLYWORM17: But, Goddess

LOWLYWORM17 IS TYPING

YOU HAVE BLOCKED LOWLYWORM17—TRIBUTE TO UNBLOCK? YES/NO?

LOWLYWORM17 IS SENDING A TRIBUTE: ACCEPT? YES/NO

LOWLYWORM17 IS SENDING A TRIBUTE: ACCEPT? YES/NO

LOWLYWORM17 IS SENDING A TRIBUTE: ACCEPT? YES/NO

It took Aṅụrị eight months after their first session to tell Ammah about the paypigs. Because she was young and struggled to understand that there were men in this world who would part with money, beg to give it to her, if only she would humiliate them in some way. Not one or two either. Droves. Financial Domination. "Findom" for short. She thought it was a joke, that there existed a network of the depraved who somehow figured out who she was and decided to lure her into this unsavory dance only to kick her legs out from under her at the last moment. But this was not the case. Yes, she had to weed out the clowns, the unserious, those who promised the world but offered nothing, and there was the painstaking process of scaling the ridge of her discomfort until she could see what awaited her on the other side: a horizon that promised increased freedom, the honeyed taste of autonomy. Always whip-smart, Aṅụrị's learning curve in this matter was a near vertical line. Within a month, her Amazon wish lists were cleared. Within three, she could use the unresolved sexual needs of Piggy_Luvs_u_99 to cover a rent payment. And she could do it all without having to gaze upon a single face. Eventually, she would use the money to set up her candle business and kit out the hairdressing hut, and she would back away from the nameless, faceless worshippers when she felt the heady thrill of control tip over into something darker. Still, she'd waited to tell Ammah. And when she did, she sat in the shadowed office and said, "I know what you're going to say."

"Oh? Enlighten me?" Ammah was wearing forest green that day. Her locs were shorter back then.

"That I'm doing this findom stuff because of my dad."

"Is that why you're doing it?"

Aṅụrị pursed her lips. Sometimes, she thought, it would be easier if Ammah just asked her to step outside and fight. Sometimes, it would be nice if she could make things easy. "I needed money."

"There are lots of things you can do for money."

"You don't think it's weird that guys get off on me calling them worthless pieces of shit? Maybe I should break my own rule and meet one so I can bring him along and get your insight."

"Would you like to use your session to delve into the complexities of psychodynamic behavior? Or do you think we could redirect? You mentioned your father."

Aṅụrị could have made triple or more from her paypigs were she willing to sell her used underwear or even pose for a few sultry neck-down shots. She stroked the arms of Ammah's chair and laughed to herself because knowing that men were vibrating with lust over someone's gently stained period pants made her feel like she had inadvertently ingested opioids. The point was that she had a choice. And she chose no. Anything remotely sexual meant she would have to evict Nkem from her head when she unloaded the vitriol for which her pigs returned again and again. She used the same contempt she had for them to fix her father in place before the insults began.

She wanted to shock Ammah out of her therapist's shell. But Ammah, even as Aṅụrị admitted that one of her punters had flirted with bankruptcy to keep her happy, remained unflappable. So she continued, adding that it wasn't the tributes that made her endorphins spike, but the cruelty of her words as they flew from her fingertips—a wave she rode until she could no longer remain upright and the adrenaline would leave her body in a singular rush. Insulting men for money. Saying all the things she could not say to her father.

"Control is your drug of choice. We have talked about this before," Ammah said. "But does it make you happy? This line of work?" There was a marked difference between how Aṅụrị approached and spoke about styling and candle making and how she did findom. Ammah suggested they explore healthy ways in which Aṅụrị might broach that which she, to date, could not voice to Nkem.

"Perhaps someday," Aṅụrị replied.

Now she opened a new browser tab and purchased an air-conditioning unit for her hairdressing hut. LowlyWorm would regroup and live on to spend again. She flexed her fingers, chronically stiff from the hours she spent creating new and wonderful worlds on the heads of her clients, and pulled up the scheduling app on her phone to see she had two new bookings: a wig install and single braids. There would come a day, Aṅụrị knew, that the sight of new bookings would not trigger a fizzing in her chest, and she prayed that if she had to see that day, it would be so cloaked with newfound joy that she would not notice. She confirmed the bookings and turned her attention to packing the candle orders she was due to ship out the next day; eighteen of them. She took pride in the meticulous ribbon tying, the handwritten thank-you card she sent with each order. She'd opted for the more expensive of the label printers and paid a premium to a company somewhere in Jersey for lightly scented padded postage bags. There was comfort in the repetition—sign, roll, seal, swipe—and in that comfort, Aṅụrị pushed Nkem's derision from her mind. *Making hair.* As if it was a worthless pursuit. As if bringing smiles to the faces of people who entrusted their crowns to her fingertips meant nothing. *Peddling candles.* Like scent could not remove you from where you stood and send you to a field, a forest, your grandmother's kitchen; as if olfaction was not a gift. Humans were like this, Aṅụrị knew. Incapable of honoring the things they assumed they would always possess.

Before she embarked on the journey of creating a candle (and it was a journey, pretention be damned), Aṅụrị liked to envision where she wanted to be. Then she would work until she could re-create the place in her mind and bring it to reality. She was uniquely gifted in this aspect and her sales were a reflection of the same. It wasn't "peddling candles" when Ophelia launched her now-shuttered candle company. And it was only the weak who espoused the lie that success was the best revenge—Aṅụrị knew this. Revenge was the best revenge; success the cake topper that sweetened the deal. Why shouldn't she indulge in both? Was it petty to commit to surpassing Ophelia in the field of wax e-commerce? Almost certainly. Was she entirely justified? Without question.

After she sealed the final package, she drifted to the fridge because she also knew that there, behind the containers of berries she bought from the market, there would be an emergency bottle of rosé. She told herself it was not for drinking, that it served as a reminder of how dangerous the sweetness of surrender could be, but it was there and not on the shelf of the off-license where the lesson was just as effective. Aṅụrị cursed herself, even as she tasted that first sip, for criticizing the weakness in others while sporting her own flaws. She had become adept at making excuses for herself; hiding under half-truths that made her squirm with shame in the cold light of day. Today's variety: Nkem's disenchantment with the best parts of her life; scuppered plans with Noelle; the precarity of calm before another legal storm arrived, another she had conjured. She told Ammah it was a habit, not an addiction; one she cultivated in her teens because it helped her sleep, and made the burden of expectation easier to shoulder. It was that or cutting. She thought she had made the better choice. *I am human*, she told herself as the alcohol kneaded her emotional knots, *and hypocrisy is a uniquely human trait*.

She woke to the sound of Loki because Loki, even before you saw him, was a collection of sounds: sighs, laughter, the near constant recitation of lyrics. His voice reached her through the fog of her hangover, but Aṅụrị did not allow herself to believe he was real. Not when he appeared in the doorway of her bedroom. Not when he opened first the blinds and then the window. No. Only when he stood over her and ran a hand over her hair did she know she was no longer dreaming. He had been gone for months, their correspondence reduced to FaceTime, texts and multiple daily voice notes, some of which were podcast length. And now he was back and in her room having let himself into the flat with the key she gave him the day she moved in. Aṅụrị closed her eyes again but tears, as is their wont, find a path to freedom, and hers squeezed from under her eyelids.

"Ah, darling," Loki said. "What have you gone and done?"

TWO

Consider this. A rainstorm. A gently perspiring woman perched on the edge of a metal hospital bed. The sheets are a bright green plaid, but they remind her of the fields behind her parents' compound in Awka, and she holds on to this like a crutch and leans willingly into the pain. This pain, she knows, is a gift; one she has prayed for through months then years of blood and tears and hopelessness that have been scrubbed from the bathroom floor by Nkem after the fact—tiny outfits bought for would-be owners who never got the chance to wear them. It is why she has not allowed herself to cry out, has swallowed each shout like tonic. Each scream would feel like betrayal. To herself, to God and to this child who has brought her to this same hospital sixteen times over the past eight months for checkups, and false alarms brought about by overzealous and slightly traumatized parents-to-be; who has pinned her to her bed, rearranged not only her organs but the very fiber of her being, the beating of her heart; who is the single most wonderful thing that has ever happened to her. Throughout it all, she has rejoiced. She had, in those first few weeks, been so gripped by fear that she would creep from the bedroom and pound yam in the kitchen until her arms seized, and when Nkem found her asleep on the kitchen floor, he would carry her back to bed and fold her fingers into his palm hoping to absorb some of the desperate hope that radiated from her. Their prayers were whispered at first.

She asked God to have mercy, he for strength.

The woman's name is Kainene which is Igbo for "let us watch." A portent.

Nkem first saw her as he held court over a platter of rice and assorted meat at Mama Nneji's. He was nineteen, young and handsome, and life had not yet stolen from him the cocky assuredness that he carried in his pockets and doled out in the form of smiles, jokes and overly loud greetings to strangers who could not help but smile back. He and his friends frequently congregated at Mama Nneji's because her food was second only to that their own mothers cooked and served under roofs beneath which they no longer lived. Mama Nneji herself liked Nkem's smile, one that broke open his entire face, and she appreciated how he would double back to help her lug sacks of onions or tubers of yam, so she would knock off a few naira and let him feel like something of a man among this gaggle of boys. That day, Kainene, surly and recalcitrant, had been sent to collect and transport a tray of peppered snails to her mother's friend whose husband had found comfort between the thighs of another. Kainene's afternoon, previously set aside for friends and films, had now been sacrificed in service of someone else. Her own smile which was near perpetual had been chased from her face. Still. Nkem would tell her months later when they lay pressed against each other that he sensed her before he saw her. That the perspiration on her upper lip made him want to bolt over and kiss it away. The air was scented with oil and Scotch bonnet, but the real reason his eyes watered was because he had lost the ability to blink, to look away, to breathe.

Here they were seven years and a lifetime later, sitting in Holy Rosary Specialist Hospital and Maternity Waterside, Onitsha awaiting their firstborn. It had been seven years of fasting and prayer. Of experts and authorities who nodded and clucked their sympathy and told the couple to try again. Almost a decade of Kainene's mother appearing in the house to stock the fridge and lie across her daughter, hoping to draw the grief into her own body until the smile returned. Of Kainene's father patting Nkem on the shoulder and allowing him to shed his tears away from the eyes of his wife. Nkem would always be grateful for this, the moments he could finally fall to pieces and reassemble himself into a husband who could give his wife what she so desperately wanted. His sister, Nneoma, already living in London, heard the news after everyone else. Nkem would grip the telephone so tightly that he lost feeling in his fingers.

"The baby," he had said a total of three inexplicable excruciating times, after each separate loss, "ọ tụfuru nwa. It's gone."

This time, the fourth, Nkem's worry had chewed through a portion of his stomach and sometimes he coughed blood into the sink in the bathroom. Every day he practiced disguising his dread with optimism, and as the months wore on, it became easier. Kainene's pregnancy shunted her from bed to doctor to hospital and back to bed, but Nkem learned to swallow his concern. The light had returned to his wife's eyes. Her smile tied a knot in his anxiety. Her laughter swept through the house and blew the foreboding out of the windows and over the red earth. He knew that love and fear sometimes tasted the same, and he loved Kainene enough to consume the fear and spit out joy. For her sake, he would pull the moon from the sky. In Holy Rosary, he dabbed at his wife's forehead with the sleeve of his shirt and looked around for the midwife who had led them to this metal bed.

"Abeg, where is this girl?" Nkem hissed and Kainene took his hand and kissed the palm.

"Try to—" her sentence was sliced in half by a contraction "—relax, di m." *My husband.*

"You've been having headache for the past two days and now your chest." Nkem's voice began to rise. "Can you stay? I need to fetch her."

Consider this. A brief but searing labor. The rain carving the sky open and descending in sheets. A baby girl born to parents who cradled her and wept with gratitude even as an air bubble formed deep inside a vein on the lower left side of Kainene's abdomen and traveled swiftly toward her heart. The doctors caught it before it was too late and six hours after the child was born, Kainene was returned to her bed. Nkem wanted a name wreathed in all the grandness of the Igbo tradition. But Kainene, who had battled and sweat and mourned her way through the loss of three pregnancies, reflected her simple and potent thanks in the girl's first name—Aṅụrị. "Happiness" or "joy" or simply "rejoice." Tragedy, as it liked to do, waited until its impact would be most keenly felt; when there was more than one life to ruin. That night, the first and the only, the three slept but only two woke. The doctors caught the embolism but missed the aneurysm, which erupted beautifully inside Kainene's brain as she dreamed about her new daughter.

At the funeral, Nkem fell to his knees then tipped forward until his cheek was pressed against the ground. He felt his heart being drawn downward through his body and into the earth. Did it not belong to her, after all? It was impossible that his life had been plunged into darkness so abruptly—that everything he was days earlier had been burned right down to the root. He had not slept; his eyes fiery with fatigue and incredulity as arrangements were made to bury his wife. There would be no Ikwa Ozu—what was there to celebrate? Nkem's parents had passed in quick succession three years after he married, so it was Kainene's father, Arinze, who stepped forward to help Nkem to his feet. It was Kainene's mother, Makuochukwu, who knelt beside him and placed her hand on his back. Nkem, made delirious with shock and agony, shrugged her off.

"Biko, leave me!" he moaned but Makuo touched him again.

"Your child," she reminded him even as tears slid down her face, "nùlụ onū m. She needs you."

Nneoma, who flew through a storm to reach him, who pressed her forehead against the window of the plane and whispered in tongues not for her safety but for the world to be unmade and remade into one where Kainene still lived, stood back and held the infant. She watched helplessly as her brother broke into enough pieces to salt the earth. In the days since Kainene's death, Nkem had allowed grief to carry him away from his daughter. When Aṅụrị cried, it was Nneoma, Makuo or Arinze who rose and tended to her, the child's anguish winding its way past them all and hitting the wall of Nkem's sorrow. The night before the burial, Nneoma brought Aṅụrị to her brother and implored him to cradle her. She could see the potential for enduring disaster already forming; his grief was a weed that, if left unattended, could choke out the goodness and claim the light from everywhere it reached.

"Nkem, Na nke a bụ ezi. Look at her."

Nneoma was not wrong. It *wasn't* right. He stared down into the bundle in his sister's arms, wiped his face and let his daughter squeeze his finger with the surprising strength given to babies when they enter the world. "Aṅụrị," he said. "Joy." He spat the word out like it was a curse and retreated to his room.

Now, as Makuo and Arinze helped him to his feet, Nneoma stepped forward and waited until he brushed the dust from his clothes before wordlessly handing him the baby. When they were children and the sounds of parental discord carried through the house, Nneoma would appear in the doorway of their bedroom and comfort him with her eyes. They'd take refuge in the yard, their backs against the cement wall. No words were spoken because they were not required; instead, interlocked fingers or a head against a shoulder until the sound of slamming doors informed them that it was safe to reenter the house. Not so much had changed over the years. When Nneoma had moved to London, Nkem would call and after the greetings and the small talk, they would sit in relative silence. Love was sometimes diluted by speech and these siblings knew that better than most.

Remaining in Nigeria seemed impossible. Onitsha was a battlefield littered with latent memories waiting for Nkem to stumble into their path. Here, Mercy's Beauty Shop where he would wait and watch Kainene shop for leave-in conditioner. Here, the fallen tree on River Beach where his hand accidentally grazed her breast for the first time and the slap she'd delivered rang in his ears for two days afterward. Here, Arinze and Makuo's dining table where Nkem had sweated as he petitioned for Arinze's blessing to marry his daughter. All of this and more, able to tear him apart. He walked around half blinded by tears and rage; would not hear reason. When Makuo suggested he leave Aṅụrị with them for a month so he could depart Onitsha temporarily and swim to the surface of his grief, he told her, in a surprising about-face, that it was God alone who would separate him from his child.

Instead, he brought forward the plans he and Kainene made. They had wanted to try their hand at life in the UK. Nneoma made it sound exhausting and exhilarating in equal measure. They would, after their unborn child celebrated her first birthday, see if the highs and lows tasted different to those in Nigeria and, after a year or five, come home. Arinze and Makuo supported the idea—for there is no greater pleasure for a parent than to watch your child being loved in unfamiliar but exciting ways. Kainene was spreading her wings and Nkem was both her updraft and her fail-safe. Now they pleaded with him to reconsider and when he phoned his sister to lament, she surprised him by echoing their concerns.

"Everything is too fresh," she told him. "Adighi oso. I rushed, but you don't have to."

"You're telling me not to come."

"I am telling you to take time. Aṅụrị is so young, and you need support from your in-laws and they need time with their grandchild."

"So you won't support me?"

"I no get strength for dramatics, Nkem. That's not what I said."

They lapsed into silence until Nneoma excused herself to go and prepare for her shift at the hospital. Nkem lifted his daughter from her basket and held her against him. He paced the boards of the bedroom he'd shared with Kainene; where the memories were perhaps the most powerful but inexplicably, less suffocating. He stepped onto the rug she'd brought home after a disastrous day at work. The one she unfurled and sat upon, and where he found her and joined her when he too came home after his calls for her went unanswered. *I just wanted to look at something beautiful*, she said to him and when he held her hand, she smiled into his face and said, *Sometimes I forget that you are the most beautiful thing*. Again he was awash with disbelief. He would never see her again and the fact of her absence ate away at him and made him realize that it was inevitable that, as with his parents, one day he would lose everyone he adored. A month later, he and Aṅụrị descended into the persistent grayness of the UK. She was three months old.

At what point does grief morph into ambivalence? For Nkem, life refused to grow tired in its insistence that he partake in it. The effort of simply existing was so great that it left neither room nor energy for anything else. The flat he found for himself and Aṅụrị was both small and dark. He thought it fitting. The possibility of joy was a constant threat he did his best to avoid. He felt disfigured by loss; marred by it. Death was cruel. It was the ugliness of a missing piece around which you have to rebuild yourself. Surely Aṅụrị felt it, too. Her mother was gone. The attempts at comfort from Nkem were well-meaning but empty. She screamed into the damp air of the flat as he shushed in vain and carried her from one tiny room to the next. Kainene was part of her as well. Nkem knew this and thus understood that her loss was perhaps larger than his own. But grief made him selfish. He had assumed he would have a lifetime. That was his mistake. Happiness was finite and he had expended his in Kainene and the brief moments they shared as parents. Pain blighted what were meant to be the unshakeable bonds formed between infants and their parents. When he looked at his child, he saw his loss staring back at him; Kainene's eyes in the head of a different human; her dimples in the cheeks of someone who could not yet speak.

Understandably, it was too much. But is that not what parenthood entails? Sometimes it *is* too much, and still you must find the strength. Later, much later when the relationship had grown so brittle and fragile that an errant breath could demolish it, Nkem would taste a hundred flavors of regret and would still be unable to adequately express his remorse.

More and more he began to leave Aṅụrị with his sister. Nneoma, who pleaded with her brother to stay with her longer; who watched his grief harden into something more disquieting, cradled her tiny niece and begged Nkem to try harder.

"I need to work. If I'm to take care of her properly, I need to work." It was a flimsy excuse. The support Nkem required, he had refused, choosing instead to accelerate plans that fell apart under close examination.

Grief, however, is a cruel but efficient motivator. A hand on your back driving you forward to goals that, once achieved, will ring hollow. With each exam passed, each certification gained; each deadpan congratulations offered from an equally dead-eyed paymaster, Nkem moved closer to the life he and Kainene had discussed so many times beneath navy skies. When he was hired into a firm of engineers responsible for designing beautiful yet impractical structures suited to people whose need to impress eclipsed common and fiscal sense, Nkem returned to his flat, touched his lips to his wedding photo and wept. He collected his daughter from Nneoma and spent the afternoon pushing her through Clapham Common and whispering apologies and soon-to-be broken promises into the soft fuzz of her baby curls.

A little before 2:00 a.m. on the Tuesday before her first birthday, Aṅụrị's right big toe twitched as she lay sleeping in her cot. The butter-soft dimple behind her knee was a little warm. By the time the clock showed 2:15, her entire body was aflame. Aṅụrị's distress yanked Nkem out of sleep. Kainene, who visited him in his dreams, touched his shoulder and vanished, and he felt that familiar resentment; that kernel of bitterness that refused to die and had instead put down roots, growing stubbornly. He shuffled to his daughter's side and he felt heat fanning out across her skin even before he pressed her trembling frame to his chest. She was limp and clammy in his arms, and panic rose inside him and beat his heart into a gallop.

"What do I do?" he shouted into the phone at his sister, who had been sleeping for only twenty-three minutes after a double shift.

"Nkem? Is it that you moved here and left all your sense back in Onitsha? Take her to the hospital, for goodness' sake! I will meet you there."

The siblings slumped against each other under the harshness of the A&E lighting. Nkem considered making a scene, but knew guilt was the driving force behind such a sentiment. Sometimes, when your behavior is terrible enough to warrant shame, you become adept at slipping its grasp; if only so you can sleep at night. Nkem felt the same loss of control that seized him the night Kainene died. Was this to be another thing he would have to carry? In the blue plastic of the waiting room chair, he began to shake. Nneoma placed her palm flat against his arm and held him still. Since youth this had been her gift.

Three hours later, there was a diagnosis: an ear infection. The relief pushed Nkem against the wall of the examination room and both Nneoma and the on-call pediatrician watched his slow descent to the floor. He was given antibiotics, instructions to watch his daughter, keep her cool and comfortable, and consult a GP should things persist after a few days. Aṅụrị was given a smile and a soft kiss by the trainee maternity nurse with the waist-length blond braid.

By the morning of her first birthday, Aṅụrị's health was restored along with Nkem's resolve. Fatherhood was not something he was meant to traverse alone. Kainene had promised him. He had been more than content with just her, with just *them*. And, because he *had* left his sense in Onitsha, because he could not reconcile common infant ailments like ear infections; because they underlined his failures and made it impossible for him to hide from them, Nkem decided that the sacrifices he would make going forward would in fact be Aṅụrị's. He called Kainene's parents, offered perfunctory updates and asked them for the money to hire some help. They gave him the money and in effect, paid for the course their grandchild's life would take. Enter Ophelia May Eriksson. She of the waist-length blond braid.

Years later, Nkem would understand that choice was an illusion. A lie. And a beautiful one at that. For what seemed like an age, he would maintain that it was his choice; to let Kainene fade into the grayness of memory; to erect a wall between him and his child; to invite this blonde woman into their lives with her scent of vanilla and her voice that left you with an earful of honey; to watch her lift his daughter up and coo into the facsimile of the face of his dead wife. He would tell Nneoma, Makuo and Arinze that he was doing what he needed to as a man and as a father. That he needed help and more than that, Aṅụrị needed someone who could be solely hers, and not fighting the pull of a hundred different obligations. And when Arinze said, "And us, nko?" Nkem would bristle. Because if it was his choice, then he still had some sort of control. And control, when you have lost everything, when hope has been extracted from you like a black tumor, is everything. Even when it is a lie.

At first, Ophelia came two days a week for a few hours at a time. She fed and bathed Aṅụrị while Nkem prepared for work; would usher him out of the door because he would remain inert, frozen to the spot in the living room as he watched this white woman cradling his daughter. In the afternoons, Nneoma would arrive at Nkem's door and relieve Ophelia of her niece, maintaining a civility she knew was required of her as a Black woman, despite her every nerve ending screaming in protest at the presence of this interloper.

For Ophelia, she saw in Nkem all the marks of a broken heart and hers split open and welcomed him and his child in. Soon, she was leaving foil-wrapped plates in the kitchen with Post-it notes; praying he would both believe that it was no trouble at all and see through the lie that it was. On Fridays, she would launder the overflowing basket of clothes and iron two or three shirts. *It's nothing*, she would say to Nkem's bewildered thanks and protestations, but she would blush each time the words left her lips and eventually, Nkem would notice. By the third month of Ophelia's employment, her two days had become five, and when month four rolled around, she would swing her braid over her shoulder and join Nkem and Aṅụrị on Saturdays for strolls around the common and hot chocolate at the coffee shop at the end of the road.

In retrospect, Nkem didn't really stand a chance. To find both love and social capital in a woman who looked and moved like Ophelia was serendipity. Lightning was not supposed to strike twice, and if it did, was he not supposed to welcome it? The first time Ophelia pressed her lips to his, he waited until she left for home then retreated to his bedroom and sobbed. He must tell her, he resolved, that while flattered, this was something they must immediately smother. It could not be allowed to grow. Kainene was lost to him, yes, but was it not his job to mourn forever? The next day, he opened the door to the sight of Ophelia on her back in his living room, her hair fanned out like ropes of gold, Aṅụrị sitting on her stomach gurgling merrily. He held Ophelia's wrist that evening, when she tried to leave the flat, and held her nakedness against him that night for the first time. That was his choice.

"You should be capturing these moments more," Ophelia told him when Aṅụrị's bottom teeth burst through. "She won't ever be this little again."

"The pictures we take of her? Those aren't enough?" Already Nkem had transformed them into a "we."

"How many photos have you actually taken?" Ophelia rolled over in the bed and Nkem caught a glimpse of her shed underwear, pink and lacy, before it was once again swallowed by the sheets—a shell under sea foam. "How often do Aṅụrị's grandparents get to see her? They must miss her loads."

Nkem frowned. What use was it to invite Arinze and Makuo into bed with them? Why position potholes in his way when he had become so adept at outpacing his guilt? "There are phone calls." He was terse, but Ophelia was a woman who understood that wars were fought and won on the backs of men and their egos. She threw a thigh over Nkem's legs.

"Y'know, these days it's better to make a space that people who love Aṅụrị can visit without visiting. Kind of like a memory chest."

"And where would we put this chest?"

"Online." She watched as the frown returned and offered the silky curve of her bare breast for Nkem to kiss. "You wouldn't have to do anything. I'll just add it to my list of stuff to handle. Change nappies, arrange tummy time, update the blog. I just think it's a sweet thing for Aṅụrị's family to be able to hop onto a computer anytime they want and see how she's getting on."

"Blog." Nkem repeated the word. It made no sense to him, bordered on absurd, but he had reached the point where he could no longer differentiate between the joy of sex and the feeling of elation of ending his evenings with a companion who gazed at him like he hung the moon and scattered the stars with a flick of his wrist. Love demands so much of us: that we pull down the barriers we have built to protect ourselves and hurl ourselves toward someone we can only pray will catch us. Nkem looked down at Ophelia and let himself fall.

They were married five days before Aṅụrị turned two. Nkem first tackled Ophelia's parents, Henry and Genevieve, who sat open-mouthed and incredulous while their only child explained her intention to wed this immigrant turned employer with whom she was evidently smitten. They considered calling the police. Had he used some of that African voodoo on their baby? Genevieve cried into the pâté and Henry cleared his throat and said "well then" so many times, Ophelia slammed her palm down on the table and accused them of being racist. If there is one thing white people hate more than anything in this world, it is the implication that their racism makes them racist. Nkem held his fiancée's hand and explained (very meekly; one does not frighten the middle class with anything as crass as enthusiasm) that he had a good job, that he planned to move out of the tiny flat and into a home befitting Ophelia and her meters and meters of blond hair. Aṅụrị was a toddler and the thought to move had not crossed Nkem's mind. But to be judged by Ophelia's parents was beyond the pale. And after Henry and Genevieve, he returned to the darkest corner of the flat and made the call to Arinze and Makuo.

They arrived in London less than forty-eight hours later. Nkem saw his life through their eyes. For Kainene they had bent their backs and made the sort of sacrifices required to paint your child's name indelibly above your own. They watched her fall in love, held her when her body betrayed her, smoothed her hair over her face before they laid her to rest. And now they stood in a flat listening to the man who swore to love her for eternity explain to them how life had a way of granting second chances you did not deserve; that God saw fit to smile down on him again.

"Odiegwu. God has nothing to do with this," Arinze said.

Makuo looked at her son-in-law. He would not meet her eye. "What is the hurry?" she asked. "Is she pregnant?" She thought she might choke on the last word but was comforted, if only marginally, by the shake of Nkem's head.

Kainene's parents could not understand why they had been reduced to reading the words of another woman and looking at her pictures on the screen of their computer at home. It made no sense that Anụrị was now a collection of pixels and this was how they were meant to know her. She was meant to be with them. They were meant to be a piece of her salvation. They had been pushed out. It felt like staring at the sun from the bottom of the ocean.

When Nkem finally called for Ophelia and she brought the child out to them, Makuo's heart seized. A stranger looking upon them with suspicion. As if Anụrị was hers. As if they meant her harm. And on the morning of the wedding, they looked across the aisle of the courthouse at Henry and Genevieve and were met with blank stares. Outside, before they filed in, Arinze caught Nkem's sleeve and all but dragged him to the side.

"Nkem. Adịghị ọsọ." *Wait.* "If you say she is for you, then wait."

"I won't." Nkem shook him off. "Come inside or don't."

Nkem was not theirs. They had tried to make him so; brought him and Nneoma under their umbrella of love because he was Kainene's and she was theirs, and so it became normal, almost necessary to them to make him theirs, too. But he wasn't. There would always be a gap at the side of which Nkem would stand and they would love him regardless because wasn't that part of it? Doing it even when it could only be returned imperfectly or perhaps not at all? It was clear, then, Nkem was not theirs, but Aṅụrị was and so Arinze went inside and sat beside his wife, and they watched the future of their grandchild become something over which they had neither control nor real input. Makuo and Arinze made strained conversation with Henry and Genevieve beside the chrysanthemums in their garden where the reception was held, and, when Makuo thought her head might burst with the effort of it all, she crept into the house to where Aṅụrị was napping and cried silent tears onto the lace hem of the child's dress.

For Ophelia, the straight A student and university graduate, education was nothing but a welcome challenge to her. Like reaching the summit of a perilous peak. There would be setbacks, a tangle of roots at the ankle, the sting of nettles on bare flesh, the persistence of flying insects, but you would arrive at the top with burning muscles and empty lungs, exhausted but triumphant. Unfamiliar territory was an aphrodisiac. Ophelia learned that her blog hits spiked whenever she wrote candidly of what it meant to raise a Black child as a white woman; how her myriad inadequacies presented themselves in a way she had heretofore never had to reckon with. She understood that her readers took delight in hearing about how her love for Aṅụrị now extended to the child's father—who doesn't love a star-crossed love story? And an interracial one at that? She was made for this. She posted photos of Aṅụrị but noted the uptick in interest when she added photos of herself; the juxtaposition of dark skin against light, the knowledge that someone so beautiful could also be so benevolent. She found herself at the eye of the perfect content storm: being soft and stunning yet somehow relatable; raising another woman's child; the complexities of loving a widower all made for compelling subject matter. Fascination beget loyalty, and loyalty beget page views, and what had been positioned as an innocent method to connect Añurị with her far-flung family members was now the source of the warmth flooding Ophelia's stomach when she read the comments that first trickled onto then flooded the page. This was the age of the blogger boom; the era of the Mommy Blogger and the space for candid portrayals of womanhood and motherhood. Añurị became the vehicle to transport Ophelia out of her previous life which, privileged as it was, was unremarkable.

By the time she and Nkem were married, Ophelia's blog (for of course it was now hers) *Fee + Nuri* was generating enough income from strategically placed banner advertisements that she was able to hand in her notice at the maternity agency where she worked and dispense with her training to be a full-time pediatric nurse. When Nkem asked why Añurị's name had been shortened, why the diacritics did not appear, Ophelia explained carefully that he shouldn't worry, that it was a matter of analytics. The truth was that Añurị was Igbo, but Ophelia was not. And most people also were not. Nkem did not seem pressed about teaching Ophelia his native tongue and she did not seem too bothered to learn. Why not make things simpler? "Nuri" was such a cute moniker and so much easier to pronounce.

Nneoma watched this all with mounting trepidation. The initial novelty of being able to peruse a webpage during the quiet parts of her shift and see the beauty of her niece soon wore off. As a woman who did not even divulge too many details about her travel plans because she was African and Africans knew it was an act of foolishness to believe everyone in the world wished only good things for you, what seemed odd but sweet soon refused to make even the smallest amount of sense. Strangers had no business staring at Añurị in the bathtub. What possible good would it do to know that Ophelia cowered under the spectre of Kainene, a woman Nkem stopped mentioning about the time he opened his home and his bed to her? Why invite comment? Did Ophelia not know that privacy was a gift? Why was she like so many other white people? Reckless with the privileges they had been afforded simply by being born a particular race?

"It's not right," Nneoma told her brother. "She is a child, but that doesn't mean she belongs to everyone. Ikike nzuzo. Does she not deserve that?"

"Privacy? She's a child. Nne, you worry too much. It's harmless, na? Don't you like seeing Añụrị without waiting for me to send you the photos? You always told me I was too slow."

Ophelia stepped into the room and Nneoma fell quiet. Wisdom, she saw, can chase you, but ignorance can outrun it if you are determined enough. The lines had been drawn and too much was at stake. Her niece, like her brother, flowed through her veins. Neither could be excised and the loss of either would be enough to render her life meaningless. There were battles that were important to fight but which required the patience and practice of strategizing. Nneoma kept quiet. Not for the last time.

OPHELIA

I loved Aṅụrị first. You must understand that. My love for Nkem followed later. It was stealthy but insistent. By the time I recognized it, it had cracked me open like the tree root that grows beneath then upends the foundation of a house.

THREE

When searching for the flat, Aṅuṛi told the estate agent, a raven-haired shark of a woman, that she did not require much but that the not much was nonnegotiable: a bit of outdoor space and a shower with water pressure strong enough to strip skin. She got both. She also got a landlord whom she charmed enough to be given free rein to splash color on the walls and blot out the omnipresent magnolia. Aṅuṛi painstakingly eradicated the same neutrals Ophelia introduced into their lives when money was no longer something that needed to stretch; that could be spent on more than charity shop finds and upcycled castaways. How strange, Aṅuṛi thought, that wealth so often ushered in the death of distinction and replaced it with the faux safety of uniformity. Freedom was colorful; happiness, bright. She splashed her truth on the walls and unrolled it across her floors.

When Aṅuṛi shut off the shower, Simi was waiting for her, a towel dangling from one finger, eyes on the iPhone in her hand.

"When did you get here?"

"About half an hour after Loki called me." Simi didn't look up. "Want to talk about it or nah?"

"Talk about what?"

"So nah, then. Cool. He's 'making breakfast' by the way."

"Oh shit."

"Mm-hmm. How dressed do you need to be to have this conversation?"

"I only need lotion."

Simi raised her head then and tucked the phone into her pocket. Her smile stole in and captured her face. "My babes. Hello. I missed you."

"In the seventeen hours since we last spoke, I missed you too, Sim." Anụrị, a woman whose own capacity for feeling often felt blunted, whose trust in her own emotions was thin and brittle, found solace in the steadfastness of her best friend's love.

She massaged lime and coconut lotion into her skin, then she and Simi made their way to the kitchen, where all six feet six inches of Loki hovered over a frying pan, the contents of which sputtered forlornly against his shirt, the stovetop, the floor tiles. To his right, the remnants of an avocado was browning on a slice of bread. To his left, an attempt at pancake batter congealed in Anụrị's best Pyrex bowl. Loki cursed under his breath as the pan began to smoke.

"Loki, please. It's actually not by force." Simi pushed him away from the stove. She wrinkled her nose at the mess in the pan before shoving the entire thing into the sink and turning the tap on full blast.

Loki leaned against the counter and ran a hand first over his face, then through his locs—shoulder length and bleached at the ends as if he had dipped them into a bucket of sunshine. Anụrị remembered the first time she saw him, aged eight at Camp Montana in Switzerland where she was sent for the month of August, along with a summer au pair who would capture the most content-worthy coming-of-age moments for Instagram and Ophelia's blog. Already towering over the other children, Loki seemed even then to crave the anonymity afforded by compactness. He tried to curl in on himself; to fold himself in half and make his size and therefore himself, more palatable. He was aware of the space he took up and, unlike others who chased attention, Loki hid from it. He had a smattering of dark freckles across his nose, and that, along with his eyes and his unhurried movements, meant that you could not help but notice him when he loped by, gaze fixed on the ground before him.

He eschewed company, and while this ought to have attracted the ridicule of children who did not understand much but knew enough that to be lonesome, even deliberately, signified otherness, and otherness denoted oddness, and oddness was to be mocked and stamped out, it instead lent Loki an air of mystery. He was popular without ever realizing it. Aṅụrị was not immune, which was no surprise—being drawn to Loki was par for the adolescent course. But what *was* strange to her was that her curiosity, her interest went unreciprocated. A child who had grown up with the praise of many in her ears, who at eight years of age already understood what it meant to have fans, could not then parse the indifference of the interesting. It was not rejection per se, although that too would have been baffling, but being hated, for many, is preferable to being ignored. In this case, Nkem's emotional desertion had been seamlessly replaced first with Ophelia's care and then with the adoration of the internet. Simply put, this was new for Aṅụrị. Loki's apathy made her hate him. Her desire for his attention intensified the hatred.

They were, as is the cliché, thrown together by chance by the camp activity coordinators who paired the two children for the circus activities—they were learning to juggle (£8,300 per child meant that such frivolities were carried out with the seriousness of an MI6 briefing). Daphne, Aṅụrị's summer au pair, took some solo shots of Aṅụrị holding the juggling clubs and then instructed Loki to smile so she might include a few "candids" of Aṅụrị and partner. Ophelia's instructions were clear: the audience responded to Aṅụrị with friends and Camp Montana was awash with the sort of company that caused Ophelia to wake up panting and flushed.

"No," Loki told Daphne even as she pleaded.

"Why are you being so weird?" Aṅụrị demanded. "It's just some pics."

"You have a lady following you around everywhere taking photos and *I'm* the weird one?"

It had occurred to Aṅụrị only minimally before then that perhaps her life was not altogether normal. The cognitive dissonance of an eight-year-old, naturally, is more pronounced. To Aṅụrị, Daphne's presence seemed typical. But on closer inspection, it *did* appear that outside of medical carers, she was the only one with an adult tracking her every move and the realization that this might be cause for derision crept beneath her skin and prickled uncomfortably throughout her body.

"It's for my mum's blog. Which is kind of mine as well," Aṅụrị tried to explain.

"So your mom is weird, too. Makes sense." Loki smiled as he said this and that smile was a dopamine shot straight to Aṅụrị's frontal cortex. It was a smile she would chase for as long as she knew him. He reached out and slung a lanky arm around her shoulder and grinned for Daphne's camera. He was being facetious, but the photograph would garner so much attention that Ophelia would negotiate a sponsorship deal with a well known brand of baby wipes on the back of it.

Post juggling, Aṅụrị and Loki formed the sort of trepidatory friendship that baffled and consumed them in equal measure. Gripped by the juvenile insecurity that comes from wanting so badly to be liked, to be accepted, but understanding that the revelation of that desire would be your undoing, the two circled each other like antelope contemplating the locking of horns. Loki would find Aṅụrị and Daphne on a bench and sit himself beside them, leaving a gap so large it necessitated the slight raising of voices to converse. Aṅụrị would locate Loki beneath a tree and would inspect the flowers on the bush some feet away from it. Neither wanted to be the one to cement the *thing* growing between them. But that is the thing with twin souls—they will find each other no matter what. Juvenile obstinacy is no match.

Before the end of August, they were inseparable and Ophelia, during her weekly calls to her stepdaughter, gathered the information necessary for herself: Loki was the child of soon-to-be divorced parents. Born and raised in New York, his accent fled south to be with those who made him: an investment banker ("Oh. Those Chevaliers.") and a six-foot ex-model from a wealthy New Orleans family who owned property ("Oh. *Those* Llorens."). Aṅuṛi racked up long-distance telephone bills because Loki was a child trying to make sense of the dissolution of his parents' union. He didn't always have the words, but he had the unshakeable knowledge that Aṅuṛi would call daily and never press him to fill the silence—she would simply exist with him in his confusion and his hurt, until he regained the ability to speak.

Loki, alongside Simi, became Aṅuṛi's chosen family. He flung his doors open when she ran from Ophelia. He eased bottles from her fists. He carried her like she was sand ready to flow through his fingers when she pushed herself to the brink of destruction. He was obsessed with breakfast food and cooked it badly when he was stressed.

This was not the first time Aṅuṛi's kitchen had taken the brunt of Loki's melancholy, but today was particularly egregious. And still he had found the time to tidy away the evidence of her mistake; the wine bottle was nowhere to be found. Her boy was sad; this became, for now, the most important thing. She watched his shoulders droop as he sighed into his hands. Loving Loki was like stepping into the warm waters of an ocean knowing you could never drown; that the water would never cool. She reached forward and curled a single loc around her finger.

"Alright, LoLo," she said. "Who is it this time?"

The Who was unsurprising. Emilie, Loki's current objet

d'affection, was leaving voice notes in iMessage explaining in detail the ways in which Loki's decision to flee Manhattan and spend the long Easter weekend in London with his friends was tantamount to infidelity.

"Gross," Simi said from her position on the living room floor where they'd moved to escape the mess of the kitchen. Loki and Aṅuṛi chose the sofa, but Simi opted for the floor. Her eyes were trained on her own phone but Simi's ability to split her attention between multiple recipients was the reason she, at twenty-six, had risen to the lofty post of marketing manager, in charge, ironically, of a collection of high-strung and high-maintenance influencers. "She knows you're not sleeping with either one of us, right? She knows that would basically be incest?"

"You and I could never fall into the category of incest, Simi. All I ask is one night." Loki threw a wolfish grin in Simi's direction which bounced off the back of her head and rolled under Aṅuṛi's sofa.

"I'm guessing saying shit like that doesn't really help your case, Lo." Aṅuṛi flicked his ear.

Loki groaned. "Em knows we're all strictly platonic and have been since the beginning of time. But she's also seen photos of you both and you know how it is with monogamous people ninety percent of the time. She thinks you're lying in wait. She thinks *I'm* lying in wait. She doesn't get why both my best friends are women."

"You too are monogamous, Loki," Simi reminded him. "And would it help if I spoke to her and explained just how much I am not attracted to you. I'd be happy to help."

"Then she'd just cuss you," Loki said.

"Why?"

"You can't insult her man like that, Simi."

Simi raised an eyebrow. "I'd consider it my duty as your friend."

Aṅuṛi nudged Loki again. "Do you love her? Emilie, I mean."

"I could. If Simi wasn't the great unrequited love of my life."

"Loki."

"Kidding. Sheesh. But nah, I can't say there's love there. At least not yet. But I like the girl. Ain't that enough?"

Simi stood and slipped her phone back into the pocket of her jeans. "Your problem, Loki, is that you're painfully naive. Omo. You're a six-foot-six, conventionally attractive man with locs. You're also a Chevalier *and* a Llorens, and have a degree of emotional intelligence when most men can't even *spell* the phrase never mind possess the trait. When will you stop acting surprised when every person you date wants to keep you. Remember Stefan? He locked himself in your bathroom for twelve hours because you said you wanted to stop seeing him. You'd been on three dates."

"So what I'm hearing is that you think I'm fine." Loki caught Simi's hand as she squeezed onto the sofa beside him and his never-ending limbs.

"Go to hell," she said but smiled.

Wasn't this the beautiful thing about friendship? The gentle, unspoken surrendering of one's deficits to those who would handle them with appropriate caution whilst never thinking less of you? Aṅụrị had come to neither Simi nor Loki whole. Before even she understood the extent of her brokenness, the breadth and inky depths to it, they had already accepted her. And when someone has loved you before trauma, has loved you through it, that love crystallizes into something toughened yet beautiful and so you count it as the gift it is and do what you can to preserve it. Because she was sand, Aṅụrị settled into the gaps of their lives, the gaps Loki and Simi did not realize needed filling before her.

Aṅụrị tightened her bathrobe, the T-shirt she'd chosen to wear abandoned in her bedroom. "Why *are* you back in London, Loki? Love that you are, babe, but you usually give us some kind of heads-up."

"Céleste is getting married. Again."

Simi fell back against the sofa cushions and rolled her eyes. Aṅụrị's teeth found her bottom lip.

Loki closed his eyes. "The boyfriend won't sign a prenup. So Céleste is doing what she does best: ignoring him and using Remy as a tool of jealousy."

Remy and Céleste. Loki's long-divorced, tenaciously dysfunctional parents. Since their separation the summer Loki met Aṅụrị, Céleste had remarried and divorced twice more, leaving her exes heartsick and cash poor in her wake. Remy, easily infuriated by his wife in the way that meant he would love her in perpetuity, sank his efforts into the continued amassing of wealth, bachelorhood, petitioning his only son to find a purpose and "stop frittering away your youth on inconsequential bullshit," and happily returning to his ex-wife's bed whenever she decided she needed to slip the knife between a current beau's ribs. That Loki, soft and sweet as he was, had managed to establish a modicum of decency was evidence that Chukwu the Supreme was watching. Watching and crafting.

"What would it take," Simi asked, "for your family to agree to a multiseason reality show deal with E! or TLC? Abeg. If they're gonna put you through this every time, the least they can do is let you profit from it."

"That means Loki would also have to be on the show."

"It's true. I don't think he needs any additional ego boosts from status-starved social climbers."

Loki, his head having fallen to Aṅụrị's lap, pressed a size-fifteen foot hard against Simi's thigh until she squeaked in protest. "I love when you two talk like I'm not right the fuck here."

Aṅụrị gathered his locs in her hands and deftly twisted them into a bun that she secured with one of the three leather cords Loki wore on his left wrist. "Are you staying at the Mayfair flat?"

"Yeah." Loki paused. "But I can stay here if you like."

Even now, the blush-tinted wine bottle was nowhere in sight. Loki made sure of that. But mistakes leave marks and there was only so much ignorance Aṅụrị could plead—to be loved, truly loved, is to be seen, and to be seen is to limit the ability to hide, and Simi and Loki loved Aṅụrị in the purest way. She blinked back tears.

"I picked up Noelle yesterday," she began.

"You told me yesterday, babe." Simi had this way of looking at you. Her eyes, they could pull planets out of orbit.

Aṅụrị nodded, fingers stilled against Loki's scalp. "So I took her home and Ophelia like, spirited her away to go do some fashion bit with a stylist. She's five. And it's like, I just had to sit there and let it happen. So of course my dad comes home and…" In her head, Ammah's reminder: "Sound it out, slow. It doesn't have to make perfect sense." Because this was a side effect of years spent having so many of your words fed to you for regurgitation to the masses: you sometimes forgot how to speak on your own.

"Did you tell her about the cease and desist thing?" Simi asked.

"I chickened out. But I'll tell her. I just want Noelle out of that house," Aṅụrị finished. She caught the glance Simi and Loki exchanged and knew that while she was loved, there was still a space between love and full understanding, and hers was an experience that could not be wholly grasped without the unfortunate necessity of having lived it.

"Who doesn't, chère?" Loki's Creole bubbled to the surface alongside his concern. "Kids though. A lot of responsibility."

Simi nodded. "Lots of it. Like the most there is. My brothers are pretty much grown and if not for you, neither me nor my parents would have made it through their adolescence."

Aṅụrị heard the words they were not saying and swallowed retorts which would do nothing to further or clarify her point. Someone too weak to resist the lure of alcohol-induced oblivion was perhaps not the same someone who ought to become guardian to an already delicate human. Pride does not care about truth. "I'm pissed off."

"Pèlé, dear. Who wouldn't be?" Simi reached across Loki's legs and Aṅụrị let her best friend take her hand. "What does Ammah say about it?"

"What's there to say? I just don't want Nell to become another me."

"What the fuck is wrong with there being another you in this shithole of a world?" Loki sat up.

"Stand down, Lo," Aṅụrị smiled. "You know what I mean."

"Babes, we just want you to be happy."

"Exactly. What Simi said. You deserve to be happy."

Aṅụrị nodded. Ultimately, happiness was the goal; of course it was. But she understood that anger was the fuel; the conduit to carry her to that ultimate destination. She was not yet ready to relinquish it.

The world had the internet, that sparking treasure trove of knowledge, a smorgasbord of easily accessible data marred by misinformation and deviancy. Aṅụrị had Aunty Nneoma who told her to look at her hands, who held her close and said that one day she would know exactly what they were capable of. Along with Igbo, Nneoma taught Aṅụrị how to two-strand twist, then cornrow, how the length of Xpressions extensions would rasp through her fingers when she wove it into a sprig of coily natural hair. Aṅụrị became the artist, a head of hair, her canvas. Because she loved them, and because they let her use their heads to practice on, Nneoma, Loki and Simi would never have to pay a hairstylist again; dropping Aṅụrị texts whenever it was time for a retwist, new braids or a wig install. Over time, Aṅụrị learned to gauge texture by sight and touch, could pinpoint porosity issues with a glance and developed a sacred respect for edges. She taught herself how to melt lace and lay a wig so flawlessly it could not be said that those thirty inches of platinum blonde did

ALLOW ME TO INTRODUCE MYSELF

not grow from the owner's very own head. She broke nails learning the styles of home: Ngala for Igbo brides, Edamburu—the braided crown from the Congo—and threading, the latter puzzling and repulsing Ophelia into silence, unable to comprehend as she was why anyone would wish to wrap their hair in thread. An affinity for hair paired with the gratification it brought meant that it became an indulgence. For many, indulgences carried with them the faint aroma of guilt; a tacit acknowledgment of weakness. But this, the care and the intimacy that came with styling, could not be faulted. Aṅụrị submerged herself in the simple pleasure of it and when others began to take note, she succumbed to gentle pressure and harnessed it in a way that meant she was able to clothe herself and finance her love for caramel choux buns.

Aṅụrị wondered, as she pushed open the door to her hair hut, that tiny room with its slatted wood and painted black window frames she sweat to create, whether there would ever come a time she would cease to feel the stomach pinch of pride when she stepped inside. There was always a second following the plink of the video doorbell where Aṅụrị paused and fear took the opportunity to sink its teeth in. Was this person really a client? Or were they here because they recognized her? Had one or more of Ophelia's YouTube videos brought them to her door? The navigation of parasocial encounters was now an inescapable part of Aṅụrị's life and so it made sense to have anxiety color every uncharted interaction. She was, after all, the same girl for whom her stepmother had planned paid meet and greets; the hours she stood having photos with strangers now relegated to a phantom ache in her knees. To love a thing is to want to protect it and ludicrous as it might sound to others, the unsullied joy of feeling someone's hair in her hands was not dissimilar to how Aṅụrị felt about Noelle. She steadied herself, consulted her booking app for the sixth time to confirm that the person to whom she was about to grant entry matched the ID she asked for during the booking process and buzzed him in. Her only client of the day.

His name was Christian and he was new. A last-minute retwist she'd accepted only because Loki was sleeping off jetlag and Simi had a PR event to attend.

Later, after she'd been afforded the gift-curse of elapsed time, Aṅụrị would, as so many do, pick over her words and actions and find them both lacking and overblown to the point of farce. Her phone buzzed at the same time he entered and later, Aṅụrị would understand she had, unfairly, linked his arrival with that of Ophelia whose text felt like a battering ram in this, Aṅụrị's safe space.

> Remember lunch is at 1pm sharp tomorrow

Aṅụrị was not a person to assign meaning to coincidence. What purpose did it serve but to give power to that which was imagined? Aṅụrị did all she could to base her life in fact, forgetting that sometimes the subconscious is stubborn—it does what it wants. This was business and with business came the expectation of friendliness even when the parties know it is without real merit; that money is the driving force. And normally prolific at this; the pleasantries, the small talk, the proffering of beverages from the fridge in the corner, Ophelia chased all sense of decorum from Aṅụrị. While he greeted her with a smile and an expression of thanks that she was able to fit him in, she, eyes already raking over the fluff of new growth at his roots, smarting at the renewed knowledge that Ophelia didn't even consider her worthy of a "hello" and angry this was something that could still hurt her, pointed to her chair with her rat tail comb and told him not to worry about it in a voice devoid of its normal warmth. She loaded up Spotify and allowed Tems's crooning to curb any possibility of further chat. She turned up the volume as if that would drown out that still, small, yet persistent voice in her mind that said, *You miss her. You still miss her.*

Aṅụrị worked methodically: a clarifying shampoo as she mentally rifled through the contents of her wardrobe; double-pronged clips with scented locking gel for the retwist as she wondered why it was Ophelia and not her father who texted her at all. While he sat under the dryer, she lowered the speaker volume and left a garbled voice note for Simi pleading with her to return to the flat that evening and help her choose what to wear to an Easter lunch at the parents of the person whose empire she had covertly vowed to destroy.

"Is something funny?" Aṅuri asked when she clocked the raised eyebrow and smirk the dryer hood failed to disguise. His glasses were steaming up. He removed them before he answered.

Again, later, during her pursuit of sleep Aṅuri would remember the way his smile revealed a pair of canines which pressed softly into the cushion of his bottom lip, and how her lungs bloomed with something hot and terrifying.

"Ignore me, yeah? I just…"

"You just…?"

"You're cute when you're nervous."

An eye roll. An eye roll, even as the heat from her chest began to climb up her throat. She wished she were not so broken that the mere prospect of physical attraction caused a malfunction in her brain. She did not want to be a person defined by the engineered amusement she brought others, but her childhood meant that this was what she was. *Who* she was. And who she was made trust elusive, an oddity.

"I think you're all done under there, Christian?" She used his name for the first time since his arrival.

"Was that a question?"

"Come on out, let's check."

He held still while she examined the clean parts she made in his hair, the gleam of the newly twisted, conditioned roots. "Am I done then?"

"Yep."

Aṅuri averted her eyes while he tapped his phone against her card reader. She dropped a homemade oud-scented votive into a bag along with the locking gel he chose to purchase and made sure their fingers did not touch when she handed it to him.

His hair swung forward when he scooped out the candle. "You make this?"

"Yeah. It's my other business. Tell your friends."

"Is it? Aṅụrị the multiple business owner. Impressive. Am I saying your name right, by the way?"

"If I can pronounce Christian, you should be able to pronounce my name."

"Touché. It's a Nigerian name. I know that much."

So he wasn't here to gawp. He was either an outstanding actor or she was nothing but a hairstylist to him. Aṅụrị ignored the bubble of disappointment growing inside her. To be conflicted was to understand that to many you are someone, but to most you are nobody at all, and to simultaneously fear and crave both. "Igbo to be exact."

"Oh *is it*? Snap."

She noticed that the size of his smile was inversely proportional to how open his eyes could remain while doing it. "You're Igbo? And you go by Christian?"

"It's my name. That a problem?"

"Only 'cause it's rubbish. What's your real name?"

"You sound like my mum."

Aṅụrị tapped her fingers against the back of the salon chair and waited.

He smiled again. "Okay. My Igbo name is Chidili."

"Chidili."

"It means 'God be with me.'"

"Cute."

He chuckled. "I can't tell when you're being serious or playing with me."

She assumed his expression; deadpanned her mockery back to him. "Is it?"

Later, she would remember the way his shoulder blades shifted under the blue of his shirt as he headed toward the door. "About your thing tomorrow?"

She arched an eyebrow.

"If you have anything green, you should wear that."

"Why?"

"I have a feeling it's your color."

The YouTube algorithm—in the days before indiscriminating users were bombarded with red pill and conspiracy content—surfaced a lot of family-friendly yet amateur content like shakily filmed home tours and *my boyfriend does my makeup* challenges which left the audience amused, bored or subconsciously nursing the beginnings of an internet crush.

On the day Aṅụrị was formally introduced to Henry and Genevieve Eriksson, Ophelia was a string pulled taut. This is what happened when the validation of strangers or perceived lack thereof held enough weight to alter the mood of an adult. A video, meticulously edited and uploaded with the expectation of a certain percentage increase in subscribers, had performed badly, if "badly" is able to be quantified in the world of the terminally online. Ophelia, slipping from beside a sleeping Nkem before the sun had hoisted itself into the sky, went to Aṅụrị's wardrobe. *Shake it off,* she instructed herself. *No time for sulking, onto the next.* But sulk she did. Even as she dressed Aṅụrị in a pristine ensemble from Mango Kids and pleaded with her husband to wear the sweater to complement it. This was before neutrals entered the mainstream and color was siphoned from the sartorial selections of even children. Aṅụrị was in blue. And despite them living only one hour outside London, she was meeting her stepgrandparents properly for the first time at the ripe old age of four. Aṅụrị's earliest memory of Henry and Genevieve would be the blue rug in their living room on which she was positioned so that Ophelia could photograph her. It was such a beautiful thing;

a thousand different hues swirling across the expanse of it and her four-year-old eyes along with her four-year-old hands were drawn to it as anyone's would be. She sank little fists into the pile, lifted her face to her parents, one of whom looked on with a decades-long wariness brought about by knowing the consequences of damaging the belongings of well-to-do white people; be it their daughters or their twelve-by-eight-foot designer rugs. The other took photos, now confident that the failure of the last video would be eclipsed by this: *Aṅụrị meets her grandparents*. And she was right. The blog post and accompanying six-minute vlog featured the bemused expression of Ophelia's parents as they held their stepgrandchild like she was a puppy with a questionable grasp on toilet training.

The relationship had not much improved since then.

On the morning of Easter Sunday, Aṅụrị chose a baby doll dress the color of well-watered pothos. It tickled the skin above her knees and made her forget she was a person who grappled with nightmares so vivid that sometimes she would spring into wakefulness just before falling asleep, and feel like she cheated death. There was a moment, the night before, when she and Simi had opened her wardrobe doors where she froze then cursed because she was now a person who could choose her own clothes, could drape herself in whatever off-season monstrosities she liked, but she was also still a child whose clothes were inextricably linked to how much income would enter someone else's account. What *she* loved was now paramount even if the scabs could still be picked, could still bleed.

The same could not be said for Noelle.

"She's irritable," Genevieve told Aṅụrị before she had even removed her cardigan and handed over the wine and humanely harvested manuka honey she brought so her pseudo grandparents might keep their criticisms light that afternoon.

"Ophelia?"

"Noelle—" Genevieve's eyebrows reached for each other in the middle of her head. "That's a lovely color on you."

"Ah thanks. You look really nice." Aṅụrị did her best to try to be present with Genevieve. They did not speak outside of family gatherings such as this, and she *had* been invited. However, now that she had been alerted, Aṅụrị could hear the high whine of her sister's cry through the French doors. Truth has a way of sharpening the senses.

Nkem stood to the right of the doors, a tumbler of scotch in his hand no doubt put there by Henry. Aṅụrị scanned her father from head to toe, taking in the loafers and open-necked shirt. She wondered briefly if scotch was his actual drink of choice or whether this was just one more concession he had made in the quest for acceptance.

"Dad."

"I didn't hear you arrive. Kedu?"

Sleep deprived. That's how she was. Antsy. In desperate need of something cool and over three percent to take the edge off. Nothing that could be expressed to Nkem. "Odi mma. The place looks good." There was a table set up in the middle of the garden with a centerpiece constructed from foliage, citrus fruit and twigs. Giant champagne-colored balloons hanging from the trees. "Not quite the Erikssons' taste, is it?"

"Ophelia is responsible. The woman never fails to surprise me with her eye for this type of thing. Village boy like me doesn't even know where to buy such balloons."

"It's just a family lunch, no? I mean it's super cute but she shouldn't have bothered."

It was the way he shifted, a barely perceptible movement if you did not have twenty-five years of experience in Nkem Avoidance. "Yes, it will just be family eating."

"But…?"

"There's something small Noelle needs to finish first. Just a little thing."

"Jesus. You're making her work on Easter?"

"I don't want you to start this today, Aṅurị, okay? Shebi, we all have to learn responsibility sooner rather than later?"

"Are you actually joking?"

Nkem stared into the flashing eyes of his daughter and saw Kainene. There it was, that pressing need to reach out and touch her. His fingers ached with it and the tumbler in his hand shook. But learning how to bridge the gap between them seemed impossible. Over the years, he had cataloged Aṅurị's expressions, noting when the light left her. To look at Aṅurị now was to witness anything from frustration to dejection and to know that he was, at least in part, the cause. Still, he was too cowardly to sit in his shame. "Don't make noise, Aṅurị. Let it be."

Aṅurị left him there. As she made her way across the grass, she glimpsed the photographer leaning against the fence; the bouncing ponytail of the lady with the clipboard, and Ophelia in fuchsia Proenza crouching to address a tearful Noelle.

"Ṅurị!" If a time ever came, Aṅurị thought as Noelle ripped herself away from her mother and hurtled toward her big sister's outstretched arms, where the light in this child's eyes did not delight her as it did now, she would know her time on earth had come to a close.

"Nelly Noo." Aṅurị kissed her nose. "Hello, princess. I missed you."

"I like your dress. You look like a forest fairy."

"I like yours, too. Same color as your mummy's."

A frown. "I don't want to change again."

"How many times have you changed?"

"One hundred million."

"Alright, Noelle. That's a slight exaggeration, isn't it, darling?" Ophelia nodded her greeting to Aṅurị. "We've had to change a couple of times but only because the eggs are gold. We didn't want to clash. Plus the Proenza is this season. It will land better."

That was the problem with chasing perfection. Nobody's definition was the same and once you reached your personal zenith, you would crane your neck and realize you were still someone else's base camp.

"Ophelia, you're speaking to me as if I have a clue what you're talking about."

"For the shoot. It's an Easter egg hunt. A quick thirty minutes and then we can all eat and enjoy ourselves."

"I don't want to take photos!" Noelle's histrionics intensified.

Ophelia stepped forward to stroke the back of Noelle's head. "Sweetie, honestly. I don't know what's gotten into you lately. There's ice cream and two kinds of cake for dessert. Let's just do this very quickly. You and Mummy, okay?"

"Can't you just allow her for today?"

Genevieve was picking her way across the grass, hands twisted into the pleats of her skirt. "Ophelia," she said when she reached them, "*Ophelia*. Molly's portrait. The miniature in the shell frame. Where is it? You said we'd have it on the table while we had lunch."

Ophelia sighed almost imperceptibly. "Did I say that? I don't think—" here she lowered her voice "—it's entirely appropriate to have a photo of…someone no longer with us on the table at Easter lunch."

Genevieve frowned. "That someone is your sister, Ophelia."

"Yes, I'm aware. You can wait inside, Aṅuṛi. We won't be long." A dismissal encased in pleasantries.

"Wouldn't want me and my dress to wreck the pics."

Ophelia tucked Noelle's hand into her own. She lifted her gaze to meet Aṅuṛi's. "I believe it was you who made the decision to no longer be in photographs. I'm respecting it."

The retort began forming in the back of Aṅuṛi's throat but before it could be expelled, she was led away by Genevieve and Henry. There was salmon to baste and the leg of lamb needed to be rotated. There was a shell-framed portrait to locate. A gulf between parent and child. Did the irony not pierce Ophelia as it did Aṅụrị? Aṅụrị shook off the sympathy she felt for Ophelia. So it went at the Erikssons'. Aṅụrị's voice extinguished before it could flicker to life. She addressed her sister instead. "Thirty minutes, Nell. Promise."

The photos when they were published would be reposted to several hundred lifestyle and motherhood accounts. The champagne balloons captured the sun and split it into golden shards which fell on the table, Ophelia's bare neck as she tossed her head back to laugh, Noelle's miniature cutlery in sterling silver. Aṅụrị did not feature. She was given a seat at the opposite end of the table and was carefully removed with camera angles. She would scroll and curse herself for caring. Before she left the Erikssons' that day, Noelle would cling to her, warm and sweaty and on the verge of sleep, and mumble, "I wish I could live with you, Aṅụrị," and Aṅụrị's words to Simi and Loki would return with increased urgency. It had been declared flippantly in the way of pipe dreams which wither and fall away before they can be fully formed. But in this garden with Noelle's words tearing holes through her heart, Aṅụrị considered that perhaps her father was right. Perhaps her calling was not on the heads of other people or in the crafting of candles. Perhaps her destiny was to save her sister.

FOUR

On opposite sides of London, two course-altering scenarios began to unfold. The cease and desist arrived—without the warning Aṅụrị promised Simi she would give—on Ophelia's desk at exactly the same time Aṅụrị pushed open the door to Ammah's office. The breaths of both stepmother and stepdaughter caught in their throats; frowns crowded brows, tension lapping at their toes. Ophelia, glass of lime and cucumber in hand, turned the letter over, noted the cursed address of the lawyer and wondered whether by refusing to open the curtains on another window of litigation, she might avoid it altogether. Aṅụrị pulled the silence up to her chin and waited for Ammah's prompt. If it didn't come, she wouldn't speak, and if she didn't speak, the wheels of her great and terrible plan would never have to be set in motion. If the wheels did not turn, she would be saved from any possible collision with failure. What was safe was also untenable. She sighed.

Ophelia liked Aṅụrị's lawyer. She was the type of razor-sharp woman Ophelia hoped she resembled. Gloria wore her intelligence and her scorn cinched at the waist, in the minute raising of an eyebrow, the pressing of her Mont Blanc on the page after

Ophelia had said what she assumed was something innocuous. She tripped Ophelia with her not-quite-neutral expressions; reactivated the stutter Henry and Genevieve stamped out in her youth. She liked Gloria almost as much as she hated her. Ophelia scanned the contents of the envelope, panic and rage burning holes in the lining of her stomach. There was Noelle, true, and how the world loved her, Ophelia's angel child. But they first fell in love with Aṅụrị and they adored her still; comments littering every single content offering pleading with Ophelia to update them on her stepchild's whereabouts. Every question a barb that struck her to the core. How long had it been since she could pick up the phone and call the girl she chose to love and to raise for nothing more than a chat? When would the fact that she could not remember cease to burn? She built her world on Aṅụrị's back and the stubborn foundation was shifting. Was it not enough that she had agreed and removed some of the most popular posts? Like the video where Ophelia explained to an eight-year-old Aṅụrị that sunscreen was still important for her Black skin before the announcement of her very own cruelty-free line of SPF (later, from the other side of Gloria's conference table, Gloria would purse her lips and say "cruelty-free to whom exactly?"). *Where did you find her?* Ophelia wanted to ask, but wasn't it just like Aṅụrị to locate a secret weapon and wield it with such abandon? The paltry offerings had not been enough. Aṅụrị was poisoning the well. Nobody would be allowed to drink.

Ammah waited for the last of the words to slip from Aṅụrị's lips; a gushing slowed to a trickle. She cleared her throat and stifled the smile that sprang to her lips at the sound of Aṅụrị's groan.

"I haven't said anything," Ammah reminded her client. Her favorite client if she was honest with herself.

"I already know you're going to discourage me."

"What you want to do for your sister is very admirable."

"But?"

Ammah drummed her fingers on her knee. "It's a matter of professional ethics and the law. You need your parents' consent to bring Noelle here."

People like to think they are prepared for disaster and Aṅuri was one of that multitude, but she had not bargained for her plan to slam so unceremoniously into so insurmountable an obstacle. Noelle needed help. Ammah could be trusted with her life. It made so much sense. And the sense it made, paired with her inability to action it, only served to push Aṅuri closer to hysteria. Once there, only two things could pull her back. One was forbidden and the other would take a while to make their way to her flat.

"What if she's in imminent danger? Don't you have a duty of care to see her?"

"If your sister is in imminent danger, then both yours and my duty of care extends to contacting the authorities. Is that something you feel we need to put into action?" Ammah watched Aṅuri's face, noted the tightening of her jaw; the door closing behind her eyes. She was used to this, the retreat to emotional safety. She waited.

"They're not beating her or anything like that if that's what you're asking."

"I asked about danger."

"I think she's in danger. In the same way I was. I had to save myself and I'd rather Noelle not have to do the same thing. I just want to bring her here so you can talk to her before I do anything else."

"What is the 'anything else' you're planning?"

Aṅuri ran her hand over the cropped softness of her hair. She inhaled and released the air slowly. A simple, obvious yet infuriatingly effective method Ammah drilled into her during their second session together. For a girl who craved control, breathing was the bedrock of possibility. "It's like I told you. I want to look after her. Get her out of that house and away from…from them, from that life. She should live with me. She said she wanted to. Being there is fucking her up."

Ammah released the gold clasp holding her hair in place. She balanced it on the page in front of her. "I can't know the full extent of what you're witnessing over there."

"I'm telling you it's messed up. You saw how I was when you found me. That should be enough evidence."

"Not everyone will respond to the same situation in exactly the same way."

Aṅuri kissed her teeth. It was almost involuntary, but the tension was rising. She was now waist-deep and clinging to anger to stay afloat. "I'd like just one person to believe I am capable of looking after my own sister."

"Has someone said you're incapable? What *I* am saying is that human beings respond to things differently. And it can be difficult at times to separate our past experiences from how we construct our action plans."

And this was what was maddening about Ammah. She could pinpoint and extract the sole silver thread without a person even knowing it existed. Was Aṅuri projecting? Probably. Did she have good reason to? Unquestionably. She sank her front teeth into her tongue.

"Let's talk about the PhD." At this point, Ammah could sift through the wreckage of Aṅuri's scattered moods and offer a hand to tug her from under the fallen debris. She was trained to seamlessly redirect.

Aṅuri refused the hand. "There's nothing to talk about."

She left with thirteen minutes still on the clock.

The PhD was now a phantom appendage Aṅuri carried with her. Black and rotting, she toted it around doing her best to ignore its heft. Her intentions were good, or at least they had been when they first budded. Three years prior, during a gin-soaked episode of painful reflection, Aṅurị opened Google and searched for herself. She scrolled through the thousands of hits, blinking as image after image of herself through the years loaded on the results pages. She observed that she rarely appeared in her own right; that she sat beside Ophelia, was knitted into the fabric of Ophelia's online tapestry, and while this made sense, it was also abhorrent. The gin brought Aṅurị's loneliness into focus, her isolation hardening and pressing upon her from all sides.

There were more like her. Of course there were. She was not the only child-turned-commodity to walk the earth. She fell down a Reddit rabbit hole and read pages of speculation about the lives of herself and her stepmother. She returned the following evening and the next, losing hours. The internet giveth and it taketh away. She lurked the forums, absorbing the smugness and converting it to rage. These parents were everywhere. And they knew on a base level that in offering their children to the anonymous masses, those same kids would become fodder for dissection and their justifications ranged from passable to ludicrous.

At first, Aṅurị reasoned that underpinning every decision to share a snippet of a child's life was something, if not entirely pure, then at least not dissolute. But as time passed, she became convinced that nothing could be excused. With every post that popped up in the *Kids in Sports* or the *ADHD or Not?* forums, Aṅurị wondered whether or not these parents understood that kids are autonomous little beings; that they are tiny humans developing their own personalities and forging together lives they would go on to live independently of their families.

She understood that at a base level, Ophelia loved her, but wondered whether that love was a result of her attracting the admiration of strangers, which translated into sometimes unstated but often overt approval of Ophelia, as a parent.

The problem, Aṅurị concluded, was not the desire for attention, but the refusal to interrogate that same desire.

And when Aṅurị eventually found her fingers and began to

type vitriolic responses for which she was banned from the forums, she sought to find the afflicted and assist in healing their heart wounds; help to make them whole. She began researching PhD programs and narrowed down her field of interest to child psychology. She filled a folder with information about entry requirements, fees and funding options. She kept Simi and Loki awake until the wee hours of the morning with her excitable babbling and because they loved her, they indulged her, grew excited with her. Perhaps, Aṅụrị thought, perhaps Nkem would look at her with something adjacent to pride. Maybe he would speak of his firstborn with the same warm conviction he reserved for Noelle. She started work on a proposal, spent nights in Simi's bed because the solid warmth of her best friend was both comfort and motivation. When she told Ammah of her plans, she pretended not to see the surprised glint in the therapist's eyes. It felt inevitable, this path, the culmination of her years under Ophelia's and Nkem's directive. Why not remake her trauma into something worthwhile? Something she could wrap up and hand out to others as both a lesson and a guide. This was the plan. And it was, for all intents and purposes, a good one. Except Aṅụrị forgot that she too was human, and humans are possessed with the kind of stubborn ego which does not leave room for the truth.

And the truth was PhD advisors were interested in her, yes, because of her educational background, but also because of her social one. Did she not think, more than one enquired, eyes bright with potential, that she might want to examine society's preoccupation with social media given that she had so rich a personal history with it? Was this not something she might wish to discuss with her parents? Wouldn't they be interested in being involved? Maybe Ophelia could even help with research using her platform. What was child psychology when the inner workings of Instagram could be splayed for the academic world to examine? The more she fought her case, the wearier Aṅụrị became until she tearfully informed her best friends that she had made a mistake and shelved the folder indefinitely.

Gloria's office differed to Ammah's in a number of subtle ways, the most apparent of these to Aṅụrị being the existence of personal accoutrements on display. On Gloria's desk, three framed photographs of who Aṅụrị assumed was her family: two serene-looking parents, a couple of kids with Gloria's eyes and the smile of the man standing at her side. Summoned by her lawyer, Aṅụrị checked her phone while she waited for Gloria to conclude a meeting that had overrun. She had two new bookings: one for crochet braids and another for a wig install, and, sitting three rows down in her business inbox, an email with the subject line Airpods. She opened it.

From: Christian Nweze [[CSquared07@gmail.com>
To: Enquiries <enquiries@Kainefeoma.com>
Subject: Airpods

Hey, Christian here. You might also remember me as the one you shamed into using his Igbo name. Chidili. Anyway, I think I left my airpods at your salon (is that cool to say? Salon? I think you called it your "hut" or something) and I was wondering if you could have a quick look for me and let me know? I can't find those things anywhere.

"Good news?" Gloria asked. She'd swept into the room and was already slipping her heels off and dropping elegantly into her chair, sliding a file into a drawer and pulling out another. Aṅụrị admired, as she always did, the self-assured manner with which Gloria moved through the world as if she was untouchable by circumstance.
"Hmm?"
"You're smiling at your phone."
"Was I? Am I?" Aṅụrị hastily tucked it back into her pocket. "It's nothing. Business stuff."

"Ah yes. And how is all that going?"

Anụrị reached down and placed a gift bag on Gloria's desk.

"Anụrị? Chere oge! What is this? You know I'm not really supposed to accept gifts!"

"You keep saying this and then I remind you what the *actual* law says and you then take my candles home and love them. You said last time that your sister liked the peony santal so there's two in there. One for you, one for her."

"Eve is going to shout. Thank you so much. But that's it, okay? Ozugo." Gloria winked. "How are you doing? Really."

Two days post Ammah and Anụrị was still trying to ignore what she knew to be true: that the throwing of her emotional toys out of the pram at her session was a holdover from her youth. That not getting her way still had the capacity to elicit the response of a brat. Ammah's assessment of her situation stung, correct as it was. "I dunno. Life can be shitty at times."

"Well, that is very true. Look, Anụrị, let me not beat around the bush. I called you here because we've had a response from Ophelia's counsel."

"That quick?"

"They actually sent it over yesterday, but I needed a little time to go over it. Long story short, she's offering you one hundred thousand to allow the continued use of Anụrị-related content."

"One hundred thousand pounds?"

"Yes. And a—" Gloria checked the file in front of her "—two point seven percent cut of any residual ad revenue."

"Wow. It's like she hates me."

"A lot of people would consider this a very generous offer."

"You know me."

"I do. So I already started drafting the rejection. This could reach court. I know I've said it before, Anụrị, but this could become a spectacle. In fact, I'm fairly sure it will. I need to be responsible and keep reminding you of that."

Añụrị clasped her hands together in her lap. "You think I'm too weak and fragile to deal?"

"You don't know weakness. I don't think it exists in you. This will be hard. That's all I'm saying."

Añụrị nodded. The memory of the wine was still fresh. She knew weakness, but it was nice that Gloria thought otherwise. She paused only infinitesimally before handing Gloria another slice of her history. "You know the album *Hexagon's Curse*?"

"Girl, you know I'm old." Gloria smiled.

"It's a platinum-selling album by some band in California. Anyway, this is the album cover." Añụrị handed Gloria her phone so she could see the photo of an infant crying. "That's me."

Gloria's mouth settled into a line. "That's you."

"She sold the rights to the photo over to the band and now I'm sitting in the houses of how many people who look at me screaming every time they want to hear a sad song. And then there was the time they pocketed a chunk of change for allowing me to be used for some advert for SIDS in the US." Añụrị repocketed her phone. She pressed her fingers into her thighs until the threat of tears subsided.

This was how her parents had sold pieces of her to the highest bidder, how she never had a chance to protest. Because that is the hubris of parents; believing that they have the ability to control the size and strength of the human capacity for selfishness. A decision that it is alright to post your kid online, but it becomes something new when others find your child equally cute and mine your content, bringing it anew via aggregated feeds on Twitter and Instagram.

"You know why I started my candle business?"

Gloria leaned back in her chair. "I'm guessing it's because you needed income."

"Oh sure." Añụrị rose from her seat. "But I also wanted to beat Ophelia at her own game. When are we filing the response?"

★ ★ ★

When a person is raised in an environment where near-instant gratification becomes part of the rubric of the household albeit in the form of likes or subscribers, it is unsurprising that they inadvertently water the seeds of entitlement. Aṅụrị had since taught herself that she was not entitled to Simi's immediate attention at all times, that it was perfectly fine and even expected that Simi not answer the phone during the workday. Still. For a person in whom weakness apparently did not live, Aṅụrị felt stained by frailty. She wanted her best friend. Her best friend was unavailable, and her other best friend had texted earlier to inform her he had finally made a decision re Emilie and set aside the afternoon to consciously uncouple via FaceTime. She knew Simi would call when her workday was over, and because Aṅụrị knew that Simi hated the tube and would likely be working late, she ordered both dinner and a cab home for her friend. Having been focused so long on the language of combat, sometimes Aṅụrị did not have the words for the love she felt for her friends. Most often, her actions did the speaking for her.

Somewhere in the city, a group of paid legal experts on opposite sides were rallying and strategizing and it was absurd to Aṅụrị that she was the prize; that even after all these years, after the hard-won inches she had gained, there still stretched ahead of her miles of ground to reclaim. "An end," Aṅụrị whispered, "that's what I would like." Her breath quickened along with her heart rate. It would climb like this, she knew, until she found a way to regulate, and how unfair it was, she thought as she opened her laptop, that there were people who lived without anxiety snatching at their heels. Would she could join their ranks.

She added £1,643 worth of useless distraction to her basket, her heart slowing with each click of the mouse, dopamine pooling deliciously in her brain; and when she completed her purchase, she sank back against the plumpness of the sofa and relished the buzz of endorphins pinging through her body. Impulse control had been obliterated early; filed down to an unusable nub Aṅụrị had been forced to resharpen over time. Occasionally enduring setbacks was predictable when she was first praised with words then with gifts. Who was to say when gifts turned into bribes? When did innocence turn sour? Healthy coping mechanisms, Ammah said, do not include squandering thousands on junk. It hurt that she was right. Already, the purring in her limbs was fading. Remorse, thick and hot, coated the back of her throat. Aṅụrị canceled the order and returned to her business email to check the inspo photos her crochet braids client had sent. Christian/Chidili's email leapt and struck her between the eyes. She typed out and sent her response.

From: Enquiries <enquiries@Kainefeoma.com>
To: Christian Nweze <CSquared07@gmail.com>
Subject: Re: Airpods

Chidili. I found them. Want to send me an address so I can post them?

He replied almost instantly.

From: Christian Nweze <CSquared07@gmail.com>
To: Enquiries <enquiries@Kainefeoma.com>
Subject: Re: Airpods

Nah, don't waste your money. I'll swing by and pick them up. I was looking for a reason and it's way too early for a retwist. Let me know when's good.

She typed the beginnings of thirteen replies before abandoning her laptop and retreating to her room. The familiar ache was reigniting. Aṅụrị had not seen Noelle since Easter lunch and the desire for the light her sister shone rose through Anụrị like hunger. She reached for her phone. Nkem, when he answered, enquired only briefly of his child's health and it didn't matter because that was not why she had called; Nkem would live another day to discard her and she would stack that rejection on top of the others and move on. She asked for her sister and wondered aloud when next she might be permitted to keep Noelle overnight. Scenes of marshmallows, Disney films and sweet, milky breath against her cheek already forming in Anụrị's head. As it is with life and its great injustices, there are things we inherit from our parents that go beyond genetics; that reach past curl pattern and the probability of wisdom tooth removal. Things that grow undetected in the threads that hold us together. From both Kainene and Nkem, Anụrị was bequeathed the myopic assuredness of youth. It flickered like the proverbial draft-stricken flame throughout her upbringing but manifested in moments such as this.

"You can't be serious," Nkem told her. "How could you think now would be a good time?"

And Anụrị felt the cold shock of her shortsightedness. Arrogance masquerading as courage. How *could* she think this was a good time? You cannot serve the mother of your heart with legal papers and expect that the heart will beat the same. What did she expect? Again, lines had been drawn and there was no way for Noelle to fall neatly between them. She had become a bargaining chip. A tool. Who is to say a broken child cannot be ruined anew. You rob her of her mother and give her the face of complacency to stare into as a substitute. Complacency marries ambition and they birth redemption. Redemption, with her curls and her capacity to love, is torn from the child like so many other things; a new wound. Anụrị stared at the blackness of the phone screen long after Nkem had excused himself. Her distorted reflection stared back. Disgust mingled with rage rampaged through her body. The terrible familiarity of helplessness was bitter in the back of her throat, expanding, causing her to choke. She left the phone on her bed and returned to her laptop.

BETABOY738 IS NOW ONLINE

IJELE_RISING IS NOW ONLINE

BETABOY738: Goddess, is that a photo you've posted?

IJELE_RISING: ...

BETABOY738: Forgive me, Goddess

BETABOY738 IS SENDING A TRIBUTE: ACCEPT? YES/NO

IJELE_RISING: What a worthless offering

BETABOY738: Please, Goddess. I don't have much

IJELE_RISING: That would be my problem, how?

BETABOY738: I just need some time to get a bit more

IJELE_RISING: Do your family know what an insignificant little bitch you are?

BETABOY738: Can I bring you cash?

IJELE_RISING: You think you should have the honor of looking at me in person?

BETABOY738: No. I'm sorry, Goddess

IJELE_RISING: Too bold. I'm cutting you off

BETABOY738: NO!! Please, I'll do anything

BETABOY738 IS SENDING A TRIBUTE: ACCEPT? YES/NO

IJELE_RISING: Fucking pitiful. Piggies like you deserve nothing. Sniveling, cowardly. What real use are you?

It ought to have worked as it always did. There, after the first few words had been written, should have been the jolt of firing synapses, the hot flood of adrenaline through her system. BetaBoy pleaded but his words immediately faded to nothingness. She shut her laptop with trembling fingers, her tongue dry. Already the longing was bubbling in that part of her she could never reach with anything else. A single glass would be enough, would it not, to bring her back to peace? She could not be blamed for that, surely not. This was not weakness, she told herself, as she rose from her seat. No, it was necessity. And it would only be one glass. Aṅụrị walked in circles around her living room knowing she had already given in and simply trying to prolong the inevitable. She retrieved her phone from her bedroom and texted the word "pomegranate" to the two people who knew what it meant; what she was about to do. At the off-license, she chose a bottle of white rum, the strength of which could strip paint from wood or memory from mind. She did not remember the walk back. What she did remember was how Loki, key still in one hand, eased the bottle from her grasp before the seal could be broken; how Simi held her face and made Aṅụrị meet her gaze; one full of love. She remembered them squeezing into bed with her and absorbing her fear. In the morning, they held her still and told her to call her grandparents.

OPHELIA

Nkem and Aṅurị torched all my prior certainties: that the inevitable husband would be all the things my parents expected of me; that our children would be our milky-skinned replicas; that their arrival would signal the end of my temporary foray into employment. There is no "right" way to be a wife, to be a mother, but to look into the eyes of the child you once pressed desperately to your bare skin and see a flatness you never thought possible in the embodiment of animated goodness, is to know that there are wrong ones, and that they are endless and inescapable.

FIVE

There is a YouTube video, which one can find if they search hard enough, of Aṅụrị's sixth birthday. It was something of a production being the first real "event" in the house coercion built. Ophelia, who had already begun to observe the flicker of obstinacy in her stepdaughter, knew that extra care must be taken in the run-up to the party in order to snuff it out. To fan the flame would be to raze the work of the last five years, and it was only a fool who knowingly engineered their own misery. The party planner was a woman who rouged her already ruddy cheeks, smoked incessantly and without apology, and barked orders at her minions in an accent so plummy, it could have been baked into a crust and served alongside the cake. The waiting list for her services stretched past the next year and into the one after that. Ophelia had been fortunate. A mild case of bacterial meningitis and a cancellation alongside a seventy percent deposit, and Estelle was secured. And because she had recently been profiled in both *Cosmopolitan* and *Hello!* (the illustrious *Sunday Times Style* still tantalizingly out of reach), Ophelia recognized, as shrewd businesswomen often did, that there was an opportunity here. This party done right could be the master key and afterward there would remain only a limited number of doors she could not open. The thought swept through her at night as she lay beside Nkem, and she felt her skin tingle as the anticipation collided with the shame she had not yet learned to completely subdue.

A fortnight before the party, Ophelia made miniature pancakes for Anụrị and her visiting playdate, Simi, an opinionated child who attended one year of the same Montessori as Anụrị before her parents decided Simi belonged with children whose parents did not name them things like *Gentleigh*, but with whom Anụrị, aged three and with what Ophelia deemed a still developing sense of good judgement, had already fallen in love. She placed the Argos catalog on the table with the syrup and strawberries. That catalog, its back pages showcasing the latest in adolescent temptation, was met with two pairs of wide eyes.

"You can choose one thing," Ophelia said. Then, glancing at the second child, added, "You too, Simi."

You do not toss a deer carcass into the lion's den and expect restraint. Those shiny pages were enough to send small children into the type of frenzy that was only exacerbated by sugar. Syrup was upended, pancakes temporarily forgotten in the scramble to flick to the back where the toy section was waiting in all its lurid, abundant glory. Ophelia waited until she observed the dilation of two pairs of five-year-old pupils before she plucked the catalog from sticky hands. *It is like training puppies sometimes*, she would write in her blog later on and quite without shame.

"Ah, now wait," she cooed, "Anụrị darling. What did we say?" Because an almost six-year-old, whose moments of praise can no longer be distinguished from performance of some manner, learns reward-seeking behavior before she can even put a name to it. And so Anụrị lowered her hands to the table and played the pup.

"I'm going to be a well-behaved girl at my party and for the photo people."

"You most definitely are, my sweet girl." Ophelia bent to kiss the unblemished forehead. "One thing each." She chuckled. "Alright, maybe two."

The girls chose roller skates, but before long, Simi paused in her pancake consumption to enquire about the "photo people." Her best friend's explanation sounded reasonable enough but even at five, Simi was not one to be easily convinced.

"So you get something nice if you get dressed up and get your photo taken."

Anụrị, flush with the naivety of the young, nodded eagerly. "Yeah."

"What if you don't want to get dressed up? Or you don't like the photo people?"

It was not as if Simi had suggested anything outrageous. Already Anụrị had begun to tire of the procession of strangers to whom her parents handed her to be trussed up in taffeta and tulle, her kinky hair tugged and tutted over. Sometimes, when she was alone in her bedroom and knew the afternoon was designated for photo taking, her chest would feel fluttery and then tight. The flash from the cameras would make first her eyes then her head hurt. But when she hid, she was always found. She was a kid, but even that kid knew Simi would refuse to suffer the same fate, roller skates or otherwise. "I like dressing up," Anụrị told her friend.

"Okay," Simi said and returned her attention to her breakfast. It was only as Anụrị sank her teeth into a strawberry that Simi added, "But it's okay if you don't."

In the final days before the party, Nkem witnessed something of a regression in his daughter. Potty trained at twenty months, she suffered more than one accident, the embarrassment of which was almost too much for a Big Girl to bear. At night, she would creep into their room and tug on the strap of his singlet, the pajamas he tried to wear at his wife's request removed during the first hour of sleep.

"Daddy," Anụrị whispered tearfully, "I'm scared."
"But of what, obim?" he whispered back.
And his child would do her best to explain the dreams where the cameras turned to monsters who stole inside her and swallowed her soul with their everlasting hunger. But she was five. And he was oblivious in the way adults are sometimes so determined to be. He carried her back to her bedroom and folded the quilt over her and felt his heart weaken when she curled her fist around his index finger. He was relieved when, the day before the festivities, Makuo and Arinze arrived, their skin warm with Nigerian sunshine, their mouths full of delight at the sight of their granddaughter, taller and more beautiful than even Ophelia's content could capture.

Makuo savored the feeling of Anụrị's small hand inside her own, but felt something else, too: fear, which pulled the girl's body taut and made it so her heart fluttered like a butterfly wing in her chest.

"Do you think," Anụrị said to her grandparents as they read to her at bedtime, "Daddy and Mummy O would be sad if I didn't have the party?" She stared at the mural painted by a semi well-known artist on the back wall of her bedroom. Her grandparents might have been the safest place for the question to be asked aloud, but they were still grown-ups, and grown-ups, she now knew, had the capacity to take something inoffensive and infuse it with harm.

Arinze's eyes met his wife's over the head of their grandchild; years of togetherness implanting in them the ability to speak without talking. They still remembered the night their Kainene had told them of the boy she knew she would marry, her joy spilling from her so forcefully it flooded the house. They had failed to protect her and the notion that history had the temerity to repeat itself made them limp with panic. But protect Anụrị from what? A party? Gifts? The attention of her parents who had welcomed them into this colossal house and installed them in a bedroom that smelled of lilacs? Before they could formulate an answer, Aṅụrị's head fell against Arinze's arm. Sleep had captured her.

On the morning of the party, the house transformed by ribbons and gold leaf, balloons and garlands, the trappings of newly attained wealth on display around every corner, Makuo smoothed down the first of the four outfits Aṅụrị would wear that day. She pinched her baby's cheek gently.

"Look at you. You don pass beauty, ehn? Omalicha. You're alright?"

Aṅụrị tucked herself into her grandmother's arms. If she could just find a way to stay there, then perhaps the spirit of celebration might reach her, too. "I'm alright, Nnenne."

"And you'll tell me if you are ever not alright?"

"Yes, Nnenne."

"How do you do that special promise?"

"Pinkie swear?"

"Swear?"

Aṅụrị giggled. "Not with words, Nnenne. Like this." She raised her pinkie finger and hooked it with Makuo's. "Pinkie swear. I'll tell you."

It would have to be enough.

It started out fine. Aṅụrị posed as she was led. She held the products sent by sponsors. She screamed with delight at the sight of her friends pouring into the house, making a beeline for Simi, who took Aṅụrị's hand solemnly and allowed herself to be led into the orangery where the white-painted picnic tables were set up. There were twenty minutes allowed for games; the clumsy smashing of a piñata during which cameras rolled, and then Aṅụrị was whisked away to grin under the zoom of cameras. Another twenty minutes for pass the parcel followed by an outfit change. As pink lambskin ballet slippers were slipped onto her feet, Aṅụrị heard the joyful shrieks of her friends carry through the open window of the dressing room. She was six now and it did not make sense to her that she was here being instructed by a woman with silver hair to "point her toe properly, darling, that's it" instead of outside twirling under the sun in this pink dress. Was it not her birthday? Had she not been well-behaved? Her new roller skates lay unused in the corner.

It was this, the start-stop nature of festivity, the repeated giving and taking which led the girl to madness. Grown-ups made the rules, of that she was certain, but there were still protocols that even they should not have the power to overrule. Parties were supposed to be fun. She had played her part. Her eyes stung, lashes heavy with the flash-pop of cameras; brow slightly damp from the heat of the ring lights and softboxes. Arinze, from his position just outside the doorway, took in the quickening rise and fall of Aṅụrị's chest, the chewing of her lip. He stepped forward but was stopped by Nkem. "Not yet. She's almost finished." It was a lie. Even after she was released to go and join her friends, Aṅụrị was ushered to stand in the midst of the throng of a group of children she did not know well. The children of Ophelia's new friends; the ones Ophelia still felt she needed to impress; to whom she was determined to prove herself. It could have been the heaviness of the day, the cruel press of responsibility on a child who simply wanted to enjoy herself. It could have been simple childish exhaustion. These things were just ingredients thrown into the belly of a child who would use them to create her own flavor of rebellion. But when Aṅụrị caught sight of Simi standing across the orangery, when her request for her best friend to join the group photo was denied ("Just for a moment, darling, Simi can join the next one") it was the first of the inner tidal waves that crashed against her heart. Charged with the strength of the furious, Aṅụrị rocked the picnic table until the three-tier unicorn cake toppled to the ground. Through the ensuing chaos, she found her grandmother and collapsed, sobbing into Makuo's arms.

"I'm not alright, Nnenne," she wept. "I'm not alright."

★ ★ ★

The adults argued that night.

"It was too much for her." Arinze's voice, the low yet comforting rumble of faraway thunder carried up the stairs and into Aṅụrị's bedroom. "From the start, you planned too much." He tried to keep his anger muted but it churned through him.

"We know our daughter," Ophelia responded, icily. "She's done more in a day before and handled it perfectly. This was a temper tantrum plain and simple."

"On her birthday?" Makuo stood. "The day is hers. If nothing else in this world, today should have been hers."

Nkem felt his wife stiffen at his side. "Ophelia is right. Ànyị nà-èmè yā kwà daa." A puny defense. The fact that they did it daily was not a justification but rather an indictment.

"Daily? Perhaps that is the problem." Makuo met Nkem's gaze, unflinching.

"We know how to raise our own child," Ophelia said.

"She told me she is not alright. She said it in my arms."

"So now you don't understand exaggeration again?" There was a part of Nkem that knew it would be wise to listen to the warning he was being offered. But what is pride if not enduring? He could not be spoken to in this way. Not in his own house. Not about his own daughter. "Every time, the two of you come here to make trouble. Today will be the last."

And so it was.

By the time the sun rose the following day, Arinze and Makuo were sitting in a Heathrow hotel, and Ophelia was doing damage control: crafting a post about the art of gentle parenting. Of understanding when your child needs positive nurturing and understanding. There is nothing gentle nor positive about sacrificing your kid to the mercy of the internet, but Ophelia thought differently. Age ten, Aṅụrị would watch the video of her sixth birthday, read this post and tell her parents that she was not a teaching moment.

That she was their daughter. That she was not an example but their baby. Those were the last words she would speak for a month.

Loki and Simi stood in Aṅụrị's kitchen drinking tea. In her bedroom, Aṅụrị tussled both with her dreams and with the sheets, knotted around her left leg.

"I won't lie," Simi said. "I'm scared for her."

"Ophelia might be bluffing." Loki pressed his mug to his lips until they burned.

"Look at it from her point of view—hear me out, boy—you're going along doing all your mumfluencer nonsense and then your stepkid who's now this big-ass thorn in your side tells you you have to take down all the content that's *still* making her a shedload of cash. Would you be open to releasing your baby into the temporary care of your nemesis?"

"Aṅụrị ain't no nemesis. She still wears a Care Bears tee to sleep in for fuck's sake."

Simi reached deep and offered Loki Withering Look Number Four. "Of course she isn't. Not to you. Us. We love her."

"Ophelia loves her too—you hear me out this time, Sim—she wouldn't be acting this way, if she didn't. Hate isn't the opposite of love. Apathy is."

"Oh is it? Come and see, Aristotle reborn."

"Honestly, I reckon I'm closer to a Kierkegaard."

"You're closer to an olódo. Hate is *an* opposite of love. Two things can be true at once."

"And honestly, Ophelia's content is way more Noelle focused these days. It's not like she needs Aṅụrị's stuff."

"Maybe not, but it's part of her livelihood. If Aṅụrị disappears, then so does she to an extent."

Loki glanced toward the bedroom and sighed. "I haven't seen her cry like that in forever. And the rum?"

"Yeah. Noelle's her main trigger point, innit? She's terrified of losing her. The rum thing is worrying though. We can't be here all the time."

"I'm just glad she called us."

"Yeah."

"Yeah." Loki and Simi not only wanted Aṅụrị to be okay, they needed it. Over time, it had become only marginally easier to impress upon her the importance of her, of her presence and her uncomplicated friendship in their lives. Aṅụrị thought herself a nuisance but for Simi, Aṅụrị was the girl who sat with her in the music room at Montessori and listened to her practicing violin scales and not caring that Simi was a four-year-old musical prodigy and therefore uninteresting to the other four-year-olds. Aṅụrị was the one who planned all of Simi's birthdays, who accepted without question that Simi was affectionate and tactile in her own way even if that way did not always translate to hugs. Aṅụrị was soft and breakable and brilliant, and Simi never needed to be anything other than her strange self with her. For Loki, Aṅụrị was the only person who didn't care who his parents were. She was the girl who punched Aaron Clarke in the jaw at Camp Montana because Aaron Clarke demonstrated to an audience that Loki's height did not automatically lend him the ability to fight, and so was fair game to tease. He spent a week calling Loki gay because Loki did not yet possess the faculties to explain that gay was not a pejorative, but Aṅụrị did. She delivered a blow to Aaron's jaw that introduced him to the floor and stood over him to say, "Either ask him on a date or shut your face." Aṅụrị let Loki cry whenever he felt like it. She was his blueprint for bravery. The feeling of her fingers in his hair wiped clean the negative thoughts he sometimes kept stored in his head. Loki never needed to be anything other than his emotionally expressive self with her.

Simi set her mug in the sink. "You get the care package she sent?"

Loki nodded. "I did. That girl. How does she always know?"

"Knowing is one of her superpowers. Execution is the other."

Aṅụrị's bespoke care packages arrived randomly and without warning, and always contained items Loki and Simi either had not managed to get around to buying, or did not realize they needed but inevitably did. This time for Loki, it was new socks for his oversized feet, Korean honey from Jeju Island for him to add to his tea and the book he had mentioned once over a month ago. For Simi, premium rosin, gold-rimmed earplugs to block out the sound of her brothers, Feminax and a one-kilogram bar of Swiss chocolate, both for her upcoming period. It was not lost on either Simi or Loki that Aṅụrị knew things like when PMS was due to begin, or that the scratchy throat from a cold was still lingering. Their elite observer.

When Aṅụrị entered the room, Loki handed her a mug of peppermint tea with two spoons of honey, and Simi put down her sheet music. The violin she brought with her in order to get in an hour of practice still sat by the door, Aṅụrị's sleep proving more important.

"You okay?" Simi asked.

Aṅụrị nodded, sipped her tea before she spoke. "I just want to see my sister. And they're treating me like I'm dangerous. Like I'm a member of the Manson household or something."

"Okay, but, babe, in Ophelia's eyes, you might as well be," Simi pointed out.

"Maybe. But I think she'd probably want to put you in a series of Instagram reels if you were," Loki added. *"How to Parent a Murderer.* What do you think the views would be for something like that?"

"Perhaps you could pitch it to her in exchange for a weekend with Noelle." Simi watched the light spring momentarily to Aṅụrị's eyes. "Your dad really isn't saying anything about when you can see her again?"

"I'll call him again tomorrow. For once, just for fucking once, it would be nice if he could be on my side."

"Our fathers graduated with degrees in disappointing their offspring," Loki reminded her. "And to be honest, you aren't doing enough to disappoint him back. Let's work on that, hmm?"

The sound of their laughter bounced off the kitchen walls. Aṅụrị pressed her back against Loki's chest and felt her body unfurl when his heartbeat knocked against her spine. "Au contraire. I do hair and make candles. He *hates* that."

"Sure," Simi said, "but what if you went and got a sleeve of tattoos? Or like, I dunno, married Loki? I feel like if you put your mind to it, you can frustrate him further."

"What the hell do you mean? A man like me would make a great husband." Loki, affronted, rested his chin on Aṅụrị's head and glared at Simi.

"My dear, look at your parents. Wonderful people, but I am not holding out hope for you breaking any generational curses." Simi leaned slightly to the right to allow the tea towel Loki hurled at her to sail cleanly past her head. She reached for Aṅụrị's hand. "You have to know I am a true friend and that I consulted Babalawo for your stepmum. But he couldn't tell me anything about Ophelia's future. I even found Ajẹ. But she won't hex one of their own. Apparently witches band together."

"I don't know what else to do," Aṅụrị admitted, and the heft of the confession dragged her head downward. She had been, for so long now, someone who, if nothing else, had an idea of where her next footstep should land. This was new. And the newness made it frightening.

Christian/Chidili had the hands of an artist. Long, slender fingers, the nails of which lay clean and flat—the result of meticulous homecare or the work of a manicurist, Aṅụrị could not tell. She stared at those hands and imagined them on the skin of her back, trailing unspoken promises up and down her vertebrae. When he closed the space between them and suddenly those hands were up close, Aṅụrị found it quite a task to make herself look away. The two of them were on the street outside the gate that led to the hairdressing hut, and he was jacketless, the residual warmth of that too-hot Easter—now almost two weeks prior—dragging knitwear and coats from the backs and shoulders of Londoners all over the city. Each step he took toward her was a prelude to heartbreak. By the time he reached her, she could think of nothing else to say but "here" as she opened her palm and thrust his Airpods toward him.

He plucked the case from her hand and flashed those canines. "They don't greet in your village?"

"What happened there?" Aṅụrị addressed his left hand where a thin scar sliced through the perfection with the determination unique to destruction. If she could not look away, then she could disguise her fixation with curiosity.

"Huh? Oh this—" he held up his hand "—occupational hazard."

"You build things?"

"No."

"Some kind of athlete?"

"Flattery really will get you everywhere but isn't necessary."

The left side of Aṅụrị's mouth twitched upward.

Christian folded that, the smallest of triumphs, and tucked it away to savor later when she was out of sight. "I'm in cybersecurity," he said.

"And that gets you maimed?"

"It does when you're trying to make a good impression with your colleagues, end up drinking too much at an after-work social event and fall up the stairs."

"*Up* the stairs?"

"Did I mention I was drunk?"

Another twitch.

"You should let me take you out." He meant to be smoother than this; had practiced what he would say when he got to see her again, but there was something about the way she held her body still when she spoke, how he knew without touching her that he would find a version of home wherever she was that made him clumsy. The words came of their own volition, like a part of him knew they needed to be spoken immediately.

"I should?"

"For a drink. Yeah."

"You just told me you're bad at that."

"Practice, Aṅụrị, makes perfect."

It would be easy to say yes, to spend an evening over a wineglass with him, before tumbling first into bed and then into the inevitable abyss that followed the abandonment of her senses. She would be happy for a moment, but the devastation afterward would be too much to bear. Besides which, she couldn't drink. She wanted to remember him as he was now, new and unsullied, his perceived inefficiencies just that. It was safer that way. She shook her head.

"Ah. I'm disappointed," he said.

"I do that a lot."

"Until the next retwist then."

She watched him until he turned the corner and disappeared.

She was still thinking of those hands when she arrived, laden with Thai guava and fig jam, at her aunty Nneoma's house later that evening. The day had slipped away from her yet still managed to leave a blemish. Her every thought had been wreathed in anxiety, the ones featuring Noelle especially so. Twice, she'd blinked at her reflection in the black stillness of her phone, but could not summon the gumption to call her father and see if the rules regarding her sister had been relaxed. They would not reach out, it would have to be her, the balance already tipped in their favor.

Nneoma, fresh from a post-shift shower, was in the kitchen when Aṅụrị let herself in. She watched her niece close the door behind her. Aṅụrị, even now, carried the same coiled energy she had since childhood; the spring-kick of a young foal that has found its balance but is unsure of how to use it. Sometimes, when Aṅụrị slipped behind the veil in her mind, Nneoma would look at her and wonder what it would take to pull her out permanently. She did her best not to think what would happen if Aṅụrị was unable to be reached. This was a child in an adult's body who had perfected speaking with a sharpness meant to cut people from her life, but who, underneath it all, craved the kind of love she told Nneoma more than once did not exist. Today, Aṅụrị brought Nneoma's favorite expensive Thai guava and the fig jam Nneoma liked to spread on oat crackers just this side of stale; Aṅụrị was a cactus filled with pulp, the tender prodigal daughter.

"If you don't sit down, you will wear a hole through my kitchen tiles," Nneoma said. Her niece was vibrating through the kitchen, wiping surfaces that were already pristine, chasing ghosts through her mental corridors.

"Aunty. Nwute." Aṅụrị gave her apology, dropped into a chair and sighed. "Today has been a day."

"Is that not every day in this place?" Nneoma slid her bonnet from her head and raked her fingers across her scalp. This was enough to capture Aṅụrị's attention.

"Aunty Nneoma, you left the house with your hair like this?"

"Please, don't even say anything. I slept through my alarm and didn't have time to comb it."

"But you *never* go out without having your hair done!" Aṅụrị's mouth was a pink sphere of shock.

"So you close your mouth and help me, sha."

They adjourned to the sitting room where Aṅụrị sectioned her aunt's hair, spritzed it with watered-down conditioner and began detangling. Through strategically dropped questions, Nneoma was able to determine the source of Aṅụrị's unease. By the time she spoke the final words, Aṅụrị was crying silent tears that fell from her chin and splashed onto Nneoma's exposed scalp.

"I don't know when they're going to let me see Noelle again."

Nneoma pressed her lips together a moment before pushing out a rush of exasperated air. "Party stew don pour for ground," she declared, and Aṅụrị, despite the sadness spreading like spilled ink through her chest, had to laugh. "It's not good. This is not good. But you'll abide by their wishes. What choice do you have?" Nneoma said.

This wrung the laughter from Aṅụrị's throat. She choked on the sudden lump she found there. She was used to feeling trapped; her childhood had introduced her to that wall, but her teen years had taught her how to kick a hole through it.

"I'll figure it out. Dad will give in. Eventually."

"Eventually is not a promise but a wish." Nneoma registered the pain in her niece's expression, reached back and squeezed her thigh. "Understand that Nkem is in a difficult position. Daughter or wife. Who would envy him?"

Aṅụrị could not see it that way. "Daughter. Always daughter." She caught her aunt's eye in the handheld mirror Nneoma had lifted to inspect Aṅụrị's progress. "I was here first."

"Chukwu took his time with you, my dear heart, but when He rained down sense, you picked umbrella."

"You're calling me dense!"

"Never. Okay, maybe small. You can't go looking for Ophelia's trouble and expect Nkem to be on your side. You bring headache to a man's wife, the headache is doubled for him."

"If he had a backbone, all of us would be headache-free."

Nneoma could do nothing but incline her head in agreement. Had she not warned Nkem? Had not all of them? During the worst of it, when Nkem would call in the middle of the night asking Nneoma if Aṅụrị had run to her; when Nneoma would shout back at him and ask why he was phoning from the house and not from the streets where he should be out searching for his daughter; when Makuo, Arinze and Nneoma had formed a trio of admonishment and told Nkem that he would lose the child altogether if he was not careful; had he not introduced his head to the sand and made it his new home? He had planted the seeds of discord and Aṅụrị had tended them with a singular dedication. Who was he to blame now? He had chosen Ophelia and there was little he could do. It is a feat to snuff out the fire betrayal lit. Aṅụrị survived most of it, but had not yet released the remnants of carrying the gaze of others, of those dedicated to devouring more of a person whilst only wanting to taste that which they have already created in their minds. Nneoma had watched her niece drop pieces of this load over the years. She prayed that one day, Aṅụrị might be completely free.

NKEM

In those days, after Kainene was buried with the remaining scraps of my soul, I bled grief and challenged people to look away as I smeared it across my face. Everywhere I walked, her shadow stalked me. There was nothing to do but run. Underneath London's skies, there would be a rebirth, wouldn't there? I was not looking for happiness; I thought that lost to me forever. Everything about living felt like a lie. And were it not for Aṅụrị, I would have refused to tell that lie for much longer. For her, I chose life, or whatever this poor imitation of it was. And yes, that is what I was supposed to do; no, I do not deserve praise, but nobody can understand. Not a soul. To understand, someone would have to have had to walk in the path of Kainene's smile. Someone would have to have known her. To have lost her. I was nothing. Ophelia loved me regardless. And it is easy to laugh at the cliché that I was saved by the love of a white woman, but it is not that she loved me; it is that she loved Aṅụrị. She knew more about my own child than I did. Looked at me with contempt when she asked my daughter's blood type and I stared back, mute. On the evenings she had to hand Aṅuṛi back to me, Ophelia would cry, silently, as if I was so foolish I didn't know what the shuddering of her shoulders meant. And when Aṅuṛi looked at her, eyes wide with delight, I knew I could look at her the same way. I defy you to watch your child taste the sweetness of love and not follow suit. Can you see? Aṅuṛi was the center of everything. It is not an excuse. It is an explanation.

SIX

A week passed before Aṅụrị heard from Gloria again and during that stretch, she painted a hundred futures for herself using only her turmoil, her fear and the near unbearable silence that could only mean catastrophe. Good news came fast, did it not? Disaster took its time; dragging its heels and gouging trauma into the surface of your heart. She tied anchors to her feet and sank to the bottom of the mundane, where she usually found comfort: buying a new cushion for her sofa, having dinner with Loki and listening to him speak about missing the *idea* of Emilie but not Emilie the reality; scouring the internet for new fragrance oils she could use in her candle range. There were paypigs clamoring for her attention, but the more acid she dripped from her tongue, the more elusive gratification became; twisting from her grasp and mocking her with its fleetness of foot. Aṅụrị was aware, as most people who practice the art of avoidance are, that running from yourself requires the kind of stamina that can only be fueled by self-destruction. The truly gifted can manage it forever. She would know. The unique thirst for alcohol lived like an unruly tenant in her mind, refusing to be evicted. She was thankful Ammah had taught her how to sit with her emotions, the most insistent and unwelcome of companions. She was facing this thing head on but each day Gloria's name did not flash up on her phone screen another crack appeared in Aṅụrị's resolve. It had been almost two weeks since she had seen Noelle.

When she finally broke her silence, Gloria did so without preamble. "We're going to mediation."

Aṅụrị recognized that, due to her upbringing, she was a person who sometimes still did better when decisions were made for her. In order for her not to rail against this with the inhuman strength of someone in the wrong, she needed to trust her decision-maker wholeheartedly. There was no room for even the slightest doubt. Gloria had earned that trust and thus that right. And so Aṅụrị did not argue. She nodded into the emptiness of her living room. "You'll come with me?"

"I said 'we' and I meant 'we.' Echegbula. It's going to be fine." It was easy for Gloria to say "don't worry" but the reassurance, this time, did not land.

The night before mediation, Simi came over and emptied the contents of Aṅụrị's wardrobe onto the bedroom floor. Aṅụrị, grateful once more to be able to surrender decision-making into the hands of another, sat on her bed and focused all her energy on thinking about anything other than the clink of glass against her teeth and the warmth that would follow if she gave in to desire.

"Alright. I've got it," Simi announced. She held up a thin, lightweight knitted dress in electric blue. "And your Docs."

"I mean it's..." Aṅụrị cleared her throat. "Don't you think I should go in there looking a bit more serious? Maybe wear a suit or something?"

"Gloria will be wearing the suit. Why do you need to wear one as well?"

"No, right. It's just. I don't want them to think this is a joke to me."

"And wearing a suit will convey that, you reckon?"

"Sim. I'm just... I'm scared."

"Right no. Sorry. I'm sorry. This shouldn't even be happening is all." Simi threw the dress down. "You shouldn't be going to sit in a room to debate with your stepmother about pictures and videos of yourself. Is that not insane? And then thinking you have to dress like Margaret Thatcher in order to be taken seriously. This whole thing is already a joke. I know it's not to you. But it is. Objectively. I feel like I'm living in an episode of *Black Mirror*, and I'm waiting for Ophelia's face to peel off so we can see the sentient collection of aluminum scraps nailed together."

Of the three of them, Simi was the one who took the time to scrutinize each emotion before deciding whether it ought to be placed into the world. She was not prone to outbursts. So naturally, when they happened, Aṅụrị would sit herself directly underneath the downpour, relishing every second.

"Love you, Sim."

"Love you back. Wear the dress."

She wore the dress. Gloria wore the predicted suit. She placed a discreet hand on Aṅụrị's bouncing thigh under the conference table and they waited while Ophelia and her lawyers filed into the room. Why was it, Aṅụrị thought, that Ophelia required two lawyers when she only had the one? She glanced at Gloria, who was wearing the beginnings of a smirk. Aṅụrị envied her. Understanding that you are formidable had to be such a comfort in life. In the end, it mattered not what Aṅụrị wore. It came down to this: Ophelia was the creator thus the owner of the content. That the content centered on another human was by the by. It was like, the more severe of the lawyers told them, an actor turning around and demanding control of what Disney produced. Aṅụrị's discomfort, whilst understandable, was simply an unfortunate by-product of the somewhat murky world of online employment and intellectual property. Ophelia could remove the content of her own volition, but she could not be compelled to do so. Gloria set her pen down on the table.

"This is laughable," she said.

The mediator, a slender man with the sort of face you would like to see upon waking from a lengthy coma, smiled patiently in Gloria's direction. "Was there something in the statement that you would like to pinpoint?" he asked.

"Forgive me," Gloria continued, "but whether we pluck out one sentence or take the statement in its entirety, it is ludicrous."

"Can we address why?" The mediator leaned forward slightly. Ophelia shifted in her chair.

"I'm not just some human—" Aṅụrị started but Gloria touched her arm until she fell silent.

"To liken the relationship between stepmother and child to that of a corporation and actor is the epitome of a false equivalence. My client is not a willful employee of Mrs. Chinasa. She did not enter into a voluntary agreement. There was no contract. What infant can reasonably consent to their image being used in varied commercial capacity for what amounts to the financial and social elevation of the guardian in perpetuity?"

The mediator adjusted his tie; the universal symbol for *shit just got extremely real*. "There was a monetary proposition to allow the continuation of—"

"I said no," Aṅụrị put in. "I don't want money. I just want that stuff gone. I know the internet never forgets, but I'd like to. At some point. If possible."

"It's not an unreasonable request," Gloria said. "To state that Mrs. Chinasa 'cannot be compelled,' well, is that not why we're here?"

And in the months and perhaps even years to come, Aṅụrị would think back on that afternoon; about how the sun slanted through the gaps in the blinds and turned Ophelia's hair to burnished gold; about how the air-conditioning in the room was cranked high, but she could not tell whether that was the cause of the gooseflesh on her arms. She'd think about how she willed her stepmother to look at her, about how Ophelia's insouciance had become an art, something she did without thinking whereas Aṅụrị's efforts to appear unbothered sapped the energy from her body and perfumed the air with her desperation. She would remember Simi's categorization of this situation as nonsensical, Gloria's echo of the same. And she would remember with more clarity than perhaps anything else that her life was a series of battles big and small, and she was so tired of fighting, that if Ophelia would just look at her, things might be okay, that maybe she could rest for a while. This was the woman who had kissed scrapes on Aṅụrị's knees; who had dried her tears. Maybe it wasn't too late. Perhaps today they could collapse time. Maybe they could be a family again. All Ophelia had to do was look at her. She waited. Ophelia stared at Gloria and, when the meeting came to an abrupt end, she stood, followed her lawyers from the room and left the child she raised to stare at the seam on the back of her beautiful tailored blazer.

Back home, Aṅụrị turned off her phone and faced her candles. She usually dedicated two or three weeks at a time to the meticulous creation of her wares. She would craft until her storage shelves groaned under the weight of the merchandise. Then she would update the website and announce the restock via social media. The candles always sold out in minutes and at forty to sixty pounds a pop, Aṅụrị's was a lucrative little business. This was an anomaly. Her body was tight with unexpended energy. So she faced her candles. It was this or wake up tomorrow leaden with regret. She weighed the all-natural beeswax, and gathered the molds; the dye she chose was called *Opalescent Death*. Where Aṅụrị really shone was in her affinity for fragrance, using only sight and scent to mix essential oils with the dexterity and intuition of a clairvoyant. Ophelia's candle range was no longer in circulation, but in times like these, Aṅụrị liked to pretend it was. She had two of those candles left, squirreled away in a cupboard and used for research purposes. Ophelia used cheaper ingredients as mass production dictates, but Aṅụrị chose only the finest ingredients. She toiled at this new creation until the scent of perfection settled into her pores. Aṅụrị named the new candle *The Turning of the Screw*. It sold out in four minutes. A victory was still a victory even if it went unheeded.

Shipping the sold-out candles necessitated leaving the house. There were options, of course, and Aṅụrị usually opted for courier collection and the delegation of other tasks, but this time, after the solitude of creation and the self-imposed isolation, Aṅụrị craved fresh air. It would pull the cloying scent of essential oils from her hair and clothes, a spiritual palate cleanser. Being outside again was the tiniest of rebirths and it felt restorative. At the post office, she shuffled to the DHL counter and began the rhythmic self-scanning process that allowed her to step cleanly out of her own head and luxuriate in the soft nothingness mindless repetition afforded. She was still, barring a couple of hurried FaceTime calls, out of contact with her sister. She was starting to forget what Noelle smelled like; the very essence of the little girl was leeching out of her and taking pieces of herself with it. This was withdrawal and by the time Aṅụrị registered what was happening, it was a fully formed thing. Once the final parcel was sent off and she made it back to the street, Aṅụrị was panic sheathed in skin. Sweat coursed down her back and dripped from the tip of her nose; breath coming in sharp yet shallow bursts. She closed her eyes and awaited the fall.

"Aṅụrị?"

In his arms, Christian/Chidili carried three large padded envelopes. His locs were secured at the nape of his neck with a length of blue cotton. He stood in front of Aṅụrị, brow creasing while she bent double and watched her sweat mingle with tears and splash onto the concrete at her feet.

"Alright," he said, "it's okay. It's going to be okay. Try to count to five with me, yeah? Slowly. One…two…three…"

He stood there and counted to five a total of twelve times. To touch her would be her undoing, but his solid presence to her right along with the even timbre of his voice was enough to bring Aṅụrị's breathing back to the neighborhood of normal, so that after a while, when the panic had abated, all that was left was bone-deep humiliation. She straightened and wiped her face with the sleeve of her shirt.

"How we doing?" Christian asked.

"It's weird that you're here," Aṅụrị managed, shame pulsing through her, making her brusque.

"Oh." He lowered his eyes to the envelopes in his arms. "Yeah, we're sort of neighbors."

"Oh."

He paused, then looked at her. "You thought I was stalking you?"

"I—" How to tell him that this would not be the first time, that "coincidence" was not a word in Aṅụrị's vocabulary, was not an occurrence in the life she had been given to live. "It's not… It's just…"

"I mean that's kind of why I came to you for my hair? Proximity." He considered for a moment how the two of them looked to passersby: a perspiring girl on the tail end of hyperventilation and a man standing a little way off to the side wearing an expression of bemusement.

"Yes. Yeah, no, of course." Aṅụrị exhaled slowly. "You live around here."

"Well, like a tube stop away. But the cafés around here are nicer. And there's this gelato place over there that I'm guessing puts crack in the product. I'm hooked." He smiled; those canines appearing momentarily before he remembered he was making a case for himself. "Stalking isn't my thing. I promise you I'm too lazy for it. It requires the kind of dedication I don't have. Sorry."

"You're apologizing for not being a stalker."

"I was raised by God-fearing Nigerians. I apologize for most things." He tucked the envelopes under his arm. "I should go post these. You're alright though?"

Aṅụrị nodded, mortification still tampering with her ability to communicate normally. "Sorry you had to witness that. I…I get these…it happens to me sometimes."

"Panic attacks."

She nodded again; consulted the loop of laces on his sneakers, an image of him bending to tie them blossoming in her mind.

"This might sound weird but sensory deprivation always helped with mine."

"You get panic attacks?"

"Used to. It's been a few years, but yeah. Parents mistook them for the work of Satan."

"They're most definitely the work of Satan."

He laughed and the sound wrapped around Aṅụrị. She wished she might keep it and bring it out whenever she needed to smile.

"Fair," he said. "Look, you still seem a little…what I mean is, we could go sit over there and keep breathing if you need to."

Aṅụrị looked to where he was pointing. "That is a cemetery."

"Yes. Well. I kind of thought of it more as a churchyard, and it's peaceful in there. But now I am seeing how graves may not be the most relaxing environment."

"Thanks though. For the suggestion. And for doing the counting thing. It helped. I should probably speak to my therapist about today."

"You don't sound too wild about the idea."

She wasn't. She needed to sit with Ammah and trudge through the events of the last while, to explain again about the weariness that comes with fighting, but she did not want Ammah to cock her head and say, *Have you considered stopping?* because then she would need to find the words to convey that hers was a tiredness that actually spurs you to action. Stopping was not an option, not really. She was the shark who must be in continual motion to sustain life. If she stopped moving, surely she would die. This is too much to tell a man who has kindly walked you back from a public panic attack, whose beautiful hands you have glanced at only briefly today lest he worries you are stranger than is already evident.

"You could say that." And because Aṅụrị was not yet ready for him to leave, because the fact of him on the pavement next to her was pleasing in a way she couldn't decipher, because the sight of his retreating back was too much to think about right then, she said, "Sensory deprivation?"

And he, Christian, tapped a finger against his unsent post and replied, "Yep. Want to see?"

At the place, aptly named Blank, they greeted Christian like a long-lost family member. They presented him with a monogrammed towel and informed him that his preferred isolation tank was free. It was Christian's turn to be embarrassed, but he wore it reluctantly, more concerned about potentially offending the employees, who beamed at him like he was the Second Coming. He thanked them for their gift and even asked who had chosen the color thread for the towel stitching. Aṅụrị turned away. To be earnest in the face of discomfort was a talent she did not possess. She smiled when finally the two of them were led to the cool-toned corridor outside neighboring isolation rooms and mercifully left alone.

"Do you think if I ask nicely, I can get a monogrammed towel as well?"

Christian ignored the tremor in her voice. "Wow. I honestly didn't expect this. You can use mine, if you like."

"You get this kind of reception every time you're here?"

"They're always lovely to me. More so because I don't come here often these days." His eyes widened. "Shit, what if I'm their only customer? Now I can never stop."

"And you brought me with you."

"Now they'll probably be expecting you every time as well. I'm not used to this kind of pressure."

Before she stepped inside her designated chamber, Aṅụrị, without looking at him, listed aloud the ways in which this endeavor could end in tragedy: falling asleep and accidentally drowning, the tank sealing shut resulting in slow asphyxiation, a claustrophobia-induced panic attack. Christian touched her lightly on the shoulder and said, "You forgot blunt force trauma caused by forgetting where you are, sitting up abruptly and braining yourself on the tank cover." Then he handed her a towel and ushered her inside, closing the door gently behind her. She did not know why, but she expected him to be gone when she emerged one hour later, yet there he was, sitting on the low sofa, in the corridor, his unposted envelopes across his knees. He was reading a forgotten copy of *Tesco* magazine.

"Did you know," he asked without looking up, "that artichokes are a flower that hasn't bloomed?"

"I didn't know that, no."

"That kind of sucks."

"Why?"

"Stuff should be allowed to reach fruition. How did it go?"

It struck her then, the absurdity of it all. It didn't make sense that she was in this strange place with this near stranger; that she had spent the last hour floating in the darkness and experiencing (after the first few minutes where she was convinced she was going to die) a kind of weightless peace she was almost sure would become her new drug of choice. It didn't make sense that Christian was still there gazing up at her, his face open and devoid of judgement. The boy who asked about her appendix scar flashed in her memory.

"Christian. Chidili," Aṅụrị said. "Don't you have anything else to do? Today I mean."

A shadow of confusion passed over his face. "I have all the things to do today. None of them are as important as this."

It wasn't a statement that required a response, but Aṅụrị felt compelled to provide one. It would mean little or would come out wrong or unintentionally aggressive as seemed to be her default when caught off guard, but she was not given the chance to mess up because at that moment, her father called and asked if she was available to collect her sister from ballet class.

Christian accompanied Aṅụrị as far as the tube station, raising his hand in a half wave as she flew down the stairs. The hand, his hand, was still aloft as she lost sight of him. Each time he disappeared from view, Aṅụrị was convinced it would be the last she saw of him—she had done nothing, after all, to earn any sort of devotion from him. She had still not recognized, even at twenty-five, that she could be loved without having toiled for it; that acceptance was not solely a reward for good behavior.

Outside Noelle's ballet class, she spoke to her father again, checking once more that her being there was allowed. Nkem repeated his earlier words: work had thrown up an immovable deadline and he couldn't leave; she was doing him a favor, and yes, Ophelia was aware. He cleared his throat and began to mention something about "incidents" of late but then there she was, clad in pink satin and taffeta, and Aṅụrị wished she could bottle it, the feeling that swept through her on seeing Noelle register her presence, understand it, then react. Nkem's voice was drowned out by the joy of reunion. Noelle asked the following in quick succession:

- If Aṅụrị had missed her
- Why Aṅụrị was crying
- If they could go and get a McDonald's
- How much exactly Aṅụrị had missed her and if that constituted enough for an additional McFlurry
- Where Aṅụrị had been
- Did Aṅụrị still like her
- Could that like be demonstrated by the addition of an apple pie

Anụrị was presented with an example of an "incident" when they were inside McDonald's. She bargained with Noelle and agreed to the apple pie but not the McFlurry (at least the pie could count as one of her five a day). She was aglow with relief and struck with the fear that accompanies it, the kind of fear prompted by the knowledge that the reason for the relief is by no means guaranteed to remain. These were precious hours, and because she had no idea whether Nkem had simply taken pity on her or indeed had a genuine emergency, Anụrị savored them. Who knew when she would see her sister again? Once seated, Noelle asked her the following in quick succession:

- If Anụrị thought she was pretty ("You're the most beautiful girl in the world.")
- If she could cut her hair off like her sister had ("For what, Nell?")
- Why she couldn't have the McFlurry ("We talked about it, babes. Next time.")
- If people thought she was ugly ("Nell? No. You're gorgeous. Who said that to you?")
- Why, if Anụrị loved her, she couldn't have the McFlurry now ("Emotional blackmail won't work with me, baby girl.")

When Noelle started crying, Anụrị abandoned her fries and moved to crouch at her sister's side. Noelle was neither warm nor clammy, signs Anụrị learned to check for early on because kids often did not have the words to describe illness; sometimes it manifested as yelling or flailing. Noelle wailed then screamed for the godforsaken McFlurry which, already feeling her chest begin to tighten for the second time that day, Anụrị dutifully fetched only for it to be cast aside so that the wailing might continue unfettered. Noelle slid from seat to floor and could not be persuaded to get up. Anụrị watched as the ballet satin turned from pink to mottled brown. Noelle thrashed against the floor of the restaurant, words attempting to squeeze around the sobs but falling short—Aṅuṛi could only catch "ugly" as it fell from her sister's mouth, crawled across the floor and up her spine, turning her cold. Onlookers paused in their consumption of trans fats to blink judgement in her direction until Aṅuṛi was forced to pick Noelle up and carry her out, stares piercing her back as she went. The tantrum blew in like a squall, raged through what was meant to be a happy reunion and left Noelle exhausted and Aṅuṛi near tears herself.

If you were a bird circling in the warm air above Swiss Cottage that afternoon, you might have caught glimpses of a woman with splashes of copper in her cropped hair as she walked the streets carrying a child, disappearing under the branches of cherry trees and trident maples then reappearing, the copper catching the sun in a way that was beautiful if slightly heartbreaking. You would witness the arrival of the pair at one of the more imposing houses, the exchange with a third person at the door whose blond head tipped forward, arms outstretched to receive the sleeping child. If you swooped lower, you would be witness to the exchange between the two adults, the tic in the jaw of the younger one as she asked once and then again why the child was fixating on her appearance; why food was being used as a bargaining chip. You would notice the hardness in her eyes that spread to her voice when she said, "What about that seems normal to you?" And if you alighted on one of the ornamental evergreens flanking the front door, you would observe the hand of the blonde rise to cradle the head of the child, still sleeping, oblivious to the fact of her world shifting again. There was the pursing of tinted lips, the drawing together of manicured eyebrows and finally a declaration made in hushed tones but underpinned by concrete resolve.

"I love my daughter, Aṅuṛi. And I want her to be happy which is why you're even able to stand here and speak to me like this. But don't think I'll allow you to put ideas in my child's head. It stops today."

SEVEN

At thirteen, Aṅụrị's unease had become multidimensional. It began with her body—she was three inches taller than she had been the year before, and now an array of brightly colored C-cup bras (*#gifted #newbeginnings*) lay in the custom underwear organizers in her bedroom drawers. She did not possess the easy confidence of her peers and was not yet observant enough to detect that much of that confidence was fake. Her steadily elongating legs made her awkward; she felt she might pitch too far forward at any moment and end up spread-eagled in one of the school corridors. There was also a trip to the optician where Aṅụrị entered with mildly blurry vision and left with two pairs of glasses, a promise from Ophelia that contacts were always an option (because who would want to dilute the intensity of her gorgeous eyes?) and a newly emerging complex. Adolescence is already rife with physical ambiguities and these were only compounded by Aṅụrị's existence as a highly scrutinized teenager. Her body did not feel like her own, and she reasoned that it wasn't, not really, too many people had opinions on what she looked like, what she *should* look like, and what they hoped she might look like in the near future.

If asked now to identify a turning point, Aṅuri would hearken back to the afternoon at Simi's house where she stood before her best friend's mirror, and, after counting her physical flaws, felt her inner turmoil and dissatisfaction develop a heartbeat, step out of her and become laws unto themselves. Ever present and unpredictable.

At the dinner table that same evening, Aṅuri pushed yam pottage around her plate until Simi, previously distracted by the conversation her two younger brothers were having about a new Icelandic girl at their school, asked if she was alright.

On autopilot, Aṅuri said she was fine. Simi's house with its regular size and its rambunctious inhabitants were her haven. Simi's parents and brothers, her second family. To be anything other than fine, anything other than perfect was to risk not being asked back. Aṅuri could list the things she would do to avoid that risk and none of them were pleasant.

"You're not eating," Simi pointed out. Then she caught the way Aṅuri was regulating her breathing and how, despite her best efforts, Aṅuri's eyes were beginning to fill. She turned back to her brothers. "Lekan, if you want to know what it's like in Iceland, just ask the girl. Nicely. Yele, don't follow him into foolishness. Clear your plates. Aṅuri, let's go upstairs."

In the safety of Simi's bedroom and under the watchful gazes of Usher and B2K, carefully affixed to the wall after a debate with her mother, Morenike ("Simisola, if you want to put boys on your wall, you could at least make them Bible believers. Look at this one. Did he perm his hair?"), Aṅuri talked around her lack of appetite as she flat twisted Simi's hair. These were the days where problems sat like stones on Aṅuri's chest, but for which she did not yet have the tools to move by herself. Simi, even at thirteen, had learned that sometimes it was easier for people to unburden themselves when they were not looking directly into the harshness of the issue itself, blinding as it could be. And so she recounted for Aṅuri another debate, this time with her dad about the split of chores between her and her brothers ("As God is my witness, Simisola, I will send you to Ikire if you bother me with this again. Yele is seven—he can't use an iron yet! He will surely die."). In this way, she was able to determine that Aṅụrị's sudden aversion to yam pottage was a result of the deal Ophelia had landed with *Teen Vogue*. An interview about entering teenhood. A short YouTube special on the meaning of mothering a teen. Some sort of product-heavy party despite the fallout of the sixth birthday still rippling occasionally through the family.

"*Teen Vogue*," Simi said. "So now you think you're fat."

Aṅụrị secured a twist with a rubber band. She was, at times, simultaneously flush with gratitude and irritation at how easily Simi flicked open the door to her head, entered and made herself at home. This was before she understood that Loki and Simi were her soulmates; something people roamed the earth to find. "I'm—"

"Yeah, we're not doing this. You're not fat."

"But—"

"Not. Fat. And even if you were, so what? Fat is a thing people are allowed to be. Also, who die of yam pottage?"

"Simi—" But Aṅụrị was already laughing, already thawing.

"Give me ideas for teaching a seven-year-old how to iron school shirts without severe harm. My dad thinks he's won, but it's like he doesn't know who he raised." Gently, expertly, Simi steered them away from troubled waters. Her love for Aṅụrị— the Aṅụrị who took Simi to the Royal Albert Hall to watch renowned violinist Max Vengerov in concert despite having no interest in classical music, whose laugh ought to be bottled and distributed to the downtrodden—was beautiful in the same way it was occasionally suffocating. There was no one else alive who saw her the way Aṅụrị did, but that privilege came with a responsibility to keep her best friend's head above water. It was a duty Simi readily assumed. One day, she vowed, Aṅụrị would realize she kept Simi afloat, too. After Aṅụrị left that evening,

Simi did not stop playing Brahms on her violin until her father, Ayo, put his head around the door and said, "My dear daughter, we have heard. Our money is not going to waste. Please rest."

Two days later, when the girls met with Loki, fresh from a stint under Remy's roof, his thirst for rebellion a barely contained beast clawing at his skin, they congregated in the den of the Llorenses' Mayfair apartment and Loki passed them bottles of too-sweet premixed cocktails, the tamest of alcoholic beverages, but still verboten for teens with inflated senses of maturity. Céleste was out and had left the three of them to recline in the living room and watch slasher movies through the thickening fog of drunkenness.

"It's *your* life," Loki reminded Aṅụrị once she'd updated him on recent events.

"I'm aware, LoLo."

"Are you? 'Cos I dunno. You're talking like you don't have a choice."

She looked down at the label she'd half peeled from the bottle in her hand. It was easy for Loki to say this. Remy might have ruled with, if not an iron fist, at least one that was vaguely metallic, but Céleste often indulged her rangy, soft-spoken son. It was why, at Céleste's bidding, Loki had appeared in exactly one editorial (*Life with the Llorenses*) and his request to remain in a tracksuit had not only been accepted but encouraged. The concept of "no," of choice, meant something different to him because he was with the parent most likely to deny him only fifty percent of the time. Aṅụrị thought of the interview she did not want to give. This was how futures were forged: through the breaking, rebuilding and reconfiguring of boundaries. She reached for the remaining bottle even as Simi stood, steadying herself on the arm of the sofa.

"Loki," Simi said, "will your mum shout if I use some of her fancy coffee? I need a cup. I can't go home tipsy—my dad really will send me to Ikire."

"Just don't drink the hazelnut shit. It's her fave and costs like sixty dollars a bag." He yawned, ran a hand over his low cut. He would start growing his locs a year later. "In fact, lemme come with. I could do with some, too. Aṅụrị, you want a cup?"

Aṅụrị shook her head. She didn't understand why her friends would choose coffee over booze. She didn't understand why anyone would choose anything over booze. Discovering drinking was her personal Nirvana. The weightlessness, the softness of its embrace, the feeling like she was in control even as she slipped out of it; even if it was a lie. These were gifts. Why would anyone choose any other drink if an alcoholic one was also on offer? This is how dependencies were created: gradually.

Later that night, after washing her face and brushing her teeth, her head still swimming slightly, Aṅụrị found her father in the kitchen. He made her a mug of cocoa which was bitter but which she drank regardless, because she was a kid and she wanted her dad to feel useful, and sadly, to like her. Nkem asked her about school and he laughed as she mounted a spirited defense of her decision to switch Latin for Spanish as soon as the option was made available to her. It was this, the moments of father-daughter camaraderie, where the idea of a normal life was something Aṅụrị could almost touch, that she felt closest to Nkem; when he looked at her and she found gentleness in his gaze. It was moments like this that led Aṅụrị to make the mistake of vulnerability, of trust.

"Dad—" she wiped frothed milk from her top lip "—about *Teen Vogue*. I don't think I want to do it. No. I know. I don't want to do it." She knew as soon as she said it, that their moment had come to an abrupt end, her admission a conversational vise.

Nkem frowned and reached for the mug his daughter was still holding. "Aṅụrị, biko. You see how hard Ophelia worked on this. Let her down now? Enweghị ike. It's too late."

"It's not impossible. If you could just—"

Nkem's frustration quietly simmering until that point, finally overflowed—why wouldn't the child just listen? "Biko, nùlụ onū m! I said it's too late."

Aṅụrị slid from her stool. "I've heard you."

In the end, Aṅụrị wrenched her choice from the fists of her parents. In the wee hours of Interview Day, she dressed, looped her braids into a ponytail and crept out, running three streets over where Loki waited in the back of a black cab, half-asleep but lucid enough to shoot her a grin from beneath the hood of his jacket and mutter an "okay then" followed by a chuckle that made Aṅụrị's stomach flip with pride and excitement. The police didn't find them until almost seven that evening and only then because the combined fury of Céleste and Ophelia was enough to power their vehicles through London until the pair were located. As Loki was hauled into the back of Céleste's chauffeur-driven car, he glanced over his shoulder and mouthed, "Worth it." And it was. It was. The day served to douse Aṅụrị's conviction in kerosene. Her resolve blazed within her even as Nkem and Ophelia paced in front of her, setting reprimands at her feet and watching her kick them away.

"I don't understand. We agreed! And then you do this. Do you know how we worried? Ophelia had to explain to those people what had happened. They might never give us another chance! Kwuo ihe ọ bụla!" Nkem shouted. *Say something.* "Shebi, you always have mouth to speak."

"*We* didn't agree."

"Ehn?"

"We didn't agree. I told you I didn't want to do it."

"In life..." It was now Ophelia who chose to chime in, pausing to stand at Nkem's side. "We have to do things we don't want to from time to time. But this was *Teen Vogue*, Aṅụrị. *Teen Vogue.* You would have been the envy of girls across the globe."

It was strange, Aṅụrị thought, how even then, she wanted to reach out and touch the silk of Ophelia's bathrobe. She wanted her stepmother to tell her it was alright, that she didn't have to do anything she didn't want to, but she knew with a sad certainty that soaked up the remaining defiance-fueled adrenaline pulsing through her that this would never happen. And it was the never that pounded in her skull.

"I'm not doing this anymore."

"You're not doing what?" Ophelia asked. Makeup-free, her delicate eggshell beauty endowed her with a vulnerability that could prove lethal.

"This." Aṅụrị raised her arms then let them drop back to her sides. "The YouTube videos. The Instagram posts. The blog. The sponsorships. All of it. I'm over it."

"You're...over it."

"Today was so fun." Aṅụrị pressed the heels of her palms into her eye sockets. "It was *so* fun. Just being with Loki and not caring about...performing. I want every day to be like today. So yeah, I'm not doing it anymore. I don't actually care about being the envy of anyone. I just want to be me." She fled to her room. Praying for Ophelia's downfall was no longer enough; Aṅụrị needed to participate in it.

Month one: Aṅụrị, on a visit to her aunt Nneoma's, took a Benin mask replica and wore it around the house, hissing theatrically whenever Ophelia's Canon or iPhone emerged.

Month two: Aṅụrị refused to speak in anything but a Latin-Igbo hybrid language she invented.

Month three: Aṅụrị embarked on a hunger strike that lasted six days and ended with the theft and consumption of Nkem's imported palm wine which landed her in the hospital for physical and then psychiatric evaluation.

Month four: Aṅụrị left home every single night and slept first in front of and then inside Nneoma's house after her aunt gave her a key, until she was returned to her parents in the morning.

Month five: Aṅụrị created a handful of fake social media handles and began commenting on every post on Ophelia's feeds where she saw herself featured. Variations of *this is exploitation, you know* and *the girl looks miserable* littered the comments section until Ophelia was forced to limit comments while she got to the bottom of it.

By month six, Nkem and Ophelia finally understood that this was not, as they thought, as they *hoped*, a phase. They conferred in the velvet darkness of their bedroom, Nkem pressing his wife to his chest and feeling her mounting alarm work its way through her body. Stats were beginning to suffer. Sponsors were asking questions, two had already absconded, sending curt emails peppered with cliches (*let's circle back in a few months and see where we stand*). Ophelia had almost exhausted her vault of backup content; the pictures, videos and posts she amassed for when Aṅụrị was sick or engrossed in a particularly intense period of schooling and she needed to feed the machine, to keep the viewers sated. Until then, every prior attempt at rebellion had been reversed and used as fodder in Ophelia's meteoric rise to fame. The sixth birthday debacle transformed into a lesson in loving your children through adversity; Aṅụrị's short-lived emo phase chronicled for an audience of simpering, giggling devotees casting sidelong glances at their own uninspiring offspring and wishing for a different, more star-studded lot. This was different.

These days, Ophelia was snatching candids of Aṅụrị at the kitchen island spearing puff puff the kid had fried herself or vlogging Aṅụrị's discarded school uniform and using these fragments to cobble together posts on puff puff recipes (she had to look up online because Aṅụrị refused to give her the one she used) or the dangers of washing with store-brand detergent (she landed a sponsorship deal with a detergent company on the back of this and wept with relief when the contract was signed).

The two of them tried to reason with Aṅụrị and when that did not work, they doled out punishments which the teenager took like repeated blows to a hardened fighter's chin. She left rooms whenever they entered, shut then locked her bedroom door when she heard Nkem's footsteps on the stairs. The walls of the house constantly reverberated with the slamming of doors. Nkem and Ophelia listened, anger flickering in their stomachs, as Simi's parents appealed to them to be patient. Spurred on by Loki, who had them made in bulk, Aṅụrị wore nothing else but black T-shirts with the words "I DO NOT CONSENT" or "CAMERA-FREE ZONE" emblazoned across her chest.

Gone was the bubbly, sharp-minded young woman Nkem and Ophelia were raising, replaced by a sullen, scornful facsimile. It became increasingly common to find empty liquor bottles in Aṅụrị's bedroom, to hear the distorted version of her laugh, sharp and shot through with contempt, to catch her eye and find nothing there but blankness. It was chilling.

Shortly after her fourteenth birthday, Nkem found his daughter in the garden. She was holding a spray bottle, spritzing water on her sectioned hair and singing. The love he felt for her in that moment almost bent him double. The slope of her neck, the way she crossed her outstretched legs at the ankles, even the register of her voice; lower than normal, near raspy pushed him to an invisible edge. When had his child become her mother? How had she slipped so far from him? He cleared his throat so as not to startle her then lowered himself to the bench where she sat.

"Your hair has grown," he said.

"My crowning glory," Aṅụrị replied.

"Just like your mother's."

She stared at him then. He did not invoke Kainene. That wound had healed and left a scar he disguised with a determination that bordered on fanatical. The hope in his daughter's eyes was a damning assessment of his abilities as a father. He focused on the far end of their garden, and when he chanced a look at Aṅụrị, he saw tears winding down her face.

"Why can't you talk to me about her?"

"Ọ gwūgo."

"How can it be finished when it never started?" Her voice cracked.

Nkem's heart folded in on itself. You did not bring children into an already broken world to break them further. Aṅụrị was so unhappy. But her unhappiness was because she didn't understand. That is what Nkem told himself. Lying to himself was easier; telling himself the truth required practice and a tolerance for pain he had used up when Kainene died. He lifted his hand. It would take less than a second to reach out and touch his child on her shoulder, pull her into his embrace and whisper apologies. It was clear that she no longer liked him, but had love survived? Kainene would have known what to do. And to think that was a betrayal because Kainene had died and Ophelia was both alive and the author of his salvation. His hand dropped back into his lap.

"I just want you to try to see where Ophelia is coming from. Everything she does is for this family. I know you're tired. But her success is our success." Nkem did not look at Aṅụrị. Something had been set in motion and unbeknownst to both father and daughter, it was now bigger than both of them. The imprudence of humans, of these two people linked by blood and separated by the same, was that they thought they had both time and control.

Aṅụrị allowed herself to emit one sob, which punched the air between them. She wiped her face and stood up. "The difference, Dad, is that her success is at my expense." She walked away.

That night, she shaved fourteen years of hair from her head and left it in a heap on the bathroom floor. She called her grandmother, then her aunt, packed a suitcase and twenty-four hours later, when the ticket Makuo booked for her was confirmed, she boarded a flight to Nigeria where her grandparents were waiting.

The child slept for the first two days, Makuo finding her flushed and immobile beneath the ceiling fan, her refusal to turn on the air-conditioning resolute since her arrival. She would wake only for the time it took to eat the food Arinze brought to her room, eyelids drooping, docile as a lamb. Makuo would watch him bring the tray back to the kitchen, watch it taken from his hands by their house help, Erinma, and she would wring her hands and wait for his assessment.

"Let her rest," he said. "She will come when she is ready."

In those two days, Arinze and Makuo spent hours on the phone with Nneoma and with Nkem and Ophelia who threatened, that first day, to call the police and have them arrested for kidnapping.

"Is it a kidnapper who can make a girl enter a plane by herself? Abeg, Nkem, be serious," Nneoma said on the conference call she set up so they could all speak at once.

"Was it not them who bought her the ticket?" Nkem's voice drowned out his sister's. "Would she be there if they hadn't interfered?"

"Daa jụụ," Arinze said.

"Don't tell me to be quiet!" Nkem's anger split at the seams, drenching them all.

"She should be here with us," Ophelia added. "I want her home within forty-eight hours or I swear to God, I am calling the authorities."

"Is it my God you're swearing to?" Nneoma deadpanned.

Arinze waited a beat, then said it again, rolling a stone in front of their threats. "Daa jụụ. If we didn't buy the ticket, do you think the two of you would know where she was now? Do you think she would be safe?"

"Instead of you to ask yourselves why it has come to this, you're talking of police. Oya, call police for them. In Onitsha." Nneoma kissed her teeth. "Arrant nonsense."

"Let us try to talk to her," Makuo said. "Let her stay for a little while. We will of course report back to you and let you know she is fine. We'll look after her."

It was a conclusion presented as a choice.

Aṅụrị emerged on the third day, wilted and melancholy, and joined her grandmother in the kitchen where Makuo and Erinma were draining the cassava ready to make fufu. Makuo dried her hands and beckoned her granddaughter into her arms. She felt the shifting of bone under too little flesh and the trembling of a person who had had to feign strength for too long.

First, Makuo said "ndo" because "sorry" was useless, a damp squib, and "ndo" meant so much more; that Makuo was a willing bunkmate in Aṅụrị's sadness. Aṅụrị had to know that she was not alone, that there were those who weathered every drop of pain along with her. Then Makuo held her granddaughter's face and said, "Hụrụ n'anya, ị nọ n'udo," *beloved, you are safe*, because she did not know the last time Aṅụrị had felt truly so and it was important to tell her that here, she was. The words needed to be spoken, to be stamped again and again into Aṅụrị's being until they too became a living, breathing part of her.

A week into Aṅụrị's stay, she, Arinze, Makuo and Erinma gathered their load and the four of them left Onitsha for the compound in Awka. The New Yam Festival was days away and Aṅụrị's shrunken, fatigued presence made for a compelling argument to head out of Onitsha a little earlier than planned. It would be Aṅụrị's first time experiencing New Yam and Arinze reasoned that a little merriment would be good for the girl. Selfishly, he missed his granddaughter's joy, watching its attrition as he had, over the years. The sound of Aṅụrị's laughter had been absent for too long. He and Makuo grew used to the exchange of commiserations over garri and groundnut in the mornings.

"If you drop pin for ground, you go hear am," Makuo said to her husband of Aṅụrị's silence.

He could only nod. Awka and New Yam could be a solution. Sun and music and the smell of palm oil thick in the air. The festival is a celebratory gathering of community to give thanks for the protection of the divine, and to mark the ending of the farming season and the beginning of harvest. Because celebration flows through the veins of Nigerians and because the atmosphere was infectious in a way even a morose teenager might be powerless to resist, Aṅụrị relinquished decision-making to her grandparents and surrendered to her roots.

The decision-making was swiftly handed back on arrival.

"You can take part as much or as little as you want," Arinze told Aṅụrị. "But this one? It's enough. You can drink small during the celebration." He was referring to the depleted bottle of cognac in his cabinet back in Onitsha. He turned momentarily away so Aṅụrị's shame could be felt privately.

"It's okay, Papa. I want to help," Aṅụrị said quietly. "And I'm sorry." Her eyes drifted to a group of youngsters assembling the platform on which Arinze said he and some of the other chieftains would sit to say the opening prayers the following morning, festival day.

Arinze laughed softly at Aṅụrị's perplexity—the girl's brow a constellation of furrows. "Nobody is expecting you to go and carry log, Aṅụrị. Go and see if your grandma needs anything."

In Awka, Aṅụrị learned that scrutiny had a softer side, one that fell softly like folds of cashmere, and did not chafe. Arinze and Makuo were known and respected there, and because of that, Aṅụrị was, too. People were curious because she was the often extolled, conspicuously absent granddaughter and suddenly she was there among them, quiet and shy and always walking at Arinze's side or following Makuo and Erinma as they prepared the "old" yam for consumption so that the new yam could be shared amongst those gathered. She made long, thin candles to be carried during the procession, and learned how best to scent them with plumeria. In the evenings, she would meekly opt for Fanta but insist on sitting with Arinze and the uncles as they drank palm wine and pito.

"When you coming home?" Loki asked when she spoke to him on the phone.

"I don't know. I like it here," Aṅụrị admitted.

"I get that. I do. But I miss you."

"It's just that I'm tired of Lekan asking when he'll see you again," Simi said when it was her turn for a phone call.

"Tell him I'll see him soon," Aṅụrị said.

"And will you? See him soon?" Simi's voice shook on the word "soon."

"I promise. I love you, Sim."

"To infinity. Bring me Ankara. Preferably in blue."

On festival day, following the prayers, the masquerades began their dance. Arinze pointed out Ijele, one of the oldest and biggest of the group, but Aṅụrị only half listened. So it could be like this, she thought. It could be like this always. Her jeans lay forgotten at the bottom of her suitcase. She wore wrappers, Akwete and embroidered lace. She watched the female drummers adorned in their suku hairstyles and safety pins, beads crisscrossed around their necks. She found her feet moving as the Ugho dance was performed. The backs of her thighs were stamped with summer. She lifted her face and inhaled the sky above Awka, blue streaks and red earth embedded in the back of her throat. The version of herself she left in the London house was one she felt she could never return to. She stepped from Arinze's side and joined the dancing, wondering if her mother had done the same; praying that if Kainene had, she was watching and smiling her approval from wherever she was now.

Makuo and Arinze waited and they watched. Arinze said, "She should just remain here with us," and Makuo looked at him until he said, "I can't apologize for saying the things I wish were true." Eventually, a few days after the festival ended, they called Aṅụrị inside from where she was picking guavas from the trees by the south wall of the compound. She saw their faces and placed her basket on the nearest table, rolled her shoulders back and prepared herself to plead.

"Come and sit down with us," Makuo said.

In the sitting room, Aṅụrị sat between her grandparents on the sofa and stared at her hands. She would keep staring at her hands, she supposed, because if she looked at Makuo and Arinze, she might see in their eyes that they were serious about sending her home; about not wanting her. Arinze plucked her hands out of her lap and held them both between his. She raised her head and his eyes spoke nothing but love.

"This was your mother's." Makuo held a curved gold bangle. "We got it for her when she passed the JSCE, that is the Junior Secondary Certificate Examination, and secured her place at senior secondary school. It belongs here." She touched Aṅụrị's wrist.

"Kainene was born here in Awka. She learned herself here, so it makes sense for you to also come alive in this place." Arinze enclosed the bangle around the slimness of Aṅụrị's wrist. This child was the best of him. His sweetheart. He told her so. "But, uso m, you have to return to your parents."

Aṅụrị thought of her father and the times she caught him watching her like she was an apparition, his face a mask of confusion, pain and something she couldn't recognize. The Nkem of today was the sum of his anguish at losing Kainene. His inability to manage the loss of her meant that he chose to apply an emotional tourniquet and cut himself off from everything that aggravated the injury. This meant fleeing their home. It meant remarrying. It meant unconsciously erecting a partition between him and his child and peering through it, bewildered when that same child regarded him as a flighty and unreliable presence in her life. Aṅụrị could have forgiven all of that if Nkem's excision of Kainene didn't also dictate Aṅụrị's forcible separation from whatever remnants of her mother he could have ensured were imparted to her. As it was, Aṅụrị could not pardon such an infraction—Nkem had experienced the joy and the sweetness of Kainene and didn't love his daughter enough to ensure she did the same, even after Kainene was gone. Anyone could see how important it was for a daughter to know their mother, even if that knowledge was secondary. Nkem had ignored that need.

Here, in the same house her mother had lived, feeling the gentle yet solid weight of the bangle her mother had worn, she felt fresh heartbreak and with it, the anger she reserved for her father. This time, however, she also felt closer to Kainene than ever before and this imbued her with the ability to speak her own pain.

"He won't talk about Kain—about my mum. If it wasn't for you and Aunty Nneoma, I wouldn't know anything. I wouldn't even know what she looked like." She did not need to tell Arinze who she meant by "he."

Arinze kept Aṅụrị's wrist in his palm. "When she died, we worried Nkem would follow her. Grief is not always rational."

"She looked like you." Makuo kissed Aṅụrị's face. "That is, you look like her. Nkem suffered greatly. But what happened is that he forgot that you also suffered." She rose, crossed the room to the writing desk in the corner and returned holding a photo album. "You can take anything from here." She slid the album to Aṅụrị's lap.

"But these pictures are all you have."

"They aren't. But even if they were, they also belong to you. She also belonged to you."

Aṅụrị chose six photos. In all of them, bar one, Kainene was laughing. She looked in those photos like someone who was yet to sit with defeat, who had not yet been greeted by disillusionment. She looked like Aṅụrị if Aṅụrị lived a different life.

"She wanted to be a doctor." Arinze paused, and Aṅụrị watched as he closed his eyes. She was old enough to know that pain did not have favorites and that loss cloned itself so there was enough to go around. And she mourned her mother, but in a way that sometimes felt abstract. Arinze and Makuo had known her; she was theirs more than hers it seemed. Aṅụrị had never lost a child. She had not been ripped from the remaining part of that lost child. She slipped her arm through her grandfather's. Aṅụrị also knew that pain didn't really fade, people just learned to grow around it; to ignore it.

Makuo closed the album. "She planned her whole life. She was not a person who let life happen to her. She was so bold. And boldness like that can only be stopped by death."

"I wish she was here." Aṅụrị started to cry. "I feel like none of this would be happening if she was still here. There's all this stuff I want to say to her and learn from her, but I can't."

"She is always here," Arinze said. "You need only look in the mirror to see her."

They told her she had learned Kainene's boldness, or perhaps inherited it along with her eyes. They reminded her that she had brought herself to them in the best way she knew how. They said, with smiles on their faces, that her months of protest in Swiss Cottage were testament to Kainene's mulishness living on through her only child. They reminded Aṅụrị that she was not a wallflower. She was not powerless. She needed to go home to London and continue her fight.

"I'm tired. What if I can't?"

"We will help you," Arinze said. "You're not alone."

It was Makuo and Arinze, assisted by Nneoma, who found Gloria. It took just over a week. And four days after that, on the day Aṅụrị touched back down at Heathrow, the first cease and desist landed on Nkem and Ophelia's doorstep.

It was the first real act in the ongoing war Aṅụrị waged against her parents. It was the stake in the ground to which she tied her future. On days when she was so hungover the act of opening her eyes felt like a step toward death; when Gloria would call and tell her first in English then in Igbo that their petition had failed but they would simply file another, when Simi climbed into bed with her and wrapped her words around Aṅụrị's shaking form, she would look through the photographs of Kainene or sit in the shower twirling the bangle around her wrist, and then she would do something that forced her to feel the undeniable truth of being alive—running in the cold or lying on a flat roof with Loki while he named the stars and held her hand.

Shortly after her eighteenth birthday, Gloria met with Aṅụrị in a café and explained that Ophelia had capitulated and agreed to pay fifty-five thousand pounds. In monetary terms, it was nothing, not against the backdrop of what had become the Chinasa fortune, but to an eighteen-year-old, it bought freedom; months of rent in a Chiswick flat that wasn't the house that had eventually become a prison, and enough to begin a fledgling candle business. Aṅụrị wept for so long that café patrons became concerned, and Gloria kept them at bay with a look that spoke of untold pain if they stepped closer.

Months later, with her nineteenth birthday not quite committed to memory, Aṅụrị would learn, when Nkem called to break the news, that Ophelia's benevolence was a direct result of her pregnancy after two IVF treatments Aṅụrị knew nothing about. The first baby was lost, but Noelle would be the second. In her new flat and in the beginnings of her new life, Aṅụrị realized that she had, inadvertently, paid for her sister to enter the world.

OPHELIA

There is something about me, perhaps an expression I have or the pitch in which my laughter leaves my body, that makes people think everything comes easily to me; that I never have to try; that my hardships are not real or if they are, then they are superficial. The blog, the videos, the picture I paint on social media is the cause and the remedy. If there's blame to apportion, I suppose it lies with me. It was important that they, the Phelia-ites as Nkem calls them, understood that Noelle was not a replacement for Aṅụrị, that even before Aṅụrị severed what bound us together as family, I spent nights praying to the God of Nneoma and of Makuo and Arinze for another child. I wanted Nkem in miniature. I wanted my love for him to grow arms and legs. I wanted it walking and shouting throughout the house. I wanted it loving us back. I wanted the plumpness and the morning sickness. I wanted the broken and weeping nipples, the sleepless nights and the familiar terror of knowing how many ways there are to break something so tiny, the endless pursuit for the confirmation that somehow, you are doing things correctly. Nkem said no. He was resolute in his refusal. For my husband, pregnancy was tied to death and in the end, he only agreed because my pillow was continuously damp with tears. He said yes but my body said no. And they, the Phelia-ites, needed to know that life for me was not an everlasting celebration.

The first round didn't take. Again Nkem said "no more" and again he relented after a shorter round of campaigning on my part. Then there was Noelle. We named her at month four only when I felt my body solidify around her, when I knew she would be safe. I hoped we might tell Añụrị together, but she was out of the house by then, and would speak only to Nkem. So he delivered the news and when I asked what she said, he brought my face close to his and kissed me.

I still don't know.

EIGHT

It was odd that Aṅụrị had not mentioned Christian to either Loki or Simi. The oddness meant that there was a reason for not doing so and that reason was too much to think about. It gave her interactions with him a significance she was too scared to stare into. So, she told them in Céleste's kitchen at the Mayfair apartment, when her back was turned and she was stirring Lemsip in a mug for Simi. It was easier to both be unwell and to play violin samples for Céleste here away from the demands of siblings and parents. Céleste had requested Simi showcase her musical talent at the wedding reception, and so, despite congestion, a low-grade fever and the threat of contagion, Simi made her way to Mayfair and Aṅụrị was not far behind—it took only a sniffle for Aṅụrị to leap into caretaker mode. She had procured Lemsip, filled a numbered pillbox with zinc supplements and taken over Simi's sisterly duties of helping Yele sharpen his CV ahead of a new job hunt. There in the kitchen, Aṅụrị dropped the information like acid rain and was now refusing to watch it burn its way into the faces of her friends.

"What do you mean?" Loki was the first one to speak. As the child of divorce, he was a seasoned breaker of silences; the experienced diffuser of tension, which he blew from rooms like smoke. Aṅụrị turned and he caught her hand and held on to her pinkie like he used to when they were kids. "Say again."

"He's just... He came to get his hair retwisted—"

"Locs?" Loki tightened his grip on her finger. "A man of both taste and class."

"And then like I said, there was the Airpods and the panic attack."

"Then he took you to a place where you lie naked in the dark?" Simi, accepted her Lemsip, raised an eyebrow.

Something flared in Aṅụrị's chest. "Okay it *definitely* wasn't like that. He didn't even go in. Just sort of hung around outside until I was done to make sure I was alright."

Simi, turned her head, blew her nose into a wad of Kleenex and deposited it into the concealed trash receptacle. Deftly shifting her mug, she spritzed antibacterial spray onto the table and began wiping. "I don't trust him."

"Apart from us, who do you trust, Sim? Aṅụrị dating is a good thing."

"Whoa..." Aṅụrị slid her hand from Loki's. "Everyone be calming down please. Nobody is dating. I said no when he asked me for a drink."

"I wouldn't say *nobody* is dating," Simi muttered.

Loki turned his entire body, all six feet six of him, to face Simi. "What? What did you say?"

Simi rolled her eyes.

"Chère, did you know about this?" he addressed Aṅụrị, eyes wide.

"Simi is basically my left lung. What do you think?"

"And I, your right one, deserved to be kept in the dark. Wow. Snakes in my circle. Simi, whoever he is, he's not good enough for you."

"This—" Simi sipped from her mug "—is why. You're prone to dramatics."

"How come me dating is a good thing, but nobody is good enough for Simi?" Aṅuri crossed her arms.

"Because the only man good enough for Simi is me." Loki winked.

"You forget that I know where you've been."

"Slut shaming! How unbecoming of you, Sim." Loki rose, bending to wrap his arms around Simi and pepper her face with kisses, before he began making himself coffee.

"The loveliest ashewo I've ever known." Simi cupped his chin, her smile settling on her face, her sinuses thickening her voice.

"Ashewo. Remind me."

"She's calling you a ho, Loki," Aṅuri supplied.

"Course she is. Never change, Sim. Look, I've got a quick business call—just a script run-through—" Loki was already heading down the hall, mug in hand "—don't miss me too much."

"'Just a script run-through,'" Simi mocked. "That boy is so oblivious."

"He's not. But it's better that he acts like he is."

Aṅuri and Simi moved to the living room. The floor-to-ceiling windows overlooked Green Park and anytime Aṅuri stood in front of them, she vanished into that comforting space Londoners often do where they are both consumed by the immensity of the city, pressed upon from all sides, whilst still being utterly alone. Across town, Noelle would already be sleeping and Nkem and Ophelia would be planning her next foray into hypervisibility, a place no child ought to exist. She reread the last text from Gloria: No response yet. I'll let you know. Ophelia would resist, of course. Resistance was all she knew, was what she excelled in, and Aṅuri wished she could cut out that spot inside herself that still longed for the knowledge that her absence was a loss to them that extended beyond revenue, hits and views. She was yet to achieve apathy and it made her feel weak, exposed; an open wound awaiting salt. These were things Noelle should never feel. Aṅuri did not want her sister to wake up ten, twenty years from now and second-guess where her parents' love ended and the love of the life she funded began. Children were not meant to doubt the surety of their parents' love for them. It should be a forgone conclusion; the foundation upon which everything else in the wretched, wonderful world hinged. She did not wish for Noelle to learn that alcohol was a steadfast but dangerous friend; that terrible thirst now a monster that opened its eyes and beckoned.

Aṅụrị's mistakes were scars on her skin and stains on her memory. After the first win, the first payout, she had indulged in the sweetness of freedom and the knowledge that these were her choices, her gaffes, her self-inflicted wounds which would, if she liked, remain somewhat secret. She forgot that opting out is not the same as becoming invisible. Prominence is not so easily erased. She appeared in a tabloid first. And then on a series of entertainment blogs whose life blood was celebrity disaster. She was photographed stumbling from a club, scrapes on her elbows, eyes hooded and unfocused. The photograph made the rounds and eventually reached her grandparents. Makuo called and told Aṅụrị that was the last time such a shot would be taken, that this, the public implosion of a young girl, was over. And it was. The former school friends from whom the worst of the vultures were receiving their material were cut off. Aṅụrị learned to be less open about her vices. She joined an AA group she left after two sessions and, later, found Ammah. Over the years, she'd been approached by journalists but always shied away from them and their hungry questions that always lacked care. The additional spotlight was not worth it. That Noelle might descend into the same madness that overtook her made Aṅụrị want to grow out her hair just so she could rip it out again.

Her reflection in the windows was half consumed by the lamps Simi lit behind her. Aṅụrị turned and joined her friend on the floor where she was stretching.

"So," Simi said, "this Christian person. What else do we know about him?"

His hands are beautiful. He has long lashes behind the glasses he wears. It's only when he stops smiling that I remember to breathe. "Not much. His Igbo name is Chidili and he works in cybersecurity. Oh and apparently we're kind of neighbors, although I don't know exactly where he lives."

"And he doesn't know exactly where you live either, right?"

"He knows the hairdressing hut. That's how we met, remember?"

Simi gathered her braids in both hands then let them rain down her back. "Hmm."

"You've got six 'hmms.' That was a category-six 'hmm.' And I'm telling you, you don't have shit to worry about. One act of kindness does not a suitor make."

"It's just—"

"Yeah, I get it. I'm a walking child incapable of making decisions about dating. But it doesn't matter because we're not dating." Her voice was sharper than she meant it to sound, and already, the shame was crawling across her scalp. But this was part of living in her skin. Aṅụrị was acutely aware of who she was and how that meant being near her or forming any sort of attachment to her was like a sucking vortex that pulled in then drowned the unsuspecting in its path. She was the one who needed babysitting lest she stumble down the hill of relapse. She was the one whose name on a phone screen could strike fear into previously peaceful hearts. It couldn't be easy to be in her life. But here Simi and Loki were, doing it regardless. She would be a fool to take that for granted. And so she turned her love outward and became the friend of grand gestures but also solid, affirmative acts, her friendship a proving ground. Even as Simi pressed her lips closed, Aṅụrị was already planning the bouquet of peonies she'd send to Simi's house, and hope that Lekan or Yele did not commandeer it to offer one of their never-ending procession of crushes.

"Let's not talk about this. You know I'm not a person who dates."

Simi frowned, touched Aṅụrị's knee. "But—and God help me as I say this—Loki's right. You could be that person. You—"

"No, Sim. Let's talk about you." Aṅụrị rubbed her eyes to ward off the telltale sting. The exhaustion of being her was something she needed to work harder to shield her friends from. "Your guy, Abe, tell me how things are going."

Simi reached across and prized apart Aṅụrị's hands. She turned on the TV and they settled with their backs against the sofa. *Grand Designs* was just starting. "Resisting the ick. With everything in me, I'm resisting the ick."

"The ick? Already? Kilode."

Without turning her head, Simi smirked. "You're vex."

"What? No, I—"

"You resort to Yoruba when you want to throw me off a balcony."

"I just... Explain it to me like I'm five."

"He sent coffee. To the office."

"And we hate that because...?"

"We were on the phone the night before. For ages. I must have said something like, 'I'll be paying for this tomorrow,' and then coffee shows up at the office the next morning."

"Right."

"And it wasn't just that it was coffee. He remembered my perfect order complete with the double pump of almond syrup, and I swear to you we've only had coffee *once*. When I asked, he said he wrote it down. Then he said he jots things about me down in his notes app. His *notes app*. Isn't that the kind of thing serial killers do? Learn your routine so they know the opportune time to remove your intestines? He also sent six flat whites for the rest of the team. He didn't know their orders so he just made it generic. Because he hadn't had the time to learn and write it in his notes app. Obviously, I poured them down the sink because

Selina made a sly comment about my skirt last week in the team meeting and they all pretended not to laugh but they laughed, and what do I look like helping to quench the thirst of witches? You know me. I water my grudges like they're flowers. Forgiveness is overrated. If I've learned anything from you, it's that."

Simi, the steady one of the three, possessed a stoicism Aṅụrị often envied. Sometimes though, she would crack like the earth on an active volcano and you would glimpse her molten interior churning away before she did the work to mend herself. Aṅụrị savored these moments. She never wanted Simi to feel sad or hurt, but she, like most people, liked others just a little broken. It distracted from her own brokenness and drew the other person's humanity to the surface. We are less alone amidst imperfection.

"You know—wow, why do people never double their contingency fund for these kinds of builds? Is it not common sense?— you know, Sim, you make unhinged look so elegant. I'm jealous." She did not realize it, but Aṅụrị's ability to simultaneously underline the irrationality of her friends while softening it was one of the reasons they adored her.

"The wife wants imported Russian larch. Even with double contingency, they're blowing the budget by at *least* twenty-five percent. Also, I'm not mad." Simi lowered her eyes, toyed with the hem of her plaid shirt. "I'm down the street from scared. But I'm no pussy, so I'm just going to say it's the ick. The notes app ick."

"Yes. Clearly you're super stable. Ultra sound of mind."

"What if I like him too much and it doesn't work out?"

"Then you come back to me and Loki and we move forward with the plan to build our own compound. Surely Céleste is leaving a bundle of land to Loki in the will." Aṅụrị lowered the TV's volume slightly. "Simi, please. Let yourself be doted on. By someone other than us, I mean."

Grand Designs flickered in Simi's pupils and she nodded once, almost imperceptibly. She saw the two of them as they were: a recovering child influencer and a violinist with a penchant for architecture. Their differences were shoved aside with the goal of loving each other. Simi suspected Aṅụrị didn't even like *Grand Designs*, but she always watched it. More than that, she always appeared interested and engaged.

"Physician, heal thyself?" Simi smiled and Aṅụrị softly pinched the skin on her friend's wrist.

"It's different with me."

"It's not. But I'm not going to hassle you about it…right now. Anyway, the ick extends beyond the notes app."

"What now, for goodness' sake?"

"His name is Abe."

"Yeah. You were aware of that when you met him and he said, 'My name is Abe.'"

"Short for Abraham."

"Simi."

"It's just so *Biblical*. What if we have children and he wants to name them Boaz or Bathsheba?"

Loki, who had chosen this moment to enter the living room, pressed a hand to his chest and collapsed on the sofa behind them. "You're talking about having kids with another man. In my house? Simi? You hate me that much?"

"Firstly," Simi said, "this is your mother's house. Secondly, shut up."

They fell asleep, the three of them, in the living room, a Nollywood movie playing on mute. Simi had called her parents to let them know she wouldn't be home that evening, and shortly before midnight, Céleste swept into the room, kissing the three of them in turn and reminding Loki to "call your father, otherwise he will find a reason to call me" before she retired to her suite.

Aṅụrị tried to ignore the twinge in her stomach when Simi rolled her eyes and said into the phone, "Honestly, Dad, I love you, too. I'm at Loki's not Sodom and Gomorrah." But it returned when Loki told his mother she was the most beautiful woman on earth and laughed when her eyes glittered and she called him ridiculous. That her friends were loved by parents who were not shy about showing it was a wonderful thing to behold. But it unpicked the stitching at the corner of her happiness until it completely unraveled. Witnessing familial love was always a poignant reminder that things did not have to be as they were. Anụrị woke before the sun rose, her chest tight with the knowledge that she could not remember the last time Nkem had told her he loved her. She pressed a hand to Simi's head and sighed with relief—Simi's temperature was almost back to normal. Then she flipped the throw back over Loki's toes where he had kicked it off in sleep and, with a cup of hot lemon water at her side, sat in Céleste's kitchen and opened her laptop.

LOWLYWORM17 IS NOW ONLINE

IJELE_RISING IS NOW ONLINE

LOWLYWORM17: Goddess, I've been waiting for you. I have a proposition

IJELE_RISING: Kneel first. Speak later

LOWLYWORM17: I'm sorry. I'm sorry

IJELE_RISING: Are you kneeling?

LOWLYWORM17: I am

IJELE_RISING: You think I'll just take the word of worthless filth like you?

LOWLYWORM17 IS SENDING A TRIBUTE: ACCEPT? YES/NO

IJELE_RISING: Passable

LOWLYWORM17: Permission to speak, Goddess?

IJELE_RISING: Not yet

LOWLYWORM17 IS SENDING A TRIBUTE: ACCEPT? YES/NO

IJELE_RISING: Go ahead

LOWLYWORM17: I want to give you £20,000

IJELE_RISING: What?

LOWLYWORM17: £20,000. To let me worship you indefinitely. To take care of you. It would be my honor

* * *

"And you didn't say no?"

"I didn't say no." Aṅụrị, in Ammah's office, drove the toe of her shoe into the oak flooring.

"What did you say?"

"I didn't say anything. I logged out. But for like, half a second, I wanted to say yes. I sort of wanted to do it. Like, 'Fuck it, let's go.' That's the scary part."

Ammah wrote something in her notebook. "At the risk of igniting the rage in you this phrase elicits, how does that make you feel?"

But there was no rage. Aṅụrị willed it, but all that escaped from her was a breath that made it sound like she was struggling to breathe. "I hate it. I hate that I considered allowing some faceless guy to give me a bunch of money to 'take care' of me. No matter how briefly. I hate that 'yes' even existed as a feasible option to me."

"Do you have any thoughts on why it was an option to you?"

Ammah left the blinds and the window open that day. Outside in the courtyard below, a child was laughing. Already, Noelle's laughter was splintering in her memory. Did it pitch like this one? Was it softer? Aṅụrị sat on her hands. The window was not hers to close. The sound was not hers to block out.

"I dunno. I guess for a second I wanted to like, tap out of all of this. Not in *that* way, but I wanted to not be Aṅụrị, Child of Ophelia, and just be Aṅụrị living a regular life where I can see my sister when I want and not have to inform her parents that it's weird for a five-year-old to have hang-ups about what she looks like. I guess I thought money might make some of that easier. Money not linked to relinquishing my life to Ophelia." Aṅụrị laughed a laugh utterly devoid of mirth. "Who knew I was even dealing with the kind of paypigs who can drop £20K on someone without blinking?"

For Aṅụrị, revisiting a terrible thing was ill-advised, but the more you doubled back, the less terrible you could convince yourself the thing was. Following his offer, she was reasonably sure she should disengage with LowlyWorm altogether. His proposition had muddied what were already cloudy waters, and when she did, LowlyWorm was so grateful that he upped his offer by ten thousand. She fought past the shame, embedded in her like shrapnel.

Telling herself she needed a distraction from Gloria's continued silence, Aṅụrị clarified LowlyWorm's position. The "arrangement" would be one where he was elevated above the others, that the "looking after" portion of the deal would come as a monthly stipend in addition to the lump sum. In return, Aṅụrị's availability would have to increase. Mr. Worm also "needed" to meet his goddess in person once a month and, for her comfort, never in private. Aṅụrị screenshotted the chat exchange, wondering if this person offering her cash like it was Skittles had a wife or kids. She logged off without giving him an answer. With the tributes he sent during the fifteen minutes of correspondence, she paid for a block of six sessions with Ammah.

Aṅụrị told herself that The LowlyWorm Proposal, as she was now calling it in her head, lending it a gravitas that was unwarranted and disquieting, could possibly be a means to an end. Her pursuit of freedom seemed a little more attainable with money behind her. A healthy bank balance would make taking care of Noelle a little less daunting. Despite knowing she would not agree to the proposal, she'd still wondered under what circumstances she might change her mind. As she showered, as she ate a bowl of cold gnocchi, she told herself that this might not be who she was right now, but the you of today is not the you of yesterday and will not be the you of tomorrow. You are an ever evolving or devolving entity.

Now Ammah softly "ahem'd" and brought Aṅụrị back from her reverie. "We've spoken about your perceived lack of choice before. Are you feeling less in control than previously?"

"This is the first—" Aṅụrị felt the lump form in her throat and forced herself to speak around it. "They've never regulated my time with Nell like this before. And I guess the separation means that when I do see her, it's pretty clear something is going on with her. I feel like a shit sister for not clocking it way before now. And now with it looking like I'll be going to court, chances are I'll see her even less. Maybe not at all. Then she'll be all alone. Ammah, you have to let me bring her here to talk to you while there's still time."

Ammah laid her notebook aside. "Aṅụrị, my answer to that is no. It's still no and will remain no. I need your parents' consent. Please stop asking me. We should discuss what your end goal is here. You've spoken about lack of access to Noelle and how that may become absolute in the event of a drawn-out court-focused litigation. Are you prepared for that? What do you hope will happen?"

Hope was such a dangerous and exasperating thing. To hope was to court the existence of better which in itself was nebulous and frightening. Aṅụrị thought of herself as someone who was not naive enough to hope, but even as she prepared to scoff, she realized that straining against Ophelia and arguing with Nkem were just tools she was using to achieve her own version of better. Hope did not have to present itself as such to be real. It just was.

"I hope... I want Noelle to have a normal life. The type of life I didn't get to have. I don't think it's too late. Am I being ridiculous? Maybe. But I really don't think it's too late. She can't have that life with them though, so I want to give it to her."

"You want to become Noelle's full-time guardian?"

"You think I can't do it."

"I didn't say that."

"Who better to help her through this kind of situation than me? I've been there. I *am* there. I'm perfect for the job." Yet even as she said it, Aṅụrị recalled the look Loki and Simi exchanged when she had mentioned it to them, and she could see it now in Ammah, trained as she was to quash any outward emotion, any telltale signs of disapproval, the thing in faces that said *you have to be kidding*.

"If this is something you plan to pursue, we can talk more about what it would mean and how that may impact you and your recovery."

"I hate that word. Recovery."

"You're allowed to hate it."

"Are you mothering me right now, Ammah?" She despised how facetious she sounded, how sarcasm crept in and blighted decorum. More than that, she despised how Ammah knew her enough not to react. "I know what it would mean for me. I'd be happy and Nell would be happy and we'd both be free of them and all of this online bullshit."

"Aṅụrị—" Ammah smoothed out an invisible wrinkle in her sensible jersey dress "—whatever you might think becoming Noelle's guardian might do for you, there are consequences and realities to ripping a five-year-old from her parents. No matter how noble the intention. We're out of time but—"

"You're seriously not giving me homework now? When I'm pissed at you."

Ammah smiled. "I find the homework works best when you are pissed at me. All I was going to say is that it would be wise to look into the practicalities of becoming a sudden parent. Maybe Google fostering."

"I refuse."

"On what grounds?"

"I'm tired of you being right."

"See you soon, Aṅụrị."

She resisted the urge for as long as it took her to walk to Turnham Green which was about fifteen minutes, annoyance propelling her forward. The application for fostering a child took between three and six months to complete. There were the requisite forms to fill, home visits to endure and numerous assessments which culminated in a panel of experts determining whether you were fit to welcome a child into both your home and your life. Anụrị knew she already had a number of factors working against her, her age being one, her lack of a second bedroom not requisitioned by candle-making paraphernalia being another. There was her near constant desire to be inebriated and if that were not enough to make the panel of experts lose bowel control as a result of laughter, there was also her fraught relationship with her own body and how she lived inside it. She might have been astute enough to understand that a child had no business worrying about what she looked like, but did it make it any better if it was a twenty-five year-old doing the worrying? She was an adult, was she not, and yet she still looked in the mirror and lamented her own appearance at times. That millions and possibly billions of other adults did the same did nothing to lessen the sting of what she considered so palpable a defect she felt she could nail it to a wall. Then there was the fact that Nkem and Ophelia would likely not melt into the shadows and leave them to live their lives unencumbered. There would be more courts, more tears and still, *still*, Anụrị knew that if she did not try, she would be consumed by remorse, that she would become guilt personified, held together with guilt and unuttered repentance.

Gorged as she had on the impossibility of the situation, Anụrị kept walking if only to try to burn off the heaviness of the mounting setbacks. Noelle needed to be saved and the obstacles in Anụrị's way did nothing to diminish that fact. This was a kid already going viral on a semiregular basis because she was small, cute and marketable, and as a veteran viral baby, Anụrị had been given the gift of foresight. She had found herself the main character many times, the discomfort of the same growing and intensifying over the years. But that was nothing compared to the stardom of Noelle, who exited the womb already lauded, whose arrival into the world was marked on calendars that did not belong to any of her immediate family, public countdowns and timers on her birth. Ophelia's pregnancy had been packaged up and presented to her fans for maximum impact. There is no real way to explain to a child what that means, and the fact of Ophelia's popularity, of Aṅụrị's before Noelle could even grasp the concept of "content," meant that the girl was growing up in a gilded cage—unable to fathom privacy because none had ever existed for her. What Aṅụrị wanted for Noelle was a future where she would know the possibility of the undetected do-over, to experience a lifetime of pristine choices she had the ability to mar or beautify with her messiness, her brightness, her humanness.

Aṅụrị's reaction to Ophelia's viral chasing was visceral for reasons Aṅụrị thought obvious; she couldn't understand how Ophelia's fans remained blissfully oblivious. It also reminded her of the other main characters that had stuck with her over the years. One in particular, a young boy whose parents eschewed asinine gender rules and allowed, nay encouraged, his self-expression via the wearing of dresses and the experimentation with makeup came to mind. There was nothing sinister taking place—he was a nine-year-old who liked the swish of a skirt against his ankles and hadn't yet decided that lip gloss was beautiful yet impractical. He was a kid learning about himself as kids should. It was the showcasing that was problematic. What should have been a series of touching private moments between parents and child now became the subject of mass debate on social media. Should the parents have indulged his request to have eyeshadow and a dab of blusher applied? Why were the parents intent on the feminization of their boy? And with this came the inevitable and maddening influx of bigotry: the slurs, the death threats, the irrational anger because humans as a species, evolved as we are meant to be, still give in to the animalistic irrationalities that drive them to hurl abuse at a child they do not know and will never meet. And feel justified in doing so.

Similarly, Ophelia had been struck by the desperation to provide "feel good" or "wholesome" content for the masses, and at the heart of it was another child chosen to be that week or month's main character all the while wholly unprepared or unenlightened about what it truly meant to be the object of anonymous attention both good and bad. Aṅụrị knew what it was to have responsibility leveled at her before she was strong enough to hold it. She knew what it was to be asked, "Don't you think it's important to show other little girls like you that they're beautiful?" And she remembered what it was to wonder why that fell to her. To sacrifice a child on the faux altar of progressiveness was still a sacrifice. Safeguarding could not just be set aside in favor of the intoxicant that was attention.

Aṅụrị didn't see herself as the protagonist, but too many others did. The fact of her upbringing made it so. The fact of her notoriety compounded it. Noelle could not become the accosted and perhaps it was arrogant for Aṅụrị to think she could be the one to stop this from happening, but arrogance is just another form of confidence and confidence is yet another form of hope, and hope, Aṅụrị was finding, could not be easily outstripped.

Her feet took her to her aunt's door. She ran the last half mile, stumbling more than once but pressing on, not allowing embarrassment to take root because it couldn't without an audience, and she kept running until she reached and fell gasping against Nneoma's door, which her aunt opened and said, "Who is chasing you?" and Aṅụrị said, "Time."

NKEM

I used to wake every morning and touch Ophelia's shoulder. There was something sacred about the second it took for her to sigh in her sleep and roll over into me. I would inhale the powdered scent of her hair and over the years, it became easier to stop myself comparing it to that of Kainene's: earth and honey and the faintest tang of palm oil. Now I usually wake to an empty bed or a wife already scanning through emails or schedules; one who fights a moment of irritation before accepting my kiss or returning my "good morning." On those mornings, Noelle's room is a solace to me. A face that still brightens before my eyes, still warms me with a smile. Over time, I have learned that there will be no traces of Kainene here. Noelle is in no part hers. It doesn't seem like it should be true. How can it be when Kainene was so much a part of me? A person that flowed through my veins? I can still bask in the way Noelle reaches for me and presses her head to my own. Like this, we are still father and daughter and we are the only ones in the world. Then, as always, she asks for Anụrị.

NINE

A brunette with a temperature-controlled room in her apartment, dedicated to the display and storage of her handbag collection, logged onto Instagram every morning approximately twelve seconds after she opened her eyes. She scrolled her feed, rendered almost unnavigable by a series of algorithms designed to expose her to new people and products, then clicked over to her favorites tab. There she found one Ophelia Chinasa, who on this particular day, had posted a reel of herself and her daughter as they tested different hairstyles on the little girl. By the fifth style, the girl had stamped her foot, crossed her little arms and exclaimed, "No more, Mummy!" and the brunette felt the familiar desire to opine, to add her voice to the litany, and this even before Ophelia turned to the camera smiling, shrugged and said, "Alright, guys, let us know which style you like on Noelle." The brunette commented that style number three was clearly the right choice; it framed the child's face perfectly. She also added that it appeared the girl had grown—and signed off with three heart emojis. The brunette lived in New York. She liked looking at Ophelia's photos and trying to figure out precisely where they were taken or where the Chinasas might be at that moment. She and her friends had become quite good at this game, recognizing a signature restaurant tablecloth or the shape of a doorway in a well-known spa. The skill might prove handy in the future since meeting Ophelia and her cute kid sat a few entries down on a bucket list. The brunette would celebrate her fortieth birthday the next month and had been following Ophelia since she began documenting her pregnancy with the girl who was now old enough to reject hairstyles. She often wondered what happened to the other girl, the darker one with soulful eyes.

In London, Aṅụrị watched the same reel and scrolled through the comments, her fingernails pressed into her arm, her gut roiling as she reported one user and then another. There was nothing conspicuous about them. The comments they left were of the mild variety (*She's such a cutie! More Noelle videos please!*) but spending as much time as Aṅụrị did in the comment sections of Ophelia's posts meant that there were things she learned by a combination of osmosis, experience, morbid curiosity and the natural pessimism and mistrust that comes from being a misanthrope. A lack of avatar usually meant one of four things: newbie, bot, spy or pervert, and all it took was a brief perusal of the profile to ascertain which. The day's winners of Aṅụrị's sleuthing were made after she discovered their entire follow lists consisted of nothing but pages dedicated to children. She watched the reel again, scrolled the comments until her vision blurred, stopping only because there were candles to send and others to create, and because she had bitten the inside of her cheek so hard her mouth filled with blood. Might there be a world where children could be posted online safely? Indeed there might, but it was not the one they lived in and it did nothing to address the issues of consent which too many were happy to flout in the case of kids, simply because they had not yet developed the faculties with which to protest. Aṅụrị was resolute and that resoluteness was repulsive to too many, which served only to spur her on.

Aṅụrị was exacting in the eradication of her own personal

social media presence. These days, all that remained were the accounts dedicated to her businesses on which she offered no glimpses of herself or her life despite knowing this was an infallible marketing strategy, and the anonymous accounts she created solely to keep tabs on her sister's ever ascending popularity. She was, she understood, a hypocrite, but she was also a human and afflicted with the sickness that drove so many other humans to both run from and seek out those things which struck a match against their disgust. In this way, she knew that compared to the same video Ophelia posted of Aṅụrị trying various hairstyles, Noelle's pulled four times the traffic; the engagement was truly a sight to behold. The internet liked Black kids. But they loved mixed-race ones. Racism and its offspring, colorism, permeated every facet of being a recognizable figure in the age of the web.

She set her phone aside and left the room.

Aṅụrị continued to think about the thirty thousand pounds because the energy required to pretend not to think about it was simply too great, and she had orders to fill and hair to do. She allowed herself the indulgence of fantasizing about a life that was not shaped by the efforts to disentangle her person and all the associated elements of her person from Ophelia. Thirty thousand was not enough to do this, not indefinitely, but it would buy respite and that, combined with what she took from her paypigs and what she made from her businesses, was enough to secure the blade that would hasten the disentangling. To wake up and not immediately be seized by dread seemed like an impossible luxury and Aṅụrị had already been swept out to sea; she would need to first make it back to the estuary before she could even contemplate swimming upstream and finding land.

On a Wednesday morning, as Aṅụrị packaged candles, her phone began buzzing against her thigh.

"Gloria," she said when she managed to fish it out from her pocket.

"You need to listen to me carefully," Gloria said, and Aṅụrị briefly smiled at the memory of Christian and his gentle chastisement at her lack of greeting, but the surge of warmth in her belly iced over when Gloria continued speaking.

Ophelia's lawyers had been in touch and offered a further one hundred thousand on top of the initial one hundred thousand. They had sweetened the deal with the promise to expunge Aṅụrị across Ophelia's online real estate from ages zero to eight. The cherry on this particular cake of bribery was the retiring of a legacy product range which carried both Aṅụrị's name and likeness—Nuri's Naturals—a haircare range for Type 4 hair which, as Aṅụrị liked to anonymously comment in the reviews, was a complete scam and overpriced to boot. The repetition of the terms moved Aṅụrị backward until she sank to her sofa. The only sound in the room was the soft rustle of scented tissue paper in her hand.

"If you were any other client, I would encourage you to take some time and think this over very carefully," Gloria said. "It's not an insignificant offer."

"I'm not any other client."

"You are not any other client. What would you like me to do?"

The same tenacity that pushed Kainene through miscarriages and heartbreak now lived in Aṅụrị. To yield now was to relinquish part of herself to extraneous forces forever, and while many journeyed through life secure in the knowledge that they were the authors of their own destinies, Aṅụrị was yet to experience this for herself. It would be nice, she thought, to have it in some measure after all this time.

"Reject it. I want it all gone. Everything has to go, Gloria. Make them understand that."

"My job also necessitates that you understand that this will likely move to a court setting."

"What are the chances?"

"It would be remiss of me not to inform you that that doesn't matter. You need to be prepared regardless of likelihood."

"D'you know how *lawyerly* you sound right now?"

"Aṅụrị, please." But Gloria was pouring her laughter into the phone and thawing the ice.

"Whatever it takes, right?"

"Whatever it takes."

"Gloria?"

"Hmm?"

"Thanks."

"You're welcome, sweet girl."

In between two clients (starter locs and Fulani braids) Aṅụrị texted Simi.

New offer from Ophelia. Kind of a big deal

It took Simi seventy-three minutes to respond.

Soz. At Abe's and he's cooking (!!!!) You said no to the offer, right?

Obviously. First time at Abe's? Huge news. What have you found?

What do you take me for?

Someone in their boyfriend's flat for the first time

He's not my boyfriend. And I didn't find shit. He's clean and there's a chore rota on the bloody fridge so he knows what he's meant to do and what his housemate is meant to do

Ten points for Abe!

Minus ten points for being called Abe. I asked him if I could call him Ade. At least that one is Yoruba

Have shame, Simi. He is Yoruba

No. Shan't. Gotta go, the monkfish (!!!!) is ready

After the Fulani braids were complete, Aṅụrị texted Loki.

Can you talk?

It took Loki ninety seconds to respond.

Nah. A man is measuring my inseam right now

Is this a sexual thing? Should I leave you alone?

I wish. Finally getting fitted for a suit for my mom's wedding

Oh for real? Everything sorted with the fiancé then?

He signed the prenup. He was always going to though. It's Celeste. I think he saw a shot of my parents in the society pages and saw sense

We still have society pages?

E! News. Duh.

I take it you're not in London

I'm not. Mom wanted me to see her New York tailor. My bad for not saying

You ok?

Aṅụrị watched the dots that indicated Loki was typing appear, disappear then reappear.

She says she's happy. I guess that's the important thing

Aṅụrị responded by sending forty pink hearts then went to take a shower. When she stepped out of the steam, slick with shower oil, she had a new email which she read, water beading on her skin.

From: Christian Nweze <CSquared07@gmail.com]]
To: Enquiries <enquiries@Kainefeoma.com>
Subject: Candle

Since we established that greeting is not your thing, let me just come out and say that I lit the free candle you gave me when I had my retwist. It's great. Better than great, really. I just dunno that I can describe a candle as anything more than "great" without sounding like a dickhead. My sister loved it too and then mistakes were made. Mistakes such as me saying I kind of knew the creator and could maybe get her a full-sized one. I was going to just order it on your site but now they're sold out and I look like a dickhead regardless. Full circle has never felt so terrible. So yeah. I've name dropped you and now pressure has me by the throat. Do you do commissions and how much do you charge?

From: Enquiries <enquiries@Kainefeoma.com>
To: Christian Nweze <CSquared07@gmail.com>
Subject: Re: Candle

How much do I charge dickheads or regular people?

From: Christian Nweze <CSquared07@gmail.com>
To: Enquiries <enquiries@Kainefeoma.com>
Subject: Re: re: Candle

Let's have both quotes and then I can plead my case.

It wasn't a phone call. It wasn't even a text, but the way Christian wrote lacked none of the intimacy of the other mediums. Gooseflesh budded on Aṅụrị's skin. She thought of his hands, and the way he stood beside her on the pavement as she heaved her way through her panic attack. When all the light was narrowing to a pinprick, she could still remember his voice: one… two…three…four…five. He was yet to touch her while she had already had her hands in his hair. She remembered her advice to Simi and noted with a pang that her friend, despite her misgivings and penchant for romantic self-sabotage, was right now with a man who cooked her meals and had a chore rota on his fridge. Simi had a shot at normalcy and wasn't that what Aṅụrị had been fighting for? The breeze from the open windows reached her and stroked a finger down her back.

From: Enquiries <enquiries@Kainefeoma.com>
To: Christian Nweze <CSquared07@gmail.com>
Subject: Re: re: re: Candle

I happen to have exactly one dead stock candle in that very scent. Would you like to pick it up?

They met the following day, Christian strolling toward Aṅụrị as she idled on the curb outside her building. He did not stop walking until he was directly in front of her, and then he was smiling and saying, "Hi, Aṅụrị," and she was smiling back and saying, "Hey, Chidili," and their awkwardness was the loud third wheel who everyone loved regardless because they were harmless. Inside, Aṅụrị gave him the tour of the second bedroom which also served as candle-making headquarters and Christian picked things up and gingerly put them down again. He asked questions such as "How much wax do you buy per month would you say?" and "You do all of this on your ones? Wow."

And when Aṅụrị presented him with his full-sized candle, he cradled it for a second like it was a very tiny baby until he caught her staring at him. It wasn't that he disliked the staring, it was that it made him feel like he was riding through a dark tunnel in an open-topped supercar, hurtling toward the sphere of light at the other end, and he was not yet sure what to do with that feeling. He thanked her and then he said that he had something for her, too.

The something, it turned out, was her very own monogrammed towel which he handed to her as if it was the most natural thing in the world; as if it was good and right that he was standing in her apartment; as if he always brought her thoughtful embroidered gifts.

"Just in case you ever want to go back to Blank," he said.

And because Aṅụrị lacked the thing inside humans that allowed them to accept unsolicited kindness, because that had been suffocated by a childhood spent in near constant performance for reward, she took the towel, left the room to place it on the kitchen counter, then returned and said, "Would you like me to show you how to make a candle?"

He was awful at it. His wick was off-center. He was heavy-handed with the essential oils. He overpoured the wax. His earnestness produced a bubble of laughter deep within Aṅụrị that she struggled to keep inside. Eventually, he set down his tools. It was as if the word "forlorn" was created for him in that moment; wax hardening on his shirt.

"We can try again," Aṅụrị suggested.

Christian sighed for so long, Aṅụrị thought he might keel over. "I don't think," he said quietly, "that would help."

"Practice, Chidili," Aṅuri said, "makes perfect."

"Sure. I mean yeah, okay, use my words against me. Maybe we'll see how good you are at my hobby. Not that this is a hobby for you."

"What's your hobby?"

"Damn. I hadn't thought this through. You'll laugh."

"I might do, yeah."

Christian paused. "I crochet."

"Hair?"

"Yarn. Well, using yarn. I make things."

"Things?"

"Like…place mats and shit like that."

Aṅuri said nothing.

"It's relaxing."

"I bet."

"And stimulating."

"I'm going to laugh."

"I'll join you. Then I'll show you a photo of the place mats."

You hear of the poets speak of love as if it is all at once the parting of clouds and the descent into darkness; like it is the greatest blessing of life and the most terrifying. Aṅuri, up until that point, found it beautifully written hyperbole, but as she watched Christian from beneath her eyelashes, she realized she envied those who confronted by the prospect allowed themselves to be swallowed by the feeling even with all its treachery and instability. She thought of Loki, repeatedly flinging himself against the great wall that is emotion always with the same gusto, willingly falling into the well that is romance and surviving always with renewed optimism, and for a few seconds, she forgot she was a girl who had never so much as had a boyfriend.

"Christian."

"I'm gonna decline a repeat performance. I've embarrassed myself enough."

"D'you think you want to kiss me?"

The brief silence that followed was thick enough that Anụrị felt she might choke on it.

"No," he said eventually. He opened his mouth to continue, but Anụrị felt she might die, actually die if he said anything else.

"Understandable. It's fine," she said. "Excuse me." She made for the bathroom where she stayed for thirty minutes replaying what had taken place in her head on a soul-crushing loop, and wishing she had her phone, which in her haste, she'd left in the candle room. Simi was somewhere being doted on while Anụrị fought the violent urge to wring her hands in the manner of a perturbed Victorian waif.

When she emerged, there he was, cloth in one hand wiping down the bench at which they had worked, phone in the other. He looked up when she entered the room.

"What I was going to say was no I don't want to kiss you because you ask me if I want to kiss you. I'm a man and my ego exists. I want to kiss you when you feel comfortable enough to let me kiss you. For the record, I want to kiss you all the time. Say something so I can stop saying 'kiss you.'"

"You're still here."

He frowned. "Yeah? I'm always going to wait to see if you're okay. Unless you don't want me to. Then I'll go home and watch HBO."

Every nerve ending was aflame. Every last one.

Later, after he did actually leave (this time with Anụrị's number in his phone), he texted her as she unrolled a croissant and picked at its fluffy interior.

You ok?

On a scale of 1-10, 10 being the Bogdanoff twins, how weird do you think I am?

Ok I just had to Google the Bogdanoff twins. Wow. You're not there yet. So like, a 6.75?

Oh

Weird is good, Anuri

I don't want you to feel like you're chasing me all the time

I have stamina. Plus it's you

Then, a few minutes later:

I figure your comfort zone will dictate your speed and I'm good with that

Just so you know, there's a reason I'm a 6.75

Yeah. We all have shit. Tell me when you're ready

Last Google assignment of the day: Ophelia Chinasa

She waited one hour, then another. As she slipped into the third and there was still no reply, she went to bed, the monogrammed towel tucked under her cheek.

The next morning, there was a text but not from Christian. Ophelia was extending an invitation to a family dinner. Just the four of us, the text read and the shower Anuri took once she read it was too hot, deliberately so, as she tried to scrub from her body the anger-tinged joy she felt to be included. It should be normal. To dine with your parents and sister should be a routine occurrence. It should not elicit a procession of *feelings* each more ludicrous than the last. But this was Anuri's life—the life of a

6.75. Of course she went. Of course she did. How many more of these dinners did she have before Gloria filed the final rejection and her life went into a free fall? She was young and despite it all, there lingered some fragments of delusion which allowed her to think she could let herself into the house and spend the evening enveloped in the unique love afforded by family. She ought to have been more suspicious. Nkem met her at the door. He complimented her chuck-on dress, asked how she was doing and if she had spoken to Nneoma of late. Ophelia apologized for the earliness of the meal. Noelle's bedtime was 8:30 and Ophelia wanted, she said, Noelle to have sufficient time with Aṅụrị.

"Although there is no amount of time," Ophelia added, "that's truly sufficient. Of course."

Aṅụrị should have run then, upending the ornamental evergreens, her fleeing form a blur of multicolored dress print. But she didn't for all the same reasons we pick at scabs and press our thumbs into bruises: because the pain is so familiar it ceases to be a warning and simply becomes part of us. Noelle was already leaping into Aṅụrị's arms, tugging her into the living room so she could see the LEGO princess castle she and Ophelia were building for TikTok, graciously gifted by a toy store chain along with a check in exchange for discreet and not so discreet plugs across socials.

At the table, Ophelia's laughter tinkled against the glassware. She leaned over to cut Noelle's chicken into child-sized bites. She complimented Aṅụrị's delicate gold rings, going so far as to lift one of her stepdaughter's hands so she might examine the jewelry in more detail. All the while, Aṅụrị wondered if Ophelia could feel the quickening of her pulse as it beat in her fingertips; if the desperate hope welling inside her had made its way to her face. They'd been a family before. Ophelia had been not just the moon but the entire universe for Aṅụrị—could luck find them a second time?

Nkem asked Aṅụrị if she would take Supermalt or some other

beverage. Noelle regaled the assembled adults with a story about being chosen to recite a poem in front of class the following week.

A person might look through the window at the foursome clustered at one section of the large dining table and after thinking, *wow, that table looks expensive,* they might think, *what a lovely family.* The same person might hang around to witness the serving of dessert (apple pie and custard) which included a minor tantrum from the youngest at the table when she was instead offered an assortment of exotic fruit which was rejected with a vehemence that might bring the observer's hand to their throat in shock. A prolonged and oddly tearful good-night later, the youngest is spirited away to bed by the second youngest at the table while the married couple remain downstairs exchanging meaningful looks and tapping fingers and feet against hard surfaces, lines appearing on the husband's face—the wife has had Botox and this round is yet to wear off.

Joining Nkem and Ophelia at the table once more, Aṅụrị's hackles were yet to rise. She was full of home-cooked food and even fuller of the sweetness of seeing Noelle's eyelids grow heavy, her breathing slowing as she crept toward sleep. It had been, Aṅụrị allowed herself the naive pleasure of thinking, a nice evening. And only when Nkem said, "Anyị kwesịrị ịgwa gị," did the blood in Aṅụrị's veins turn to ice.

"Talk to me about what?" she whispered. But she knew. She *knew*.

They, that is the two of them, Ophelia explained, missed Aṅụrị so much. So very much. All this bickering wasn't good for them as a family, was it? It was confusing and frightening for Noelle who just wanted everybody to be together all the time. Wasn't there a way, Nkem put in, his fingers curling around his wife's, that they could put this silly lawsuit aside and just be a family? Couldn't Aṅụrị see that it didn't have to be like this?

Our intrepid phantom onlooker would no doubt have a time recounting the tears that the girl allowed to fall (ten for accuracy) and the sound she made as she jumped from her seat (a harrowing marriage between a scream and a sob). The wife was on her feet a second later, following the girl into the entrance hall pleading, touching her arm only to be shaken off. When the door slammed, it shook the bespoke chandelier suspended from the sixteen-foot entrance hall ceiling.

She didn't drink. That is what Aṅụrị would tell Arinze and Makuo when she arrived in Awka less than two days later. It wasn't a lie, but it also wasn't the entire truth. One vice can take the place of another and currently, over two thousand pounds worth of superfluity was on its way to her PO box, purchased in a fit of pique before she clicked Confirm on her plane ticket to her grandparents.

NKEM

Am I proud?

A man can be destitute and alone, lacking both wealth and company, but as long as he has his pride, he can never lose everything. He will never have nothing. I have gone to great lengths to safeguard mine. I have built walls and rampart. I have cloistered Kainene to a place where I no longer dare tread. Makuo and Arinze, I have all but confined to the past, I chose to make a second attempt at life and, with the help of my wife, have made that life beautiful—painted in a rainbow of security.

Am I proud?

Of the love in my wife's eyes every time she turns to me? Of the approval and respect my colleagues offer me? Of the ability to enter my PIN at the ATM, slap down any number of cards with the certainty that nothing will be declined; that I will not be denied? That my youngest still finds safety and maybe even joy in my arms? Yes, I am proud. Only a liar would say otherwise.

In the eyes of others, I have made it. With years of mis-

takes and toil in my wake, I am now a chief. Odogwu! Shouldn't I then be insulated from pain? Should I have had to watch my child pull away from me or see the warmth in her eyes drain away or feel the absence of her laughter like another living presence? Should my accomplishments not shield me from the looks of contempt leveled at me? As if everything we have done has not been for her. As if I am not a man in my own house. Anụrị took great pains to prove that I was not needed.

All the money and all my manhood are useless in the eyes of a daughter who no longer needs you. It cannot command from her the respect you deserve; and she won't be compelled to give you and your wife what you want. Your family remains broken and that you—Odogwu, champion!—did nothing or could do nothing to stop it.

But my pride. At least I have my pride.

TEN

Nneoma did not insist on much but her monthly dinners with Nkem were an immovable entry in both their diaries. She established them shortly after he married for the second time, when she could see that steps needed to be taken to ensure he was not completely lost to her. To his credit, Nkem had missed only a handful in the years since he first appeared on her doorstep, shivering and incredulous, demanding to know why she had not forewarned him that this country could reach such frigidity, to which she responded, "You who've lived most of your life in singlet, why won't you now be cold?" The atmosphere those first few dinners was equally frosty—Nkem demonstrating the bullheaded defensiveness of a man unable to adequately justify his actions, and Nneoma calmly critical of said actions. They would sit on opposite sides of her then tiny kitchen table and roll verbal grenades at each other until Nkem would inevitably slam from the house only to phone the next day and confirm that they were still on for the following month. He always called. And Nneoma always said yes. Nkem was many things but he was her brother first, and their childhood had been spent as many Nigerian childhoods are, in a clutch of community where they were constantly surrounded by cousins, play-cousins and friends, and yet, Nneoma remembered that no matter how many children were gamboling around their parents' compound, Nkem would always locate his sister, and up until he reached the age of eleven when he won a coveted place at boarding school, he would crawl into bed with her, their parents or the house help finding them top-to-toe every morning.

With five days still to go until the next scheduled monthly dinner, Nneoma's surprise tugged her eyebrows skyward when she opened her front door and found her brother looking at her balefully.

"Ọ̀ọ ala?" Nneoma said, because surely it was madness that brought Nkem to her door unannounced with a face like she had stolen his kola nut.

At once, Nkem was a child again, recalcitrant, his manhood dissolving in the face of Nneoma's composure. "Nneoma. Please. Let me in, sha."

Nneoma stepped aside. Inside she left him in the sitting room given that his unannounced arrival had pulled her out of the shower and down the stairs, damp and still in her bathrobe (one of her prized possessions: thick, waffled and white. A gift from Aṅụrị).

"I'm thirsty," Nkem said plaintively from his place on the sofa.

"The kitchen is still in the same place it was when you were last here," Nneoma called down the stairs.

Lotioned and fully dressed, Nneoma informed her brother that she had only an hour before she needed to leave the house for her shift at the hospital, and before that, she was expecting a FaceTime from Aṅụrị and her grandparents.

"Grandparents? She's at home?"

"You didn't know?"

"Does the girl tell me anything? You sef. Why didn't you tell me? You've always kept Aṅụrị's secrets."

Nneoma registered the hunch of Nkem's shoulders. He fancied himself a closed book when in fact he was easily read. It was tiresome, Nneoma thought, that so many people erected shoddy walls around themselves forgetting they had built windows as well.

"If you came to argue, then go home. It can wait until next week when I'm really ready for you. Otherwise, open your teeth and tell me what's troubling you." She watched as Nkem deflated, bravado rushing out of him. A post-defense puffer fish.

"Everyone is so angry at me," he said and Nneoma felt the inclination to protect him surge through her as it had during their top-to-toe days, as it had when Kainene died. As it had when Aṅụrị mewled from her Moses basket that Nkem, blinded by sorrow, could not see.

She placed a hand on his shoulder. "Gwànụ m," she said. *Tell me.*

He did, haltingly at first, but soon the words were clambering over themselves. "We thought maybe if we could just speak with Aṅụrị, then she would see that there's no need to pursue this lawsuit. That she is part of this family. Now she won't speak to me, won't even tell me when she flies to Makuo and Arinze. And Ophelia thinks I should have done more. And Noelle is confused." He sighed again. "She is always confused."

Nneoma squeezed Nkem's shoulder. Then she made her hand into a fist and knocked sharply on his head.

"Nneoma! Kaì! Ah ahn, stop it! What is wrong with you?"

"What is wrong with *you*? Nkem, you and Aṅụrị are spectacular in that God blended brilliance and stupidity and gave you both too much of the mixture. When was the last time you asked Aṅụrị to come for dinner because, as you put it, she is part of this family? Why raise the girl's hopes then break them with ulterior motives?" She rapped smartly on his head again even as he shouted.

"It's not like that!" Nkem insisted, but his words were limp, devoid of conviction. He rubbed the spot his sister's knuckles had bruised. "Things at home are like they have never been before. Sometimes it's like Ophelia doesn't want to speak to me at all. And Noelle is not acting like herself."

Nneoma nodded. Her own relationship with her second niece was regrettably not as strong as the one she had with Aṅụrị. By the time Noelle was born, Nneoma was not required to be a secondary caretaker. Ophelia already treated her with the strained civility of someone who knows they must endure a person but only that. Noelle was a bundle of joy Nneoma only enjoyed at family gatherings and through phone calls she initiated, and selfishly, she did not know if she had the strength to once again toss herself into the web Nkem and his wife had woven for themselves and their children. Her brother was like many men: in possession of an ego that was easily punctured, built around nothing of true value. She should tread carefully. But Nneoma did not know how. She had lived life like a person with beasts at her heels and stepping softly was not something she was willing to learn at this juncture.

"Nkem, if you say you're worried about Noelle," she said, "then now is the time to address it. In ten years' time, you don't want to be facing her and asking what happened again."

Nneoma thought of her eldest niece. To love the tortured was to become tortured yourself. How many times during the girl's youth had she pulled Aṅụrị into her lap, even when she was growing at an alarming rate and was no longer the tiny, pliable baby girl Nneoma used to strap to her back in Aṅụrị's infancy? How long had Nneoma spent rocking her niece, trying and failing to absorb her hurt? The girl had asked questions about other online children, wondering aloud about whether they smiled because they were happy or because they were made to; if she was the only one whose relationship with the internet was turning sour. Nneoma was not a woman who had the time or patience to deal with misplaced pride. Especially when the well-being of children was involved. Nkem and his spectacular specimen of an ego was no exception. History had already begun to repeat itself. She turned again to her brother.

"Remember the proverb 'Isi kotara ebu ka ebu na-agba.' That is it is the head that disturbs the wasp that the wasp stings. You understand me?"

Nkem knew that his sister was issuing him another warning; that if he and Ophelia continued to poke the lion and set their youngest in the line of fire, there would be consequences. Still, he shook his head. "No. I don't understand."

But he would.

To say he had not tried would be a gross misrepresentation of the extent Nkem had not tried. His abdication of responsibility should be studied in classrooms around the globe and titled Nkem-ism. That a father could be so present and at the same time so utterly absent in important matters would be awe-inspiring were it not so tragic. If pressed, he would say that he did what he could with the tools available to him. The tools in question were cluelessness and fear. He was an Onitsha Igbo man and still referred to himself as a "village boy" although Onitsha was a city. The point was he had no idea what to make of this "social media" business. Facebook was as far as he had traveled across the plains of the web before Ophelia entered his life and showed him just how much he didn't know. If pressed further, he would turn the corner in his own mind and happen upon the memory of one of his few parental triumphs. Were it a film scene, it would be shot in a gray-blue filter with some kind of string instrument sawing away in the background.

It was back when he and Ophelia were in the midst of what they would later refer to as Anụrị's Difficulty, although they did not yet realize that Anụrị's Difficulty was actually a shift in their daughter's perspective which would wreak untold damage on the family unit as it stood. It felt like every other day, the expensive school to which they sent their daughter was either phoning up or sending a crested letter to outline the latest episode of Aṅụrị's unsavory behavior. The theme of this, the most recent incident, was Aṅụrị's capacity for quick-witted comebacks. She had talked back to her English teacher who, after he refused to concede a point Aṅụrị was attempting to make, told her that she ought to focus more on mastering the pathetic fallacy. To which Aṅụrị responded, "You're a pathetic fallacy." It was wrong, Nkem knew, to lock himself inside Ophelia's newly built pantry to expel all the laughter he knew he couldn't bring to the discussion they needed to have with their daughter. But that is what he did. After they grounded her and sent her stomping to her bedroom, Nkem poured himself and Ophelia drinks and they reclined in the living room, spent from a taxing hour of parenting.

"Oh go on then," Ophelia said, accepting the globular glass of wine, "only the one though. I have to get up and start documenting all this."

"Hmm? Documenting which one, darling?" Nkem was rubbing the arch of his wife's left foot.

"This. 'Fallacy-gate.'" Ophelia chuckled at her own joke. "You know I have *The Ellen Show* web thingy next week. This is the perfect thing to talk about."

Nkem would find it hard to pinpoint why after everything, but the notion was abhorrent to him. "No. Don't do that."

"Don't do what, my love?"

"We should halt all of this anyway. Until things settle down. Until Aṅụrị feels better." He surprised himself by saying it, but now it had been said, it felt not only right but necessary.

"Feels better? She's just doing what all kids do and having a rebellious phase. That's why it makes sense to talk about it. I bet tons of parents are dealing with the same thing. It'll be encouraging."

"I don't agree. The girl is going through something and I don't want to speak to another of her teachers. Don't you have headache? Me, I have headache."

Ophelia lowered her glass. "Darling. It's *Ellen*. She is a master at putting a positive spin on things like this."

"I don't know who this Ellen is. Is she your friend? And anyway, I said no. Is it everything outsiders must know?"

His mistake, he realized later when he was sleeping in a room that did not contain his wife, was that he had tried to take a stand far too late in the game. The ship had already started to sink. What good was bailing water now? Still. Despite her protestations, he told Ophelia he forbade it. That Aṅụrị was his daughter. And the pain in Ophelia's face when she said, "And so what is she to me exactly?" was almost luminous. She did not write the blog post and she did not speak to Ellen about Fallacy-gate but she also did not speak to Nkem for several days and that put paid to any future attempts Nkem made to put his foot down. In fact, his metaphorical foot would remain suspended in the air and perhaps in time.

Arinze moved more slowly these days. It broke Aṅụrị's heart to watch how precisely he stepped, knowing that a fall meant something different for him than it did for her. It is said that to watch your loved ones age is a gift, and it is, but it walks hand in hand with pain. The sweetest of life's agonies. Arinze's hands, however, remained steady, and Aṅụrị sat beneath them on her first day back in Awka after she asked and he agreed to cut her hair. Ever since that first time she took clippers to her curls, Aṅụrị knew there lay a power in staying shorn. She buzzed her hair whenever she felt overwhelmed. Her reverse Samson moments were restorative. Under the Awka sun, she cropped her hair again and as Arinze dusted the remnants from her shoulders, she let the breeze kiss her scalp. She felt alive, as if Chukwu Himself had leaned down and breathed into her, reminding her that despite it all, she was her own. In Awka, the days were slow.

Aṅụrị walked with her grandparents around the compound. She rubbed lotion into her grandmother's hands and brought her grandfather his lunch on a tray beside his beloved guava trees. At night, the darkness was complete. Aṅụrị felt invisible. She'd raise her hand in the blackness and not know where she ended and the night began. She spoke of her desire to bring Noelle under her wing in a more permanent capacity and her grandparents hugged her and told her that nobody knew how to be a perfect parent; that was why the concept of a village was important. Arinze asked her if she had a village, and Aṅụrị realized that she did but that they may not, themselves, be ready to be the type of village Noelle required.

"What if I have to do it alone?" she asked.

Makuo cupped her chin. "Then, nwa m, you do it alone."

On the third day as Aṅụrị watched the blades of the ceiling fan slice silently through the late afternoon air, her phone buzzed.

> If I call, will you pick up?

She would have liked to say she had forgotten about Christian. But his silence was still a new injury; scar tissue was yet to form. It was also another chapter in Aṅụrị's growing tableau of confirmation bias. Relationships were already complex. Romance was the death knell of burgeoning connections. She'd learned from her time with Ophelia. Never again would she do something repeatedly and leave scarred by the discomfort. She would opt out. Which she did when it came to romance, until Christian made her forget. Temporarily. She chose not to reply to his text. He called regardless. She picked up after six rings—best to apply the tourniquet now.

"I was going to keep calling, you know," he said. Because of course. They didn't greet.

"For how long?" she asked.

"Between seven and ten days, I think. People are busy and my pride would want me to believe you were busy. After ten days, my pride would have died its final death. Plus, like I told you, I don't have what it takes to stalk."

"And my pride, nko?" She did not like the bitterness that crept into her voice. Bitterness was vulnerability and this call was a means to an end. She cleared her throat as if she could cough it out onto the floor.

"I'm sorry. I have a reason. It's not an excuse, but it's an explanation if you want it."

"Oh this should be good."

"The way my brain works is that it has to take in like, *all* the information before it—before *I* can form a response worth giving. And even then, I still don't know if the response is worth giving. I spend all that time absorbing and parsing info and then I could still end up chatting shit."

When she caught herself smiling, Aṅụrị rearranged her features into one of placid unreadability. He couldn't see her, that she knew, but smiles could be heard. They were loud that way.

"Like now," she said.

"Yeesh. Okay, I deserved that. I'm bleeding. But I deserved it. What I mean is, I googled like you told me to. And then I couldn't stop googling as it were. There was so much. Fuck. My brain thing kicked in and it was like, 'Okay, C, you need to get your head around this before you open your mouth and say anything.' I've always been that way. Overanalytical. Or an overthinker if you like. To my detriment many, many times."

"You refer to yourself as 'C' in your head?"

"Or Chidili, surprisingly."

"So you googled."

"Right. I googled and it took me a week to get through it all. There's a lot there, Aṅụrị."

Aṅụrị sat up and a bead of sweat swanned down the smooth channel of her back. "You're saying you went through *all* of it?"

"I mean yeah. I had to. To understand. I read all Ophelia's

blog posts. I watched all the videos on YouTube. I looked at her Instagram and I guess what she wanted people to believe was your and your sister's Instagram accounts where she was pretending it was you talking as a kid? Creepy as hell by the way."

"It's a thing, apparently."

"Then I saw the TV stuff, the TikTok stuff with your sister and after all that, I fell down my own personal Ophelia rabbit hole and read all about the companies, the products and the rest of it. Aṅụrị, you can't achieve weirdness level ten. Ophelia is the ten's ten."

She wondered if vindication would ever stop feeling good. She hoped it wouldn't. "You're very thorough."

"I had to be. It's you."

Aṅụrị didn't realize she was scared until she next spoke and her voice shook. "And wh…what did you think?"

"Honestly? I just wanted to give you a hug. I mean I already wanted to hug you, but now I want to hug you and then put you in a bubble so you can't be hurt. How much like Annie Wilkes did I sound just then?"

"Only a little."

"Are you okay?"

"I'm not," she told him. "I'm not, but I'm trying to be, I swear."

Christian sat in the tiny glass meeting room at his office that he had booked because he could no longer wait to speak to Aṅụrị; because he understood that a girl that was taken down by panic attacks in front of post offices was a girl who had other things going on. He had understood it then as the attack happened. Now the layers to Aṅụrị's other things were sharpening into focus.

"What is it the world's weirdest momager said? 'You're doing amazing, sweetie.'"

Aṅụrị laughed then. To approach a thing with trepidation, expecting judgement and instead finding the sweetness of acceptance is to understand a little more how deeply you have been cut and how much longer it will take to see yourself as someone worth adoring.

Regardless. In the glass meeting room, Aṅụrị's laughter reached Christian and spread through him. The effect was almost medicinal.

"That day you came for your retwist…was I a bitch?" Aṅụrị asked.

"Your unique brand of detached hostility is what drew me to you."

"It's just… I'm used to people knowing who I am."

"How conceited of you."

Aṅụrị laughed again. "Nah I mean, I wasn't pissed that you didn't. That was a relief. I guess I was just wary in case you were just acting like you didn't. So you could get close."

"Aṅụrị. Are we close?"

"I mean physically."

"Fam, if we're physically close then I'm definitely dead and in the upper realms. Or else I'm dreaming."

"Chidili. Ozugo." But her smile was loud. Deafening in fact.

Around two in the morning the following day, worry hoisted Nkem from his bed and carried him down the stairs and into the room Ophelia designated for watching television that was not the living room. Nkem had never been able to understand this but there were many things about his wife he didn't understand, and they mostly endeared her to him. He turned on the television which he remained proud that he had selected: a seventy-inch Samsung which looked like a piece of art when it was not displaying Netflix or Sky Sports. He switched to BEN Television which was another of his viewing staples—a largely Nigeria-led channel which kept "expatriates on the pulse of Africa." At almost fifty-three years of age, Nkem felt he should be well-enough equipped to manage anxiety without Nneoma's reassurance. He chose distraction from his arsenal of tactics, stared at BEN Television with the volume low. Ineffective. He watched without seeing for twenty minutes, and then he picked up the phone and called Aṅụrị. In the intervening seconds as the phone rang, it wasn't that Nkem held his breath, it was that he forgot how to breathe. There were millions of parents who felt the same as he did right then; recognizing that their child may not answer and not only because of the absurd hour, but because they had no desire to speak with their parent. It felt like an iron fist had been driven into his chest.

Aṅụrị, however, picked up the phone.

"Dad? Is Noelle alright?" Her voice was thick with sleep but even so, her first thought on seeing that it was Nkem calling was that something had happened not to him, but to Noelle. Wonderful. And damning. The fist drove deeper.

"Ọ na-eme nke ọma," is what Nkem said because reflexes are there for a reason and are often difficult to circumnavigate. But Noelle was not fine. She was not fine and that was part of why Nkem was calling.

In the preceding week, Noelle was sent home from school twice. The first time because she had pushed a girl (Xanthia Braithwaite, six, child of Naomi and Gregory Braithwaite) and called her poor when all Xanthia had done was ask Noelle to wait her turn with the Rubik's Cube. The second time, Noelle was sent home for throwing the type of table-shaking tantrum that necessitated her removal from the classroom. That very night, she had wet the bed for the third time that week; their Noelle, who was potty trained at two. Regression was normal, Ophelia said. Her arms had been around him at the time, her voice soft but still betraying her own concern. They would speak with Noelle again, she assured him, and maybe take her to the doctor just to ensure everything was physically sound.

Right now, Ophelia was sleeping, Noelle's ruined bedsheets were in the laundry hamper and Nkem was downstairs in the blue wash of BEN Television explaining to his eldest daughter that no, perhaps Noelle was not "ọma." He did not have any plans beyond the call. His numerous inefficiencies as a father and general adult presented themselves to him and, sleep deprived and weary, he allowed himself to be thrashed by them. He did not even know it was what he was hoping for until Aṅụrị said, "I'll come home," and a few days later, Nkem and Noelle were waiting for her at the airport when her flight touched down. As the sisters embraced, Nkem hung back, his hands in his pockets, his heart knocking inside his chest like a wrecking ball.

They went to Aṅụrị's flat. Nkem had only been inside a handful of times and then, mostly in the capacity of depositing or collecting Noelle. His daughter's personality was splashed on the walls in the form of art, or arranged on her sofa as cushions and throws. It was in her music choice, an up-tempo Afrobeats tune reminiscent of Fela which she played as she fetched Noelle a snack and settled her in front of the controversial *Peppa Pig*. Aṅụrị's hair was newly cut and as always, Nkem ignored the pang elicited by being confronted with a life lived not only without him but without the notion of him. They sat at Aṅụrị's small breakfast bar sipping a new variety of malt (Nkem usually rejected all deviation from what he felt was the superior Supermalt, but it was Aṅụrị's house after all, and this offering was frustratingly pleasing). They looked at Noelle so they didn't have to look at each other.

To her credit, Aṅụrị lasted until then before raising the subject of therapy for her sister. Since Nkem's phone call, the urge to shout about it had been present in everything she attempted to do. Bring Arinze a glass of water? TELL NKEM ABOUT THERAPY. Fold towels for Makuo? EXPLAIN THAT ONLY A PROFESSIONAL CAN HELP. Eat draw soup without making a mess of her shirt? MAKE HIM SEE THAT WITHOUT THERAPY, ALL ROADS LEAD TO DISASTER. Her restraint, she felt, was admirable. Nkem, unfortunately, did not see it that way.

Añụrị, keen to decipher what lay behind the male species' reluctance to partake in psychological counseling, once asked Loki to explain. His answer was both illuminating and simple: "It's because we think we know everything, chère." So she expected resistance. Indeed, she bit her tongue as her father cycled through exclamations of disbelief, "She is not mad!" to admonishment, "You want us to pay a stranger to listen to our secrets? Are you alright?" When he reached nonsense ("How can someone who doesn't know us, tell us anything about Noelle?"), Añụrị pointed out that like physicians, therapists were trained to understand and assist with things closeness often prevented people from knowing or perhaps interrogating. Nkem scoffed. Añụrị sat on her hands so she did not pour the malt over his head.

"I'm in therapy, Dad," she said finally. "I'm proof it does help."

Nkem-ism when left untreated can cause irreparable damage. The choice to say nothing was there and that would have been preferable for all involved, but what Nkem chose to say instead, which was that it was no wonder Añụrị behaved the way she did—she had white people filling her head with rubbish, which she was packing up and presenting to the family to deal with. No wonder she was intent on suing her own mother.

Añụrị glanced at her sister. Noelle was still engrossed in the world of Peppa and George and was thankfully unaware of what was playing out a few feet away from her. Añụrị chose not to tell Nkem that Ammah was Black. She also chose not to point out the extreme irony of him accusing *her* of having white people fill her head with rubbish. What she did say, quietly and still without looking at Nkem, fingers on Kainene's bangle, was that Ophelia was not her mother. Shortly after that, Nkem and Noelle made their way home.

ELEVEN

To distract herself from this new failure, Aṅụrị decided to confront another one. She made her way down to her PO box to survey the damage caused by her pre-Awka rage-fueled spending spree. Who needed not one egg slicer but three? What even was microdermabrasion and why did she feel she needed a home kit? Shame, that many-legged thing, began wriggling over her and with it, the thirst. Tesco Express was not far and it was a nice day. Surely she couldn't be begrudged a cold bottle of cider? She took out her phone and called Loki. In her absence, he'd returned to London and he came over with fragrant bags of Thai food. They sat on the floor and Aṅụrị, who decided long ago to act as both Loki and Simi's de facto assistant, reminded him that he had a dentist appointment later that week, and that she had ordered cake samples for him to try ahead of finalizing the cake for Remy's impending birthday. Business sorted, they turned on the Switch, and played Super Smash Bros. between bites.

"You all set for the wedding?" Aṅụrị asked. The laab she was eating was perfectly seasoned.

Loki took a sip of mango juice and nodded. "Pretty much. You and Simi are my dates, okay?"

"We're invited independently of you, Lo. Your parents should have called you Narcissus instead of Loki."

Loki mock pouted. "Doesn't matter anyway. I don't want to have to fight Abe. I'm a lover, not a fighter." It was true. Despite his height, which automatically put him in the category of intimidating, Loki did not possess any skill in the act of physical combat. He was a teddy bear through and through; the greatest giver of hugs and a prolific and unabashed crier.

Laab tucked into the corner of her cheek, Aṅụrị wiped her hands and picked up her controller. "You don't really have a thing for Simi, do you? You're not actually in love with her?" It was the first time she had asked him outright. Over the years, Loki's playful banter became part of their dynamic. His default setting was "flirt." Aṅụrị didn't think, until now, that he may actually be harboring real feelings.

"Nah." Loki was playing as Kirby because he always played as either Kirby or Wario. "Actually maybe that isn't one hundred percent true. Maybe I was a little bit in love with her at some point, but then I was a little bit in love with you at some point, too. I'm probably a little in love with everyone I meet for a while."

"Mate," Aṅụrị said, "that sounds exhausting."

"It is a bit." Kirby looped through the air. "But it's fun as well."

"Will your dad be at the wedding?"

"Remy's going to give this one a miss."

"Oh?"

Loki shrugged. "Don't ask me. It's not like Remy talks to me about his emotions. Especially any emotions linked to my mom."

Aṅụrị remembered Nkem's expression when she mentioned therapy; his incredulity at the notion that help existed beyond him and his lackadaisical approach to parenting. She tutted.

"Ugh. Of course he doesn't. Emotional intelligence is kryptonite to this lot."

"Thinking about Nkem?"

"Yup."

"Look, if Remy can pay for me to see a therapist for six years, there's hope yet. Nkem'll come around. It was the first time you brought it up, right?"

"Didn't you say Remy sent you to someone because he caught you with that guy? His colleague?"

Loki kissed his teeth. "The man's such a fucking drama queen. It was *one* kiss. And everyone was drunk."

"Lo. He was also in his forties. And you were fifteen."

"Okay. Points were made. Still. He sent me, didn't he?"

"You don't believe he's just going to give in and take Nell to see someone? He was twitchy the whole time he was here like he was cheating or something. He can't even tell Ophelia when he's seeing his own kid."

"All I'm saying is that you're not the type to give up. You'll tell him again and maybe you'll wear him down. If not, you'll annoy him. A win either way."

Loki was back in London for some new voiceover work. Because it could only be described with all manner of clichés; because when Loki spoke, you found yourself not only listening but leaning into him until you were close enough to count his freckles, Loki's voice was in high demand. He was the voice of a popular cheese brand and a fast-rising coffee company; he had narrated seven audiobooks, three of which were bestsellers, and was in talks to become the voice of a cartoon fox with the ability to shape-shift. It was the type of work Loki excelled in, something that paid handsomely but was infrequent enough that he could have enough time to do what he really loved, which was nothing. He fell into voice work quite by accident after being introduced to a casting director at one of Céleste's dinner parties. The nepotism amused Loki as much as it enraged Remy who would call his son frequently to demand that he use his connections for good; the "good" being a job in finance or tech. It didn't matter to Remy that Loki happened to be excellent at what he did. You can do a thing to perfection, but if it is not desired, it becomes detestable. And yet Loki answered all of Remy's calls and allowed himself to be raked over the coals. Aṅụrị asked him why.

At first, Loki said nothing. Then, after another sip of juice, he said, "I figure the day I start working some job Remy approves of is the day he stops calling me daily to tell me to get a job he approves of. He chews me out, but at the end he always says something like, 'This much of a fuckup and I still love you.' I dunno. I don't want him to stop saying it."

Aṅụrị was fluent in longing. She understood. She hit Pause so she could lean over and kiss Loki's cheek. "Look at the actual state of us," she said. "Daddy issues. How terribly clichéd and pedestrian."

"Exactly. God, we have such daddy issues."

"Literally all of them."

They passed another few minutes vanquishing their opponents on-screen. Loki asked about Christian and Aṅụrị informed him that Christian was now clued in about Ophelia.

"He know how messed up you are by it?"

Aṅụrị laughed. "Screw you. Not the full extent, but he has some idea, yeah."

"And he ain't run for the hills? See? You just might be a lover girl, after all."

"Relax. Love is your thing, not mine. Which is weird because given how unafraid of it you are, you never seem to want to stay in a relationship."

"You're making me sound like a fuckboy."

"You're the tenderest of fuckboys, Lo. But you do break hearts."

"Unintentionally!"

Aṅụrị gave him a look.

Loki rolled his eyes. "Who wants to end up like Remy and Céleste?"

"Divorced?"

"Two people who love each other but just can't make shit work. My mom's getting married in a couple of months and the dude is cool, but he's gotta know that she and my dad have this dynamic. Then there's Remy who just grits his teeth and goes on random dates because my grandma bugs him about it. But for him, there's never going to be anyone but my mom."

"You're not Remy, Lo." Which wasn't altogether accurate because he was the anti-Remy whilst still being miraculously Remy-like. He was a walking nerve ending, sensitive to so much. But Loki wore the clothes Remy rejected when he pledged allegiance to finance, listened to NPR and read Charles Bukowski all because Remy introduced him to those things. Loki vacillated between contempt for his dad and ill-disguised yearning to be understood. Their childhoods had been conducted to the tunes of "fuck Remy" or "Remy's pretty cool, y'know," and Anụrị, similarly disenchanted yet unable to fully disengage from Nkem, recognized elements of Loki in herself. Anụrị could not, however, imagine Loki having a son and only telling him he was loved after reprimanding him for not unfolding in the ways Loki wished. But then, Anụrị had once sat with a distraught ex-paramour of Loki's for an hour, explaining as gently as she could that no, Loki was not a bad person, but he also was not a person who was going to come down the stairs and give in to the girl's pleas for rekindling.

"I know I'm not. And I don't want to be. Maybe I'm just in my frog-kissing era or whatever."

"Okay, but do you have to make the frogs fall for you? And have you considered that perhaps you are the frog?"

It took Loki fifteen years to decide his anxiety about his laughter was unfounded. These days, he let it roam around a room startling then delighting whoever it happened upon. "They fall for me 'cos I'm amazing."

"True."

"But you're right, I'm not a good romantic role model, chère. I don't know what I'm doing half the time. If it feels good, I kind of just let myself fall into it. Inadvisable."

Aṅụrị's phone pinged. "New upload from Ophelia," she said. She paused the game and loaded the new Instagram photo. Ophelia and Noelle shot from behind as they played in a swimming pool. Palm trees in view. The sky insisting on its blueness, the composition of clouds. Aṅụrị had no idea when the picture was taken. When had they left the country? When was the last time Aṅụrị had been on holiday with them? Did Ophelia's fans know she had a mole on the underside of the left arm? Was the mole even still there? It could have been lasered away. After all, perfection is the product of determination, money and fabrication. She began, as she always did, scrolling through the comments, offering her commentary on the psychology of sycophants. When she glanced up, Loki was watching her.

"What?" she said.

"Nothing. Nada. Can we get back to the game?"

"No, Loki, why're you looking at me like that?"

Despite Remy's emotional constipation or perhaps because of it, Loki was not a young man who balked at expressing himself. One of the reasons for his comfort with Aṅụrị was that this outpouring was always welcomed. He was proud of the table they'd set up between them, on which either one could lay their burdens and have them received in good faith. It was because of that table, of that unspoken understanding that Loki decided to say what he needed to say. The avoidance of truth did not equal the unmaking of it.

"It's just…you're kind of slating all those people looking at Ophelia's content, but you're right there with them, looking at it, too."

"Okay. And?"

"And that's not a little fucked up to you?"

"You know I look for completely different reasons."

"Yeah, sure. But like, an obsession is an obsession is an obsession, feel me? Ophelia's fans probably don't all have the same motivation. Like, they can't *all* be perverts."

Aṅụrị's phone was warm in the palm of her hand. As Loki's words traveled the space between them, she wondered what it would be like to stand up, step out of her body and slide seamlessly into his. She wanted to sit behind his eyes and know how it felt to say things like he was saying, see if they stung the same way leaving as they did on arrival. She crossed her arms.

"Sounds like you're defending them," she said.

"Come on, you know I'm not. But I do think you should stop adding to Ophelia's traffic. And I don't think it would be the worst idea in the world for you to take a break from everything. Just for a bit."

"Everything meaning what?"

Years of knowing her meant Loki didn't have to examine Aṅụrị's face to know what she was feeling. He could read her mood by the change in her tone, by the way her fingers sank into her own bicep, by the way she shifted backward in minute increments. Hand him a sheet of paper and he could sketch every one of her expressions from memory. She was part of him. And her being part of him meant that to hurt her was to hurt himself. Some pain, however, was necessary. He had waded this far; turning back would take more energy than it would to move forward.

"Everything," he repeated. "Stalking Ophelia's profiles. The lawsuit." Here he paused, took a breath as if it may be the final one he was allowed to take. "Maybe chill on the whole Nell guardianship thing."

"It's good of you to finally admit you don't think I can do it." Aṅụrị furiously wiped her face. The raw edge of her sweater was rough against her skin. When Loki reached out to touch her, she shrank away from his hands.

"The last couple of months have been a lot, chère." Looking

at her, Loki felt like he might cry, too. He blinked. "Overwhelming even. It would be for anyone."

"But especially for someone like me, right?"

"Aṅụrị. I love you, you know that."

"So what?"

"So, Simi and I watched you relapse once and come close how many times in the past few weeks? We're scared, okay? And if we're scared, then Noelle..." he trailed off.

The downside of friendship is that whereas when the world pins assumptions to you, they are, much of the time, easily removable, but with friends, with those who know you, their observations come with a level of insight not so easy to shrug off. Loki was not wrong. And this made his presence at that moment intolerable. The mirror had been held up and Aṅụrị, devoid of any reasonable response, chose instead to smash it.

"You don't get to tell me I'd basically scare my sister to death if she lived with me, Lo. You don't get to say that to me."

But he did. Because friends, the good ones at least, were also tasked with saying the hard things; with holding the uncomfortable truths up to the light and allowing them to be illuminated.

"Aṅụrị," Loki tried, "all I'm saying is—"

Aṅụrị spoke over him. "And it's not like I asked you. I never actually asked you to look after me or do anything for me," she said, ignoring the fact that the reason Loki sat beside her that very moment was because she asked him there, because confronting her most recent mistake was too much to bear on her own. "You don't have to use me as an excuse to distract yourself from being fucked up over your mum getting remarried, or your dad being your dad. I said you're not Remy but honestly, sometimes it's like you're so busy trying not to be Remy that you're turning into him. I'm not your project."

Even as she was speaking them, Aṅụrị regretted the words. They tumbled out of her and polluted the air, and there was no way to unsay them. She watched helplessly as Loki's face closed—a rare occurrence; a facial eclipse.

"Cool," Loki said.

In the bathroom, where Aṅụrị fled to blow her nose, she constructed an apology, but by the time she returned to the living room, Loki was gone; the sofa throw folded carefully, the controllers stacked neatly on the coffee table. Here was the vortex once again only this time, she'd ejected Loki when he was willing to help pull her out. She picked up her phone and texted her apologies.

Loki didn't respond.

He still hadn't responded a couple of days later when they were due to attend Simi's concert. Simi and her violin were part of a classical string quartet, one quarter of which Simi despised. They were playing at the Royal Academy and Aṅụrị would be seated between Loki and Lekan—there was not a performance of Simi's her family did not attend, and even as Aṅụrị waited on the steps outside of the theatre, she spied Morenike and Ayo making their way toward her, Ayo's fist full of Morenike's hem, because which Yoruba mother would attend a showcase of their child's musical skill in anything other than a gown? The sun was setting and throwing handfuls of vermillion across the London sky.

Aṅụrị received Morenike's hug. "Wow, Aunty. Fine girl no pimple!"

"My dear," Morenike said, palming her bag, "Simi told us not to come and disgrace her so I needed a new outfit."

"And boy do you have one. You're a stunner."

"You're not coming inside?"

"I'm just waiting for Loki," Aṅụrị said, hoping her voice didn't sound like she felt, which was like she was trying to haul herself up the sides of a greased well.

"I pity whoever is sitting behind that boy," Ayo put in. "Aṅụrị, we'll see you inside."

Seven minutes before the concert was due to begin, Loki was nowhere to be seen. Aṅurị set her shoulders back, lifted her chin and found her seat, smiling wanly at Lekan's wink. Just as the room began to darken and the hush started moving through the audience, Loki dropped into the seat to her right. The dimness of the room disguised his expression, and Aṅurị knew she couldn't spend the duration of the performance staring at the side of his head, so she tucked her desperation away and watched her brilliant friend bring tears to the eyes of those assembled. In the midst of the applause, just as she turned to him, Loki reached past her to touch fists with Lekan. And then he was gone, weaving his way through the crowd, not even throwing a glance over his shoulder.

"Hmm," Simi said, appearing at Aṅurị's side. "He texted and said he had to dash right after I was done. But, hmm."

"You were so good, Sim," Aṅurị said, because she had been electrifying on that stage and she had the right to know it.

"I still sometimes surprise myself," Simi admitted. "But I wish they would let me wear something else for these things. It's not like I would go and dress anyhow, but this—" she gestured to her black shift dress "—if they want me dead, they should say that. Instead of making me dress for my funeral."

Aṅurị threw her arms around Simi and pulled her close until their cheeks were smashed together and talking became an act of determination. "You alwaysh look gweat," Aṅurị said.

Simi laughed, and they were so close that Aṅurị felt it reverberate through her own body. "Thanksh." Simi tilted her head away. "Thanks. Go after him."

"No," Aṅurị said. "It's your night. Yele said something about a quick drink?"

"One, *nonalcoholic* drink at the bar. And you don't have to."

"Sim. I want to. Let us toast you. Chief Violinist."

One side of Simi's mouth curved upward. "Alright. One drink. Let's go."

She sipped ginger ale at the bar and stayed until Simi and her family started making noises about organizing Ubers to ferry them home, then she decided that in the time it would take her to walk from the Academy to Mayfair, she might be able to formulate the kind of apology that Loki would listen to. Céleste's doorman complimented Aṅụrị's dress and the gold earrings in the many holes she'd punctured through her lobes and the cartilage. She flew to the lift, praying for her courage to last, and when she faced Céleste's front door, she allowed herself a single steadying breath before letting herself into the apartment with the key Loki gave her when they were fourteen and she needed a place to be even when he couldn't occupy that place with her.

He was already in bed, his door open, Netflix playing on the projector screen suspended from the ceiling. There was a giant Rothko above his bed, an eighteenth birthday gift from Remy along with the signet ring Loki wore on his little finger. He was shirtless and drowsy, and it took what felt like an age for his gaze to meet hers.

Aṅụrị held her offerings aloft. In one hand, a small ribboned box; in the other, the rat tail comb she carried everywhere.

"I'm prepared to grovel," Aṅụrị said.

"Bribery?"

"Yes. Beignets and pralines—" she shook the ribboned box "—and a retwist. Although that one's partly for me as both your friend and stylist. You're walking around with regrowth and it's…it's a trigger."

Loki sighed. "I do love pralines."

Aṅụrị lowered her arms, took a tentative step over the threshold.

"Stop," Loki said.

"I'm so sorry, Lo," Aṅụrị said. "I'm the worst. There's no excuse. I really am sorry." He was not a person Aṅụrị was prepared to lose. She had no need to be loved widely, only deeply, and Loki was bottomless.

"Shoes," Loki said.

Céleste's was a shoeless abode. In her haste, Aṅụrị had traipsed right to Loki's room in her block heels. She returned to the front hall where she unbuckled and abandoned her shoes, and by the time she reached Loki's door once again, he had shifted in the bed and left a T-shirt on the duvet for her to change into.

"Love you," Aṅụrị said.

"Love you more. Pass the pralines."

She climbed in beside him. Despite his height, Aṅụrị was big spoon that night.

The next morning with equilibrium restored, Aṅụrị left Mayfair and surreptitiously returned to tracking Ophelia's post schedule. The fact that she told herself she was doing it solely to keep tabs on Noelle took nothing away from the reality that the same content she condemned was what she felt compelled to consume. She was, if Loki was to believed and there was good reason to do so, no different to the subscribers and the followers, no matter what pedestal of social justice onto which she hoisted herself. Looking became watching became following, following lived on the floor above obsession. So forms a seemingly innocent habit you never intended to have. The more you watch, the more the algorithm serves you, and thus the more you watch. A vicious cycle that underneath it all, was quietly sinister. Aṅụrị was like any other internet punter—only her origins differed.

In trawling through Ophelia's offerings, it was true that Aṅụrị was inadvertently feeding the beast, oiling the cogs of the machine. But she maintained that in order to choke the beast, you did in fact have to feed it. However, she was now aware that she lingered on TikTok longer than was necessary. Her thumb had developed a callous that had as much to do with scrolling as it did with braiding and wick testing.

Scattered amongst the Noelle content were solo posts of Ophelia. They were usually linked to some fashion, skincare or lifestyle brand, and in the photos, Ophelia was usually clad in linen or chiffon and draped across an impractical yet undoubtedly expensive item of furniture. There were some close-up shots of her face as she massaged a blob of eye cream into her skin, or peeled a whitening strip from her teeth, and this was the closest Ophelia was prepared to come to the influx of "real" posts that were taking social media by storm. It wasn't feasible to expect Ophelia to bravely reveal that she too had cellulite and sometimes left her underwear in small piles on the floor instead of the laundry basket, because she didn't and her fans were not interested in reality; they were interested in rosy-cheeked, strawberry shortcake escapism.

Aṅụrị, having once been at the center of it, could see the appeal whilst remaining repulsed by it. Had she been allowed to cultivate her own online presence as most were, she might allow for a more gracious reading of those who indulged. Loki and Simi had their accounts and Aṅụrị, biased as she was, had to accept that there were levels; that one might find themselves entertained by a boxing match without necessarily wanting to enter a ring themselves.

Social media had its own currency. Validation and praise could be dangerous and addictive, and as it had with Ophelia, when popularity translates into financial returns, the drug becomes more potent. For Aṅụrị the internet was useful and terrifying in equal measure. People unzipping their coats and leaving them on the floor, baring their souls and their flesh and their rudimentary understandings of feminism to all and sundry. Aṅụrị shoved her phone into her bag. Was the attention worth it? She didn't know. For her, it was not. *So many of us*, she thought, unlocking her front door, *enjoy being consumed.* But too few did the work to understand why.

OPHELIA

There are many things that if you're determined, you can overlook. And it's easy to be determined when the visible good outweighs the invisible, or partially visible, bad. The more I overlooked, the easier it became to rationalize my choices. Yes, it was disturbing that a woman in central Argentina would comment almost instantly on all of Aṅụrị's photos with the vilest racial abuse, creating new accounts post blocking. But she was in central Argentina, and Aṅụrị was three. She would never see it. And yes, I didn't know what to make of the increasing number of faceless account follows my profiles amassed as my popularity expanded. I put measures in place, but those measures were restrictive. Growth was the goal. I'm not perfect. I'm like anyone else who rationalizes because their lives are now charmed. I became someone who no longer had to check her balance before making a purchase. I am adored in a way I always assumed was beyond my sphere of being. I rationalize because I've known insignificance and, I, like everyone else, deserve to be seen.

TWELVE

The thing about Genevieve, Ophelia thought, was that her inability to keep her hands still rendered anyone in her presence unable to concentrate fully on what she was saying. This made things difficult because Genevieve would then complain that she was not being listened to, and she would do it in such a way that made the recipient of the complaint feel like they were the worst person to grace the face of the earth; like they were depriving her of oxygen or had called her haircut an abomination.

They were in Genevieve's kitchen—the one Ophelia had paid to have renovated, importing terrazzo tiles at great expense from some tiny Italian retailer—and they were dancing, as middle-class women often do, around the subject they had convened to discuss. The choreography this time involved the assembly of an elaborate salad which included things like pine nuts and pomegranate, and Ophelia marveled at how far her mother had come. Her childhood was spent listening to Genevieve dub so many foods as "a little too adventurous." And now here she was, drizzling truffle oil and instructing Ophelia to decant the Chablis.

In her bag (tasteful mushroom-colored leather), Ophelia's phone, muted though it was, was filling with notifications—

empires could crumble in the time it took to plate a salad—but she was determined to ignore it. She knew the route this afternoon would take: pleasantries, the perusal of new photographs of Noelle during which Genevieve would comment on the "interesting texture" of the little girl's hair, an attempt at lunch, before veering off into the inevitable forest of disappointment and ending, as these one-on-ones often did, at the bottom of a conversational ravine. They sat, they picked at the pomegranate and pine nut salad, Genevieve's hands moved with the pace of a drugged hummingbird and eventually, Genevieve asked again for Ophelia's reasons for not attending the memorial luncheon for her sister. Ophelia, suppressing a sigh, explained in person as she had done on the phone (thrice) that things were challenging right now; that despite everything Aṅụrị was persisting with the lawsuit; that Noelle was having a tough time. She did not ask why her mother insisted on hosting this memorial luncheon every year when Molly had passed over four decades earlier, when sometimes Genevieve would phone Ophelia up several days after her own birthday and say, "Ah, darling, I'm so sorry, time ran away with me again."

"That's disappointing," Genevieve said, her hands fluttering above her wineglass.

"Yes. I'm sorry." Ophelia, her appetite walking briskly toward the door, put down her fork.

"I would have thought you'd like to mark your sister's passing."

Ophelia said nothing. She could have said that there was only so much marking one could be expected to do when you were eighteen months old at the time of the passing. She could have said that despite this and the prolonged grieving which spirited her parents away from her emotionally, she had continued the marking by attending almost every memorial luncheon, by allowing Genevieve to gift Noelle a few of Molly's dresses, by paying for a new marble (also Italian) headstone for the grave, by repeatedly bringing her family at her parents' request to stand by that marble headstone and lay flowers and say a few words although she struggled greatly to find the words to describe the sister she could not remember but loved in the way one does when memory fails. After a few seconds during which Ophelia allowed Genevieve to make her point, she found her voice.

"I did send you a couple of hampers. From Harrods. I didn't want you to have to think too much about cooking or anything for the luncheon. Did you get them?" At home, Ophelia would chastise herself for her eagerness, especially since Genevieve's response was to pat her hand and nod.

"They were lovely, sweetheart. We do cater though. You know that."

On the drive home, Ophelia's car picked up the incoming call from her lawyers and she listened to them explain that Anụrị was not budging; that her beautiful, obstinate girl was immovable. She had put down roots, screwed the courage Ophelia was still shocked she possessed to the sticking place.

"Offer her more money," Ophelia said. Traffic was slowing. There was no time for this.

"Mrs. Chinasa, at some point, you must consider the possibility that Ms. Chinasa's is not a financial motivation."

The traffic was not yet slow enough that hitting the boy who darted out in front of Ophelia's car would not cause catastrophe. Her foot slipped from the brake and shaking hands (a holdover from Genevieve?) sent the vehicle to the right and into a parked car, the impact jolting her backward and pushing a gasp from her chest.

"Mrs. Chinasa?"

"I'll call you back," Ophelia whispered and then burst into tears.

It hadn't taken long for Ophelia to realize she could not be separated from Anụrị. When Nkem brought her, feverish and miserable to A&E, Ophelia felt something break apart behind her ribs and flood her body. She watched him carry her out hours later and it was as if a piece of her heart left with them. They reentered her life soon after this and were it not for another girl at the agency quitting unexpectedly, it may not have been Ophelia who was sent when Nkem, adrift in his personal sea of sadness and incompetence, reached out to hire a nurse on a part-time basis to make sure that his daughter, wide-eyed and beautiful, was not merely kept alive but cared for. It was a distinction some parents failed to make. And it was heartbreaking and infuriating every time.

Within a fortnight, she was smitten, her affection for Nkem taking root almost unconsciously, and growing more slowly so that by the time she recognized her feelings, it was too late. She could not un-feel them and so she embraced them instead. It made sense, she thought, to fall in love with them both. There was a rightness to it that sat comfortably inside her on the nights she made herself return to her own flat and remind herself that she had a life outside of them, unremarkable as it was. What surprised Ophelia was the intensity of her love. Soon it became impossible to imagine a future without them featuring heavily in whatever paltry plans she had for herself. Soon after that, the plans ceased to be paltry at all. Genevieve and Henry interpreted their daughter's romantic decision as late-stage rebellion or a form of Stockholm syndrome. Ophelia interpreted her parents' trepidation as what it was: good old middle-class bigotry.

With Nkem and Aṅụrị, Ophelia was not Molly's sister. She was just Ophelia. Just Ophelia was someone she liked. It was like stepping into the sun after shuffling along through, if not a gale, but a very determined chilly breeze. They warmed her from within and injected purpose into her world. This is what she would tell first *Heat*, then *Cosmo* and then *Elle*, *Harper's Bazaar* and *Good Housekeeping* when they asked about how she fought her way to the pinnacle of the mumfluencer mountain.

They would turn their eyes on her and wait for a tale about how she, blonde, benevolent and lovely, had swooped in and saved this pair of bereft emotional casualties, and she would try to explain (but never very well) that it was they who had saved her.

The gratitude was, in part, the origin of her blog. She told Nkem it was a quick and easy way of keeping his faraway relatives abreast of Aṅụrị's development, and whilst that was true, it was also a method of showcasing the life she was building for herself with these two people she adored. This life was small but perfectly formed. She was no wordsmith and a photo or two paired with a paragraph would never be enough to adequately convey how it felt when Aṅụrị stretched her tiny arms out for Ophelia, or when Nkem smiled at her and called her "obim," but they were a start. Her popularity was accidental. And then it wasn't. It was a painful thing to realize that you alone were not enough to hold the interest of others, that your personality or looks could not suspend the fickleness of the human condition. Popularity, Ophelia learned, was something that needed to be worked at; it required the labor of maintenance.

Aṅụrị made this easier. Ophelia's followers were soon as invested in the kid as Ophelia was. Part of love is wanting your loved ones to experience it from multiple sources, was it not? This is what happened. Did things at some point become strange? Yes. Was there an insistence from some that crossed the line into parasocial? Yes. Ophelia was not invested in her audience, after all, not really. Their lives would forever remain foreign to her while hers and Aṅụrị's were open enough for people to form one-sided bonds. Was that enough to make Ophelia stop? No. No it was not. Anytime she felt herself disappearing, a holdover feeling from her childhood, Ophelia need only turn to her fans for a reminder of her new indelibility.

The introduction of money into the equation necessitated further explanation to Nkem (and, bizarrely in Ophelia's opinion, Nkem's sister). Nkem seemed puzzled yet unconcerned and his trust in her was another prompt to move forward, to demonstrate her ability to not only exist but to flourish. Ophelia's biggest mistake, she knew, was allowing Aṅụrị to think the threat was of losing the accoutrements that went along with the notoriety: the house, the cars, the acclamation. But after Aṅụrị excised herself from their lives and from the world Ophelia worked painstakingly to build in the most agonizing way possible, Ophelia was now learning that there were worse things in life than obscurity.

The car would be fixed. There was a dent and a few scratches along the driver's side but nothing a trip to the detailer could not rectify—Ophelia would not even need to drop the car off herself. She and Nkem were now the sort of people who, with a swipe of a credit card, could have their vehicles collected, repaired and dropped off in the space of forty-eight hours. There were so many conveniences in this life; all one had to do was have the money to access them. The physical evidence of her afternoon would be popped, buffed and polished away, and all that would remain would be the invisible damage Ophelia tried to combat first by drinking another glass of wine, then taking the type of shower that left her skin pink and tender. When neither tactic worked, when hours later, her hands and feet still pinged with anxiety-induced pins and needles, she tiptoed into Noelle's bedroom, sat on the floor and watched the rise and fall of her sleeping child's chest and then she watched the moon out of her sleeping child's window. When she rose to leave, her joints protested in a way the yoga and Pilates for which she paid an exorbitant sum should not have permitted. She had not called her lawyers back.

In her home office, a room of such tranquility and beauty she could have rented it out for wellness retreats, Ophelia closed the door and made for her secret stash. Some enjoyed the mellowness of weed, some the metallic spark of cocaine hitting the membranes of the nostril, but Ophelia preferred to light one of

Aṅụrị's candles which, in order to remain undetected, she had her assistant buy and ship to a PO box. She closed her eyes and the scent unfurled itself. This was the thing about the candles—it was almost as if they were alive, as if they had a personality of their own. Aṅụrị's candle had notes of freesia which disappeared behind a cloak of the softest amber and sandalwood. There was also something else which Ophelia could not identify. There was always something in Aṅụrị's candles Ophelia couldn't quite place. She wasn't alone. That injection of mystery was a unique selling point if ever one existed. Ophelia felt as if she were being led through a garden and then a wood before ending up on a beach facing the ocean. There was no denying it: Aṅụrị's was the better product. Everything was deliberate and flawlessly executed from the packaging to the scent to the quality. And each candle was handmade, adding another layer to the brilliance. If Ophelia was still selling her own candles, they would have been easily eclipsed. It was something they should have bonded over, but the fissure ran too deep.

Ophelia sat, switched on her computer and surveyed her stats. Seventeen hundred new YouTube subscribers. Eight hundred and twelve new Instagram followers for her and almost three thousand for the dedicated profile she ran for Noelle. Six thousand new comments on her latest TikTok. The pins and needles stopped. Her nerves stilled. She was home.

Sometime later, Nkem appeared, barefoot and red-eyed.

"You won't come to bed?" he asked.

To anyone else, it would have been an innocuous query, but loving a man for years means knowing the meaning of every breath. The accusation was never overtly articulated. It stung all the same.

"In a minute," Ophelia said. She was midway through typing a response to a potential sponsor, her train of thought already hanging by a thread.

Nkem lifted the candle from her desk. He inhaled, set it back down. His shoulders rounded. He drummed his fingers on the desk. There was a new wrinkle dissecting his brow. At least it was new to Ophelia; she could not remember the last time she really looked at her husband; drank him in the way she used to when their future was uncertain yet brilliant—the last streaks of sunset fading into the encroaching night sky. The day he proposed, Ophelia had dropped to her knees, her chest heaving with relief and joy.

"Aṅụrị thinks we should send Noelle to see someone. A therapist is what she said."

Ophelia peered at Nkem over the top of her iMac. "Oh? How nice. What else does Aṅụrị think?"

It was not even an implication but a declaration shoddily wrapped in cotton wool. They were terrible parents. Outside help was required. Ophelia could no longer remember the last time she and Aṅụrị had spoken about anything other than Noelle. Or the lawsuit. The same might be said for Nkem. But the blade of jealousy that sliced through her was white-hot. They were speaking. They at least had that. Her peace had been perforated long ago and her energy was escaping through the puncture. She wanted nothing more in that moment than to lie on the floor and close her eyes.

"I already told her no," he said.

Before stepping inside, Nkem had cracked open the office door and watched Ophelia for some three or four minutes. He saw the way her body seemed to elongate, the way it settled into her chair as soon as the computer flickered to life. She was like a cat stretching in a patch of sunlight. What did it mean that his wife became herself when presented with a screen? Her long plait hung over her shoulder. Ophelia had not cut her hair over the years, opting instead for maintenance trims and summoning a specialist to the house to perform subtle touch-ups on the color. She was barefaced, truly, not the illusion of it that she spent half an hour every morning carefully constructing at her vanity table.

All these years later and Nkem still had to plant himself to the floor to stop himself from covering her shoulders in kisses. It pierced him, the way Ophelia spat out Aṅụrị's name like a curse. He passed the tip of his finger through the flame of the candle.

"Today at work," he said, "a woman showed me Noelle's photos on her phone."

Once again, Ophelia looked up. "What?"

"Her name is Helen," Nkem continued. "I think she works in Accounts. Or is it HR? She came and showed me. She has Noelle's photos on her phone. So many of them. She said she took them from online." He remembered the cloying sweetness of Helen's perfume. "She's such a doll," she had said, "just a gorgeous girl." Nkem had thought of nothing else since. "Is it normal? To me it isn't normal. Does that happen often?"

What answer could Ophelia offer that would be accepted? To say it was an anomaly would be a lie. It did happen often. It had happened first with Aṅụrị, and Ophelia had dusted down Aṅụrị's uniform after another scuffle at school and chastised her, not knowing how to respond to the girl's concrete glare and the question: "Why do people have photos of me on their phones? Why is my face something people use to express annoyance?"

Eventually, Ophelia said, "Is that a reason to fight?" and Aṅụrị, already turning away, had said, "Is it a reason not to?"

Now it was happening to Noelle. Her daughters lived on personal devices the world over. She could not explain the motivation to save photos of children that were not your own. She wanted to go to him and press her face into his neck. She wanted to tell him that even now, there were no fewer than ten fake accounts passing off Noelle's photos as their own; that every time one was successfully taken down, another two would pop up—a twenty-first century Hydra. She wanted him to rub her back and murmur affirmations into her hair. The way he watched her kept Ophelia in her chair. Whether Molly or Kainene, the silent comparisons continued. She would be forever living in the shadow of the dead.

ALLOW ME TO INTRODUCE MYSELF

★ ★ ★

Much later, when the dust had settled enough for Aṅụrị to see the extent of the damage; the emotional and mental debris that lay strewn across her life, already a paragon of tumult, she would divide her existence into Before the Article and After the Article. It followed a pattern she established when she was younger; neatly apportioning the pivotal moments in her life and setting herself on either side of them. She left Aṅụrị Before the Sixth Birthday behind and became Aṅụrị After the Sixth Birthday. She intrepidly ventured forth as Aṅụrị After the First Payout. She found driving a stake into the ground at the site of disaster was helpful, as if she could return and leaf through the catalog of faults that led here to serve as a warning not to traverse the same path again. She had not yet managed to become the Aṅụrị After the Alcohol although with each passing day, she grew closer.

The day of the Article, she was doing stitch braids for one of her favorite clients. Bisola could only be described as "effervescent," not in the way that made you want to impale your own eyes with something sharp, but bubbly in the same way as champagne, slowly intoxicating you until you are grinning and swaying at imaginary music. Aṅụrị settled comfortably into the stitch braid cadence: under the middle and grip, under the middle, grip again. It was soothing work and the reason Aṅụrị was able to empty her head of anything but the task at hand which proved essential given that the flock-wallpapered rooms of her mind were cluttered with such detritus as legal issues, paypig propositions and how often it was appropriate to text Christian without alarming him. She reached for the mousse, the final step in the process, just as her phone began vibrating. Because Aṅụrị prided herself on professionalism, one of her self-imposed rules was no phones when she was with clients. They appreciated the extra care and she appreciated them appreciating it. The phone continued to vibrate, insistently like an enraged hornet, pausing only momentarily when the caller was sent to voicemail and chose to begin their crusade anew. Aṅụrị apologized to Bisola who, gem that she was, told her it was totally fine and wasn't it nice to be so popular? Moussing and payment complete, Bisola was in the process of gathering her belongings when Simi threw open the door.

Simi did not throw open doors. That caliber of dramatics was reserved for Loki who, now he had come to terms with his size, found amusement in people's reaction to it. Simi entered rooms quietly, sometimes silently, and often not at all having given herself the opportunity to survey the contents or inhabitants of the room and reject it outright. Aṅụrị could not recall even seeing Simi pant the way she did now, one hand on her knee, one braced against the door as she tried and failed to catch her breath.

"Why," she gasped, "won't you answer your phone?"

Aṅụrị gestured to Bisola who stood patiently waiting for Simi to stand aside so she could exit. "Um, since when do I answer when I'm working?"

"You're calm? How are you calm? I ran here thinking something had happened to you and you're standing there not giving a shit?"

Aṅụrị guided Simi to the recently vacated styling chair and waved to Bisola who gently closed the door behind her. "Sim, you're scaring me. Why aren't you at work?"

Simi searched her friend's face and did what she did in moments like this, of which there had been many; moments when Aṅụrị's world was about to shift. She prepared herself to be, temporarily, the legs that would carry her best friend forward until she was once again able to walk unaided. "Oh, babe," she said. Then she showed Aṅụrị the Article.

It was written by someone called Penelope. This struck Aṅụrị as both preposterous and cruel. Why did someone named Penelope get to ruin people's lives with her attempts at journalism? By rights, she should be sunning herself on some yacht deck or shopping for organza in some appointment-only boutique. That is what Penelopes did. They did not write pieces on landmark legal developments arising out of prominent influencer and businesswoman Ophelia Chinasa's now-tenuous relationship with hairstylist and candle brand owner, Aṅụrị Chinasa, who she raised almost from birth. The details were still unknown, Penelope wrote, but sources and recently obtained documents outlined a case which saw Ms. Chinasa (25) pursue some form of compensation for her contribution to Mrs. Chinasa's (47) lucrative business empire. The compensation, Penelope finished, is understood not to be monetary. At least that is what Aṅụrị assumed to be the end of the article; it was hard to tell because she was shaking so much, her knees knocking together in a way that should have been embarrassing if embarrassment had not been left behind so long ago, Aṅụrị recalled it as a long-lost friend.

"Aṅụrị," Simi said. "Sit down."

But there was no sitting down. To move, to so much as breathe was to usher in the crumbling of the walls, the floor; to bring about the unstitching of the fabric of life. Aṅụrị's phone, even after Simi's arrival, did not stop buzzing, and Simi, who almost two years into her career in marketing and publicity, had come to see vibrating phones as a trigger, reached out and answered.

"I'm handling this, Aṅụrị," Gloria said from the speaker. "It must have been leaked by Ophelia's team to pressure you. It's a dirty trick, but I can make it backfire. I just— Don't go online, okay? Simi. Make sure she does not read the comments."

"Yes, ma," Simi said, because deference was a reflex even if only in the presence of Gloria's voice.

"Less of the ma, if you please," Gloria said. "Aṅụrị, I will call you as soon as I can. Do not go online."

So of course Aṅụrị went online. After they'd returned to Aṅụrị's flat and Simi was asleep on the other side of her bed, and their four-hour FaceTime with Loki concluded, Aṅụrị, T-shirt clad and shivering, carried her pillows to the sofa and read through the comments on the article and on the subsequent articles which were spreading across the internet like a rash. She gorged herself on the insults, let them slug her repeatedly until they burned themselves into her brain. The conviction of the commenters was impressive. Aṅụrị was ungrateful. She owed Ophelia everything. Her candles were not even that nice (a lie does not care who tells it). They questioned what sort of person sued their own mother especially when that mother chose to raise her when not obligated to? And, sprinkled in amongst the vitriol, some support. *I think it's a good thing*, Malika from Houston wrote, *let that girl live her life*. Terri from the Bronx added emojis to her response. *Y'all are weird as hell. You know this is a stranger, right?* The replies to Terri's observation were rich in caps lock; nobody enjoys having that sort of mirror held up to them. They heaped scorn on her and try as she did to leave it there on her sofa, it followed Aṅụrị around the flat and stuck to her skin until eventually she gave up and sat with it, letting it harden into a shell. Simi found her there the following morning, red-eyed and hugging her knees.

"I didn't drink, Sim," Aṅụrị whispered, her eyes not moving from the coffee table where her phone lay. "I didn't drink."

Beside the phone, an unopened bottle of rum.

Simi rubbed the sleep from her eyes and sat beside her friend. "No you didn't, babe." She kissed Aṅụrị on the head, and the two of them sat there, time piling up around them.

THIRTEEN

It hadn't been done before so interest was high. It was a spectacle, no matter how one looked at it. The adult child of a well-known influencer initiating legal action against her parent? Like moths to a flame, the public flocked first to Penelope's article and then to the others popping up like toughened weeds amongst the lawn of more somber, more important news: war, politics, the ever concerning state of the economy.

It was like trying to extinguish a thousand tiny fires without setting anything else alight and in the end, Gloria accepted defeat and pivoted instead to damage control. She called Aṅụrị and explained, holding the phone so tightly she thought it might splinter in her hand, that she was unable to have the articles pulled from the internet. But she had, Gloria added, been in contact with Ophelia's lawyers and her publicist—a woman named Veronica, who was a veteran in the game, punctuated her sentences with staccato laughter, and for whom Gloria nursed a deep-seated hatred—and reminded them that leaks of this kind were in fact gifts that would make discovery a circus and Gloria intended to play ringleader. She too could play games, she thought savagely and instructed her team that all calls originating from Ophelia's circle be screened for the next two days. Let them ponder what she meant. Let them twist in the wind. Gloria's anger, before it settled to the bottom of her mind like silt, temporarily made her ineloquent. They were pricks. She couldn't think of a more charitable characterization of everyone involved.

During those two days, Gloria did her duty and scoured the web. In doing so, she noticed that there appeared to be an uptick in support for Aṅụrị. The lion's share of vocal commenters—many being influencers or celebrities themselves, because of course—still backed Ophelia, but in the recesses of the internet, the Reddit forums, the badly moderated community chats, Aṅụrị was developing a new kind of cult following. Anonymous users, some of whom claimed to also be the offspring of the chronically online, voiced their distaste, distrust and weariness for their own parents. They were thrilled to see that someone somewhere was brave enough to take this on, to hold their parents' feet to the fire. The tide, Gloria hoped, was slowly turning. She said as such to Aṅụrị who she was calling every three hours, trying in vain to keep her voice light, striving to disguise her worry.

"I know I said not to go online," she said, "but, biko, maybe you should reconsider."

Aṅụrị, contemplating the smudges underneath her eyes, painted there by a lack of sleep, clicked her tongue.

"Reconsider? I'm nobody's role model, Gloria. I don't want to be the poster child for this."

Yet, as soon as they hung up, Aṅụrị made her way to some of the threads Gloria mentioned and saw that what she had been told was true. It helped to loosen the knot in her stomach, the one which had been tightening by the hour since the introduction of Penelope into her life, and she called Simi to look, smiling humorlessly when Simi muttered that anyone with even a facsimile of sense could see that if it was a matter of sides, Aṅụrị's was clearly the one to take.

They had not left the flat since the publication of the story, had gone directly from the hut to Aṅụrị's living room, Simi calling her brothers who arrived hours later with a weekend bag of belongings. Lekan filled the fridge with "supplies" (premixed protein shake, trays of eggs and tubs of blueberries) while Simi looked through what they brought, stopping now and then to raise her eyes to the ceiling and say things like, "Is it…is it that I was speaking Tagalog? Why bring so many bras but like, two pairs of pants?" and rolling her eyes when Yele shot back defensively, "Fam, we're your brothers. Which brother wants to look through his sister's panty drawer?" Lekan lowered himself onto the sofa next to Aṅụrị and wrapped an arm around her shoulders.

"D'you want me to ask one of the girls at work to batter her?" he said and none of them knew whether he meant Penelope or Ophelia, but they all laughed, and for just those few seconds, the tension was blown out of the windows which Simi pushed open a crack when the air in the flat became oppressive and she felt like she was wading through it, like it was sticking to the lining of her lungs.

At night, Simi would plead with Aṅụrị to abandon the laptop, discard the phone and lie beside her on the bed. "You don't even have to sleep," she said, but Aṅụrị was afflicted by the thing inside us which wrongly asserts that if we can only keep our eyes on something, then we can put our arms around it and contain it. And Simi would retire to Aṅụrị's room, furtively texting Loki and Abe, providing whispered updates to Nneoma, Makuo and Arinze who at various points were offering to descend on the flat. The times Aṅụrị did fall asleep, fitfully and usually on the sofa or sometimes even the floor of the living room, Simi would slink through the flat and check for alcohol. She removed the unopened bottle of rum, carrying it to the trash chute, waiting for Aṅụrị to mention it. Her back and shoulders became a mass of knots and she took to dedicating twenty minutes every morning to stretching. Watching Aṅụrị became her job and so she emailed her boss and said that her period was especially wretched and necessitated her remaining immobile. When her boss responded and asked how wretched, Simi wrote back, "It's like a crime scene over here." Her boss told her she could work from home. Full-time work about which Simi would never complain. How many times had Anụrị stood in the gap for her when she was bending under the weight of practice or schoolwork, staying up late to help her study, keeping Lekan and Yele busy and fed while their parents toiled at work? How often did Anụrị see to it that there was an Uber to take her to or from a destination? Who else's flat could she run to just to breathe without something being asked of her?

Simi deleted the emails from reporters that trickled into the candle and hairdressing inboxes, and was constructing a reply to one of the pushier *Daily Mail* correspondents crammed with Yoruba phrases like "oloriburuku" when Makuo called again. She asked the questions grandmothers asked: Was the child eating? *Barely, her appetite, like her desire to shower, was in the wind.* Was she running a fever? *Possibly.* Had Simi tried feeding her isi ewu? *It was on the list, but it was a little difficult to source goat's head in Chiswick.* Had Nkem been in touch? *Of course not. Of course he hadn't been.*

"Who was that?" Anụrị stood in the doorway of the bedroom rubbing her eyes. With the exception of bathroom visits, it was the first time she had moved from the living room in the better part of a week.

"Your grandma. Love her. Don't think she gets that you live in one of the whitest parts of London. She thinks you have a local okporoko vendor around here."

"You're calling Nnenne?"

Simi stretched. An unattended muscle in her shoulder popped and she winced. "Well, yeah. And she—they, your grandparents are calling me. They're worried."

"They don't need to worry."

What Aṅụrị should have said was that she did not want them to worry; that she did not have the strength to carry her grandparents' worry along with everything else. But the past few days had fed the part of Aṅụrị that told her there would come a point when Makuo and Arinze would tire, that whatever reserves of love from which Simi and Loki and Nneoma were drawing were now surely about to run dry. The spectre of loneliness was hovering and Aṅụrị felt powerless to fight it off; ill-equipped to battle against what she could visualize but could not see.

"Omo, I need you to be for real, right now."

"Seriously, Sim, you shouldn't have bothered them. I'm fine."

In response, Simi raised one hand and gestured to Aṅụrị's appearance. It was not the love, as Aṅụrị thought, that would wane, it was the patience and only for as long as it would take to recharge. Simi, now nothing but an assortment of muscle spasms, ground her knuckles against the side of her head to dispel the oncoming headache. There was no thank-you, not that this was motivation for her continued presence, but it would have been nice, wouldn't it, to have been offered one regardless.

"Your commitment to suffering alone is admirable, Ṅụrị, but like, today can we drop the martyr act? It's *me*."

Friendship could not exist, Aṅụrị thought, without an element of envy. It didn't have to be insidious. What person was not drawn to others in part because they possessed attributes you wished to have yourself? Simi's ability to self-regulate, her stoicism in the face of incongruity lit up the parts of herself Aṅụrị considered inadequate or faulty. It was she who made the drunken phone calls at the back of some sticky-floored bar. It was she who bitched out of writing a PhD proposal because she was too scared her advisors would accept her for reasons she deemed incorrect. It was she who *did*, despite her protestations, need babysitting, still, at twenty-five because her judgement was impaired, because she could not be trusted to pilot herself through life's storms. She had learned too early that love was conditional, and she had learned to accept crumbs so early that a meal felt frightening. Simi was here. Her circle were loving her from afar. And still, the emptiness inside of Aṅụrị reared on its hind legs and threatened to spoil it all. She had so much, but it still did not feel like enough. Trying to find everything so often meant ending up with nothing.

"You can go home, you know? You don't have to watch me."

Simi stood. "I actually do have to—" She was interrupted by a knock on the door. Not the buzzer alerting them to a visitor outside, but a knock on the front door. "You expecting someone?"

Aṅụrị shook her head. She was trembling again.

"Okay. It's okay. Just stay there." Simi crossed the room and peered through the peephole. She was expecting paparazzi, was poised to deliver the sort of verbal thrashing she felt she, as a Yoruba woman, had been working toward her entire life, but she only saw a man holding a Whole Foods bag and wearing both a very beautiful cardigan and an expression of angst. "You should come and look at this," she said to Aṅụrị.

"God. *God*," Aṅụrị said after she looked.

"Is it? Looks like some guy to me."

"It's Christian. What is he… Can you get him to leave?"

"I sure can," Simi said. "Should I?"

Aṅụrị remembered the monogrammed towel which had yet to make its way to her bathroom. She shook her head.

"Hello, Christian," Simi said, opening the door. "How the fuck did you get into the building?"

Christian insisted on preparing the contents of the Whole Foods bag while Aṅụrị showered and Simi straightened out the living room. Aṅụrị returned to avocado toast, vine-ripened tomatoes with balsamic vinegar and scrambled eggs so fluffy, Gordon Ramsay would have trouble finding fault. Simi was hunched over her plate, eyes narrowed, watching Christian as she methodically chewed her way through her own portion.

"Loki is going to hate you," Aṅụrị said. "Or maybe love you. Can you teach him to make breakfast?"

"I was just saying to Simi that I probably shouldn't have bothered bringing eggs. You seem to have a lot of them in your fridge. A disturbing amount in fact." Christian pushed a glass of orange juice toward Aṅụrị.

"This is delicious," Simi said suspiciously.

Christian beamed at her. "Thanks."

"Does your wife know you're cooking breakfasts like this for other women?"

"Uh. I'm currently wifeless."

"Mm-hmm." Simi reached for her glass of juice and sipped without taking her eyes off him. "Is there anybody who would be upset that you're cooking breakfasts like this for other women?"

"Simi. Abeg," Aṅụrị pleaded.

"Person cannot ask question again?" Simi said.

"Is it happening?" Christian said, looking from one woman to the other. "Am I getting the best friend interrogation? I haven't studied."

"The other best friend is a six-foot-six giant. Has she told you that?"

"Sim." Aṅụrị forked some eggs into her mouth. "Okay this is buff."

Christian turned bodily to face Aṅụrị. "Is it cool that I'm here?"

"He said you weren't answering his calls or texts," Simi put in.

"I saw the shit happening online and I wanted to make sure you were good." His eyes didn't leave her face. "Are you good?"

"I'm something," Aṅụrị said slowly.

"Is it in the neighborhood of good?"

"Please pass the tomatoes," Simi said.

Aṅụrị looked at him. The sun streamed through the window behind her and warmed the back of her neck. "It's cool that you're here."

"It's cool that who's here?" Loki said, unlocking the front door with his key and stepping inside. "Oh *hello.*"

While Christian was showing Loki how to scramble an egg without scorching the pan, Simi and Aṅụrị changed the sheets on Aṅụrị's bed and prowled around the argument they had been about to have. Aṅụrị told Simi she had to know how grateful she was that Simi was there; that she had been there from the beginning, and Simi told Aṅụrị that because she had two younger brothers she felt partially responsible for, she was too selfish to babysit anyone—chapter one in the eldest daughter's handbook.

"Believe it or not, girl, but you are actually of use to me. I'm not that selfless," Simi said then threw a naked pillow over to Aṅụrị to sheath with a fresh pillowcase.

This too was friendship: the ability to push back the four walls of a disagreement and allow room for the recollection of that upon which the bond was built. There were no overt apologies because sometimes the word "sorry" projected a heaviness onto a situation that was not altogether warranted. Aṅụrị and Simi had chosen a long time ago to do life together. Accepting their imperfections was an ongoing process, but one to which they were committed.

Back in the kitchen, Loki was standing by the breakfast bar, eyes closed and mouth full. He raised his fork over his head, accidentally scratching the ceiling and said, as Aṅụrị and Simi walked through from the bedroom, "If you don't date him, I will."

Christian, slipping clean dishes into Aṅụrị's drying rack, pressed a damp hand to his chest and said, "Bro? So flattered." The four of them retreated to the living room.

"So when exactly are you going to let us meet Abe?" Loki asked of Simi.

"That's actually an excellent question," Aṅụrị said.

"Who is Abe?" Christian asked.

Loki stretched. "Abe's the person with whom Simi is doing a shit job of playing hard to get."

"Oh is it?"

"What you're all forgetting—" Simi raised her voice slightly to be heard above the laughter that rippled around the room "—is that this isn't about me. We're here for Aṅụrị. Can we focus? Let us focus." She turned to Christian. "Ogbeni, sensory deprivation? What sort of first date is that?"

"I wouldn't class it as a date," Christian said. "She was having a panic attack. I thought it would help."

"It helped," Aṅụrị said.

"Have you used the towel?" Aṅụrị would remember the way Christian looked at her when he asked. Like he was holding out a forever in his palm and hoping she might accept it.

"I haven't been back yet. A few things have been happening in case you didn't know."

Loki's eyes flitted between the two of them. "If you people are ever looking for a third—"

"Let me apologize for Loki now," Simi said. "He's around a lot and I don't want you thinking he represents us as a group. He'll be banished to his own corner of the compound."

"There's going to be a compound?"

"Yeah," Loki said. "But truly, don't mind me. Simi's scared I'll put you off our girl."

"Impossible," Christian said.

Life is also lived in the gaps in memory and no matter how many other missing pieces she had lost, Aṅụrị hoped she would remember this particular moment.

Loki whistled low. "I will find another date for the wedding," he said.

"There's no need, Lo," Aṅụrị protested.

"What was it I was told?" Simi, head now in a magazine, said. "Let yourself be adored."

***

In the late afternoon, when the sun threw shadows against the far wall of the living room, after Aṅuṛi napped, Christian, aided by an eager sous chef in Loki, made them katsu sandwiches, Simi brought her laptop to the coffee table, Loki pulled out his iPad, and Aṅuṛi and Christian picked up their phones so they could all look through the most recent responses to Ophelia's content which had not been updated since Penelope's write-up. They reasoned that Aṅuṛi would not be deterred and the least they could do was apportion the reactions so she did not have to bear it alone. The breadth of support for Ophelia was what shocked them most. Models and actresses left comments wishing Ophelia well. A sitting congresswoman told her to keep her head up. Other lifestyle and family influencers littered the replies with inspirational quotes and hashtags so that Simi was forced to take a steadying breath lest she black out from having to read another *#DarkestBeforeTheDawn*. It was the callousness that hurt the most. Aṅuṛi was referred to as "troubled," as "attention seeking," and because racists will use any opportunity to fly their flag of hatred, many other things Aṅuṛi would see on the backs of her eyelids even after she logged off. It didn't take long for Christian to toss his phone onto the rug at his feet.

"This is foul," he said. "It's basically a cult."

Loki glanced at Aṅuṛi. "Let's stop looking now. Aṅuṛi? It's done for now, okay?"

He and Simi left to procure dessert from the gelato shop and Christian tried to commit to memory the sight of Aṅuṛi in her oversized Snoopy sweatshirt, her toes painted a pinkish-nude color, the sunlight sparking off the copper in her hair.

She moved to Simi's laptop and when Christian summoned the courage to walk over and peer over her shoulder, he saw she was looking at estate agent listings. Ivy-covered period buildings in Ealing.

"You're moving?"

"Nobody thinks I can do it—be a good mum." It was like she was talking to herself. Like she had forgotten he was still in the room with her.

"Have we discussed kids?" he joked.

She smiled a smile that moved toward her eyes but gave up halfway. "I know I'm a mess. But who isn't?"

He slid down to the floor beside her. "Anụrị—" he said, his voice soft "—help me catch up."

"Noelle," she said. "I want to find a place where we can just be. Nobody thinks I can look after her properly. But I have to try. You've seen it now, what she's got to deal with. I have to do something."

Christian nodded. "Because nobody could do anything for you."

She cried then, quietly, because this was still new and he could still be scared away. He held her hand and waited. "God. Sorry. How embarrassing."

"What? Crying? Nah. I cried yesterday when I finished watching *Scenes from a Marriage*. I hated it that much."

"I don't want to be a mess that someone else has to clean up."

He kept her hand in his. "I don't know them like that so I could have this wrong, but you have your friends. And I don't think you're just a mess to them. You've had them so long and not in that fucked-up way where history makes it too hard to leave. You guys keep choosing each other. Day after day, year after year. A lot of people don't get to have that. Messiness aside, you're special to them." He cleared his throat. "Besides, I actually wouldn't mind cleaning you up from time to time."

He was nervous. She saw it in the way his eyes wandered over their intertwined fingers but not to her face. "Remember when I asked if you wanted to kiss me?"

"Oh no. I don't remember that at all."

"Let's call a do-over."

"God, Anụrị, are you coming on to me?"

So much hangs on a first kiss but Aṅụrị did not give herself time to get worked up about the prospect of excess saliva, the clashing of teeth or the age-old conundrum of what to do with your tongue. What she would think about (again and again and again) was how soft Christian's lips were, the way he kept holding her hand throughout and even when they broke apart, and those canines up close. She rested her head on his shoulder and they stayed that way until Loki and Simi returned with the gelato.

Aṅụrị felt cosseted by their presence. The storm raged on in a thousand comment sections, but she could choose when and what to look at. She could turn off her phone and instead laugh at Loki calling Simi "fiddler on the roof." She was able to glance away shyly when her eyes wandered to Christian and found him already looking at her. She was able to divide her concern between them. They were all willing participants in her lived experience. There was no complaint and there was an absence of judgement. Aṅụrị had always been able to scare them but was yet to shock them. And it was because of all of these wonderful realities that she chose, that night, to tell them about her paypigs. They actively discouraged her from taking LowlyWorm up on his offer, but aside from that, their reactions were pleasantly neutral.

Loki said, "You can never call me a deviant again, chère."

Simi said, "You mean I've been insulting men for free all this time like a dickhead?"

Christian said, "Does this mean I'll be a kept man?"

Aṅụrị chuckled. "Am I still a 6.75?"

"Today you've earned an 8.25."

Later, as they washed and dried dishes, Loki eased a plate from Aṅụrị's soapy hands and said, "This paypig thing. You… what you're doing…are you…is it safe?"

Aṅụrị turned to look at him. Her tenderhearted Loki. He had disguised his concern until such a time came where he could reveal it to her away from the eyes and ears of others.

"It is, Lo. I never actually *meet* them."

"And it doesn't make you feel…do you *enjoy* it?"

"It's a job." Anụrị would eventually tell him about the catharsis, but for now, she gifted him reassurance. "I'm okay. I promise."

Loki nodded and dried the plate. "And if you ever stop being okay—"

"I'll tell you." Anụrị wiped her hands so she could wrap her arms around him. "And I'll stop."

"Okay," Loki breathed. "Okay."

He waited for two hours, but when Ophelia did not come to bed, Nkem rose and went to find her. Downstairs in the TV-less living room, Ophelia lifted her head only a fraction at the sound of Nkem's feet on the floorboards.

"Did you do it?" he asked.

"Hmm? Do what, my love?" One of the lesser Kardashians had left a comment on her last Instagram post telling her she was inspirational.

"Ophelia."

She looked up then. He did not call her by her name. It had been years, decades. "What is it?"

"Did you tell them to leak the news? About Anụrị and the lawsuit?"

Dread hardened like concrete in her belly. "Nkem, no. You know I wouldn't."

"We don't do this. Personal business, *family* business is not for them."

Even as he said it, Nkem knew how useless the words were, how much of a lie. Their lives were built on the exposition of personal business, of family business. The boundaries could not be crossed because they never existed. It was difficult to make right what had never been so.

"Nkem, I said no. I said I didn't do it."

He had already turned away.

FOURTEEN

Because Céleste Llorens (soon to be Llorens-Scott) knew with the certainty of a woman who has tasted the peace of romantic solitude and also the joy of platonic kinship that this next marriage would be her last, she convinced her fiancé that they should marry discreetly at the Algiers Courthouse in New Orleans before fulfilling their civic duty as persons of note and throwing an extravagant bash in London thereby furnishing their high-profile guests, multiple fashion houses and several glossy magazine editors with enough fodder to satisfy their desire to be seen, photographed and inserted into the pages of newspapers, magazines and entertainment write-ups alike. Céleste left the bulk of the organization to a revered planner called Kym (no last name), known for her avant-garde centerpieces and the unsubstantiated rumor that she only consumed green and yellow foods. In New Orleans, Céleste wore a bespoke jumpsuit in a delicate shade of champagne, and in London, she yielded to Kym's insistence that she "exit singledom with panache" and agreed to an outfit change midway through the reception which was to be held at Soane Hall.

It was Aṅụrị's first public outing since the furor and what

luck that it was to be amidst people who thrived on gossip, scandal, Schiaparelli and camera flashes. She did not do well in crowds; Simi and Loki were where her otherness was the least pronounced. In the days leading up to it, sleep proved elusive and what snatches of slumber she did manage to grab were riddled by bizarre nightmares which left her shaken, sweaty and dry-mouthed. She composed lengthy apologies detailing why she couldn't attend and texted them to Loki. His response was always the same: Rejected—go and buy a dress.

"Omo, I know it's like, the worst possible time," Simi said after they spent yet another afternoon pinging back and forth links to sale finds on Net-a-Porter, "but can't you break into Ophelia's wardrobe and steal something for us both?"

"Sim, what makes you think you can fit that yansh into anything Ophelia owns?"

"You think I no get tailor? My mum has someone in Dagenham. Uncle will ask you if your outfit brings glory to God, but he'll still sort you out."

"Are you bringing Abe?"

"Undecided. I have to go. Lemme know if you find anything."

In the end, it was her aunt who provided Aṅụrị and Simi with inspiration. While Nneoma critiqued Simi's latest attempt at assorted meat pepper soup from her chair, Aṅụrị finished up her aunt's braided bun and complained about the dearth of outfit options available to them for such an event.

"It's as if the two of you have forgotten you're Nigerian. Instead of you—" she pointed to Simi "—to tie gele, and you—" she rounded on Aṅụrị "—to tie ichafu and wear coral, you're telling me you have nothing to wear."

So in the end, Uncle in Dagenham was called upon and, after he had pointed out that hurrying a man of his age did not bring glory to God, he allowed himself to be bribed by attention, a plate of meat pies and an additional one hundred pounds for a rush job. Aṅụrị chose green, remembering—a warmth rising in her cheeks—that someone once told her it was her color. That same someone nodded amicably on FaceTime when Aṅụrị informed him that he had been replaced by Simi as Aṅụrị's date to the reception. Abe, according to Simi, was unavailable—a podiatry issue involving his roommate for which he needed to provide taxi and fetching and carrying services—and Aṅụrị, citing the hallowed pact of sisters before misters, said it was no problem. Simi's mother tied her daughter's gele, pinning it so expertly, Simi could lift the finished product from her head and transport it with care to Aṅụrị's flat.

At Soane Hall, Simi was ushered onto a central platform bathed in soft light where she played Bach's *Ave Maria* and *Air for G String* to a rapt audience. She stepped down to rapturous applause which she accepted with brief repeated nods around the room. Aṅụrị felt her head might inflate and float from her shoulders with pride. When Simi finally reached Aṅụrị's side, they were greeted by an impeccably behaved white peacock and offered some sort of chicken canapé topped with gold leaf, and, after that, they were absorbed into the throng of beautiful people, stopping here and there to answer questions about Simi's performance and about their outfits from interested parties.

"Actually, it's an Okunlola original," Simi drawled to a blonde in McQueen. "No, no, you wouldn't have heard of him. He only takes bespoke orders."

It was a stunning affair. Kym had worked her magic and the hall was no longer a hall but an enchanted forest with its own imported weeping cherry trees and white-barked Himalayan birches. Foliage was strung strategically around the lighting and the centerpieces were elaborate constructions of crystals and flowers, chosen because they released their scent at night. The room was fragrant with star jasmine, petunia and honeysuckle. They spied Loki gliding between groups, his locs in the rope twists Aṅụrị had done for him a couple of days prior to the event. His suit, a hunter green Ozwald Boateng was tailored so expertly, it was as if he was born into it and it had grown along with him. He was a sight to behold, his smile never shifting, always knowing when to touch an arm, slap a back or drop a kiss against a powdered cheek. Aṅụrị was seized with the urge to run to him and envelope him in her arms. It was a gift to love someone and watch them become the person time, circumstance and environment willed them to be.

Simi watched Aṅụrị watching Loki and lifted another pomegranate fizz from a passing tray. There were times when her best friend's beauty was almost an assault and was best viewed from a little distance, with a little protection, like using a pinhole camera to view an eclipse. Tonight was an example. Aṅụrị in her jeweled, fitted wrapper and ichafu, her shoulders bare, her eyelids two streaks of green glitter, was turning heads and drawing unabashed looks of wonder. Not that she noticed. Crowds sucked the brightness from Aṅụrị; parties simply highlighted the ways in which she was not able to indulge as a normal twentysomething should. The tension in her shoulders would not abate until it was time to leave and there would be no more opportunity for someone to mention her stepmother, her decisions, her deficiencies. In a room full of alcohol, Aṅụrị was confined to mocktails and soft drinks, and this, a time of celebration, would serve only to emphasize her failure to moderate herself. One never felt more sober than in a room of the increasingly inebriated. Simi fought the urge to hug her friend; she would not want it, would not like to be reminded of her differences. Instead, she handed Aṅụrị the pomegranate fizz and registered Aṅụrị's face fall.

"What's wrong?"

"I— Sim, you don't have to be teetotal tonight." Aṅụrị painted a smile on her face. "It's a party and you're not paying! You should absolutely get shitfaced." It was one thing to deprive herself out of necessity, but it was quite another to inflict that same denial on her best friend.

"Please. I know how to have a good time without getting drunk."

"Yeah. But, Simi."

"And I have to get home tonight! Imagine getting in and having Mum sigh and say, 'Simisola, is what you're doing a reflection of the Most High?' I'm good, babe."

Aṅụrị pursed her lips. "You're staying at mine." She stopped a passing server and ascertained that his tray contained caipirinhas. "Here, drink. No arguments."

"Aṅụrị, are you—"

"Just drink! We're celebrating Céleste's ability to attract wealthy, beautiful men, and nobody asking me about Ophelia. So far." She clinked her mocktail against Simi's glass and smiled when Simi, after hesitating, took a sip from her glass.

Céleste's speech, one expounding the virtues of nonromantic soulmates as she toasted her best friends, called on the need for cultivating a life full of soft moments and encouraging those whom if determined to partner, to find someone who was above all kind (here, she turned to stroke the cheek of her new husband), left everyone in the room moist-eyed and sentimental.

"My one true love, of course, remains my darling son," she said before she took her seat. "Loki, my darling, you are not only mine but your own greatest achievement. I could extol your virtues all night. I love you, zanj."

"That was so gorgeous." Aṅụrị left half-moons of green glitter on her heavy cloth napkin.

Simi, on her third cocktail and loosening by the second, nodded and threw her arm out, gesturing to the woman to their left who was helping her husband back to his feet after an unfruitful attempt to locate a lost diamond earring beneath the table. *Don't worry*, the husband said, *I'll buy you another pair as soon as we're back in Paris*.

"God, look at this," Simi said. "The opulence. I wonder what it's like to live like this. Perhaps we should give LowlySlug a call, after all."

"It's worm. Lowly*Worm*."

"Worm. Slug. Who cares? I still can't believe you were doing that all this time. Anyway, call him up and tell him you'll take the money so we can get our own pear-shaped diamonds."

Anụrị looked again at Loki who was beaming as his mother kissed both of his cheeks. "Money is so fucking weird. It makes some people go nuts and then it has no effect on others. Like Loki."

"We only know Loki with money," Simi pointed out. "He could be a complete prick without it." She watched him kneel to help an older lady back into her shoe. She smiled. "But I doubt it. Ah crap, Abe is calling."

"Answer it."

"He can wait."

"You just heard Céleste tell us to find someone kind. Abe brought you Tesco's finest brioche loaf because you were PMSing. Answer the phone."

Simi canceled the call and drained the remainder of her cocktail. "I'll call him back."

"Did he even have a podiatry incident today? Sim? You look so fine tonight and what you played up there for Céleste was one of the most beautiful things I've ever heard. Why *wouldn't* you want Abe to see that?"

"Did I tell you an agent gave me his card? We're having a call in a couple of—" Abe was calling again.

"Answer the phone, Simi."

Loki found Anụrị alone picking gold leaf from a blini. He looped his arms around her and lifted her off her feet. She smelled like a rainforest post downpour if it had been dabbed delicately with oud. He felt he could take a bite out of her.

"You look gorgeous," he told her.

With his face an open door revealing nothing but delight,

Anụrị, for the millionth time, understood just how and why Loki would forever be batting off suitors. She felt like she had trudged through a hundred wars and looked it, while Loki was unchanged. Beatific as ever. She rose to her tiptoes and kissed his cheek. "So do you. And so does Céleste, and all of this."

They looked on as Céleste's husband deftly removed her empty glass from her hand and replaced it with a full one, all while Céleste was in conversation with a guest. She paused, turned to him and he pressed her free hand to his lips. It was the kind of moment that made witnesses feel like they should avert their eyes. Sometimes we have no idea on which shelf to place intimacy that is not ours. Anụrị turned to Loki and found his face wet.

"Lo? Are you crying?"

But Loki made no move to wipe his face. His tears splashed onto his suit and darkened the green of the trees to a forest floor. "Look at them," he said. "They're actually in love."

"Looks like it." Anụrị bit her lip. "That's good, right?"

"I guess maybe because of all the crap with the prenup and just… I guess I thought her and Remy might end up back together, after all. But I think that's a wrap. Yeah. That's probably why he isn't here. My dad. I think he knows it, too."

"Babe, it might also be because you don't generally invite your ex-husband to your wedding."

"He sent flowers, you know. But I hid them from her." Loki brushed his hand under his eyes. "It's like a tower of peonies and roses and delphinium. You want it? I can have it couriered to the flat."

Anụrị squeezed his hand. "You okay, Lo?"

He squeezed back. "I'm good. She deserves this. These are happy tears. Her outfits and jewelry were gifted." Loki shook his head. "I will never understand how the people who need things the least are given the most. And often for free."

"I mean yeah," Anụrị said. "Look at Ophelia."

Upon reflection, Loki would hazard that his impulsivity reaped positive results perhaps only thirty to forty percent of the time. The problem was that it was as much part of him as the dimple he inherited from his father and his ambidexterity. He reasoned, after the fact, that there really was no perfect time to tell her but still he hesitated. He wanted to take her hand and run with her to some impenetrable place where she would be safe from prying eyes and free from the demands of celebrity. He took a breath and squeezed her hand again.

"Speaking of, look, let's step out for a second." He led her into the foyer. The white peacock had been spirited away. "I wanted to fly back when the news broke."

Aṅụrị, distracted by a sudden breeze that swept through the doors and swirled around her ankles, and by the realization that Simi was yet to return, shook her head. "What? No. You got there as soon as you could."

"It's just, Ṅụrị, I need you to look at me. It's just I was delayed because there was something I had to get. Something for you."

"Are we doing gifts?" Aṅụrị was looking at him then, excitement and surprise jockeying for position on her face. "I didn't know!"

"No, it's not… Look. I know this guy, okay we dated briefly until I started crushing on his sister which in my defense is because she's probably my future ex-wife—"

"Loki?"

He fixed his eyes on her and ushered in yet another Before and After.

There are influencers, online celebrities, and there are their fans; sometimes legions of them who form varying degrees of attachment on occasion to the people but more likely to the lifestyle the people present to them. And because there are fans, it stands to reason that there exist the opposite—the anti-fans; those hooked not on the rush that comes with seeing a tropical getaway or the dopamine stemming from imagining themselves doing the same, but who are obsessed with picking apart, for whatever reasons, the lives, the lies, the choices polished to an enviable sheen and proffered to the masses for consumption. You could take a left on your online travels and end up in shadier parts of the web, forums so rife with vitriol the creators needed to set up and fund their own servers because the rage was not permitted on places like Reddit or anywhere with even the most lax terms of service. One such forum, the name of which hardly matters in the grand, ceaseless torrent that is the internet, came to Loki's attention during pillow talk. His companion at the time, the sister of the dude—a Cirque du Soleil understudy whose flexibility would have been criminal to ignore—watched Loki blow weed smoke toward her ceiling, and listened to him lamenting over his ineptness, his failure to find a way to, if not comfort his best friend, then to at least help her as she was figuratively battered by this new onslaught of unwanted attention brought about by Penelope and her article.

Ms. Soleil retrieved the joint from Loki's fingers and said, "I feel for her. You know her mom is on The Gossip Alley all the time. She's like, a fave on there." Thus followed a confusing explanation of what The Gossip Alley was, and after Loki moved through shock and into incredulity, Ms. Soleil lifted one toned leg and tucked it neatly behind her head. A conundrum. There was more information to glean, but Loki was also a young man and who knew when again he would encounter someone so adept in showcasing their double-jointedness. Afterward, Loki scorched Ms. Soleil's best pan trying to make ramen, realizing only as his eyes began to sting with tears that he had smoked way too much. To her credit, she made him chamomile tea and, as she shimmied into her jeans, said, "I hope your friend's okay. Must be weird to be the kid of someone who's basically responsible for your pics ending up on the dark web." In the hours that followed where Loki pushed determinedly through revulsion, horror, anger and sadness all while bent over his MacBook back at his father's Manhattan residence, he was able to ascertain the following:

1. There was indeed an entire subforum about Ophelia and her exploits. It numbered in the thousands of pages.

2. Several hundred posts had in fact been dedicated to the revelation that the photos of Ophelia's daughter had turned up on not one but two websites which ended up as part of a targeted takedown by authorities.

3. The daughter in question was actually Noelle and not Aṅuri.

Loki did not ask Remy for much. But this time he sought out his dad in his study, and Remy, seeing the expression on his son's face, paid attention. By the end of the following day, Loki knew that the information on the forum was accurate, and that apparently, the families of the children were informed at the time. Loki also knew he would have to tell Aṅuri and that it would break her in fresh and perhaps irreversible ways. To suspect that your kid sister was the target of the depraved is one thing, to reckon with proof was another. To recognize that your parents have chosen inaction in the face of such revelations was unconscionable. Who knew how many anonymous users had shared and downloaded the photos?

He'd held Aṅuri a thousand times, picked her up and carried her in a variety of beautiful and devastating circumstances, and she had always felt small in his arms or against his back as he ran them toward the ocean or laid her gingerly in her bed after an episode of overindulgence. He knew when his steadiness and his size were required, and so when he stopped talking and Aṅuri's knees buckled, Loki carried her to one of the sofas in the lobby and settled her against him, reminding her to breathe. That is how Simi found them.

"I don't get why this is even a question," Simi said, her voice cutting through the darkness of Anụrị's bedroom. "You have to tell your dad."

It was not yet three in the morning and minutes earlier Loki had finally let himself into the flat. It had taken him hours after he'd put Anụrị and Simi into an Uber to extricate himself. It was his mother's wedding and there were still gifts to corral and transport to Mayfair, Céleste to hug and send on her way first to Monte Carlo and then Fiji to honeymoon with her husband. On arrival, he'd clicked on the bedroom light and seen Simi and Anụrị in T-shirts, their faces still lovely in makeup that was only now beginning to smudge so he felt like he was looking at a blurred photograph, and had quickly clicked it off again when Simi protested. He now lay across the foot of the bed, Simi's feet kneading his lower back, Anụrị's pinkie in his hand.

"It's not that simple," he said. Sleep was creeping up on him. "He might already know."

"He doesn't," Anụrị said with a vehemence that surprised even herself. "He can't. There's no way he'd know something like that and just let things carry on as they are. Even Nkem has a line. I think. I hope."

"But," Loki reminded her, "the authorities contacted the families. Nkem is Nell's dad, right? There could be a chance he knows."

"So then if he knows then it's not like Anụrị would be breaking any news. All the more reason to call him up now and sing like Mariah."

"Chill, Simi, I'm not fighting you. It's a shitty situation is all, and we should probably approach it carefully." The last word was nearly swallowed by a yawn.

Anụrị let the bickering wash over her. Not long after that, she noticed silence had descended in the room. Loki and Simi were asleep. She rubbed her eyes, ran her hands up and down her arms just to make sure she was real, a person still moored to the earth and yet again experiencing a new and awful thing with which she must decide what to do. This, the knowledge of Noelle appearing with other innocent kids on such a website, now permeated everything like a room besieged by damp or a morning mist, the kind that passed unbidden through your clothes and chilled you to the bone. Not for the first time, she listened to the sound of Loki and Simi breathing and felt a visceral yearning for a new set of problems; ones that made sense to her, ones that didn't rob her of sleep and peace, and yawn in front of her, ripe with the power to completely devastate not just her own life but that of others she loved. What wouldn't she give for the extent of her issues to be limited to the mundane—how to rinse red wine from a shirt or how best to organize transport to an airport so she might make a flight at an ungodly hour? Simi shifted in her sleep and brought Aṅụrị back to her bedroom and to the fact that other people's problems often seemed less cumbersome simply because they were that: other people's. She knew this and also knew with a certainty that turned her stomach that neither Simi nor Loki would swap their positions for hers. She rolled onto her side and noted again the deep loathing she felt for herself and her inconsistency as it pertained to decisiveness.

And so it was that just as the sun began to haul itself into the sky, Aṅụrị slipped from her bedroom and, remnants of Before still streaked across her eyelids, she made her way to her aunt's house. Nneoma took one look at her niece and swallowed her admonishments. Yes it was dawn, and yes it was becoming more difficult to pull herself from bed in the mornings or the evenings, but she could not look at Aṅụrị and see the anguish stamped on her face and not let her trudge past her into the kitchen; Nneoma could not deny Aṅụrị the space to make tea not because either of them wanted the drink but because Aṅụrị required a task and the time to summon the words she had come there to speak. Nneoma sat at the table and, when Aṅụrị brought the mugs, she tapped against her braided bun to quell the itch that prickled her scalp. And she watched this adult who was still a child sit astride the fence that separated what was with what could be. She reached for Aṅụrị's hand.

"Whatever it is, it is not the end of you," Nneoma said.

And Aṅụrị spoke, having already decided to leave the details back in her bedroom but offering enough to convey the gravity of her dilemma. Lives would change, she said, definitely hers and Noelle's but ultimately there would not be a soul within their familial circumference who would not be affected in some way. She said all this while gripping Nneoma's hand as if it were a lifeline; as if it were the only thing keeping her from sinking to the bottom of a depth so complete it was impenetrable by light.

Nneoma said: "You won't like what I have to say."

Nneoma said: "I will say it anyway because I am usually right."

Nneoma said: "I can't tell you what to do. You have fought to be your own person and you have nearly won."

Nneoma said: "If there is nothing forcing you to decide today, then take some more time. You came here and you haven't even bathed. It's love that even allowed me to open the door for you."

Nneoma said: "Remember that not all things can be unmade."

And Nneoma said: "It's also fine not to take my word. Isn't there an oyinbo woman you pay to give you advice?"

Aṅụrị laughed even as her throat closed and she said: "She isn't oyinbo."

Nneoma rose so she might hug her niece and inhale the scent of her even in her unwashed state. "Eh hehn," she said. "So, she can probably instruct you further."

Ammah *was* able to instruct further, but only in that roundabout and sometimes infuriating way therapists have where instructions are not explicit but rather are couched in language like "guidelines" and "reminders"; where it feels like a person is trying to exit a maze with only a distant light for guidance. Anụrị, who had showered at her aunt's house and waited until a decent hour before texting Ammah SOS and immediately following it up with a second text that said *OK exaggeration.* Not physical harm SOS but spiraling SOS, sat before Ammah and once again set out her conundrum in a way designed to obfuscate the details but present a broader picture: she had potentially incendiary information, it might destroy any number of relationship dynamics, she did not know how she would pick her way through the aftermath should that be the case. It occurred to her as she shredded Kleenex in her lap, that having now been presented with the tools she required to both exact her revenge and liberate her sister, she found herself devoid of the elation and satisfaction she anticipated. It was like biting into an aesthetically pleasing pastry and finding it stale and tasteless—where was the pleasure, she bemoaned? A pyrrhic victory. And Ammah, ever the professional, only proffered the wastebasket for the shredded Kleenex and said that revenge was not always sweet.

Ammah also said: "It isn't for me to tell you what to do."

Ammah said: "The work you've been doing means that you can now make decisions by yourself. Even when the situation seems impossible."

Ammah said: "I think you already know, as you mentioned, that it's the hypothetical consequences you're struggling with."

Anụrị asked then, if she might lie on the floor, and Ammah nodded once, adding that she should do whatever ("within reason, Anụrị") would help her in that moment. The floor was cool and solid beneath Anụrị, and there were no cracks in Ammah's ceiling, but there was a single cobweb suspended from the brass light fixture and wafting gently, moved as it was by a draft Anụrị could not feel.

"I just wish I knew how it'd pan out," she told the cobweb.

"You've said before that certainty provides you with comfort. We've spoken about how that isn't uncommon," Ammah said.

"Yeah. We also said that maybe I shouldn't make decisions while highly emotional and distressed. I'm kind of both right now. Also sleep-deprived."

"It's not a decision for today," Ammah said, "but we also spoke about how emotions can often be a good barometer for your version of morality."

"You have a cobweb on your light."

Ammah looked up. "So I do."

"I'm going to tell him." Only as she said it, did Aṅụrị's conviction resurrect itself. "But I'll give Ophelia the chance to tell him first."

Ammah gazed down at Aṅụrị. There was no scenario where hugging her would be appropriate, and so Ammah drew a single, minute heart in the top right corner of her open notebook. "I think that's very admirable."

"If this goes to shit, I will camp out on this office floor."

Ammah laughed. "Noted," she said. "Noted."

FIFTEEN

Ophelia would begin her week with a private Pilates lesson and an aloe facial, and end it with a Sword of Damocles hanging above her head—situations so perfect for the satiation of online appetites, it felt like a new kind of cruelty invented solely for her; an irony so pungent it all but singed her. Hers had been an interesting week. She received reminders from her holistic wellness coach that it was important to remain kind to oneself in the midst of turmoil—"We must extend latitude to ourselves when it counts most, Ophelia"—and reasoned that "latitude" was open to interpretation. Thus perusing Harrods food hall counted. As did banishing Nkem from their bedroom one evening so she could work her way through one sleeve of Oreos and then another. The ruckus around the revelation of the lawsuit was beginning to recede and whilst the details remained concealed, there were still one or two reporters (dogged stragglers determined to make names for themselves) sniffing around and angling for statements or better yet, exclusives. Nkem did not mention the leak again, but something between the two of them had shifted. She felt his eyes on her as she dressed in the mornings, and not in the way of his that was leaden with adoration. When she turned and met his eye, his gaze would slide away from her and he would retreat to another part of the room or leave altogether. He now insisted they ferry Noelle to school themselves ("Both of us, Ophie") and what could she say? She rearranged meetings and found she enjoyed the car ride where Noelle sang in the back seat and Nkem smiled at them both and forgot his suspicions long enough to reach across the console and hold her hand.

Post facial, Ophelia's movements were glacial. She floated on a cloud of calm brought about by clean pores and a limber body. Yes, the problems still existed but right now, it was as though they existed in a separate realm, like a philanderer's second family installed in a distinct abode, awaiting his return; his attention. Her new problem was in the process of being stitched together so it might be presented to her in the most impactful of ways. Ophelia should have learned that Aṅụrị's predilection for comeuppance had only lain dormant. The dam had been broken.

Loki's suggestion was to have Simi contact Ophelia posing as a potential sponsor and organize a meeting at which Aṅụrị would reveal herself and deliver the news like a cartoon villain. Simi, leafing through the latest copy of *Architectural Digest*, deadpanned that there was no need to behave as if they were in an episode of *Scooby Doo*—Aṅụrị should simply call and ask to have a chat. Aṅụrị, riddled with nerves that manifested in a mild stomachache and the inability to sleep more than thirty minutes at a time, said she would think over both options. She felt like her skull had been filled with quick-setting cement. She tossed and turned that night, having reassured both Loki and Simi that she was fine, that all she needed was some uninterrupted sleep, and she tried not to bristle when she saw their concerned looks; fatigue and frustration making her ungenerous.

"I won't drink or anything like that. I *promise*. I'm just gonna go to bed."

In the ensuing silence of the flat, she watched the holographic clock which beamed the time softly onto her bedroom ceiling and then, because she was too weary to feel shame, she texted Christian.

Chidili. You asleep?

He called less than a second later.

"I want to be angry with you," he said when she picked up. "Nah, I *am* angry. But it's not sticking like I want it to. Where've you been at?"

Ah. There was the shame. Thick and bitter and coating her tongue. "I'm sorry."

"The thing is, I know I dropped off the radar on you before, so my anger is that of a hypocrite, but here I am, in my feelings."

"Can I bring you out of your feelings?" She liked talking to him in the dark, knowing he was somewhere not too far away, probably also in bed, his locs secured away from his face, his lips soft from the final nighttime application of Clip balm.

"I hope not. I'm kind of made of them. Are you good?"

"I don't think so," she said and told him her tale.

"I don't know what to say," he said when she was done. "Actually, scratch that. I totally do. 'Kpee ọbọ ife mèlù gị.' Was that helpful?"

"You telling me take revenge?" Aṅụrị chuckled. "Yeah, it was, actually. And, Christian, I really am sorry. It's been a bit crap lately."

"We're going to make mistakes here, Aṅụrị. But I want us to at least give ourselves a chance. A proper one. Can you think about that?"

"If I don't, how many days will you keep trying?"

She heard him shift, perhaps rearrange his duvet, then she heard him chuckle. "It's gone up to two weeks. I really need to find shame. Good night."

* * *

The longer Aṅụrị ruminated, the more daunting the task became. Carrying the knowledge around unaddressed was like dragging an anvil behind her; like wearing a coat suffused with a smell that refused to wash out. It was all-consuming and chased out every other thought and threw ash on every other activity that might be enjoyable. In the end Aṅụrị chose the path of least resistance which was the one that led her to the house when she knew Noelle would be at school and Nkem at work. There was no need for an audience and although she couldn't be sure Ophelia would be in the house alone—the publicist, accountant, personal trainer or any other of the paid procession of people she kept around her might be dropping in—the last of the energy Aṅụrị reserved for avoidance was spent.

Ophelia opened the door and failed to conceal her surprise for ten long seconds at the sight of Aṅụrị standing, key still in hand, having decided at the very last second that letting herself into the house would likely be inadvisable given the objective of her visit.

Ophelia only briefly took in Aṅụrị's outfit: a striped men's oxford shirt, sleeves rolled up to the elbows, and a pair of jeans, washed and worn so often there remained only a suggestion of the original stonewash blue. She did, however, drink in the rest of Aṅụrị—had she lost weight? Why had she not even bothered with concealer to obscure the shadows beneath her eyes? Why, despite the lack of concealer, was it that youth had a way of blurring imperfections? Aṅụrị looked exhausted, but she also looked radiant.

"Nkem and Noelle aren't here," Ophelia said and was immediately pincered by sadness. A sadness born of knowing there could be no good reason Aṅụrị would visit in the middle of the afternoon; of knowing that she had not really been robbed of a friendship with this woman she raised but had surrendered it willingly. There was nobody else to blame for the gulf that existed between them, and accountability only becomes palatable after it has already stamped its sourness on you. In another life, she could kiss Aṅụrị's face and escort her inside.

But Ophelia did not live another life. There was only this one flush as it was with both triumphs, and personal and inescapable disasters. She kept one hand on the door, but the other twisted the hem of her shirt into a curlicue.

"Yeah, I know. I'm actually... I wanted..." Aṅụrị channeled Makuo—*nyìe ọtọo, stand up*—and straightened her shoulders. "I'm here to talk to you about something."

Alarm spread across Ophelia's face, altering her features as it went, like a bottle of spilled ink. "Look, Aṅụrị, if this is about the press, I—"

"It's not." Aṅụrị was already stepping past Ophelia and into the entrance hall, willing herself not to be moved by the familiarity of the place she used to call home. A pair of Noelle's shoes sat by a discarded swim bag. The air was scented with vanilla and rose. Somewhere in the house, the muted sound of television chatter. She stood and waited and finally, when Ophelia mumbled something about them sitting in the sunroom, Aṅụrị slipped off her blue sandals and followed her.

It wasn't as if she wasn't adept at confrontation; indeed she could have written the book on new and inventive ways to do it, but Aṅụrị didn't like that she could not control how certain varieties of it made her feel—exposed and raw, and, inexplicably, like a fraud. Like someone could fling open a door into her mind and find a minute version of herself flattened against the far wall, trembling and useless. And there was nothing to do but launch into it, the revelation, because what small talk could they possibly make at a time like this? It was not so much ripping off the Band-Aid as snipping off an entire limb in one excruciating motion.

For Ophelia, there was something about how Aṅụrị sat on the very edge of the wicker chair in that sunroom that dictated she should go ahead and memorize the elegant jut of Anụrị's cheekbones and the length of her fingers, each one adorned with a slim gold ring. Finalities don't always announce themselves, and even if they do, it is usually luck that determines if we are paying enough attention to register the warning. So, Anụrị's words did not land at first. Every time Ophelia saw her, there was something new or changed to observe. And it was in the observing Ophelia lost herself.

"Did you hear me?" Anụrị frowned.

"I—" What use in lying? "No, I'm sorry. I didn't. What did you say?"

Anụrị would look back on the encounter and the thing that would stick out the most was the shades through which Ophelia traveled. A veritable rainbow of emotion cataloged by the transition from peachy pink to a pale, milky cream and then the splotches of red blooming first on the chest and then moving upward over the neck before claiming the face in its entirety. Then came the greenish tinge before a sort of grayness settled in. She would also remember how there wasn't even the attempt at a denial. Ophelia, it seemed, was aware of the existence of The Gossip Alley but took great pains to avoid it as she traversed the internet; masochism being outside her frame of reference. Who *sought out* that designed to denigrate you? Not she. She knew of the site but knew nothing of the comprehensiveness of the content there.

And wasn't that part of the problem, Anụrị thought bitterly, the assumption that it was solely her own deeds Ophelia deemed admirable and worthy of the allotments of time and energy. No, it wouldn't have been pleasant for her to see what was written on the site, but one could argue, it was necessary. Maybe then she would understand how much these outsiders knew about their lives; how invested they were in unmasking what they believed was deliberate obfuscation. Ophelia should have been aware that she was not the only one beaten with the stick of diligence, but she had made a decision to close the door on reality.

Aṅụrị waited, and still, *still*, she felt no pleasure and this, the lack of gratification, made her hot with anger.

"Does my dad know?" she all but hissed. But there was no need for words. Ophelia's stricken face was all the answer Aṅụrị needed. "Why? Why wouldn't you tell him?" A rhetorical question but one she would repeat until Ophelia answered.

When Aṅụrị was three years old, a fan turned stalker tried to steal her from the playground she and Ophelia frequented. There were two things Ophelia remembered most about the incident: the first was the icy panic she felt when she looked away from the other mums assembled on the bench by the sandpit and saw that Aṅụrị was no longer pointing at flowers with the redheaded little girl. Her dungarees and afro puff were nowhere in sight. The second was the thought she'd had at the police station later that day, after the stalker—a middle-aged doughy woman who hadn't even made it out of the park without being waylaid, had been arrested. Aṅụrị was crying, terrified by the desperate way Ophelia was pressing her to her chest, confused by Ophelia's sobs which took the best part of an hour to abate; and Ophelia was thinking, *Do I have to tell Nkem? He wouldn't understand.* She had told him. And he had done his best to understand. And they had learned. Security became paramount. The park was abandoned until they moved to Swiss Cottage and found one inaccessible to nonresidents. This thing with Noelle was different. There could be no explaining it, and so Ophelia had not tried.

"I... It was..." Ophelia swallowed. "It was pretty much over by the time they let me know."

"Over?"

"The sites were in the process of being taken down. It was finished."

"It can never be finished. Her pictures were probably downloaded so many times. Don't you get that? Why wouldn't you think my dad had the right to know?"

The same sickness she felt the day Aṅụrị was taken roiled in Ophelia's belly. She had hoped to never feel it again, but it was simply awaiting the occasion for which it could once again surge. There *were* precautions she could have taken; alterations she could have made. But her fans responded to Noelle in the latest designer swimsuit. They loved it when she put on makeup and pretended she was "grown up like Mummy." If she changed her content so abruptly, Nkem would have asked questions she did not know how to answer.

"Nkem wouldn't have understood. There was no point."

"How come you think everyone is a dumbass except you?" It was not exactly what Aṅụrị planned to say but it did what it needed to do. There again, the redness rising in Ophelia's cheeks.

"Aṅụrị—"

"I don't actually get it. What the hell do you mean he 'wouldn't have understood'? What is there to misunderstand about something like that?" At times like this, civility was overrated. In fact, Aṅụrị thought, civility was what people like Ophelia depended on in order to shield themselves from their own shortcomings. It felt right to rip the curtain back and demand the truth.

Ophelia drew her shoulders back. She recovered enough to remember that she could defend herself even if she shouldn't. Outrage was an undisputed corrector of posture, no matter how guilty the accused. "Everything I do is for this family. You might not agree with it, but you don't get to come in here and talk to me like this. This is my house."

"Is it though?"

Ophelia held the question up to the light, examined it fleetingly, and decided there was too much there. There was no adequate response. Aṅụrị was not there for pleasantries. Ophelia realized she had spent years holding her breath, waiting for the blow that would finally defeat her. Endless storms weathered and now at last, she was careening toward the rocks. She had fought her way to the top only to be felled by someone who ought to be at her side, who *should* be grateful for the opportunities Ophelia's discernment afforded. Instead, she was being skewered in her own—or whatever—house. She flushed again, successfully peeved.

"What good would telling Nkem have done?" Ophelia said.

"What good?" Inside Aṅụrị's head, an uncomfortable thrumming started up. Soon, she would need to lie down. Her body had ceased protesting and was on its way to giving up. "It doesn't actually matter. You have to tell him now."

"Aṅụrị, you can't dictate what goes on between me and my husband."

"You're still not getting it. You *get* to tell him. Before I do, I mean. And I promise he won't be the only person I talk to about this. Apparently, this family is besties with the press now. We *love* cluing them in on sensitive matters."

When she was five, Ophelia taught Aṅụrị the importance of making eye contact with the camera. It was, she was told, so that the audience felt connected; that they felt brought into the experience. It also served as a method of imbuing significance to the words or actions being spoken or performed. There was not much Aṅụrị willingly retained from her time performing for Ophelia's followers, but there in the sunroom, she leveled her gaze at Ophelia and with it, summoned that which they both knew. Penelope.

Ophelia was the first to look away.

"It can't have been that bad, Aṅụrị," she said quietly. "Can it? Your life here, with us? Being online?"

Aṅụrị stood.

"You should have stopped when I told you it was."

She had almost made it to her sandals when Ophelia caught up with her. In the time it took Aṅụrị to reach the door, Ophelia had allowed herself the luxury of a few tears, the evidence turning the corner of her eyes and the very tip of her nose red. But there was no time for crying. The situation was not lost. Things could still be fixed. She'd raced into the entrance hall.

"What if I agree to your terms?"

Aṅụrị, stooping, shoe in hand, turned. "What?"

"The lawsuit. What if I say yes to everything you want removed? I can make one call. It can be over."

For me, Aṅụrị thought, *but not for Noelle*. She shook her head.

"Tell him," she said and left, sandals in hand before more could be said; before her resolve could disintegrate.

She didn't see Simi sitting outside the gate until she was almost tripping over her outstretched legs. "Sim? What are you doing here?"

Simi leapt to her feet, clutched Aṅụrị's shoulders and peered into her face. "You're alright? She didn't try to hit you, did she?"

"Why the hell would she try to hit me?"

"I work with influencers. I've seen what can happen when they're backed into a corner."

"No violence. I think she cried though. And offered to agree to the terms of my lawsuit if I kept my mouth shut. Simi, why aren't you at work?"

"I'm sick." Simi coughed pathetically into her fist.

"You're going to get fired."

"Oh no," Simi deadpanned. "How will I go on?"

The fact of Simi waiting for her outside the locked gates, knowing neither when nor how Aṅụrị would emerge, finally unfastened the stopper of Aṅụrị's sadness. She sagged in her friend's arms.

"It's okay," Simi said against the cinnamon-scented crook of Aṅụrị's neck. "I've got you. Let's go home."

They did. And finally, finally, Aṅụrị slept.

Simi lowered the volume and then put the call on speaker. She was in Aṅụrị's kitchen, littering the floor with scone crumbs, and breaking up with Abe. He protested and made some sounds about love, and Simi told him more forcefully than she intended, that he should not say it again; that her love was reserved for the sleeping, fretting woman in the other room, and that she would probably soon be unemployed and how would he explain that to his Yoruba parents? She was bowing out, she said, and then she was yelping because Aṅụrị's arrival into the kitchen was both swift and silent and Simi did not realize it until her phone was being plucked from her fingers.

"She will call you back, Abe. I promise you." Aṅụrị ended the call and turned to Simi, or rather to Simi's back as she had returned to the box of scones. "What are you doing, Simi?"

"Eating. Why don't you have any jam in this place?"

"Why are you using me as an excuse to break up with Abe?"

"I also used my probably imminent unemployment as a *reason*. A very valid *reason*."

"Simisola. Tell the truth and shame the devil."

"I just don't think it's going to work. That's all. He won't die."

"You don't actually know that."

"The dying part or the working out part?"

"Both." Aṅụrị eased the scone from Simi's hand. "What's going on?"

Simi sighed. "He's too nice."

"Sim, I'm not above striking you."

"I don't want you to feel abandoned!" Simi burst out.

Aṅụrị blinked. "Abandoned?"

"Like. Your dad is a wasteman and your stepmum is Beelzebub, and you're doing this all alone. I don't want you to feel like I'm one of those girls who gets a sniff of dick and leaves her best friend for dead. We said we're growing old together so why complicate things with boyfriends?"

And because Aṅụrị knew this was true but also knew that Simi was terrified and that terror stemmed from walking into the unknown, and that unknown was love, she deposited the scone back into its box, and dabbed Simi's face with the hem of her T-shirt.

"We *are* going to grow old together, weirdo. And I'm definitely not doing anything alone. I have you and Lo and my aunt, *and* my grandparents."

"And Christian," Simi said very quietly, gripping Aṅụrị's wrists.

"Okay. And Christian. You're not leaving me for dead. You're allowed to be happy. Abe is allowed to be on the compound."

"He can be in a separate compound. Like, the compound next door or something."

"Would that make you happy?"

"You make me happy."

"Would that make you *happier*?"

"I'm so proud of you for today. For always. But especially for today."

"Thank you, babe. Can you call Abe back now?"

Simi picked up the scone. "In a minute. Who die of waiting for a call back?"

OPHELIA

She was only fourteen, but the totality with which Aṅụrị withdrew from the life we had crafted so carefully left Nkem and me unmoored, which in turn drove us together, united as we were in our puzzlement and frustration. It was the sole solace—our unity. A terrible reality but one that brought us closer. With every slammed door, every act of defiance, every unearthed and empty can of cider, we presented each other with our despair knowing there was little to be said and even less to be done. We were moving in the dark, but always we found each other. It wasn't that we were ignorant of her anguish; we simply did not know how to right it without also shredding what we had worked to build. We, in what we considered our wisdom, would make casualties of us all.

What I wanted was reassurance that it wasn't my fault. I wanted to know that our girl had not fled because of something I did, and because he loves me, Nkem gave me that.

"It is not you," he told me, fatigue softening his voice. "She is her mother's child. Headstrong. Obstinate."

Sleep claimed him, but I remained awake, pain pulsing through me. It was not only what he said, casually confirming all I had spent the years since I met them fearing. It was how he said it: with pride.

SIXTEEN

There are levels in *Super Mario Odyssey* that take place mostly or even completely underwater. Reality is not suspended long enough to afford the tiny mustachioed plumber the ability to breathe underwater and so, whenever he dives beneath the surface, an indicator appears above his head showing how much oxygen he has left. Should that supply fully deplete, the inevitable happens. Slightly macabre for children to contemplate perhaps, but then they are usually distracted by the bright colors and the jaunty music. Were Anụrị a game character, a similar dial could be seen hovering above her head in the days following her visit with Ophelia. The longer the silence stretched, the emptier her reserves of both patience and hope became.

    She played through Zelda, collecting korok seeds; she repaired to her candle room and ended up crying because she ruined not one but two scent fusions she'd been working on for the better part of a month; and she made lengthy FaceTime calls to her grandparents who, not quite abreast of unfolding events, took turns to hold the phone at strange angles and try to distract Anụrị with stories of the mundanities of Onitsha life. They had taken on twelve new chickens and Arinze was already seized with buyer's remorse. Makuo was caught in the middle of a petty dispute between two longtime friends now at odds because of the perceived disparagement of a tray of peppered prawns. Only Makuo's forehead was visible on the screen of the phone.

"Miscommunication," her forehead sighed, "is the cause of too much strife."

That evening, Makuo joined Arinze at the window and the two of them watched the new chickens being corralled into their hutch.

"Ọ bụghị ya onwe ya," Arinze said, and Makuo could only nod because he was right. Aṅụrị was not herself at all.

Exasperation compounded the impotence and Aṅụrị once more took to scouring Ophelia's social media for signs. She was ultimately left dissatisfied. Ophelia's posts were innocuous, consisting mainly of sponsored content she was under contractual obligation to deliver: a hand cream, a blender that could chew through rock but was lovely enough in its pastel and rose gold offerings to adorn the most curated of kitchen countertops, and one photo of Noelle, pajamaed and curled up in Nkem's lap while he read her a bedtime story. *The loves of my life* the caption read. Aṅụrị logged off. The next time she picked up her phone was to call Christian and ask him over to play *Mario Kart*. When she opened the door to him, the urge to throw herself into his arms was so overwhelming, she became lightheaded.

"I've got something for you," she said in a voice that sounded like she'd fed it through a wood chipper and tried to reassemble the pieces.

Christian stepped inside. "If you're about to say an 'ass whooping,' let me just remind you that I regularly test my prowess against the Japanese *Mario Kart* contingent. I always lose but I am, by degrees, way better than I was when I first started humiliating myself."

And wasn't this what she needed? Christian's unassuming

presence was like slipping into a warm bath, the water drawing the ache from tired muscles.

"Ooh," Aṅụrị said, "I love when you talk humiliation to me."

Christian raised an eyebrow. "I'm broke, Aṅụrị. I don't have tributes to give you. Hey. *Hey*," he said when he saw her face. "It was a joke."

They sat. Christian produced a small cloth folded in quarters and began cleaning his glasses. Aṅụrị watched him and in watching him realized that she could go on like that, watching him clean his glasses or make scrambled eggs. She could watch him looking at her with those expressions that cycled between unreadable and astonishment. She could watch him breathe. Aṅụrị put a small gift-wrapped item onto the coffee table and pushed it in Christian's direction.

"Oh wow. You meant like a real something," he said.

"The ass whooping is a real something. But I did mean a gift."

Christian replaced his glasses and picked up the present. He held it in his hand and examined the wrapping paper. "Are these tiny locks?"

"You said you work in cybersecurity—so I'm not buying that broke line you fed me before—I dunno. Locks seemed appropriate." They had at the time of the purchase. Now, Aṅụrị's armpits prickled with embarrassment.

The thing about Christian was that his smile claimed his face. His other features were powerless against the force of it. It was a smile that pushed his eyes closed. He deployed it now, unconsciously. "You're something, isn't it?"

"I dunno. Depends on the something."

The gift was a monogrammed glasses case. The leather was exquisite and buttery soft. The initials embossed into the lower left hand corner. It was a beautiful item, the sort of piece which declared its expense without the need for a price tag. Christian, prolific talker, was quite speechless.

"If you hate it, I can give you the gift receipt and you can get something else you do like. I just thought since you wear glasses you might need someplace to keep them. When they're not on your face, I mean. Obviously when they're on your face, you don't need them to be anywhere else but on your face." If she kept talking, Aṅụrị thought, maybe she would run out of actual oxygen and black out. The idea of oblivion never ceased to comfort her.

He was yet to tell her, but her voice was one of the things Christian liked most about Aṅụrị. He would listen to her read *Atlas Shrugged* aloud. It was that good of a voice. Therefore it almost pained him to silence her. Or rather it would have if he had to do it any other way than with a kiss. And after the kiss, there would be the way she suddenly had to examine her hands as if the meaning of life was scrawled on her palms.

"Thank you," he said to the side of her face. "This is much better than a towel."

She traced her nail beds one by one, face burning. "I...I meant what I said about the gift receipt."

"Aṅụrị."

She looked at him. He smiled again. "You're welcome," she said.

"You know you don't have to buy me stuff, right? There is zero need to impress me." He picked up his controller and turned on the game.

He was on the screen where a player needs to choose the kart for their character to race in. Aṅụrị's stylist eye caught two things: that his hair had grown since that retwist what felt like a lifetime ago, and that he appeared to be sincere in his statement. Was impressing people not the default? If you did not impress, did your chances of being rejected not increase? Wasn't there an unspoken agreement between parties that love was contingent on service of some kind? Was Christian/Chidili then, trying to mislead her?

"Aren't you going to choose your player?" he asked. "Sorry but I'm Black Yoshi for life."

Aṅụrị chose Toad and they tossed a coin for the chance to choose which course set they'd race. "You don't like presents?"

"Fuck. Rainbow Road? The worst of the worst tracks. Best of three?"

"Nope."

"I love presents. Who doesn't love free and heartfelt shit?"

"Okay."

"What I'm saying is that gifts won't change how I see you."

Aṅụrị felt a trapdoor open somewhere inside her.

"Because I'm sort of already in awe? Shall we do this?"

The act of processing emotions is different for different people. For Christian, it meant opting for isolation. For Loki, tears were usually involved. And Nneoma? Prayer. But the lessons we learn as children are not grease. They cannot be sluiced off with soap and water. They burrow and even lay dormant until they manifest later in life as hyperindependence or avoidance or fear of abandonment. It was no secret to those who knew and adored Aṅụrị that for her, stress and impulsivity were enmeshed. She'd spent years trying to unpick them. Thousands spent on purchases, the majority of which were returned when the dual juggernauts of dopamine and serotonin had worn off, and nights (and days) spent wandering through the fog of alcohol-induced amnesia trying to figure out how badly she'd erred, were testament to Aṅụrị's processing failures. It wasn't that she felt no attraction to Christian—on the contrary, there were times she had to stop herself from licking his face—it was more that in times of high stress such as this, with Ophelia's lack of communication coloring every waking moment, Aṅụrị's desire melded with her desperation to forget, if just for a second, that this was the life she was living.

And because Christian's years spent trying to avoid panic by relegating himself to an observer of rather than a participant in life left him perceptive sometimes to a fault, he knew when Aṅụrị called him that things were not proceeding the way she envisioned and she was at a loss on how to manage that. He even felt guilty, as he made his way to her flat, that he was so happy to spend time with her when that time was brought about, at least in part, by her state of mind. It was for these reasons then, that when Aṅụrị kissed him again, he responded, but when the kissing became frantic; when her hands began to roam and he noticed that those hands were shaking, he held them still and he pulled his head back slightly so he could look at her.

"Hey," he said softly, "you okay?"

It wasn't a rejection. She'd understand that later when the mortification dispersed enough for her to see clearly. Right then though, his tenderness was excruciating. She shook herself free.

"I'm good. You can go though."

"What? Aṅụrị, look—"

She picked up her controller again and began playing, turning the volume up. Christian squinted at her profile. Then he left as instructed. On meeting Aṅụrị, Christian resigned himself to the task of wooing her, but he was not a person to stay when he had been explicitly told not to. When she completed Rainbow Road (coming in first place), Aṅụrị saw he had taken the glasses case as well as the wrapping paper. The effort it took not to cry gave her a headache. She left the TV on and went to bed so she could fool herself into thinking she was not alone; that there was someone still in the other room hoping she was alright. Still no word from Ophelia. Dusk turned to night. It was only then, when she finally accepted that there was now a new fight to add to the others, that her phone rang.

It was Nkem.

On the drive to Nneoma's house, Aṅụrị stared out of the window and watched London in its various versions of nighttime. Gaggles of revelers half-clothed and luminous under the orange-wash of street lamps, the sound of their laughter punching the air, their beauty all the more radiant for their lack of inhibition; the lone walkers, hands in pockets and heads down, ears plugged and resolute in their pacing. And then the expanses of nothing, where the quiet was dense as a hug and the lights in the houses were mostly out; the occupants having already retired.

Loki, who insisted on borrowing his friend's car and driving Aṅụrị to her aunt's place, turned on Al Green and lowered the volume so the car was filled with a muted crooning that served as the conversation they were not having. Loki's guilt was what brought him to Aṅụrị's door that night. Since his revelation and the resulting turmoil, he'd kept something of a distance; checking in periodically via text or call, but studiously avoiding having to sit with Aṅụrị and look at her tormented face and feel the slow drip of her worry filling up the room, drowning them all. It was one thing to be there to cushion Aṅụrị when she fell, but it was quite another to be one of the things that tripped her in the first place.

Simi clocked this almost immediately. "I know what you're doing," she'd said to him two days after the Ophelia Confrontation, when he picked up the phone and her face appeared on the screen. She was bonneted and holding her toothbrush, her face bathed in the whitish-blue light of Abe's bathroom.

"What am I doing?"

"She hasn't noticed that you're avoiding her yet, Loki, but she will. Get it together."

"You don't know everything, Simi." He'd spent much of his life waiting and wanting to be seen, truly seen, and here he was choosing anger when it was happening.

Simi ignored him. "None of this is your fault. It's just a byproduct of the shittiness of Aṅụrị's parents. You're not responsible."

"Okay. Thanks. I feel so much better now. Like, tons. Giddy even."

"Is *this* making you feel better? Being a dickhead?"

"Don't you have a man to be leading on?" He hung up the phone.

Aṅụrị's text came as he was about to embark on the pilgrimage to East London where there was a party, several trays of edibles and the means to blitz recent events from his head. He was in the car in less than thirty minutes. Now he glanced at her. Her head still rested against the window. It took Aṅụrị years to learn that there were silences she did not have to fill, but as Loki pulled to a stop outside Nneoma's house, he wished she would say something.

"Aṅụrị," he began.

She turned to him then. "I know, Lo," she said. "It's okay."

His eyes stung, but the least he could do was wait until she was safely inside before he cried. "I'm super proud of you. I want to be like you when I grow up."

"I'm scared, Lo."

"I'll be right here when you come out."

"Nah. You should go home and sleep. I'll call."

"Promise?"

"You know it."

He watched her disappear inside, and then he drove away.

Noelle was asleep on the sofa in the living room. Nneoma had tucked a blanket around her and was sitting by Noelle's feet, reaching over now and again to smooth the curls away from her face. She raised her eyes as Aṅụrị walked past.

"He's in the kitchen," Nneoma said. "Brought this child here in the dead of night. When he's less sad, that is when I'll flog him."

Aṅụrị crouched by her sister. "She's okay?"

"We'll see. Are you?"

"We'll see."

Aṅụrị paused at the kitchen door. It was not that Nkem looked tired, it was more that he looked now like he had never experienced a moment of joy or peace. It was the first time he appeared old to Aṅụrị and he wasn't, but the sag of the skin beneath his eyes, the suddenly prominent sprinkling of gray at his temple, the dryness at the corner of his lips and between his fingers, leant him the appearance of someone twenty years older. He wore a faded brown sweatshirt, one Aṅụrị knew he kept hidden from Ophelia at odds as it was with her desire for him to be clad solely in cool cashmere jumpers and chinos. She knew it was a throwback from his days in Onitsha. She hadn't seen it in years. Inexplicably, she wanted to hug him and she resented the reminder that she was yet to fully suffocate the part of her which associated Nkem with any form of comfort. There had been no extension of grace on his part, so why should there even be the notion of such on hers? She stood for another few seconds, savoring this, the last minute where everything was still possible. Another—and perhaps the most important—fork in the road. Aṅụrị considered that life for Nkem had already changed. Irrevocably so. She simply needed to catch up. She forced herself to put one foot in front of the other until she reached a chair, then she sat.

"Aṅụrị," Nkem said in a voice ravaged by what Aṅụrị, if she was closer to him, might identify as an unfortunate amalgamation of pain, sadness and uncertainty. "Ke kwanụ?" he asked knowing the answer. She'd lost weight. The gap around the collar of her T-shirt made him want to weep.

"It's the middle of the night, Dad."

"Yes," he said. His head dropped into his hands. "Aṅụrị, why didn't you tell me? You knew and you didn't come to me."

Aṅụrị expected the anger and even banked on it, rage being a particularly excellent crutch on which to lean during fraught situations, but the force with which it overtook her was astonishing. Even to her. Everything in the room became a potential weapon. Nkem's dejection now of no consequence. Her fingertips dug into the cool wood of the table.

"You're not blaming me. I know that's not what I'm hearing."

Nkem's hair was too short for him to grip. If it had been long enough, clumps would have littered the space between them. As it was, his hands worked over the expanse of his tightly packed curls. Back and forth, back and forth like he was trying to claw out the information.

"You should have told me. You're my daughter."

"And she's your wife. She kept the secret, not me. It needed to come from her." Aṅụrị did not say that a time would come where she would have told him. What bore into her as she sat was that of all the things to which Nkem might choose to exercise diligence, it was his misunderstanding of his oldest child.

"Nwa m," Nkem moaned. Then again, a stream of regret. "Nwa m, nwa m, nwa m." *My child.* Aṅụrị knew he did not mean her.

A long while back, when she was first entering into the world of findom, Aṅụrị quickly learned the lesson that one pig's pleasure was another pig's pique. They were individuals with separate and distinct modes of enjoyment, so that calling the one who preferred looks-based degradation a failure in the arena of employment just wouldn't land the same. Similarly and most unfortunately for Nkem, Aṅụrị had spent years hoping he would see her discomfort and put a stop to it. His inability to parse what she was feeling, she realized more acutely than ever before, was yes, partly due to ignorance, but more so due to the reluctance to move past that same ignorance. Nkem did not understand the perils of the online landscape as it pertained to visibility. What he did understand was the uniform disgust for those who might harm children. The harm was the point. The varieties of it existed as distinct entities for him, some being placed above all others. Noelle fell into the latter. Her existence on that website was now a reflection on him. His distress was that of a father but also that of a selfish, completely human man. Had there been nights Nkem *nwa m'd* over her? Aṅụrị doubted it. What a wretched thing to envy.

"What else has she kept from me?" Nkem's question was

rhetorical. He was asking himself, but Aṅụrị chose to answer anyway.

"Have you asked her?" Would it make any difference if Nkem knew of Ophelia's desperation? Of her offer to settle with Aṅụrị? She kept quiet.

Nkem raised his head and looked at her then, almost recoiling at the intensity of her gaze. "I am not perfect, Aṅụrị, but—"

"Who the hell is, Dad? I never actually wanted perfect from you. All I wanted was a dad who listened and gave just a little of a damn about me. I'm really happy you know how to be pissed about this thing with Noelle. I'm happy she gets that from you. Would have been nice if that kicked in a few years back though, can't lie."

Nkem dropped his gaze to Nneoma's table. It was impossible to know how to react when you found your first wife, gone as she was, sitting across from you in your sister's house and addressing you through your daughter. With Kainene's bangle glinting on her wrist, Aṅụrị had never before been so much like her mother. He was shocked to find himself still winded by her absence. His pride was limping and bedraggled, but it still existed.

"Where did you learn to talk like this?" he said weakly.

Aṅụrị smiled. She thought of Ammah and she thought of LowlyWorm and Piggy_Luvs_u_99 and how they were beacons along the path to finding her voice.

"You wouldn't like it if I told you," she said.

"Kaine would have said the same things to me," Nkem said. A tiny smile tugged at his lips. "She has more to do with who you are than I do. And she's not here."

Aṅụrị looked down at her wrist. "Oh she's here."

They sat for a beat. Nneoma's singing carried through from the living room.

"How did you manage to convince Ophelia to let you take Noelle at this hour?" Aṅụrị asked.

"Let?" Nkem drew himself up in his seat. "Noelle is my child.

Ophelia had no choice in the matter." And as he said it, he saw again how true this was for Aṅụrị too, and how right she was about his repeated letdowns. He cleared his throat. "I don't know what to do."

"Sure you do. You're going to find a way to make sure this doesn't happen again."

His eyes were wide. "How?"

"Dad. Figure it out. Saying no might help."

Aṅụrị was on her feet, moving toward the door. Her body felt like some unseen force was trying to drag it through the floor. She didn't want to look at her father anymore or answer any more of his questions. Before she left the room, she heard him call her name. She turned.

"Gbaghara m. Biko."

It was the first time Nkem had asked for her forgiveness and it had come late and under the worst possible circumstances. And still Aṅụrị tucked it away to reexamine later. She turned once again and went to the living room to wait for her sister to wake up.

When Ophelia was nine years old, she tumbled from a tree and broke a bone in her ankle and one in her wrist. The twin casts along with Ophelia's general pleasant demeanor and her flowing blond hair were too much for her classmates to resist. While sequestered in the hospital, a procession of children came to visit. All asked to sign not one but both casts and most brought Ophelia a card, a gift or both and sat with her awhile. Her best friends at the time, two girls called Alice and Fiona, visited the most often and always stayed the longest. They'd climb up into the high hospital bed during visiting hours, and for the four days Ophelia was there the trio would watch reruns of daytime television shows, play Cat's Cradle and whisper secrets to each other before recording them carefully in the purple notebooks they'd harangued their mothers into buying for them. Alice had a brother and Fiona a much older sister who had no interest in her, and of course, Ophelia had a spectre she felt guilty about not knowing how to love, so the three were happy to gorge on the joy of sisterhood; that nectar found only in friendship, when nobody else is as fun and amazing as your pals.

When Nkem took Noelle and decamped to his sister's house, Ophelia had no desire to speak to her publicist, her accountant, her dermatologist or any of the other people with whom she had professional relationships. And so the house was empty in a way it had not been for a long time. Ophelia, with only her thoughts and her remorse for companions, realized she had nobody to call. There was not a soul to whom she could pour out her fear. There were the school mums. There were the PRs at various brands with whom she was on a first-name basis. There were dozens of people she knew but amongst them, not a single friend to sit with her in her misery without then going on to sell a story to the tabloids. Ophelia walked through the house. She moved through the cavernous rooms and she felt despair descend like mist. Nkem would not answer her calls. Nneoma was the one phoning every morning to say Noelle made it to school alright or to relay the message that Nkem was not yet ready to speak. Destruction was so swift and so merciless and it made Ophelia want to shout into Anụrị's face, *Do you see? Is this what you wanted?* But there was nobody else to blame. Her solitude a damning confirmation.

What good was pride? Had she not decimated her reserves of the stuff by filling Nkem's voicemail with pleas? It didn't even occur to her to read praise from her fans. They ceased to exist the minute Nkem left. It took three days for Ophelia, now overcome with hopelessness, to phone her mother. But it was Henry who answered.

"Ophelia," he said. "Your mother has gone to drop a Bundt at Mrs. Johnson's. She should be back within the hour."

Ophelia started to cry. Genevieve had a Mrs. Johnson to whom she could drop a Bundt. *She* had nobody. She wanted to kiss Noelle's upturned face. She wanted to feel the press of Nkem's shoulder when he rolled over in bed. She wanted to shout at Añuri until she was breathless. Henry cleared his throat. His discomfort made its way through the phone and twisted itself into Ophelia's hair.

"Okay." Her voice did not sound like her own. It was a quiet, strangled thing forcing its way through a wall of hurt. "I can call back."

Henry cleared his throat again. "Are you alright? Ophelia?"

"I'm fine, Dad. I have to go."

When Ophelia answered the door some two hours later, there stood Henry. He shrugged apologetically.

"You didn't sound fine, darling," he said.

SEVENTEEN

"No change?" Aṅụrị, in her candle room, stacked candles into a pyramid nobody would see and waited for her aunt's response.

It was nearing a week since Nkem and Noelle moved to Nneoma's. Aṅụrị visited every day, the first being the sweetest. There was nothing in life to compare with watching Noelle break the surface of sleep and register Aṅụrị's presence. No greater joy than the kid's head against Aṅụrị's shoulder, her curls tickling Aṅụrị's chin. Aṅụrị went back daily to spend time with Noelle but also to help Nneoma launder clothes, vacuum the house and stock the fridge. She also listened to her aunt alternate between delight and irritation at the two new mouths she had to feed.

"I want Nkem to remember that I chose to live alone," Nneoma said. "And that I will live alone again. Soon."

Every time, Aṅụrị found Nkem inert in the kitchen and the living room. He would nod a quick greeting but was quick to leave his daughters to themselves.

"Mba," Nneoma said now. "Today I had to threaten to lock him outside just to get him to bathe."

"Yikes." Underneath the exasperation, Aṅụrị heard Nneoma's

concern. You would need to know Nneoma intimately to recognize it, but it was there. "I'll come over."

On arrival, Aṅụrị found that Nneoma had not exaggerated. Nkem wore his gloom unabashedly, like it was a garish coat only he could appreciate. It was fascinating to learn the man was capable of feeling this deeply; that a single albeit weighty issue could ransack his emotional stocks, rob him of whatever apathy remained and leave him mired in suffering. And again, there they were. Jealousy and anger. Noelle deserved this reaction. But so did Aṅụrị.

She watched Nkem stand and make his way to the sink. Slowly, he began washing the small collection of dishes. He cut such a pathetic figure that Aṅụrị had to clench her fists to stop from hugging him.

"Dad?"

A plate slid from Nkem's hand back into the sink. It did not break but both of them lurched forward in anticipation of disaster. He shook his head.

"Noelle says she is bored. Nneoma brought a few things from the house, but whenever you're not here, she misses you. I...I don't know how to amuse her."

"Let's go for a walk," Aṅụrị said. "The three of us."

Parts of West London were so leafy you sometimes forgot you were in the capital and instead fancied yourself somewhere more rural, where buses came once maybe twice an hour and nobody drank oat milk, didn't even think to ask for it in their coffee. It was part of the reason Aṅụrị moved to Chiswick and it was also why, when the desire to remove Noelle from Swiss Cottage arose, Aṅụrị fell in love with the red and blond brick and pitched roofs of Ealing. The trees hung into the street, green and lush, and they walked beneath them, Noelle in the middle holding one of Nkem's hands and one of Aṅụrị's. She babbled continuously and they indulged her, stopping for an ice cream and continuing on, Noelle's happy slurping the soundtrack to their steps. Did they look like a family? What did a family even look like? Life had taught Aṅụrị that there was no cookie-cutter definition. Picket fences could be replaced with digitized security gates, but the lives of those who lived behind them were equally messy. That was the problem with facades: the lie was the point but it was also the problem.

For his part, Nkem blinked at the blueness of the sky and the warmness of the air and wondered how life could be so beautiful and simultaneously so hideous. At his side were his two daughters and it was fast becoming apparent that he didn't know how to talk to either of them. He'd known this about Aṅụrị for a long time, but it was easier to ignore when he had the twin buffers of Ophelia and Noelle; when Aṅụrị existed as a satellite, albeit a troublesome one, in their orbits. The days spent at Nneoma's, he'd sat in the spare room where he and Noelle were installed and he had held his child's hand until she slept and even when it went slack in his own, he kept on holding it because he did not want her to wake and find him gone. He had failed her enough. His deficiencies would stain him eternally. He found himself racked with an unfamiliar uncertainty. Up until this point, he'd always had an answer, a plan. Kainene dies? Move to the UK and start afresh. Cannot adequately care for a baby? Find an Ophelia who can. Marry the same Ophelia. Build a new life. First daughter drifting away? Let her go. Don't chase. Have another one. Now *he* was adrift. What was the solution to a problem like this?

Aṅụrị turned them onto Denbigh Road and, after another minute or so of walking, stopped in front of a house.

"Do you know who lives here?" Noelle asked. She liked that the front door was bright blue and that the stained glass in the top of it depicted birds.

"I don't," Aṅụrị admitted. "But I know that in a couple of days, there's probably going to be a for sale sign in front of it."

Nkem shook the fug from his head. "And so?"

"And *so*. Everyone in this family needs to grow up. Not you, Nell." Aṅụrị hunkered down and tickled Noelle. She and Nkem watched as Noelle skipped a few feet away and began to inspect the pink ballerinas of a fuchsia bush.

"Me first. I love my flat." Aṅụrị found herself becoming emotional and paused because it was so fiercely true. She *did* love her flat. The first place she was able to truly be herself, by herself. "I love it, but I want a guest room. I want Nell to have her own space when she visits, and I want her to have a garden she can sit in when she's with me."

Aṅụrị looked at her father. "And she *will* be with me. Maybe not all the time but whenever she wants. I'm not letting you and Ophelia take her away from me." She grinned. "You know me. I'll never stop fighting."

"This is a big house," Nkem said. And the unspoken question hung between them.

"I don't know how I'll afford it. Not yet. But I have some time to work that out."

Nkem knew he had buried his head for so long that he had become one with the sand. He was a man who allowed himself to look at his eldest daughter through narrowed eyes and mostly when she was unaware. He'd done nothing to overcome his shame and in the intervening years while he hid from it, Aṅụrị had become a woman. She had done so without him. Despite him. The distance between them did not allow him to fully envision Aṅụrị's life inside such a house, but there were things that made sense. She would paint the walls ridiculous colors. The floors would be covered in rugs old and new. The air would be tinged always, with the scent of creation. There would be plants and music, and that tall boy Aṅụrị loved would walk through the rooms along with Simi and they would be comfortable in a way Nkem never dared hope he might be. He didn't even know if he would be welcome. But Noelle would. The house, according to Aṅụrị, would be crafted around Noelle and her needs. His eldest was showing more care for his youngest than arguably he or Ophelia had done. He had no right to be proud, so he settled for gratefully despondent.

Añurị said she would work it out and there was not a single reason to doubt her. She said she would not stop fighting for her sister and Nkem knew it was an incontrovertible truth. His Añurị who was not really his anymore, with her shaved head and her mother's eyes and her inexplicable dress sense. Apologies would not be enough. Prostrating himself on the concrete might work, but he was still an Onitsha man and pride, gone before his fall as it had, would never be truly extinguished within him.

"Yes," was what he managed to say. "You will work it out. Ị ga-eme nke ọma." It was true. She had done and would continue to do well, with or without him. With or without his approval.

Añurị called to Noelle and told her to stay close, then turned to Nkem. His shoulders were slumped. His lack of sleep was etched into the space under his eyes and the lines in his forehead. Whatever her crimes, Nkem had spent over two decades with Ophelia. It made sense that he felt bereft without her.

"Have you spoken to Ophelia?" Añurị asked.

Nkem shook his head. "She has been calling."

"She misses you," Añurị said. Ophelia had not made a single update since Nkem and Noelle left the house. "She loves you."

"She loves you, too. She does, Añurị. She made mistakes."

Añurị bristled. A defense of Ophelia was not required.

"You'll go back?" she asked. She held her breath while she awaited his answer. Even in his righteous indignation, he loved Ophelia, too. And still, Añurị hoped.

"Kainene would be very proud of you," Nkem said, neatly sidestepping the question. "Me too, I'm proud. But I still don't know how to fix this."

"Bring Noelle to see Ammah—my therapist."

A memory. Añurị at six months dozing against Nkem's chest. One chubby baby fist curled around the neckline of his shirt.

He quelled the ridicule sprouting inside him. His methods were not beyond reproach. Nobody could look at the current status of his life and conclude that he was a success. A person did not always have to be right, but they could try, at least, to be different.

"It will make you happy?"

Aṅụrị nodded.

Nkem sighed. "Then I can think about it. I can do that."

And he did. For the best part of an hour that night, he thought hard. He would have continued to think, but Ophelia called from Henry's number and the moment Nkem heard her voice, a new fuse was lit.

One of the lesser examined side effects of popularity, of having to make minimal effort, is that one becomes accustomed to having others do the heavy lifting of maintaining relationships. With Simi and Loki, the effort did not really exist. The same went for Aṅụrị's aunt and her grandparents. Because her circle was so finite and so intrinsic to her being, speaking to them and seeking them out came as naturally to Aṅụrị as breathing. And because she had been content, for so long, with only them and her sister, she found herself wrong-footed by Christian's withdrawal from her life. He'd told her he would try for two weeks, but what happened was that he didn't try at all. His ejection from her flat evidently signaled the end of something for him, and Aṅụrị cycled through suitable responses to this and landed on anger. Some cursory self-reflection might have signaled that the anger was the shoot stemming from pain and watered by fear of rejection, but Aṅụrị blew right past reflection. Anger was easier. Nobody had yet found a way to make accountability fun.

"You're angry," Ammah said when Aṅụrị's twenty-minute diatribe on the futility of trying to engage ethically with men came to a close.

"You could say that, yeah."

"You used the term 'ethical' a number of times in your…in what you said."

Aṅuṛi squinted at Ammah. "I did, yeah."

"Do you think you could explain again why you believe what this young man did was unethical?"

"Well, ghosting is rubbish, isn't it? I swear you were the one that told me we need to *communicate* our feelings."

"You said he was a very heart-on-his-sleeve sort of person."

"Well, yeah. He was. Then he disappeared."

"After you told him to go."

"Okay but—"

"Which came after his refusal to be physically intimate during a time of distress for you."

Aṅuṛi was quiet.

"Is there anything preventing you from reaching out to him?"

Aṅuṛi laughed. "Me? Call him?"

"Interesting," Ammah said.

Aṅuṛi left Ammah's and headed for Blank. In her bag was the towel Christian had given her. In her head, which she prayed she could empty once engulfed by the water and the darkness, her own words creating their very own tempest: *I don't want you to feel like you're chasing me all the time.* She unlocked her phone.

I'm at Blank and about to use your towel gift for the first time

It ought to have been an apology but Aṅuṛi, terribly, was counting on the fact of Christian's politeness. She was rewarded. Her phone pinged a few seconds later.

Enjoy

If he had backhanded her, it might have hurt less.

Could we talk?

Again, his response was almost immediate.

Probably better we don't. I think maybe you were right to be skeptical about this

Aṅụrị realized then that she had become the ten and that the ten was too much for a five like Christian; someone who just wanted to manage his panic attacks and crochet in peace. Aṅụrị squeezed her eyes shut and waited for the urge to plead to pass. It did, but the need to apologize did not. It stayed with her in the tank, on the journey home and was joined by the renewed desire to explain herself while she was in the shower. She texted Simi and asked her to come over for pizza, then she texted Loki and asked the same of him. The two of them were not talking for some reason unbeknownst to her, but this was a veritable Code Red, and it was something of a relief after the consecutive Code Blacks of the past few weeks.

Loki arrived first and proceeded to begin the pizza order on his phone. When Simi walked in, she rolled her eyes, spun on her heel and headed toward the door. Aṅụrị caught her sleeve and—remembering that Simi had brothers, which necessitated she build strength in order to wrangle—locked her arms around Simi's waist.

"Aṅụrị. Let go please," Simi said through clenched teeth.

"Nope." Aṅụrị held on tighter.

"You no dey get work? Like an actual occupation? Useful employment that you could be doing right now instead of holding me hostage?"

"I need you two to start speaking so you can help me, the most important person in the world, find a way to apologize to Christian for being a weirdo."

"Apologize to a man? You sure this is the route you want to take?"

"Did you not apologize to Abe?"

"He wouldn't really let me."

"But you tried."

Loki chose that moment to speak. "You can always practice on me, Sim."

"Someone somewhere, Loki, has tied your destiny to a calabash. Maybe it was me. Maybe it wasn't. We'll never know."

"What's a calabash?"

Simi rounded on him, but the dimple was on full show. She kissed her teeth. "I want the fig pancetta pizza with truffle fries on the side."

The answer was so obvious Aṅụrị knew that had she given herself a little longer to freak out, she would have happened upon it by herself. But what were friends if not willing stand-ins for the parts of your brain temporarily made useless by emotion? Loki told Aṅụrị to use her hands and when Simi rounded on him for the second time, Loki ducked Simi's punch and said, "Whoa, I meant to make something!"

The candle she made for Christian took almost thirty-two hours to complete. It was the first time she had successfully distilled her own essential oil and she combined eucalyptus with lemon and ginger root, the subtlest hint of cedarwood, and something else she would never, not even under pain of death, reveal. Aṅụrị mixed flecks of gold leaf and minute cedar chips into the wax before it set. She opted for matte onyx packaging and had Christian's initials embossed in gold on both the label and the box. Aṅụrị's apology would linger in Christian's bedroom, on his clothes. If he accepted it.

"Even though this was partly my idea," Simi told Aṅụrị over FaceTime, "I feel like this is a lot of effort to go through. Especially for a dude. What if he doesn't care?"

"Then at least he'll know I did."

Christian could very well snub her, but there was comfort in knowing an attempt had been made. She knew what it was to spend time wishing for an apology and receiving nothing. Aṅụrị reasoned that unexpressed regret was not something she should make generational.

She put the candle inside its box, nestled the box in tissue paper inside a bag and left the bag with the receptionists at Blank. They were ecstatic, it seemed, that someone else held Christian in as high regard as they did.

"He doesn't visit too often these days," the taller one warned, "but his number is on file so we can always call and tell him to collect it if he doesn't show up in a couple of days."

Aṅụrị, heart thudding, thanked them and left. She returned to her flat and to her life and tried to act like she wasn't waiting. A few days passed with no contact.

"Well. I tried," she told Simi and Loki and then the darkness of her bedroom.

The next day, she returned from the post office to a padded envelope in her mail slot. Inside was a crocheted plant pot holder. It was turquoise and monogrammed. There was no note.

Aṅụrị stood in the lobby and held it to her chest. She smiled.

It went like this: during his visit, Henry had followed Ophelia into the house, looking around and wondering, as he always did when confronted with his daughter's place of residence, how women seemed to have an innate sense of decor. He would never think to mount what looked like a piece of driftwood on the wall or cut an entire branch off a tree and find a vase large enough to house it, but Ophelia had, and they looked fitting, even pleasant where they were. In the kitchen, Henry stared for four minutes at the coffee machine while Ophelia sat dazed and quiet in the breakfast nook. She was not capable of dishevelment, but surely this must be the closest Ophelia had ever come. It was disconcerting for Henry, a man whose admittedly limited sphere of female interaction consisted of women for whom appearance was of the utmost importance. When he entered his car and made the journey into London, he didn't know what he planned on saying to his daughter. He only knew that her voice over the phone carried a haunted quality that disturbed him enough to leave a note for his wife and search for his keys.

Thankfully, he located a common kettle, found the mugs and tea bags behind some sliding contraption, and set about brewing Earl Grey. For Henry, there was not much in this life that could not be solved or at least helped by a mug of tea. Genevieve was the talker of the two of them—indeed Henry always viewed his children from behind a screen of awe and slight panic. There were so many ways to destroy them, so many ways to disappoint them. He never felt worthy of them, of their love. Better to offer head pats, assistance with maths problems, and the unspoken agreement that he would allow Santa Claus to claim credit for the gifts he bought with the money he earned. He suspected he ended up disappointing them anyway, but, given his ancestors' escape to Britain centuries earlier, he was too English to enquire. He placed a mug in front of Ophelia and eased himself onto the banquette beside her.

"So," Henry said.

Ophelia blinked in surprise. Henry's presence in her house was anomalous. She blinked again, trying to reconcile the shape of him against the brushed suede of the banquette.

"I think Nkem's left me," she said. Then she proceeded, in between bouts of sobbing, to recount the events of the preceding weeks.

Henry listened. Henry sipped his tea. It had been a mere two years since he fully understood what Instagram was. He refused to even go near TikTok. He still found it incredible that people felt the desire to post photos and videos of themselves for strangers to look at, but then he was not a man possessed of the need to even look at himself in the mirror. When people asked him what his daughter did, he led with "oh something with the internet," then he would drop her name and watch as recognition and delight lit up their features. Ophelia's success had nothing to do with him, but reality had very little to do with pride. She was his child and her success brought him joy.

When Ophelia finished talking, Henry patted her hand twice.

"He isn't talking to you?"

"He did for the first time this week."

"Alright, darling. I understood about half of what you said just before." And when he saw her face fall, he said, "My brief stint in the army taught me two things. Number one—" he raised a finger "—I would be killed in hand-to-hand combat. And two—" he raised a second finger "—offense is the best defense. You've come this far. Perhaps it's time you thought about fighting back?"

OPHELIA

Aged five, and the night before she was due to have her second MMR vaccine, I drew Aṅuṛi's bedroom curtains closed and sat on her bed. She looked so tiny then, the personality that dwarfed us all tightly furled inside her. Back then, there wasn't anything about her I didn't know. Every expression, every sound, the different shades of her laughter, I knew them all. The slope of her shoulders could reveal sadness or fear. That's love, isn't it? Speaking the language of another without the need for words.

That night, I touched her cheek and she reached up and held my hands. I felt like luck would follow me for the rest of my life. I was so confident she would always reach for me; that I would forever be the one she turned to first. To be loved by a child is a gift. To be loved by this one, a miracle.

She was worried about the jab, that it would hurt, and that perhaps there might be blood. Her grip on my fingers tightened and when I told her that yes, it might hurt, but that it was important, she pulled my face close to hers and gently wrapped my hair around her little fist.

"I don't want to," is what she told me.

"I know, my heart," I said back. "Sometimes though, we must do things to protect ourselves. Even if it hurts. Do you understand?"

A lesson in pain that I would teach her and myself, over and over again.

EIGHTEEN

In the time it took for Aṅụrị to construct Christian's candle, Ophelia resumed posting on her social media feeds. There was no mention of Nkem and references to Noelle were obscure. There were shots of birds freewheeling through the blue of the sky and reels of Ophelia's bare feet walking across grass. The captions were cryptic and designed to breed speculation which they did amongst the fans who in the overreaching manner of the internet started making their own conjecture-laden posts and videos on what was happening in the Chinasa household. It was Makuo who alerted Aṅụrị to the resuscitation of Ophelia's updates and when she did, Aṅụrị forced herself to finish the clients she had scheduled for that afternoon before she looked herself. Complacency was stealthy and Aṅụrị chastised herself. She should have known better but didn't. She phoned Nkem but the call went straight to voicemail. She then phoned Nneoma who said Nkem was sleeping. Nneoma's voice was tight.

"What is it?" Aṅụrị asked.

"I told Nkem he had to tell you. He said he would do it when he woke up."

"Aunty? Tell me what? What *is* it?"

"Noelle. She is back with Ophelia."

It was in the midtwenties. London was luxuriating under a blanket of comfortable warmth. Aṅụrị shivered. "He let her go?"

"They decided together," Nneoma said. "They couldn't give Noelle reasons she understood about why she couldn't be at home. The child missed her mother. They decided it was better for her to be there."

"But he's still at yours? My dad?"

"He is here." Nneoma sighed. "I don't know for how long."

Aṅụrị did not know what it meant.

"I don't know what it means," she told Makuo and Arinze.

"Nneoma is not wrong. Noelle chọrọ nne yā, even if it's just for now," Arinze said.

Why did it feel like a betrayal to be told that Noelle needed Ophelia? Knowing that nobody needed just one person, that life was made richer when joy and hope and pain were shared between multiple recipients, did nothing to lessen the burn of being told that a five-year-old girl needed her mother. Then Aṅụrị conceded that at twenty-five, she too needed her mother and would never again have her.

"I don't know what it means," she told Simi and Loki when they met for lunch in the city.

The three of them opened Ophelia's profiles on their respective phones.

Loki speared a ring of calamari from the bowl they shared. "She's definitely up to something. Look at this. 'Life makes sense when we stop expecting too much of it.' What the fuck does that mean?"

"Maybe she's had a change of heart. Maybe she's pivoting into crunchy hippy mama. That's totally her bag. Getting Botox injections every six months and telling people she maintains her line-free complexion with burdock juice and raisins." Simi put down her phone. "Are you still both down for the Brutalism Exhibition at the Tate?"

"Yeah, sure, we're still coming with you to look at ugly buildings," Loki said. "What'chu mean by pivoting?"

Simi yawned and picked at a groove worn into the wooden tabletop. "I used to see it all the time at work. Some fitness or makeup guru gets bored or has a baby or the numbers just aren't numbering like before, so they find a new avenue to pursue. Last month, Laila Vegas decided lingerie is no longer her thing. She's turned to baking."

"Not Laila. No more lingerie?" Loki dropped his head onto the table. "Can't you suggest she do both? I'd double subscribe to that if it were possible."

Simi lifted Loki's chin and wiped a smudge of tartar sauce from his cheek. "Why don't you just slide into her DMs and tell her you're the voice of McKinnon's Smoked Sausage. Who among us can resist that?"

"You think I have a chance?"

Aṅụrị handed Simi another napkin. "Loki. It's you. No matter who it is, you always have a chance. Simi, what do you mean you 'used' to see it at work?"

"Well, actually, I called you here today to tell you that I'm officially jobless."

Aṅụrị and Loki instinctively reached for the other's hand. "What?" they said in unison.

"I didn't want to be there and they knew I didn't want to be there and so they didn't really want me there. It was a matter of jump or eventually be pushed. But since I was so good at my job, the pushing wasn't forthcoming. So I bounced."

"Why do you look so serene about this, Sim?" Aṅụrị's pulse was cartwheeling on her friend's behalf.

"I don't waste energy worrying about things that make sense. I kind of have you to thank, Loki. Or rather Céleste. Playing at the wedding is what led me to finding my new agent." Simi paused to allow her friends to lower their jaws to the tabletop. "And also what made me think that I should probably find a job that doesn't make me want to peel my skin off in strips. Violin playing can't be my day job."

"So what are you going to do?" Aṅuri asked.

"Well. After my parents finished praying in tongues and threatening to instigate a twenty-one-day fast, I told them I'm going back to uni to study architecture. They were pretty chill after that."

"Of course," Loki said. "Of fucking course you are. And you're making us go look at weird architectural shit to celebrate. You're amazing. Congrats, Simi."

"Congratulations, babe." Aṅuri leaned into Simi's side. "I can't believe how brilliant you are. Every day you outdo yourself."

Simi beamed. "Thanks, my loves. We'll need someone who knows about this stuff when the time for the compound is upon us."

"You're so right," Loki said. "Now back to what you were saying, Aṅuri. Something about no matter who it is, I have a chance?"

"That's what I said."

"Except with the two of you."

Both Aṅuri and Simi smacked various parts of him. "LOKI."

"Yeah, yeah. But you're both in love. Everyone seems to be in love."

"Who is in love?" Simi demanded.

"Not I," Aṅuri said. "You feeling left out, Lo?"

Loki chewed on the end of a french fry. He remembered a debate he'd once had with Remy about the concept of luck. Remy's position was that there was no such thing but if, by some twist, he was incorrect (Remy did not think it possible for him to be incorrect; he worked on the assumption that it was everyone else who was the problem. He had not yet made the connection between this way of thinking and his divorce) that the power of luck was negligible. No, it was hard work and tenacity that brought people their successes in life. Loki argued that while he could see his father's point, the ability to be tenacious was in itself lucky. Remy, three drinks in and mellower than his default self, touched his tumbler against his son's and conceded the point. It was a truth that never left Loki. It followed him and tapped him on the shoulder now and again. It kept him reasonably humble and forever grateful, because he also had to admit that one person's luck was another's misfortune. It was luck that brought Aṅụrị to camp that summer and gave him what he lacked: an anchor. But if he dwelled on it for long enough, he was forced to trace the series of events backward and acknowledge where they changed from fortuitous to frightful. There was nothing lucky about Kainene's death. Still, this was one of those moments when his good fortune was clearest to him. Sitting under a London sun with two of the people he could not see his world without. The fact was that Loki did not think he could love anyone as much as he did Aṅụrị; or at least not as purely. That whatever came after would be tainted by sex and disappointment. That the inevitable disagreements would never seem worth solving.

"I'm not," Loki said. "I have all the love I need."

"Sweet," Aṅụrị said.

"Gross," Simi said.

Aṅụrị ordered drinks for them all; fizzy bright cocktails for Simi and Loki, some sort of ginger mint mocktail for herself.

"I dunno, guys," she said. "I still feel uneasy about this Ophelia thing. Something isn't sitting right in my spirit."

"She probably still has contract and sponsorship commitments, babe. Try not to worry," Simi said.

But to be Aṅụrị was to exist in a perpetual state of worry.

"Sponsors care about useless shit like birds in the sky?" Loki asked.

"They care about anything that generates engagement," Simi said. "Ophelia was all radio silence and now she's back and *vague*. People love vague. Intrigue sells. I bet the impressions and engagement is off the scale with those posts."

On the walk over to the Brutalism Exhibition, Simi and Loki's conversation buffeted gently against Aṅụrị. She was grateful she had people with whom she could exist without active participation, and she was also grateful that their walk was long enough to allow her to puzzle over Ophelia's reappearance, over Noelle's return to Swiss Cottage and over Nkem's purported weakening resolve to remain with his sister. Eventually, they reached the Tate and Simi slid her arm through Aṅụrị's.

"Oya, head up and phone off! There's a ten-minute intro film before we get into the meat of the exhibition."

"If we have to look at buildings, why can't they at least be beautiful?" Loki grumbled. But he was already turning off his phone and sliding it into his pocket.

"You're too shallow," Simi said.

"We've known each other too long for you to only be aware of this now," Loki said and deftly skipped out of Simi's reach.

"Yes, but we can unknow each other at any point."

"Bold of you to assume you have that choice." Loki pushed his way between Aṅụrị and Simi. He flung his arms about their shoulders and pulled them in until their cheeks were crushed against the cotton of his shirt.

"It is well," Simi said. "Let's go in."

Aṅụrị spent the next two hours lost in the easy companionship of her friends. She listened to Simi's whispered explanations of the showcased buildings, compact histories that lit up Simi's face when she spoke; she dug her elbow in Loki's ribs when he yawned too loudly. She would later think what a marvel of nature it was that the brain was able to temporarily suspend reality and inside the coolness of the Tate, allow her to forget what hung in the balance; blot out the limbo in which she floated. She could be anyone. She could be normal. Just a girl with her best friends taking in some Brutalist architecture on an early August afternoon. The happiness Aṅụrị felt during those two hours would later seem like an absurd alternate life when she stepped back outside into the sunshine, turned on her phone and saw she had two new voicemails from Gloria.

    Ophelia, like many people, developed an affinity for beautiful things at a young age. When she later grew up and possessed the sort of wealth that not only allowed but encouraged the amassing of many beautiful things, Ophelia stepped into the role of curator. The house was its own showcase; a stage on which she was finally able to project her physical beauty outward and demonstrate that walls and floors and the space between the sofa and the living room door could be made lovely; that yes actually, you did need six kinds of candlestick holders and an entire organized drawer dedicated to the housing of the candles which would go inside them. But aside from the house, there was still the matter of herself. Genevieve and Henry had done well in passing down the perfect combination of genes so that their daughter was bestowed with blond, green-eyed Scandinavian beauty. Beauty, as we all know, can be frightening. It had the ability to pull forth unsavory emotions: envy, anger, possessiveness, pride. But Ophelia's attractiveness was inoffensive, not least because it was accompanied by a personality caged and subdued by a sibling's death and the resulting dejection of her parents.

    Life with Nkem and Anụrị provided Ophelia the space and occasion to pursue beauty more voraciously than she had ever thought to before. Suddenly, she had reason to wear gowns, to have her hair twisted into elaborate structures at the top or the base of her head. She had, she told herself, occasions which necessitated the choice of several perfumes and a closet filled entirely with shoes. The naturally gorgeous, at some point, realize that it is something they must maintain and over time, unguents and potions, and visits to smiling practitioners on Harley Street in the pursuit of eternal youth and loveliness wove their way into the structure of Ophelia's new life.

    For Anụrị, a child, all she saw was her stepmother's charm;

the sweep of hair when she loosened it from the thick braid she liked to wear; the creamy skin where pinkness sometimes rose in the softest of ways, the fine wrists and fingers increasingly adorned with gold or diamond. Aṅụrị would sit on the secondary pouf in Ophelia's dressing room and watch her prepare for a dinner out with Nkem, or some sort of award evening she knew nothing about but understood was important enough to require a floor-length dress and an hour of careful mascara application. During these times, Ophelia would occasionally turn from the mirror and cross to where Aṅụrị sat so she might tickle or kiss her, and Aṅụrị remembered the welcome assault of her senses; her head and nose filling with the expensive scent of Ophelia's bergamot and vanilla perfume, the colors—so many of them—from Ophelia's dress, her eyeshadow, the leftover lipstick print on Aṅụrị's skin. It was when she felt closest to Ophelia, a time made even more precious because it was short-lived. Soon, Ophelia hired makeup artists and would dole out a single kiss before ushering Aṅụrị from the room so the black-clad experts could work. Neither Aṅụrị nor Ophelia knew it then but this signaled the end of something between them—they were too ignorant (one due to age, the other due to a combination of naivety and the blind confidence that everything will work out) to set the train back onto the track. This was the beginning of the downward spiral, the erosion of closeness; the decline and eventual loss of tenderness. Adult Aṅụrị looked back and remembered the click of Ophelia's door as it closed, and how final it felt to the not-yet-five-year-old standing on the other side.

She was thinking of this when she listened to Gloria's voicemails. London slowed and then dissolved to white noise around her.

"What do you mean they withdrew?"

"It's just like I said, Aṅụrị. I received a call this afternoon from Ophelia's lawyers informing me that Ophelia was withdrawing the counteroffers she made to you."

"What, everything?"

"Everything. The money, the dissolution of Nuri's Naturals, the deletion of the earlier content. It's all off the table now."

"Can—can they do that?" Aṅụrị steadied herself against the wall. Her leg strength could not be depended upon. She was back in the flat, Simi and Loki having gone on to the cinema where she was meant to join them.

"They can do anything. Aṅụrị, did something happen?"

Of course something had happened. Several somethings had happened. If Aṅụrị's life was a computer game, the past couple of weeks represented a series of side quests she assumed would end up bringing her closer to her overall goal but which seemed to have actually confounded her further and almost exhausted her energy reserves. Reality did not offer conveniently placed pick-me-ups; the suffering could be relentless. Aṅụrị had told Gloria nothing of the information Loki divulged, of the ultimatum given to Ophelia, of the ray of hope in Nkem's and Noelle's departure, or of Noelle's return to North London. Gloria would hardly be interested in the minutiae, but it was that which Aṅụrị held dearest: Nkem's slow gait as they ambled through Ealing, Noelle's little girl giggle, the burst of fuchsia outside the coveted house. Aṅụrị could choose to continue saying nothing until the somethingness completely ended the pretense.

"Something happened," Aṅụrị said slowly. She filled Gloria in, shrinking further and further into herself as she spoke; willing the sky to step down and swallow her whole.

"Aṅụrị," Gloria said, and Aṅụrị imagined her in her office, head pressed into one hand. "Aṅụrị," Gloria said again.

Aṅụrị liked her name. It was a name that required the enunciation of every letter. She did not like it then. For those few seconds, she did not like it at all.

"Do you know what you did can be classed as extortion?"

Aṅụrị slid down the wall. "No! I didn't ask her for money or anything like that!"

"You're smarter than this. You basically told Ophelia she had to tell or you'd tell for her."

"Yeah, but I meant my dad!"

"Did you or did you not hint that you would also leak this information to the press?"

"You mean like she did first?"

"Anụrị."

"But it doesn't matter, right? She told my dad. I didn't have to say anything."

"Unfortunately, given the nature of your relationship with Ophelia, her telling your father doesn't mean you won't turn around at some point and speak about this anyway. I'm sorry, Anụrị. She probably doesn't trust you to stay quiet. If the shoe was on the other foot, I wouldn't trust her to shut up either."

Anụrị put the phone on the floor. She pressed her palms flat against the floorboards and closed her eyes. She was at home. The ground was solid beneath her. She counted to five and back down to one. When she picked up her phone again, Gloria was still there. "What do I do?"

"Nothing. This isn't a situation you can fully control, Anụrị. Okay? Promise me you won't do anything else or talk to anyone else. I need to call in some favors and see if there's anything I can find out."

Anụrị nodded although Gloria could not see her. "Will you call me back when you do?"

"Of course." Finally, Gloria's voice softened. "Of course I will."

She wanted her father. There may come a time where you stop needing your parents, but you do not stop wanting them, Anụrị found. You only resigned yourself to their absence or grew weary of their shortcomings. She could call Nneoma or her grandparents, but instead, not trusting her legs to carry her to her destination, she ordered an Uber and went to Simi's house. Yele opened the door and said, "Yo, Anụrị!" And Morenike, who was at the precise moment walking down the stairs, cuffed her son gently on the back of the head and said, "Yo? What is yo? Did I not teach you how to greet properly?" It was a relief to Aṅụrị to not have to explain what she was doing there without Simi.

Morenike patted Aṅụrị's cheek. "My dear, how are you? You don't eat again? Why so skinny? Come, there's ewedu and asaro in the kitchen. Simi made it last night. Has she told you about this architecture thing she wants to do?" She started moving down the hall toward the back of the house. Here it was. The familiarity Aṅụrị craved. She took a deep, steadying breath and followed.

Like Remy, Gloria did not believe in luck. To admit to being auspicious was to sacrifice an opportunity to celebrate yourself and in the lit match that was the world, why deny yourself that right? Here was a woman who rose to her position as the youngest senior partner at her firm, who did not succumb to the pressure to transition to the bar, who had watched Aṅụrị grow from child to adult. She was Igbo, of Anambra stock, and it wasn't that failure frightened her, it just did not make sense to her. For this reason and *because* she had watched Aṅụrị grow from child to adult, she dedicated fourteen minutes to her annoyance at Aṅụrị for opening her mouth and trying to orchestrate a forced triumph. The girl's actions had essentially removed Gloria's teeth, her bite was now ineffective. Fourteen minutes over, Gloria decided she would simply grow new teeth.

She closed the door to her office, kicked off her shoes and paced a circle into the carpet. She then returned to her desk, picked up the phone and placed a call to one Vincent Nelson-Grey. She did not particularly like Vincent Nelson-Grey. The man perpetually smelled like coffee and concluded every sentence he spoke with a low laugh. He was a man who had abandoned the desire to be liked, and because of this and his prowess as a private investigator, Gloria respected him. After all, it is easier to be liked than respected.

"Mrs. Ezenwa-Okorie," Vincent said. "To what do I owe this pleasure heh heh heh?"

Gloria clenched her teeth. "As always, Vincent, 'Gloria' is fine." She did not wait for a response. "How au fait are you with pseudo-celebrities?"

It took Vincent Nelson-Grey a little less than forty-eight hours to arrive at Gloria's office holding a slim file. Inside was a photograph and a single sheet of paper.

"She's very boring, that Ophelia Chinasa heh heh heh," he said to Gloria. "Send me something a little juicer next time?"

Gloria paid him the remainder of his fee, saw him out and all but sprinted back to her office. She opened the folder and pored over its contents. The photo was semi-blurry; a long-range shot of Ophelia meeting with someone in a Starbucks. Gloria did not need to read the typed report but did anyway, dread pooling in her stomach. She would recognize that orange hair anywhere. It was a hue that did not occur in nature. It was the hair of Penelope Bishop, author of the Article.

NKEM

I didn't tell Nneoma when I decided to marry Ophelia. Already, there was too much doubt, too much negativity surrounding us, and I did not want to build my new marriage on a bed of pessimism. I knew what my sister would say; what Makuo and Arinze would think: that I was rushing, that all I wanted was a replacement for Kainene or perhaps a gateway to the other side of losing her, where I couldn't feel her absence like a thorn with every movement I made. Nneoma would ask me whether or not I thought marrying Kaine's opposite would bring me peace. She would hold me in place with her eyes, as she has always done, and I would crack open and stain us all with the truth.

Which was this: I did not know how to be a father to Añụrị without the child's mother at my side. Failure pressed in from all sides. I was too weak, too frightened to learn. My love for Ophelia, at least in the beginning, was secondary. I needed her to be the person my daughter could rely on.

For this reason, but for a different daughter, I returned to her.

Again, my love for my wife was secondary, but it was unaffected by circumstance and by the choices she made.

I returned to her knowing it would forever feel like a betrayal.

NINETEEN

At age twelve, Aṅụrị was cresting the wave of an aggressive growth spurt which left her with spidery stretch marks on her hips and a pair of breasts she kept hidden beneath a range of outsize men's sweatshirts. She was also battling a small yet persistent patch of acne on her chin. She was dueling with puberty and hormones and losing most spectacularly. The hormones and the general glut of preteen angst coincided with Simi's parents finally taking their child's classification as "gifted" seriously, resulting in Simi's enrolment in a series of extracurricular tutoring and sporting activities. This meant that Simi was less available and that when she was, she was often preoccupied or fatigued. Twelve-year-old Aṅụrị took Simi's droopy-eyed presence to mean she had become less interesting to her friend, and that this must be rectified immediately. She set about on a short course of intense reinvention. She learned Yoruba phrases from Lekan and Yele to better engage Simi in conversation. She looked up information on Wikipedia about the kind of very boring buildings Simi was interested in, and made herself sit through the very boring documentaries Simi enjoyed. She visited the fancy charity shops near her school and bought secondhand Mills &

Boon books so she might regale Simi and Loki with her newfound knowledge of "tumescence" and "heaving bosoms." For a strange fortnight, Aṅụrị wore only black clothing, started listening to alternative rock and trained herself to refuse all beverages bar Dr. Pepper and black coffee. She was a child, but more than that, she was an Online Child used to being the sustained object of acclamation. She had not yet learned that perfection was subjective and that you could spend weeks, months or even a lifetime carving away at parts of yourself until you resembled what was popular, not knowing that what was popular had a new definition and you were now disfigured and surplus to requirements.

Aṅụrị did all these things and all that happened was Simi pulling her up the stairs to her bedroom one afternoon and saying, "Aṅụrị, kilode? Mummy says to ask if something is wrong with you so they can direct their prayers." A month later when Simi told her parents she would find the nearest boy to run away with if they did not allow her to drop advanced mathematics, things went back to normal and Aṅụrị started dressing like herself and diversifying her beverage choices. She cast off the disguise but found she genuinely did enjoy both Doc Martens and alternative rock—something about the drums, the clashing of the high hat, the guitars braying anguish even if the song happened to be jovial.

In times of high stress, Aṅụrị retreated wholly into this music. Her afternoon was spent listening to Manic Street Preachers, Arcade Fire and Red Hot Chili Peppers. The catalyst? A phone call from Gloria the day before.

"Are you sure it was her?" Aṅụrị asked, following Gloria divulging the outcome of Vincent Nelson-Grey's assignment.

"It was Penelope, Aṅụrị. I'm sorry. I'd recognize that hair anywhere. Besides, Vincent is very thorough."

Aṅụrị raised her free hand and saw that it was shaking. "No. I mean…was it Ophelia? Are you sure it was Ophelia?"

Gloria, making the call from her living room sofa where she

watched her husband slice spring onions, wished there was a world in which she might tell Aṅụrị she was mistaken. Alas.

"I— The job was for him to follow Ophelia and find anything of note in her comings and goings. It's her, Aṅụrị. I'm really sorry." And she was. Bad news was never a delight to deliver, but there was bad news and then there was this; a confirmation that Aṅụrị's stepmother was the source of yet another painful time in Aṅụrị's life.

Aṅụrị sat down on her bed. She did not want to, but her body did. There were too many reminders today that a person was never fully their own. "Okay but what does it mean? Aside from her being the leak?" Her voice had taken on a reedy quality she did not like.

"We have to think logically. Ophelia's back to posting content. Noelle is home with her and she's meeting with Penelope Bishop and not to swap casserole recipes."

Keep breathing, Aṅụrị told herself. How pathetic to have to coach your body to carry out the functions it was there to naturally perform. She almost laughed. But then she would forget to breathe.

"You don't think…she couldn't be…" The words were too horrific to speak. If Aṅụrị put them into the world, then there was a chance they would be true.

"That she's leaking something else? I think that's very likely given what we know now. I—"

"No. No." Aṅụrị swallowed. She felt herself tilting to the left, so she lay flat on her bed. "When she wrote the article, I googled her. Penelope is kind of famous for her long-form interviews. Written and televised. You don't think…" She was unable to finish the sentence.

In her living room, Gloria was on her feet. Her husband's knife stilled over the onions. He looked at her quizzically.

"M nzuzu," Gloria said because in that moment, foolish is all she felt. How hadn't she thought of it herself? The coolness with

which Ophelia's lawyers had informed her of "Mrs. Chinasa's change of heart," the abruptness with which they snatched the offer off the table and now this new information about Penelope. Retaliation never occurred to Gloria because, despite everything, she was a mother first and she could not comprehend a mother choosing this course of action. It did not compute. But she was not dealing with normal people. And it was brilliant. Diabolical but brilliant.

"Aṅụrị," Gloria said, "Ophelia could be planning something with Penelope. Is that what you were about to say?"

"Yes." It came out as a whisper.

"I'm going to see what I can find out." Gloria's blood was hot. The rush of unearthing new and important information, of slotting in another puzzle piece for the good of her client was imminent. She felt giddy with it. Then remembered the sound of Aṅụrị's voice: tiny and defeated. "Aṅụrị. It's not over, okay?"

But it was, Aṅụrị thought. How could Gloria not see that it was?

Aṅụrị did not need to wait to see what Gloria could find out. The announcement was made that morning across both Penelope's and Ophelia's social media, as well as the entertainment pages of global publications. Ophelia was sitting down with Penelope Bishop for a long-awaited TV exclusive on motherhood. *Find out*, the Instagram post said, *about the pressures of public motherhood, the pain of strained relationships with your kids and all about that legal trouble! An unmissable and frank discussion coming this Sunday.* Aṅụrị read the announcements over and over again until her eyes rejected it and the posts became smeared colors and shapes on the screen. It was Tuesday. She phoned Nkem.

"What do you want me to do?" he said.

Aṅụrị did not answer. If he didn't know, then there was nothing to be said.

"Biko, Aṅụrị, I have problems here, too."

"Are you still at Aunty Nneoma's place?"

Nkem was slow to respond. "It was better for me to be here at home with Noelle. She was asking for me."

Aṅụrị hung up then turned off her phone and turned on Manic Street Preachers. She pressed her belly to the floor so she could reach under her bed for the unopened bottle of rum she purchased the day before, and when she found it, she set it on the chest of drawers opposite her bed. Then she lay back down. She stared at the bottle and it stared back. She would drink it, she knew, it was only a matter of when. And she felt nothing but relief, because was weakness truly weakness if you welcomed it?

Around 3:00 p.m., Aṅụrị heard knocking. She realized then that she must have fallen asleep because the knocking startled her, thrust her into unwelcome wakefulness. She turned over and ignored it. It stopped. Around 4:00 p.m., the knocking restarted and this time, it came as the drumbeat of a Wizkid song Aṅụrị loved. She shuffled to her front door and opened it to find Christian.

After the plant pot holder, Aṅụrị returned to Blank and left Christian a monogrammed yarn bag she ordered from Etsy. That had been days ago and she decided not to live in hope. He didn't call and he didn't text and plant pot holders were wonderful but they were a poor substitute for conversation. She may have been forgiven, but she may also have been confined to Christian's personal past. Whenever she thought about this, Aṅụrị felt like all the air in the room had consolidated into a ball and rolled away from her, out of her reach.

"Oh," she said now.

"Hi," Christian said.

"How do you keep getting into the building?"

"You have very nice neighbors. They always compliment my hair. They even ask to touch it." He smiled.

"Oh," Aṅụrị said.

"Your phone was off."

"It's been a crappy day."

"I figured."

Aṅụrị briefly considered folding like origami at his feet but chose instead to return to her bedroom, lie back down on her bed and resume her staring contest with the rum. Christian followed. He opened one window, surveyed the clothes on the floor and Aṅụrị's vacant stare, and lay beside her, leaving space between them.

"Why are we looking at a bottle of rum?"

"I find staring helps kill the craving."

"Does it? Let me try." Christian fixed his eyes on the side of Aṅụrị's face. "Fake news."

Aṅụrị turned her head and met his gaze. "Hi," she said.

"Today has you craving rum?"

"Every day," Aṅụrị said, because she was too weary to lie. "But I haven't drunk it yet."

"Ah." They both resumed staring at the bottle. "You're right. You haven't drunk it. I'm not sure there has to be a 'yet.'"

"Doesn't there?" If she kept still, perhaps he wouldn't notice she was crying.

"No. There doesn't. We can talk about that sometime, if you like. Thank you for the yarn bag. My sister's been laughing at me nonstop since it arrived."

"I'm sorry for being weird. I try to help it, but I can't."

"I'm a grown man in cybersecurity who enjoys crochet. We're all weird, Aṅụrị."

"My weird is special."

"I like your weird. Listen, do you want to know how long I would have knocked if you hadn't answered the door?"

"How long?"

"Literally four hours. They let us leave work early today and I came straight here to give you this." Christian reached down and handed her a crocheted monogrammed plush pig. "In case you were missing LowlyWorm."

Aṅụrị couldn't speak. She fumbled for his hand.

"This might be shitty timing but I just…" His voice faltered. Aṅụrị squeezed his fingers. "Right. I'm saying it doesn't have to be complicated, you know. It can just be two people, and sometimes more, working together to make each other's lives a little less trying. And pointing out beautiful things the other might not have seen. And like, crocheting substitute paypigs. I think that's my definition of it anyway."

"Love?"

"And the lead up to it. I think I'd like to have the chance to do those things for you, and you know, have you do them for me in a way that isn't a chore."

"Despite me being a ten?"

"*Because* you're a nine point one."

"What if—"

"Nope. Let's not do that today."

"Alright. Deal-breakers?"

"The consumption of runny egg, methamphetamine or Woody Allen films."

"Wow. Strict."

"Yours?"

"Don't go on TV to talk about your relationship with me."

Christian held Aṅụrị's hand a little tighter. "Oh that's a piece of piss. I don't like talking to most people."

When she woke again, it was gone nine and the bottle of rum had disappeared from Aṅụrị's chest of drawers. Christian had also disappeared, but she could hear the muffled rumble of voices from the living room. Congregated there, she found Christian, Loki, Simi and a person she had never met.

"Omo, she lives," Simi said, and picked her way across the room so she could clamp her hands on Aṅụrị's shoulders. "This is a council of war. You need food first? We ordered tacos."

"You good?" Christian asked from his place beside Loki.

"I'm—" Aṅụrị stared at the stranger "—thinking you look familiar," she directed to him.

"Oh. This is Abe," Simi said. As if his being there was a forgone conclusion. As if he were a piece of furniture Aṅụrị had forgotten she owned. As if this was not groundbreaking behavior on Simi's part.

"This is…this is *Abe*?" Aṅụrị squeaked.

"Exactly," Loki said. *"Exactly."*

"Hey, Aṅụrị," Abe said genially. "Nap was good?"

"Don't ask about her nap," Simi said. "It was an avoidance sleep, I fear."

"Chère. Was it an avoidance sleep?" Loki joined Simi at Aṅụrị's side.

"This is Abe," Aṅụrị repeated.

"Getting jealous down here," Christian said.

"Imagine my shock when I get here and this one opens the door." Simi jerked her head in Christian's direction. "Lekan will be devastated by the way."

"Hi, Abe," Aṅụrị said.

Abe grinned. "Nice to finally meet you."

Simi let her hands drop. "Why is everyone making such a big *deal*?"

Abe slid an arm around Simi's waist. "Apparently I'm important."

"You see. You *see*. Now look what you people have done." It was a miracle that a person could hiss and look giddy at the same time. Simi was a worker of miracles.

The tacos arrived and with the ingestion of carnitas, shrimp and pineapple salsa, came the opportunity to scrutinize Aṅụrị. Simi, who had arrived first with Abe in tow; who had been immediately taken to the side and updated about the rum; who had instructed Abe to dispose of it, noted a new quality in her friend she was struggling to place. Midway through her third taco, Simi realized with a jolt that it was *surrender*. Aṅụrị wore it awkwardly because she was unused to its shape and its weight.

For Loki, the absence of Aṅụrị's laughter ricocheting around the room pulled his eyebrows together. Earlier that evening, he'd left dinner with Céleste and her husband early, as soon as he received Simi's text, and Céleste had held his face and said, "Go to her."

On his way to Aṅuri's place, he rehearsed in his head what he would say when he arrived: *It's okay to not do this anymore, let's go to New York for a bit.* But when he did arrive, and when Aṅuri stepped out of her bedroom, he saw that he'd never truly thought he'd have occasion to make his offer. He'd never expected Aṅuri to stop fighting. He'd asked her if she knew what she was going to do. "Do?" she'd responded with a look of bewilderment on her face, and Loki found himself shaken. Aṅuri always did. Even when it wasn't clear what the doing meant.

"Stop staring at me," Aṅuri said now.

"Think she's talking to the rest of you," Christian said.

"Was I staring?" Abe asked.

"We just want to know your plan of action," Loki said.

"Oh that's simple. I don't have one. Are there any more corn chips?"

Simi waited a beat. "And that's why you have us. To help you think of one."

"You will live very long," Aṅuri said, accepting the chips from Abe, "but, Sim. I think I'm done."

"How can you be done?" There had never before been a time when Simi needed to convince Aṅuri to stand up to Ophelia. It was as if Aṅuri was destined to be the deliberate obstacle in Ophelia's path. To hear Aṅuri announce her resignation from her position as Chief Agitator with such calmness was chilling.

Aṅuri glanced around the table. How to explain that the anvil of futility had finally fallen and flattened her? What was the use of fighting when Ophelia would only rise again? The information about Noelle should have heralded the end, but there was to be no end, and there was a peace in accepting that. Sunday would come and Ophelia would be vindicated and life would continue on its set course, this time without Aṅuri hanging off the back of it, trying fruitlessly to slow its pace.

"I'm tired," is what Aṅuri said.

"So we tackle this and then we find a beach to lie on for as long as you want," Loki said.

Aṅụrị smiled. "I love a beach. Let's do the beach right now."

Simi turned to Christian. "Can you crochet her some sense?"

"Simi," Aṅụrị said.

"I don't get it. I'm trying, babe. But I don't."

"Isn't it enough that I'll be happy?"

"Will you?" Loki said carefully. "Be happy?"

The answer to Loki's question should have been obvious: she would not be happy, but she was prepared to abandon happiness for something approximating serenity. That too would be hard-won, but it would come eventually. Aṅụrị once again surveyed the assembled faces. They were there for her. They had other places to be. They had entire chapters of their lives Aṅụrị was not privy to. Her stomach twisted with guilt. She set her half-eaten taco down in its nest of wax paper. Loki and Simi had seen her through every one of her rock-bottom moments; there had been more than one—Aṅụrị was an overachiever in that respect. In giving up her fight against Ophelia, she was rendering that part of them obsolete and because that part of her was its own totality, it was frightening for them, too.

"I can't win," she said quietly, eyes on the table. "She'll only preempt me some other way."

For a few minutes they sat in silence, appetites forgotten. Eventually, Loki began gathering up the remnants of their meal to throw away. Abe joined him. Just before they left the table, Christian cleared his throat.

"Obviously I don't know shit about it," he said. "But what if you preempted her preempt?"

Twitter. How ironic that this ended up being the solution. Because while Aṅụrị was hiding from social media, society continued to embrace it to the point of dependency. It was where news landed first, where revolutions were documented in real time, where human beings discovered the loves of their lives and

ALLOW ME TO INTRODUCE MYSELF

charted their mistakes publicly and without shame. It was also a place entertainment journalists and editors put their email addresses and allowed work to find them. This is how on a Tuesday night in June, just before midnight, that Gabrielle Curry, young whiz kid entertainment writer at a prominent UK broadsheet, with bylines everywhere from *Vulture* and *The Cut*, to *The Atlantic* and *Variety*, who also happened to be a noted and vocal critic of one Penelope Bishop, therefore flouting the unspoken rules that existed amongst journalists to never publicly criticize one of their own, received a DM interesting enough to make her peel away from the clutch of bodies with which she was sipping champagne whilst waiting for a minute with the publicist of a newly divorced model.

The DM was from Loki Chevalier and despite Gabby being nearly a decade younger than her peers and navigating the dual journalistic complications of being Black and having neither an Oxbridge degree nor famous or wealthy parentage, she knew who Loki Chevalier was. She was still quietly irate that a senior colleague had commandeered her press invitation to the recent wedding reception of Céleste Llorens-Scott. The DM was succinct: Evening, Gabrielle. I have something I think you'd be interested in. It's about Ophelia Chinasa.

Ophelia Chinasa was ubiquitous. She was inescapable; on everyone's radar even if you'd rather she were not. Gabby had followed the unfolding drama and speculation under duress from her editor and had taken her scolding for being scooped by the Bishop woman on the chin. This Sunday, she planned on eating her bodyweight in roast potatoes and getting drunk on gin and hate-watching the interview that would no doubt bring additional acclaim to both Bishop and Chinasa. Therefore, the DM intrigued her. For Gabby, it was a win-win. If what Loki had to say was nonsense, she could professionally and courteously refuse, inventing a reason it would not work for her editors, whilst still having made something of a useful acquaintance. Should the information be pertinent, well, the glee would be profound. She responded. Hi there, Loki. What do you have for me?

"You can back out," Gloria said.

"No," Aṅụrị said, "I don't think I can."

"You've had no sleep."

Aṅụrị glanced over her shoulder to where Simi, Loki, Christian and Abe were congregated at the hotel bar, nursing some form of caffeinated beverage. Christian abstained given that caffeine tended to exacerbate his anxiety.

"They made me sleep for a couple of hours."

Gloria nodded and straightened Aṅụrị's collar. "I will be sitting right there at the next table. Just give me one look and I'll lock the whole thing off."

Aṅụrị laughed. "You're worrying too much. Abeg, relax."

"Don't tell me to relax. I'm fine. I'm relaxed." Gloria chewed her lip. "But you *can* change your mind. This is one hundred percent your decision, Aṅụrị. Nobody will think less of you."

Aṅụrị rotated her mother's bangle around her wrist. Gabrielle's swiftness deserved lauding. Loki's message landed a mere sixteen hours earlier. She was waiting in the beautifully lit restaurant of a London hotel with the videographer she roused in the wee hours of that morning after first rousing her editor who used the words "whatever it takes" when Gabby breathlessly explained what was at stake. The printed interview would run alongside a filmed piece which had neither the lead time nor the associated complexities as a television production. Thus, it would appear in the world a full twenty-four hours ahead of Ophelia and Penelope's piece. There was no turning back. The die were cast.

"I'd think less of me," Aṅụrị said.

Simi sauntered over. "Hello. Hi. Please excuse us," she said to Gloria and pulled Aṅụrị to the side. "You can say no."

Years earlier, Simi had introduced Aṅụrị to the concept of

choice, and here she was again with a reminder. Aṅụrị smiled. "You don't even believe that, Sim."

"You're right. I don't. I love you, okay?"

"I love you back."

Loki came over to join them. In his right hand he held the remnants of an iced latte. On his face, he wore an expression of tenderness. "How you feeling?"

There it was, the familiar desire to plant roses over the decay. Aṅụrị shook her head—if anyone deserved the truth, it was Simi and Loki. "I'm feeling like now would be a great time for some tequila." She raised a hand to quash the pep talk she knew was forthcoming. "But I think I'm okay. I might *want* to drink, but I know I'm not *going* to. I...could probably use some help making that permanent."

In her head, Aṅụrị counted to five. "I need to make a call." She moved away, heart swan diving in her chest, and stepped behind the giant bird of paradise plant in the hotel lobby; its leaves dipping low enough to graze her cheek.

Nkem answered on the second ring. "Aṅụrị."

"I'm going to do something," she said.

Nkem opened his mouth. His chastisement was already forming on his lips—the child could not even greet?—but something in her tone stopped him. He swallowed the words.

"I'm going to do something," Aṅụrị said again, "and it won't be good for Ophelia."

Nkem knew now that transformation did not always herald its arrival; that as the river erodes rock, life could also be altered gradually just as it could change abruptly. His life had changed by degrees, but the constant was how he had failed his daughter. He knew that he would fail again, repeatedly, and that Aṅụrị's disappointment would follow him—a scarlet letter only he could see. But he had a choice. He could continue to allow her to slip away, or he could try. Perhaps there was hope yet if he could just listen.

"Will it hurt her?" he asked.

"Not physically."

"Will it hurt you?"

"Not physically," Aṅụrị said, her voice tremulous in a way Nkem had not heard in years.

"It is your life, Aṅụrị. It is my fault you did not know it more before now. Do what you need to."

Aṅụrị was still standing behind the bird of paradise when Simi touched her elbow.

"Ready?"

Aṅụrị nodded. "Ready."

Aṅụrị did not know what Gabrielle would ask. She also did not quite know what she would say. Where was the best place to begin? The sixth birthday party? The appearance of her period aged ten which was turned into a blog post so that her introduction to womanhood was not allowed to be her own? Did she talk about alcohol? The spending sprees? LowlyWorm? Aṅụrị's fingers found her wrist. The bangle was cool against her skin. Kainene. She was the beginning of everything, and now she would also be the end.

In the restaurant, Gabby wore a loose-fitting white shirt. Her braids were piled on top of her head. She'd swapped champagne for coffee and adrenaline. She was the orchestrator of perhaps the most important of Aṅụrị's Befores. The sun split a cloud in two as Aṅụrị approached the table and turned her skin to bronze. Gabby stood up.

"Hello, Aṅụrị," Gabby said. "Shall we sit down and talk?"

OPHELIA

One of the first things Penelope said to me when we sat down together was this: "The current state of the relationship between you and your stepdaughter must be difficult for you, and the result of this—" here, she gestured between herself and me "—is guaranteed to make things worse. So I have to ask you before we continue: Is it worth it?"

Was it worth it?

If you surmise that something is already broken beyond repair; if you feel that what has been lost can never be regained then you reason there is no harm in grinding that something beneath your heel, compounding the collapse and completing the ruination. If that sounds almost rational then let me temper it with the facts.

The fury I felt toward Aṅụrị, like the mutation and division of cells, spread through me, overwhelming the good that remained. It was easier to blame her than it was to scrutinize my own choices and sit in the mire of my own failings. So, it became Aṅụrị's fault that Noelle's behavior changed and that at night when her crying could not *be quelled, that it was Aṅụrị she asked for. It was Aṅụrị's fault that Nkem began to relent, his resolve thawing and revealing the possibility of taking Noelle to a therapist. Aṅụrị was the origin of this new distance between me and my husband. She was the cause of the increasing number of comments left by angry observers on anything I posted online. The reasons sound poor because they are. But my rage, my fear, all of it was fanned by the realization that I had lost her.*

The thing about vengeance is that its sweetness only lasts if you have been wronged. And Aṅụrị's crime was reclaiming her life.

"It is the right thing," Nkem said tonight from his position at my side. "I think it is the right thing."

He stayed there at my side as I dismantled it all, until nothing remained but the outline and consequences of what I built, indelibly inked in internet archives.

If losing my world means she can rebuild hers then maybe it was worth it, after all.

TWENTY

Gabrielle titled Aṅụrị's interview "Allow Me to Introduce Myself: Aṅụrị Speaks." Two hours after it was published, Nkem stepped outside into his back garden, strolled past the hydrangeas and, in the shade of the sycamore, called his daughter. It was the tall boy who answered and gave, in almost accusatory tones, a cursory explanation about call screening before informing Nkem that he would enquire whether Aṅụrị felt like speaking to him. Nkem's relief, when he heard her voice, kicked his legs out from under him. He sank onto the grass.

"Dad," Aṅụrị said, hesitantly, her voice guarded and laden with weariness.

"When your mother was at university, there was a professor there who refused to teach female students unless they wore skirts to his classes. Most people didn't want to fight but Kainene decided it was only jeans she would wear. Someone who only wore skirts up until then, o! Now suddenly, jeans," Nkem laughed.

"I begged her to reconsider, and she stopped speaking to me for a week. She missed one month of classes, wrote I don't know how many letters and even threatened to leave university altogether if her parents wouldn't support her. That one was theatrics; what was it Kaine would do that Makuo and Arinze wouldn't support? By the time she was allowed back into class, every girl was wearing jeans."

Nkem paused, remembering Kainene's delight, her shout of triumph when she received the news that her efforts had not been in vain. Even then, he knew he wasn't worthy of her; that she would eclipse him. And he had felt grateful to be able to sit in her shadow if it meant she would be close.

"What you did…what you said…Kaine would be so proud of you."

Aṅụrị's eyes fell on the now-framed photographs of her mother on her windowsill. It would take time, she knew, for her to feel anything other than robbed of these precious kernels of information. She would battle, perhaps forever, with the fury that accompanied every conversation with Nkem. She suppressed a retort. Nkem had given Aṅụrị a gift—the knowledge that Kainene would be proud was something she would carry with her; something she could return to again and again. Nkem had done what he considered his best, and like the best of so many other parents, it had not been good enough. It made him flawed, but it also made him human. Undeniably so.

"Thank you," Aṅụrị said. "For telling me."

"There is more to know."

"Dad, if this…if what I've done has made things harder for Noelle—"

"Then that is for me…for us to rectify. There is still time."

Aṅụrị waited, but there was no further apology. Nkem, just like her, was coming to terms with all that their lives had been and stumbling in the uncertainty of what they would become. "Dad," she started.

"You can call me if you need to," Nkem said, "I may not always… I know I won't be the best. But I will try. I want you to know that I will try. And that I am proud of you, too."

As the article swept the entertainment circuit and spilled over into the psychology and parenthood publications, Aṅụrị's days became thick with the exaggerated exuberance generated by the internet gossip machine. Hers was a story not bound by the usual web news cycle which dictated a few days of intense analysis followed by the predictable transition out of the spotlight in favor of something new and salacious. The world was united in its adoration of perceived scandal. She expected backlash, and it came, but it was drowned out by how completely her words upset the apple cart that was the parental influencer model. Now people had more questions. Now people wanted to know what it truly meant to innocently post the photo of little Johnny. Now the tween and teen children of influencers were shouting a little louder. Aṅụrị's words gave legitimacy to the notion that delaying the inevitable might not be so awful a thing here; that maybe kids deserved a chance to say no. That was to come.

But before that, there was Ophelia. Ophelia read the words first, then watched the accompanying YouTube video. In a way, the written words were easier to digest than the spoken ones uttered as they were by the person she once bathed in a sink, the one to whom she cooed when London nights pressed in close and dawn seemed a lifetime away. In the video, Aṅụrị's eyes were wide with what could have been fear or determination—Ophelia only settled on the former because she also saw, brief as it was, a shot of Aṅụrị's hands twisting together and then apart on the tabletop. That had not changed. She was still a fidget when nervous, and she was nervous because talking about that which you have escaped (and there was no question that Aṅụrị's departure from online life was an escape) often drags it back from the past and gives it the position of vanguard anew.

Aṅụrị chose the same medium she despised to put decibels behind her voice. It was not easy, but the difficulty of it compounded its importance.

Ophelia read and she watched Aṅụrị articulate what life was like for her in the Chinasa household before she torched the apron strings and reimagined her future. It did not read like revenge; it was spoken like redemption.

EPILOGUE

Almost six months to the day after Ophelia's internet presence went dark, Anụrị raised her phone to eye level so that Makuo and Arinze might see the giant bay window in the front room. She stood in a house in Ealing, the sixth she had seen in the last four days and, if her elevated pulse and stinging eyes were anything to go by, *the one*. It was smaller than the house on Denbigh Road, with a clutch of tangled, mostly dead wisteria in the square of front yard, and a trio of conifers in the back garden. Its windows would need to be replaced, although not immediately, and the floors were scarred and uneven. *Like me*, Anụrị thought. She'd FaceTimed her grandparents after she and Christian walked through the house a third time, and she glanced at him now standing by the open front door, googling how to resurrect wisteria.

Arinze, far away but watching the joy etch itself into his granddaughter's face, reached for his wife's hand. "Of the six," he declared, "this is the best."

Makuo nodded. "It's already beautiful, obim. But I think you can still improve it."

Up until she met Gabrielle, Anụrị feared that everything she had struggled and fought for could still fall away. And in that event, she thought, she would still always have her imagination. Fantasies were untouchable that way. But then, in the weeks after her interview met the world, Aṅụrị, buttressed by her village, became virtually unreachable, turning down book deals, speaking engagements and anything that would necessitate reentering the spotlight before she was ready. That sort of faux-insulation from the world did not distract Aṅụrị from the reality that when the time to emerge arrived, it would be terrifying. Therefore, she constructed her return, opting to publish a follow-up article with *Psychology Today* one month post-interview. In it, she spoke candidly about the effects of online life for herself as a minor and beyond, and the confusing lack of legislation designed to protect children as yet another tendril of capitalism reached them. She would never be sure without asking her outright, but Aṅụrị guessed that the article was the catalyst for Ophelia's decision to, through Gloria, offer Aṅụrị what she called "payment for services rendered." The number made Aṅụrị's eyes water and drove home the extent of her stepmother's financial aptitude. It was not an apology. But it was the chance at a future; at a house in West London with lopsided floors and a bedroom and back garden for her little sister; an end to the nameless, faceless men she degraded for money. A fantasy creeping toward fruition.

Aṅụrị ended the call with her grandparents as Simi and Loki descended the stairs.

"So?" She looked from one to the other. "What do you guys think?"

"I call the attic bedroom," Loki said.

Simi tutted and shouldered her bag. "Just like a man to choose aesthetics over practicality. As tall as you are, and you pick the room with the least headroom. Okay, o. If you like it, I love it." She turned to Aṅụrị. "You'll let me cut my teeth on this place?"

Aṅụrị let her gaze trail over the ceilings and the walls she had already started knocking down in her mind. "Naturally, Sim."

"Then it gets my stamp of approval. I'll see you tonight?"

"Of course she'll see us tonight," Loki answered for Aṅụrị. "I'm bringing homemade flatbreads. Don't look at me like that. Christian will supervise their preparation."

Christian, on hearing his name, ambled over, eyes still on his phone. "Correct."

"Guys, please," Aṅụrị said. "I love you all, but it's not a party."

"Damn right it's a party," Loki said. "Submitting your PhD application is not a small thing. And you invited Yoli. Speaking of, what do you think about—"

Simi lifted her eyes heavenward. "Loki, you can't date Aṅụrị's AA sponsor. Have shame. If that's possible."

"Who said anything about date?" Loki protested. "What if I want to pick her brain on the finer points of addiction?"

"What if I slap you into next month?"

As they moved toward the door, Christian took the opportunity to lean in close to Aṅụrị. "It doesn't have to be a party, but maybe a little celebration? Since I have a feeling you might be considering putting in an offer on this place."

Aṅụrị threaded her fingers through his, pausing so he could use his free hand to roll up the sleeves of the hoodie she was wearing; the one she'd stolen from him that morning. "I want to bring Noelle here first. She has to love it."

"She will. Because you do." He dropped a kiss on her forehead. "You sure you don't want me to come with right now?"

Aṅụrị shook her head. "To Ammah's? I'm good. I'll be okay."

"Then I'll see you tonight."

Every day since they disappeared, the first thing Aṅụrị did when she woke up was check Ophelia's social media handles, anticipating her return. It would not surprise her if Ophelia engineered some form of comeback—the internet was too addictive, too suffusive. Ophelia's livelihood and self-esteem were inextricable. It was not realistic to expect her to fade to black forever. To know this was to know the closest thing to peace the situation allowed. Anụrị and Ammah had been preparing so that if the time ever came, Anụrị would be able to keep hold of something solid while the tide rolled in. The court of public opinion had determined Ophelia's actions reprehensible and, Anụrị thought, mostly because there was no real way to defend herself, Ophelia had remained silent. She had not reached out and Anụrị shocked herself by feeling, at least temporarily, saddened. The bright side was that Anụrị's time with Noelle was no longer curtailed by the infighting.

Now, as she made her way to Ammah's office, Anụrị wondered what Ophelia was doing and whether there would ever come a time when she didn't wish things were different. She wondered if she'd forever wear the bruises of the past and if they made her repulsive, or, like a certain kind of scar, interesting and even beautiful. She wondered if her PhD proposal, "A Critical Analysis of the Impact of Appearing on Social Media on Adolescents and Children into Adulthood," would not only drive the wedge further but turn it to steel. She was still sorting through the debris in her head when she arrived at Ammah's, noted the empty second chair and readied herself to ride another groundswell of sadness. She set her bag on the floor and when she turned back to Ammah, there he was, gently shutting the door.

Nkem ushered Noelle into the room, and met his eldest's eyes. "We're here," he said. "We are here."

* * * * *

DISCUSSION GUIDE

1. After reading Aṅụrị's story, have your thoughts about social media changed? What do you think about adults documenting their children's lives on the internet?

2. The story begins with Aṅụrị having already made the decision to pursue her autonomy via litigation. How do you think this affects Ophelia emotionally?

3. How do you think the loss of Kainene shapes Nkem's relationship with first Aṅụrị and then Noelle?

4. Simi and Loki are important anchors in Aṅụrị's life. What role do you think Aṅụrị plays in their lives?

5. Aṅụrị's focus shifts to her little sister and securing a life for them both free of Ophelia's desire for ongoing online popularity. Why do you think this becomes so urgent for Aṅụrị?

6. What significance do Makuo and Arinze have in Aṅụrị's life? What part do they play in her pursuit of independence?

7. What are your thoughts on the way in which Aṅụrị interacts with Christian? Is her hesitancy understandable? How do you think her past colors the way she perceives romantic relationships?

8. Throughout the story, Aṅụrị constantly battles the allure of drinking and binge shopping. Why do you think these are

her vices of choice? How do you think her relationship to these dependencies changes as the story continues?

9. Ophelia seems determined to cling to her relevance and popularity at all costs. How do you interpret this resolve?

10. LowlyWorm's proposal captures Aṅụrị's attention enough for her to briefly consider accepting it. What do you think led her to even contemplate this? What are your thoughts on Aṅụrị's decision to practise findom?

11. At the end of the story, Aṅụrị chooses to sever all contact with Ophelia. Do you think their relationship could ever be repaired? What do you think it would take?

ACKNOWLEDGMENTS

This book would not exist without having glimpsed, and sometimes observed in greater detail than was right, the lives of the many children whose moments are stamped in the annals of the time and immortalized on the internet. Because of you, a new conviction sprouted inside me. Thank you.

I am forever indebted to my parents, Betty and Nwachukwu, who placed a pen in my hand and gave me the room to write my way into the homes of other people; sitting with me through endless questions, debates and discussions, and watering the seed of my imagination with their love. And to Ngozi and Chuks, your unwavering confidence has pulled me through countless moments of doubt. Charlene and my precious babies, life is sunnier because of you all. My family, I love you all more than I can adequately express, and your place is cemented in every acknowledgment I have the privilege of writing.

Precious, thank you for indulging my many questions about the Yoruba language, and for being unequivocally, unabashedly you. You have spent days and nights reading my WhatsApp meltdowns and bolstering me with laughter and with faith. Like Anụrị and Simi, we're in this for life.

Farah and Aimee, it goes without saying that without your steadfast friendship, without the inspiration the two of you provide and without our combined determination to craft a future where we all shine, I would not be writing. I am so lucky to love you both.

Satia, Isaac, Jade. There are nights when I scroll our group chat and dissolve into laughter. You are my soft landing place. Thank you for letting me be every version of me I contain, and for loving each one.

Toyin, Hani and Eniola. One day I will find a way to repay you for the love you continuously heap on me, even on my very worst days. You're forever sealed in a chamber of my heart. I adore you all.

Amy, I remain consistently incredulous and so grateful that you took a chance on me.

Cat and Juliet, I couldn't ask for better editors. You teach me so much and I am honored to learn from you both.

To everyone at Graydon House and Oneworld, you changed my life. Thank you and thank you again.

As always, to God be the glory.

© Precious Mayowa Agbabiaka

Onyi Nwabineli is a Nigerian-British writer. Born in Benin, Nigeria, she grew up in Glasgow, the Isle of Man and Newcastle, and now lives in London. Onyi is the co-founder of Surviving Out Loud, a fund that provides financial support for survivors of sexual assault, and the founder of Black Pens, a writing retreat for Black women. Her debut novel, *Someday, Maybe* (Magpie, 2022) was a *Good Morning America* and Book of the Month Club Pick, and was shortlisted for the Diverse Book Awards.

ALSO BY ONYI NWABINELI

Longlisted for the Diverse Book Awards

Stunningly honest and bursting with wit, *Someday, Maybe* is the story of grief and resilience that you won't be able to stop talking about

After her husband's unexpected death, everyone around Eve – her friends, her stifling Nigerian-British family, her toxic mother-in-law – is pushing her to move on. But Eve isn't ready to face the future yet.

Instead, she begins looking back, combing through her memories in an attempt to understand where it all went wrong.

So begins this very unconventional love story.

'A love story in retrospect, heartbreaking in its inevitability but also shot through with moments of joy and humour.'

Stylist